Wicked Restless

A NOVEL BY GINGER SCOTT

For Sadie.

part one

Chapter 1

Andrew Harper, Age 16

Normally, I don't care what clothes I wear when I leave for school in the early morning. I spend my days with people I don't really know. Most of my freshman year of high school was on a college campus—my curse for being *smart*.

I say "curse" because unlike my older brother, Owen, I don't have normal friends. I don't get to go to high school dances or hang out at football games. Not that Owen ever did, but he could have if he wanted to. I get to go to what's called the Excel Program. I'm the lucky one learning physics and advanced calculus. The trade-off is I'll probably be accepted into any college I want, get any job I want, and find the entire process to be easy.

The curse—I'm alone.

My friends were Owen's friends: always three years older; always inviting me to things out of pity; always keeping me out of trouble, but just out of its reach. Protecting me. That was the line. My life was on the periphery. I heard it from Owen since the day I started grade school, and my mother echoed those words whenever I would protest I couldn't go to the party with Owen or hang out in the woods with him and his friends.

"He's only protecting you," she'd say.

Protecting me.

Choking me.

When Owen graduated, so did his friends. My small sliver of a social life evaporated piece by piece as people went off to college or to find jobs in some town that wasn't small. Then my mom sold our house to help pay for my grandfather's care, and I moved into a two-bedroom apartment with a vacant unit on one side and neighbors in their sixties on the other.

Sophomore year is shaping up to be more isolating. My only friend my age, a guy I barely tolerated named Matt who I met during a torturous year when both of our mothers decided putting us in Boy Scouts was a good idea, moved to Guam. Not the next town over. Not California. Not any place I could convince my mother was safe enough for me to visit—*escape to.* The fucker moved to Guam.

I used to go to Matt's house and spend hours playing video games. We didn't talk when we played, which is what made my friendship with Matt work. Now, I go to school, then come home. I study and have dinner with my mom and her boyfriend, Dwayne Chessman, a man we've known for years. He teaches at the high school—the one I don't get to go to because I'm *so smart.*

In the evening, I walk to the rink in the middle of Old Town, to a place called the Ice Palace, and I skate until my feet have blisters. I sprint and stop so many times I wear paths in the ice— so deep, they need to fill them with water when I leave. This is the only place I can go to feel something. On weekends, there are enough guys there to get a game going, but during the week, when I can come, it's usually only me. I've always skated, but when my brother Owen left, I became obsessed with hockey. Seems the skills I lack at throwing a ball are made up for in my ability to move a puck. That, and I'm incredibly fast. It's not the competition. I couldn't give a shit about winning something. For me, it's the rawness, the hunt—chasing something, taking something from someone, hurting them to get it, and not caring how they look lying on the ice in my wake. I don't operate under those morals anywhere else. But I think, maybe, there's a dark part of me that needs it. And I *need* to keep it on the ice.

Usually, though, I'm alone out there. So instead, I push myself until I can barely breathe, sometimes until my chest burns and I vomit. I push until Gary, who cleans up the joint, is coughing under his breath, leaning on the exit as he taps on his watch—his subtle hint to me to get my ass off the ice so he can go home.

My feet are sore today, but that's the last thing I'm going to remember. This is the day so many things are going to change— the day I start caring about what I wear when I leave my apartment in the morning. Illinois passed a law that every high school student needs to take PE, even the smart students who

2

don't go to a real high school. I protested at first, dreading the bus ride I'd have to endure, the awkward blue uniform, and my assured complete-lack-of-allies for dodgeball. But those anxieties are escaping me now. The second I broke through the athletic department door, I saw her sitting against the wall of the PE office, her legs outstretched, the blue fabric of her perfect dress tucked underneath her knees. The vision of her hits me harder as my eyes scan their way up. Her hair is the color of mahogany, and it twists in spirals, like a tornado rushing down her shoulders and spine; a dark storm against her cream skin.

I sit opposite her, sliding down against the wall, stretching my legs out until the soles of my shoes tap the bottom of hers. I do this on purpose. I want to see her eyes. Her gaze comes up quickly, and she pulls her feet in fast, careful to tuck the bottom of her dress underneath more tightly, hiding her modesty. Her eyes are gray, a dark gray, like charcoal.

I don't know her name, and I'm not sure I'll like her when she speaks. But I know I'll never forget her. Her smile, however fast it comes and goes in this moment, coincides with the first full breath I've taken in years.

I try to hold her attention, leaving my grin in place, a crooked one, just to let her know I'm sorry I bumped her. Sorry—*not sorry*. I slide the beanie from my head, and I know my hair is probably a mess by the way she lets out a breathy giggle when she sees it. I run my fingers through, but stop quickly. I like the way she giggles, and I don't care how I look. If my messy hair makes her smile, I'll wear it that way every day.

"Are you new, too?" she asks. I nodded *yes* at first, but correct her quickly. Her voice had me in a trance.

"No, I'm just...special," I say.

She sizes my response up for a few seconds, her lip quirked up on one side. "What makes you so special?" she finally asks.

I hold her gaze for a few seconds, liking this feeling of just sitting here looking at her. I stare until she has to look away, her cheeks growing more pink and her eyelashes fluttering as she stares back to her lap, where she's holding a small pink pass with something written from a parent or teacher. She keeps folding and unfolding the corners, wearing the paper out on the edges. She's nervous.

"Nothing makes me special. I'm not very special at all," I say, which only makes her peer back up with a sideways glance. Her lip ticks up again. Her mouth is pink, and tiny, and there are freckles that dot her nose.

"I bet you're special to someone," she says, her smile reaching the other side of her mouth now. She's being nice. No...she's being sweet. Goddamn is she sweet.

"I have an opening for that job...*someone.* Want it?" I tease. I see her eyes flash wider for a second, and I can tell I made her tense, so I tap my toe against hers again. "I was just kidding. But thanks."

"Emma Burke...Andrew Harper?" The voice breaks through our silence, startling us both to our feet. Mr. Crest, the PE teacher, is standing with his clipboard, two uniforms wrapped in plastic tucked under his arm. I bet these come in a big box, on a big truck, from a warehouse filled with ugly blue uniforms. Thank god my shorts aren't as small as hers. Thank god her shorts are that small.

"I'm supposed to give you this," Emma says, stepping closer to the teacher and handing over her paper slip. He reviews it and stuffs it in his back pocket, then marks something on his clipboard.

"You, this way," he says in my direction, shoving a bundle of pale blue material at me while jerking his head toward the boys' locker room. I don't even care that he's talking to me like this, like I'm some slacker he plans to fail. I don't care because she's still biting her lip, trying not to look right at me for too long.

"I'll see ya around, Emma," I say, taking my ugly-ass PE uniform into my arms.

"Bye, Andrew," she says, only letting her lip go from the grip of her teeth long enough to utter my name. Her voice is just over a whisper, and she's timid, and sweet, and I love PE. I want to change my schedule to nothing but PE. All day. Every day—as long as I can have this class with her.

I may have oversold my enthusiasm for PE. I've been taking a bus here for three weeks, and so far, I've been the first guy out in dodgeball a dozen times, and forced to stand on the free-throw line in basketball for an hour until I could sink a shot. The only saving grace was the day we played field hockey. Of course, I got a warning from Mr. Crest and a lecture that made me miss my bus after I checked a guy on the field. Apparently, there is no contact in PE field hockey. When I told him they shouldn't call it hockey then, he sent me to the principal's office.

The only bonus about today—we don't have to wear our uniforms. We get a break for the entire week, in fact. It's the square-dancing unit. For about ten minutes, we've been sitting in the gym, our backs flush against the wall outside our locker room, while Mr. Crest struggles with an ancient sound system. Based on the few times he was able to get the speakers to make a sound, I'm pretty sure we're not missing anything by not hearing this music. He finally turns a microphone on and sets it next to a tiny speaker he plugs into his phone.

"All right, gentlemen. On your feet, and form a line against the wall," he says. There's a collective grumble as we stand, but that sound stops as soon as the girls' locker-room door swings open and a single-file line that matches ours begins to fill the space along the other wall.

When I see Emma, I start counting. She's in the middle, and I make it to fourteen before the row of girls streaming through the door ends. I count two more times to be sure, then I count my line.

Seventeen.

Three people away.

Our number fourteen is a guy whose pants are rolled up at the bottom. And the dude isn't wearing socks. He isn't worthy of Emma. But he notices her. I watched him count. And I watched him clench his fist in a silent *yes* when he figured it out. There is no way I am letting this asshole swing her around the gym to shitty music for forty-five minutes.

"Dude," I say, leaning forward, watching to make sure Mr. Crest is still facing the front. "Psssst! Dude!"

Fucker's ignoring me.

"Come on, man. Hey!" He finally looks my way. He's wearing a button-down shirt. The collar is wrinkled. "Hey, trade me spots."

"Fuck off," he shrugs.

I blink at him, a little stunned that he was so quick to shut me down. Owen would have punched him, or saved this memory for later and made him suffer through ridicule—or he'd just date the guy's girlfriend. I glance back down to his shoes, and his hairy ankles. I'm pretty sure he doesn't have a girlfriend.

I look at my row again, making sure I didn't mess up on my first count. I'm still seventeen. I glance back at sockless dude, and he's tucking his shirt in and smoothing his hair out on the sides. I can't believe he's going to touch Emma's arm.

Our line moves forward, and couples are pairing off and finding spots on the gym floor marked with tape. When I'm about ten people away, I count again, relieved that at least I have a shy girl who looks just as uncomfortable with this lesson as I do.

The music is mostly fiddle, and there's a male singer giving directions—spinning, two steps in, two steps out, around the barn and *ain't she pretty.* I laugh a little under my breath. It's my turn to pair off when I glance back up and meet Emma's eyes. I don't show my surprise, and I ignore the grunts in protest of the a-hole two people away from me. *Dude, socks. If you just wore socks, this wouldn't have happened.*

Maybe it would have, though. Maybe...maybe Emma was counting too.

I guide her to our tape marks in the far corner, and while everyone else has unlinked arms, I keep my hold on hers—our elbows locked together—the soft tickle of her skin along mine is possibly the best thing that has happened in my life to date.

I lean over and whisper in her ear while we wait for the remaining couples to find their spot. "The dude doesn't wear socks."

She laughs the most perfect, quiet, careful laugh, then glances over her shoulder as sockless guy walks by with his partner.

"Yeah, thanks for saving me from *that,*" she giggles.

I nod and smile, but while we sit down in our square formation I also feel a little smug. *You had to trade spots with three people, Emma. This wasn't just about the socks.*

We're both leaning back on our hands now, listening to Mr. Crest read through a packet on basic square-dancing moves. I don't think anyone is *really* listening though. The guy across from me has slipped his phone from his pocket, and he's playing a game, the girl next to him is mouthing something to her friend across the room, and I'm staring at the small fraction of an inch of space between my pinky finger and Emma's.

With every word Mr. Crest says, I slide it a millimeter more, until finally the tip of my finger is resting against hers. I glance up at her at the feeling of our touch, and she's still staring at our teachers, *listening.* She also lets a smirk take over one side of her mouth.

"All right, on your feet. Let's give this one a try," Mr. Crest says.

I stand at the same time Emma does, and when I reach for her arm and loop it through mine, she doesn't flinch. It's like that's where her arm belongs.

I spend the next hour noticing things. I notice she wears pink Converse, and they look perfect next to my black ones that are twice the size. I notice her black leggings tuck into her shoes, and her legs are long with perfect curves for every muscle. I memorize where the tip of her hair stops when she brushes it over one shoulder—grazing her shoulder blades in the back and the small swell of her breasts in the front.

When I get to look into her eyes, I memorize everything they hold. The gray is caught somewhere between silver and black, and the longer I look, the more convinced I am she's the perfect storm and I'm lost at sea.

I spend so much time looking at the details, I'm surprised when the bell rings to signal the end of class. When she unhooks her arm from mine, she lets her fingertips slide along my skin, and I memorize that, too.

Square dancing for an hour with Emma Burke is worth being pummeled in a thousand dodgeball games.

Chapter 2

Andrew

Square dancing lasted a week. For five days, Emma Burke and I counted lines of teenagers to make sure we both met in the middle. We never talked about it. There was never a formal plan. It was just something we both did—a silent commitment.

Then Monday came, and we started weightlifting for two weeks. I only saw Emma in brief trips to the drinking fountain while the girls were in the other wing of the gym, tumbling.

I'm pretty sure Mr. Crest thinks I'm diabetic, because I'm thirsty all the time.

I don't have afternoon classes today. There's an event at the college, so the Excel Program is getting the afternoon off. I intend on spending those extra hours learning about Emma.

Dwayne said I could sit in his classroom, since he has a prep hour for the last hour of the day. But I don't know where Emma is, and part of me wants to stand outside to look for her. I don't have my own car yet, just my mom's or Dwayne's when they let me borrow it—so I can't even hang out in the parking lot and offer her a ride home.

I keep glancing through the sliver of a window on Dwayne's door. Every noise I hear in the hall draws my attention.

"What has you so jumpy?" he asks after my twentieth peek through the glass.

I look at him, my heart a little stuck, my chest tight. This is awkward, and I feel edgy—like I'm caught doing something I shouldn't. We don't talk much—Dwayne and me. He was always closer with Owen. I think because Owen had so many struggles. I'm just the smart, quiet one.

"Do you know Emma Burke?" I ask, finally. I want to vomit. I don't talk about girls. Not to Dwayne. Not to anyone really. There's never been a girl to talk about.

Dwayne tosses the marker onto the ledge of his whiteboard then kicks his desk chair around until it's facing him so he can sit. He glides in it to his desk in small scoots, laughing under his breath. He's laughing at me. Because I'm ridiculous.

"Yeah, I know Emma," he says.

I nod at him, my lips tight, then I glance back out the window, figuring now that I'm good and mortified, I'm sure to see her. When I look back at Dwayne, he's still smiling, but he's looking at his grade book and tapping his marker on his desk, not wanting to make me feel any more embarrassed. We both drift back to the silence of before, except now there's a ginormous cloud of *Andrew likes Emma* floating in the fucking air. I'm sure this will be a late-night chat topic for him and my mom.

Awesome. Fucking...awesome.

The tick of the seconds on the clock above his desk is loud, and I start counting with it rather than checking the actual time—testing myself to see how close I come to being right. With two minutes left before the end of the day, Dwayne slides his chair out, letting the rollers carry it to the wall behind him when he stands, and he walks over to the desk I've commandeered by the door.

"Here," he says, dropping his keys in front of me.

I slide them in a circle with my finger, then gaze up at him.

"Your mom will come pick me up on her way home. I have grading to do, and I don't want you to have to stay here. Besides...don't you need to give *someone* a ride home?" He's teasing me a little, and I kind of hate it. But, I also want to hug this man who is sort of the only father figure I have. Because yeah...there's someone I need to give a ride home to.

I stand, untangling my long legs from the small desk that doesn't suit me, and pull my gray beanie back on my head.

"She's in room one-twenty-seven," he says, smirking, but only for a second, never fully looking at me. He turns around, and I slip out his door just before the bell sounds, hauling ass to her room on the other end of the hall.

I get to her door seconds before she steps through it, and I lean against the wall on the other side, bending my knee and looking natural. Natural; I look like a fucking creeper. I'm

9

rethinking my pose when she surprises me, kicking her foot into mine. This is our thing, it seems.

"What are you doing here, Harper?"

I wince when she asks that way. People call us *Harper*, and it's not usually a good thing. If she's calling me that, it means people have been talking to her about me—about Owen. About my father's mental illness, probably his suicide, and maybe James's drug habits and the way he died last year. The town has been more respectful over James, and I think the fact that Owen landed a basketball scholarship shut them up a little too. But rumors and gossip are hard to kill completely. And us Harper boys—we make headline-worthy gossip. Owen may be the golden college boy now, but he's also the troublemaker with a rap sheet.

"Thought you might want a ride," I say. The confidence I had when I darted to her classroom is gone. I'm pretty sure there's no way this girl is getting in a car with me. I just hope she doesn't laugh out loud.

The look she gives to the blonde walking up behind her confirms my suspicions. Her friend, I've seen her around. I think she might be the sister of one of Owen's exes, or maybe related to someone my brother's friends know. She knows me, and that's enough; her eyebrows are high on her forehead when she looks at Emma. That expression is all about warning her to stay away.

"Oh, I was…I was going home with Melody. We were going to get ready…there's…there's a dance here tonight," she says, delivering the news in fits and starts.

It's cute the way she takes her time with every word, not sure which thing will hurt my feelings more. I'm use to it all, though. I didn't know about a dance, because I don't *really* go here. And yeah, it's probably better she rides home with Melody…

"But if you can wait a few minutes, I'd…I'd love a ride," she says, surprising me enough I falter on my feet. I catch myself quickly, pushing my hands in my pockets and leaning against the wall.

Her friend tugs on one of the straps of her backpack, but she ignores it, shirking away.

"Is that heavy? I could carry it for you," I say, reaching for her backpack. I glance at her friend when I do, letting her know I saw her tug the strap, and I know what she meant by it—*don't go, Emma, not with him.* She sneers at me; I know we have an understanding—an agreement to disagree.

"Sure," Emma says, letting me slide her heavy pack from her shoulder. I layer it over my own backpack, slinging it over my arm, and I wait while she has a whispered conversation with her friend a few feet away from me.

"I just need to get some things from the office. I missed a few classes this morning," she says.

"Sure," I say, following her down the hall. I smile when I see her step carefully with her Converse; she's placing one foot inside every square, alternating from black to white. I do that sometimes.

"Step on a crack, you'll break your mother's back," I mutter. I'm laughing to myself when she halts instantly, spinning to face me, her face serious.

"My mom broke her back last year..." she says, and I look to both sides, feeling like an asshole. When I glance back at her, a grin starts to crawl along her lips. "I'm just fuckin' with ya," she winks.

"Oh my god, that was the funniest *not-funny* thing anyone's ever done to me," I say, pulling my knit cap over my face and rubbing my eyes before sliding it back on.

"Sorry," she smiles, sheepishly.

I hold her stare for a few seconds, until she looks away blushing again. I love that she blushes. And I love that half smile she gives me. It's unsure, cautious. She starts to move toward the office again, and I follow a few steps behind.

"It was more funny than not funny," I say, not wanting her to feel bad. Honestly, that little stunt just gave me one more thing to be infatuated with when it comes to Emma Burke.

I follow her through the office doors, and Margot, the main secretary, lights up when she sees me. I don't know many of the teachers here, but the office staff knows me well. They helped process the transfers and paperwork for the Excel Program, and

I spent a lot of time waiting in the office for Owen my freshman year on days I didn't have a full schedule.

"Andrew Harper, how's that brother of yours?" Margot asks, leaning over the wraparound counter by the secretaries' station.

"He's good," I smile. "I'm driving up with mom and Dwayne...I mean...Mr. Chessman...to watch his game this weekend. He's starting." I'm genuinely proud of Owen. In many ways, my brother was my hero. I think that's why life sucks so much now that he's gone. Of course, Emma is making things suck just a little less.

"You can call him Dwayne, sweetie. That's what we call him, too," Margot winks. She moves to a file at her desk, pulling papers together for Emma while continuing to talk to me. "And I hear you're pretty damn good on skates, so maybe we see you starting for some university too in a few years?"

"Yeah, I don't know...maybe. It's more of a hobby," I shrug. I'm not great at compliments, or attention, or...praise. Margot's husband is one of the guys who shows up at the rink on weekends, and we usually play on the same squad. He's a good guy, and a hell of a goalie for a forty-five-year-old. Their son plays for Northwestern's club team.

"Right, well...as long as you're having fun," she smirks, reaching over the counter to hand Emma a folder of assignments. "That's what I tell Robbie. Lord knows that man better be having fun, considering how little he can walk the day after one of your games."

I chuckle as I tap the tabletop and offer a small wave when we leave. I feel Emma's eyes on me as I hold the door open for her and lead her out to the parking lot. I open up the trunk of Dwayne's car, a decade-old Buick, and slide my skates and stick to the back to make room for our bags. I could have thrown our things in the back seat—there's plenty of room—but I wanted her to see the skates, because I kind of like the sideways glances she gave me when she found out I play hockey. And if she thinks that's even remotely hot, I'm going to run with it.

I slam the trunk closed and look up to meet her eyes.

12

"Why do you have holes in your ears?" she asks, swiftly deflating my miniscule ego. She could care less about the skates and stick in the back of the car.

I chew at the side of my mouth, smiling through it, then turn from her and walk to the driver's side while she moves to the passenger door. We both climb in at the same time, and before I put the keys in the ignition, I slide my hat back enough to see my ears as I look at them in the rearview mirror. I have small gauges in my ears. I got them because my brother's friend House talked me into them a year ago. I thought they were cool...all the way up until now.

"I mean, what happens when you don't want a hole in your ear anymore?" I let out a short laugh and run my hand over my face before turning to look at her.

"Did my mom send you here? Is that why you've come? Because, I swear to god, you sound just like her," I laugh.

"Hmmmmm," she says, her lips in a tight line, her eyes focused on my right ear for several seconds before they slide over to meet my gaze. We're maybe a foot away from each other, and when she looks at me, the gray around her pupils is all I see. "I guess I'm curious how you can make such a huge decision about your body at sixteen."

"It's just an ear. Now, putting a hole in *other* parts?" She blushes at my innuendo and turns from me to face the front again. I let her off the hook and start the car, but just before the motor kicks in, she speaks.

"I like them...the holes, that is," she says, blush growing and her lip back in her teeth.

"Thanks," I say with a shake of my head as I shift the gear and back out from the parking space. "Where do you live?"

"Fireside and Barrel...do you know where that is?"

I know where it is. It's *the* house—the big one everyone in town knows. There's really only *one.* When I was a kid, Owen had me convinced it was haunted. For a while, I thought it was a museum. Then, one day, it went up for sale. It's been for sale for about six years. I guess it's not for sale anymore.

"Yeah, I know where that is," I say, not looking at her or making a big deal out of it. I can tell she's embarrassed about living in the town landmark. It's not a mansion or anything, but it *is* incredibly old, one of those big houses that could be for rich people if only it hadn't been forgotten. Now, it's falling apart.

It's silent for the first few blocks we travel—the only sounds, her shuffling her feet along the floor and messing with the heater vents, trying to make the air come out stronger.

"That's as high as it goes," I say after watching her shift her vent and flick the button a few more times. "Dwayne's car...it's pretty crappy."

"It's okay," she says, slouching back in her seat. She fidgets for a few minutes, running fingers through her hair a few times, then scratching at her nose and arms while she looks out her window. "So...you play hockey?" she finally asks.

Finally.

I grin.

"Yeah, I play," I say, once again glad I opened the trunk. Pretty sad when your big pick-up move is showing off your used hockey equipment.

"That's cool. I always wanted to skate," she says.

I make the turn on Fireside and the large bay windows and red brick of her house come into view. An older car—a lot like the one I'm driving—sits parked in the street, and a newer compact car is in the driveway. A little boy is kicking a ball in the front yard, and a woman sits on the front steps watching him. She stands as I slow along the curb.

"That's my mom," Emma says softly.

"Little brother?" I nod out the window toward the toddler rushing back and forth around the front yard.

She nods *yes* and smiles. I push the gear into park and step out with her to open the trunk. I lift her bag for her, and purposely touch her hand on the exchange, noting the small twitch her fingers make when I do.

"Have a good time," I say, and she looks up at me, pulling both straps of her bag over her shoulders, her face bunched, not sure what I mean. "The dance...have a good time at the dance tonight."

The scheming part of my brain is already playing out the conversation with Dwayne to help him chaperone—or to see if there's anything I can do to be there in that gym tonight. I wouldn't know a soul, other than the couple guys I've gotten to know in PE. But I'd know Emma.

"Oh…yeah…thanks. I might not go, though," she says, glancing over her shoulder to give her mom a sign that she's coming. Her mom waves, and I lift a hand to wave back. I hope she doesn't know about the Harpers.

I stand there a bit frozen while Emma steps up on the curb, thanking me for the ride. When I move to close the trunk, I glance at my skates again, and take a deep breath before shutting my eyes and blurting something out.

"I could teach you to skate. If…if you want. Sometime. Not tonight, but I was just thinking…I could teach you," I stammer. I feel like an idiot, and I'm already working out a way to backtrack my words and give her an out when she interrupts my self-doubt.

"Why not tonight?" I look up to meet the silver of her eyes, the small curve of her lips, the smile, the flirting.

"Tonight works too," I say. "I can pick you up. Say…six?"

"Yeah…" she turns and takes a few more steps toward her house, before glancing back at me over her shoulder. "Six. I'll be ready."

With her back to me, I push down to make sure the trunk is latched, then move toward the open driver's door, watching her meet her mom and little brother at the front of her steps and head inside. I pull away from her house slowly, careful not to stare at the ornate window trim and the many other things that make this house stand out above every other home in Woodstock. It's sort of fitting that Emma lives there, though. She's the kind of girl who gets noticed.

It only takes a few minutes to get to our street, and I mentally calculate how easy it would be to bike to her house or to walk or jog. I call Dwayne as soon as I get into our apartment, asking him to use his car again tonight to go to the rink. He doesn't ask how the ride home went or for any details about my sudden need to play hockey on a Friday night. I think part of him thinks that we're bonding over this. Maybe we are.

Dwayne was always closer with Owen, but he didn't start dating my mom until Owen left for college. I was left with the awkward shit. Dwayne's come to a few of the hockey scrimmages with me, and he's helped with a few assignments, but other than that, our conversations have been limited to grocery lists and my mother's work schedule. Of course, now we can add Emma Burke to the small catalogue of conversation items, too.

I spend most of the time at home alone pacing my room before leaving to pick up Emma, switching out my dark gray T-shirt for a long-sleeved black one and slipping on my gray jeans. I look like Owen when I wear this, and I think there's a part of me that feels his confidence in my veins when I resemble him.

I leave a note letting Dwayne and my mom know I went to the rink, propping it up in the small bowl for keys and mail that my mom has by the front door, then lock up fast and jog to Dwayne's car. Within minutes, I'm back in front of her house, the motor idling while I try to find the right thing to say for each possible person who might answer the doorbell once I ring it.

Pulling the keys from the ignition, I push open my door with my foot and step onto the roadway just as Emma is skipping down the front walkway of her house.

"I saw you drive up," she says, working a large sweatshirt over her hips and slipping her hair through the hoodie on the top. She's wearing black leggings and a purple sweatshirt, and she looks like a damned princess.

"Wow, I had a whole speech prepared for your parents and everything," I smirk, opening the door while she slides inside.

"They're not home," she says quickly.

I close the door and step around the front of the car. As I open my door, I notice a figure looking out the window at the front of her house, the shadow lingering long enough to let me know that someone's watching us leave.

I slide into the driver's seat and start the car again, looking beyond Emma and out her window before shifting the car into drive. She follows my gaze, then looks back to her lap quickly, focusing on her seatbelt and the small purse she's brought with her. I wait a few extra seconds, hoping she'll look at me. When she's still focused on the zipper of her purse, I relent and pull away from her house.

My excitement from a few minutes before was swallowed up by the lie I know she just told. The only thing that makes it okay is I know exactly why she told it. I'm a Harper, and her parents— they don't like that she's going out with me tonight. She lied because she doesn't want to hurt my feelings. Wrong or right, the fact that she cares about my feelings sorta makes it okay.

"I'm sorry," she mumbles. She knows I know.

"It's okay. I get it," I say.

We don't talk about it any more. I've heard the stories her family has probably heard, and when she's ready, she'll ask me for the truth, which is somewhere closer to the middle— between rumor and gruesome fact. Of all of us, I'm the one who was probably the most sheltered. Yet, I still get the same rep as the rest of us, buried by the same fallout.

"Hey, we didn't get to talk much in PE. But...you're new here, yeah?" I ask, glancing from her to the road and back again. I threw a shitload of gum in my mouth before I left my room, because I didn't want to have bad breath, and when I'm nervous, I chew gum. Now the chomping is the only fucking thing I can hear, though. I roll down the window and spit the wad out onto the street. When I look back at her, her brow is pinched and her arms are folded.

"Uh, that's still littering, you know?" she says.

I stare at her trying to decide if she's fucking with me again, but after a few seconds, I decide she's serious. I swallow hard and look back to the four-way stop I've been sitting at for a solid twenty seconds. "I'm pretty sure I will never spit my gum out again," I say, thoroughly scolded by the girl who is in *no way* going to kiss me tonight now that I'm a litterer.

"You can spit it out, just not where people step. It's gross," she says, her voice growing a little softer.

"No...you're right," I say, glancing at her again.

"I...I didn't mean to sound bossy. I'm bossy sometimes, but I don't mean..." She's shaking her head while she's babbling, and it's adorable. I reach over and touch her knee with the back of my hand, which has the effect of electroshock therapy on both of us. We straighten in our seats. She tugs at her seatbelt and slides closer to her door as I pick my hand up and promptly put it on the *two* of the *ten and two* of the steering wheel.

A few long seconds pass in silence, and ironically I wish like hell I had my gum back in my mouth to give it something to do. "You're not bossy," I say, smiling as I glance at her sideways. "You were right. It's gross."

"Delaware," she blurts out, and I shrug my shoulders, shaking my head as I squeeze the back of my neck with my left hand.

"Yeah, you lost me. I think I missed the transition," I chuckle.

"Sorry," she says. "That's where I moved here from. I'm from Delaware."

"Delaware." I repeat the state, loving that she's just as damned uncomfortable and awkward as I am now. "That's my favorite colony."

I can feel her looking at me, and I notice her start to laugh lightly out of the corner of my eye as I pull into the parking lot of the Ice Palace.

"You're strange, Andrew Harper. Very strange," she says through the end of her laugh as we both step from the car.

I move to the trunk, open it, and lift out my skates. "I'm not quite sure what makes me strange, but...I'll take strange from you." I grin as I motion toward the front doors to the rink, urging her to walk next to me.

There's a peewee team on the ice when we enter; a group of maybe fifteen kids puffed up with hockey gear and pads and barely balancing on their skates. I nod to Chad, the guy coaching them. He plays with me on the weekends, and he's been coaching here for years.

"Oh my god, they're so cute," Emma says, stepping close enough to put her hand flat along the glass. She watches as each kid takes a turn skating toward the goal, the only mission stopping before running into the metal. It's harder than it looks, especially when you're six. "Was that you when you were little? One of those little round kids wobbling on the ice?"

"No," I say with a shake of my head. I lead her over to the skate rental counter. "My brothers taught me how to skate by throwing me out on a frozen lake. And we played our own brand of hockey, I guess. Or, they hit me hard and laughed when I fell on my ass..."

"That's so mean!" Her eyes show genuine sympathy, and it's sweet as hell.

"Yeah...and no. I mean, they were my older brothers. It's like...a thing, ya know? And I was the little runt. I loved it as much as I hated it. Size?" I look down at her feet.

"Oh, uhm, sevens probably," she responds.

"Sevens," I say to Gary. He pulls out a pair of white blades and slides them along the counter to me, quirking one eyebrow up, his subtle way of giving me shit for being on a date. Am I on a date? I think this is a date.

We both sit on a nearby bench and unlace our shoes, then slip our feet into our skates. I get mine on quickly, then kneel in front of her to help her tie hers tight. Our fingers tangle for a brief second in the laces, and it makes my lip curve up on one side. I keep my gaze low, hiding it.

"So you just played with your brothers. No team or anything?" she says, leaning back and letting me finish working out the knot on her skates.

"Just my brothers," I say as I take her hand and help her to her feet. She lets go of me as soon as she finds her balance, and I exhale my disappointment. With one step, though, she loses her center and grabs hold of my arm, clutching it with both hands.

"I got you," I say, careful as I slide one arm around her back, noticing the feel of the curve of her body on my way. Her fingers dig into the fabric of my shirt on my shoulder, and her grip hurts a little, but I don't care.

"I don't think I can do this." Her words come out in a quiet, nervous laugh.

"Sure you can," I smile. "Look...it's just ice. And it doesn't hurt any more than falling on the ground. I promise. We won't go fast, and I'll hold you the entire time."

I will hold you. Please don't find your balance ever, because I will hold you. This is my job, holding you.

I lead Emma to the edge of the ice, and we pause while the group of young hockey players race up and off the ice, a few of them stumbling onto the carpet, others showing off how comfortable they are on their skates, sliding in sideways just before the wall. Chad nods at me as he follows behind the group of kids.

"See you tomorrow, Drew?" he asks, glancing quickly to Emma.

"Yup," I nod. "Hey, you think maybe you let me score this time?"

Chad glances back to Emma, whose only focus is on her quivering ankles, then he looks back to me. "Only if you earn it, big man. Only if you earn it," he chuckles as he glides past me.

Chad's the same age my father would have been if he were still alive. I have a feeling that he and my father knew each other. I've never asked, and he's never said anything, but there's just this vibe I get from him. I can't explain it, only that when most people know my family's story, they start to treat me with either pity or fear. Chad does neither.

"Okay, are you ready?" I ask, tightening my hold on Emma, bringing her closer to my side. I tell myself it's to give her confidence, but it's really just so I can feel her close to me.

"Ready," she stutters, her eyes still down on her feet.

"Okay, that's good; look at your feet, and keep your weight forward. You get into trouble when the skates move ahead of you. Falling back—that's what sucks," I instruct.

Emma bites her lip and nods quickly.

"Got it, backward sucks," she says. I laugh.

"Not quite what I said, but that's okay," I chuckle. "Okay, you're just going to glide between me and the wall. No steps, just get used to the feeling of this."

I push her, but stay at her side, and we move around one end of the rink inches at a time. After a few minutes, I convince her to bend her knees, and when she finally moves one leg, her feet slide around in a panic as she collapses on the ice, taking me with her.

"Damn, I'm sorry. I'm going to end up hurting you. It's okay. I don't need to learn this," she says, looking around for a way to get up, her face painted with disappointment and frustration.

20

"Stop it. You can't hurt me," I say, pulling myself up and holding the wall so I can lift her back to her feet. "The average number of falls for a first timer is something like eight," I say, completely making up a statistic. "That was just number one, so we've got a long way to go."

When I raise her to her feet, I circle my arms around her, and her eyes are only inches from mine. Her pupils flare with a short-lived rush. If I were Owen, I'd kiss her—*right now.*

Instead, I look down, dust off some of the ice crystals from her sleeves, and link my fingers through hers. "Come on, let's finish our lap," I say, still wishing I had the guts to kiss her.

I lead her a few more feet at a time around the rink, and we fall, me falling with her, at least a dozen more times. By the time we finish one full lap, though, she's grown steadier, her ankles finding their strength, and when she feels brave, she lets go of my hand and glides a few feet at a time on her own.

This is when her smile takes over ruling every single thing I do.

"Oh my god, Andrew..." she says, a little breathless and excited. "Oh my god! Look!" She moves one foot slowly, and her steps are choppy and awkward, but with me within an arm's reach, she manages to scoot her way around a quarter of the rink, leaning forward when we finally make it to the entrance, clutching the gate and collapsing over the side, exhausted.

"Well?" she asks, twisting her body around to face me. "How'd I do?" she asks.

"Better than average," I smirk, my eyes flitting to her hand, wanting to hold it again. She reaches up and smacks my chest once, but quickly grips the wall again when she feels her balance start to give out.

"You said average was eight falls. I'm pretty sure I fell way more than eight times," she laughs, holding herself along the railing until she finds a bench to sit at.

"Yeah, but you fell...like...*way* better than most people," I joke. She tosses her hair over her shoulder as she raises one leg to unlace her skate, and I get a little lost in watching her move. She leans forward to catch the line of my eyesight to bring me back.

"Show me what you can do," she says. I bunch my brow, not sure what she means. "Out there. Just...I don't know. Skate a lap or something? I want to see if my teacher is all talk."

I laugh and shake my head, a little embarrassed by her attention, maybe a little nervous about flirting, too. When my eyes meet hers, she raises her eyebrows in expectation.

"Yeah?" I ask, not sure if showing off is a good thing.

"Please? Just one lap," she says, and I'm struck by the word *please*. I'm pretty sure that's all it would take for me to do anything for her—anything at all...ever.

"A'right," I say, bending forward and pulling my laces a little tighter. A few girls have entered the rink, and they're spinning in the middle, tracing lines and working on footwork. I've always been more impressed with what they can do. Me—I'm just fast. Those girls—they're full of grace and beauty. Nothing beautiful about what I do at all.

I skate backward, watching Emma as she tiptoes to the glass to watch me more closely. My heart begins to race knowing her eyes are on me. I move to one corner and skid to a stop before shrugging my shoulders at her. This isn't very impressive, but it's what I've got, so I take off quickly to the other end of the rink, stopping fast and sprinting back to where I started, repeating the move again, then pausing at the other end. I wait a few seconds to catch my breath, then glide toward and away from her in circles, like I do when I'm playing defense, and eventually end back at the exit gate where she's clapping.

"Okay," she laughs. "That...was skating. I see the difference now. I was falling. You...you were skating."

I laugh with her, sliding into the bench to pull off my skates. "My brothers were good teachers," I say. There's a simple smile spanning the space between the pink of her cheeks. It's not fake or uncomfortable, but rather exactly the opposite—like the kind of smile you give someone who gets you and your story without even asking. I stare at it a little too long, though, and she starts to let her hands twist in her lap again, nerves creeping back in. It gets quiet when I slide my feet from my skates, and when I grab her blades to return them to the rental counter, she waits for me by the door.

I've only had her for an hour, and I'm not ready to give her up yet.

"You know, Illinois is way different from Delaware," I say when I meet up to her again, holding the door open and fighting the instinct to put my arm around her as I did on the ice. "You should probably get the full tour of Woodstock from a local."

"I was thinking the same thing. I wouldn't want to wander into the wrong woods or something like that," she grins at me from one side of her mouth.

"Precisely," I mimic, holding the car door open, the muscles in my cheeks working hard to keep the excitement I feel—over the fact that she wants more time with me—from fully taking over my face. If I gave in, I'm pretty sure my feet would dance with anticipation.

I pull out from the rink's parking lot in the opposite direction from the one we came, and I take us to the outskirts of town first, pointing out the lake that sometimes freezes over, the homes that are older than hers, if not quite as big, and the Old Town shops around the main square. After we hit the touristy stuff, I drive through a few of the woodsy areas, along the edge of the industrial strip and past the warehouse where my father worked. I don't tell her about him then, but when I pull up to the edge of the Wilson Apple Orchard about ten minutes later, she asks.

"Is it true?"

Everyone has their own way of asking about our story. Some people gossip and whisper, others are more direct—hugging me, touching my arm, offering sympathy and grief counseling even if it's fifteen years later than I really need it. The funny thing is, though, that few people actually really *ask* for the story. Most assume.

I shift the gear into park just outside the orchard driveway gates, the festival season long past and most of the trees starting to show their winter branches. My fingers grip over the top of the steering wheel as I breathe in slowly, then exhale, noticing the slight trail of fog my breath creates as it threatens to leave a steamy circle on the window. I push the heater up one level before resting my arms over the steering wheel, laying my head flat against them and looking at her next to me.

She's beautiful. And I want this one to be the girl—the one I remember. And my sad family history is going to ruin it. But she asked. So I'm going to tell her.

My lips tight, I force a smile, not wanting to make anything about this moment sad, despite the history I'm going to share. She twists in her seat to face me slightly, unbuckling her seatbelt so she can bring her knee up to her chest.

"I've only ever heard the stories, too. I was one, maybe, when my dad died. He was sick. He had bipolar disorder, and his brain—it made a lot of things up. He wasn't taking his medicine, and nobody knows exactly why he stepped from the Ferris-wheel carriage. But he wasn't well when it happened. That's the one truth I know for certain. My brother and mom, they don't talk about him much," I say, turning my head to look down at my lap. "I think what really happened is a secret that will forever be kept between my father's ghost and a five-year-old Owen."

"You said brother. But before...you said you learned to skate from your *brothers*. So that's...that's also true?" Her voice breaks slightly when she asks. I lean back into my seat and stretch my arms forward to flex my muscles before letting my hands fall to my knees.

"Yeah. That one...I have more of a memory of. But..." I stop, holding my breath.

"But it's not a memory you want to share," she finishes for me.

I nod slowly, then look up to her waiting gaze, her stormy eyes lit by the moon. If she was the ocean, I would be happy to be lost at sea. "If that's okay, I think I'll just let the rumors fill that one in for you," I exhale.

Her freckles. Her small nose. The waves of brown of her hair. Her long lashes, and the way her fingers search for something to do when she's nervous. I watch it all; I savor it. "I'd rather just leave it blank...until you want to share," she says, her lip curling briefly on one side. I take that small movement in too. "I don't much care for rumors," she says, her grin stretching just a hint wider.

The radio is barely audible in the car, and part of me wants to turn the music louder to fill the silence taking up too much space between us. Another part of me, though, wants to leave the silence alone, because when it's quiet like this, and she's close, I can hear every breath she takes.

Her phone steals away my choice, buzzing regularly in her pocket until she pulls it out and answers a call from her dad. I only hear her end of the conversation, but her answers are clipped, relegated to single words. Without asking, I shift the car into reverse and back away from the orchard and onto the road. Emma needs to go home; this much I'm sure of.

"Sorry, my dad doesn't like me out late," she says as she puts her phone into the side pocket of her purse, not adding the part where I'm sure her father said he didn't like his daughter out late *with me.*

"It's okay. I'm getting up early to drive to Champaign with my mom and her boyfriend. I should get home too. He'll want me to gas up the car," I say, not wanting her to feel guilty about her parents' opinion of me.

It takes us twenty minutes to get back to our neighborhood, and instead of finding out more about her, I give into my insecurities and turn the music up loud enough to give both of our minds something else to play with. There are a few times, though, where I catch her lips moving with the lyrics of one of the songs, and I tell myself that visual is almost as good as finding out more of her story.

As I sit in the car next to her in front of her ornate, giant house, I know that there's no way I'm going to sleep tonight. There's no guarantee that if I dream, I'll dream of her.

"Thank you for teaching me to skate," she says, pausing with one leg out of the car, the other still here with me.

"I'm not sure we can call it skating yet, but..." I tease, and she pushes my arm with a tiny grunt in dissent. Yeah, I lock that touch away, too. "I'm joking. You did great."

"Well...I'm no hockey phenom," she says, her voice dragging out that last word.

"Neither am I," I sigh. I don't know why it makes me uncomfortable, but I just don't want her thinking I'm more special than I am.

Our silence is drowned out by the ad for legal advice blaring through Dwayne's car speakers, and I watch, helplessly, as she finally steps from my car. There are so many things that I *could* do right now. But just beyond her, the front door to her house has cracked open, and the porch light has flipped on, the blinds to the front window wide as well.

"I hope this was as good as some school dance," I say, every drum of my heart rattling my insides. I'm not sure how I'm going to drive home unable to feel my feet and fingers.

Her feet on the curb, and her purse pulled across her body, Emma stops just before closing the car door, leaning in just enough so I can hear her, and whoever is standing at the doorway behind her can't.

"I'm not sure," she says, squinting one eye as a smile breaks through slowly. "I think we're going to need to try it again so I can be sure. Skating or dancing...it's a tough one."

"You're on. I play Sunday morning, and I'm all yours after noon." When I realize how my words sound, my stomach drops. Emma's smile pushes further into her cheeks, though, and suddenly I don't care so much about sounding desperate for her. I am desperate, and I want nothing but more seconds with her.

"I'll meet you at the rink. I'll come watch you play," she says, winking as she shuts the door finally and skips up her walkway. She quickly passes a man I assume is her father, and he lingers in the light of the porch, his arms crossed in front of his body, until I pull completely out of view.

When I get home, Dwayne and my mom are both up and at the kitchen table eating bowls of cereal. I can sense my mom's desire to ask me a million questions as I grab a soda from the refrigerator and move down the hallway, but I catch the subtle look from Dwayne telling her not to pry, and I'm grateful for him.

With my lights off, I crawl into bed, kicking off my jeans and shoes, and pulling my pillow over my eyes so I can imagine Emma in my mind. Eventually, I fall asleep, but not before I make a list of the million things I need to learn about her—top of that list: what her lips taste like.

Chapter 3

Emma

"All I'm saying, Em, is that you can't take any risks right now. I'm not saying that you can't have a life. *Of course* you can have a life. It's just...for now...for the next little while, however long that is, you have to take life slow."

My mom has been sitting on the foot of my bed, explaining her decision to me for at least an hour. I quit listening five minutes in, when she finally choked out the part where I have to stay home today instead of going to the hockey rink to watch Andrew. Correction: she didn't say I had to stay home, she said she wouldn't give me a ride.

My dad took my little brother, Cole, to this Tiny Tikes soccer program, something they do at this indoor gym by the mall. Not that it matters, because I know he wouldn't take me either. It's part of their concerted effort to make decisions about my life while they whisper behind their bedroom door at night—decisions that I am not a part of making.

"Em, you do understand, don't you honey?"

My mom has asked this question at least six times. Each time, I say *no*. I say it again.

"I'm never going to agree with you. It's ice-skating. I'm not going to get hurt. Nothing is going to happen. It's only slightly riskier than walking," I roll my eyes.

"Honey, you know that's not true. You could fall and break something, and the time it would take you to heal, it all plays into everything," she says. She's making things up at this point, but I don't argue. There isn't a point.

I was standing out in the front yard with her and my father, watching my brother race around the dying grass, when the woman who lives across the street came over. Mom mentioned I was a sophomore, and the woman asked if I'd met anyone nice yet. I said I square danced with Andrew Harper.

I said too much.

After an hour of hearing this woman expose every wound and skeleton that exists in the Harper home, two things became certain—my parents would never approve of Andrew, and I would never be able to forget him.

They won't say it. They won't, because they know how it will sound—bad. It will sound bad because it *is* bad to sum Andrew up based on a nosey neighbor's opinion, and to assume because bad things have followed him through life, he'll do nothing but bring them to me too.

So instead, my parents talk about how careful I need to be—reminding me why we moved to Illinois in the first place, and the promise that is now only weeks away.

I keep my attention on my phone, wishing like hell I were brave enough to ask him for his number so I could text him right now, let him know I won't be there. I hate that he's expecting me, and I'm going to disappoint him.

"What if I promise not to skate?" I ask, surprising myself. I'm putting a foot down, something I haven't been very good at lately. But I'm doing it.

My mom doesn't answer, and for a brief second or two I think she might pretend she didn't hear me. She finally looks at me, and I can see her trying to work out a new reason I can't go. There's a lot of work happening behind her eyes—but unless she's willing to say she doesn't want me hanging out with Andrew, she's got nothing.

"No skating," she repeats, standing and holding a finger up at me, as if I've done something wrong.

"No skating," I say, my stomach sinking a little, knowing I might be lying, because skating with Andrew was so...

"I want you home by noon," she says, her finger still pointing. Why is she pointing? I want to snap it off; it's infuriating me so.

"His game isn't done until noon. I won't get to talk to him at all," I say, standing and getting my shoes on, not bothering to pause while I speak for fear she'll reverse the direction we're moving. I am getting progress for the first time all morning; I'm not halting it.

"Were you planning on spending the whole day with him?" she asks, and I can sense that small hint of distaste in her tone. I stare her down until she looks away.

That's the other part about moving here. We had a long conversation about giving me some freedom, within reason. I am what everyone in my high school would call a *goody-goody*. I call my parents. I come home on time. I don't sneak around—though, I'm pretty sure I'm going back on that whole *no skating* promise. I've never given my parents a reason not to trust me, and if I'm going to go through with the things on my plate over the next few months, then I'm owed a little slack when it comes to the social things that are supposed to define this time of my life.

"We might have lunch. I'll be home before the sun sets. My homework is done, and I won't do anything that will result in a trip to the hospital or casts or...or even a Band Aid," I plead. Dragging my finger over my chest in a crisscross pattern, I stare into my mom's eyes, hoping to hear the sound of her keys jingling in her hand. She reaches into her purse, and I hug her.

"Home by six," she says, one more point with her finger. I don't even mind it this time—I'm so happy.

Andrew's game is halfway over by the time my mom gets me to the rink. She wanted to come in and watch with me, but I begged her not to. She compromised by waiting at the curb by the front doors until I was completely inside. There's a part of me that thinks she might still be out in the parking lot now.

There are a few people sitting sporadically in the bleachers around the rink, mostly wives and family members I think. I first notice the coach who was working with the kids on the ice yesterday. He has a thick beard, which makes him hard to miss. He's waiting on one of the benches; sweat is running down his face, and when one of the other players offers to trade out with him, he waves a hand signaling he's not quite ready to go back in.

I follow the various players gliding around the ice, watching their feet stop and skid. A few of them trip up a little when they have to change direction, but not Andrew. I recognize his feet quickly—smooth, fast. He doesn't control the game, but he changes it, darting in and out of plays before the others can catch up. Andrew isn't the youngest out there—most of the guys are his age. But the older ones *really* can't handle him. He's disruptive.

When he slides from the ice onto the bench, he pulls a helmet off and looks around the glass until he spots me. He smiles on one side of his mouth—he smiles for me. I raise a hand and scratch at the glass, trying to be cute with my hello. He scrunches his hand back at me.

His hair is floppy and lying in all directions; I'm hoping he's almost done with his game, because I don't want him to put his helmet back on. I want to watch him like this. I like looking on while he laughs and talks to his friends, while he yells things and points to other guys—while he's happy. Andrew might be the most beautiful portrait of happiness I've ever seen, and he comes from so much sadness.

He thunders out a "Booooooom!" as one of his teammates scores, and when he comes out on the ice to congratulate him, he hugs him around the neck, mussing the younger guy's hair. Andrew would have been an amazing older brother, and I have a feeling his brothers, at least Owen, were like this with him. It makes me smile, and I wear it bright and wide while he skates around the edge of the ice until he's facing me on the other side of the glass.

He starts moving his lips, saying something, but I can't hear him, so I shrug. He nods, then pulls his glove from his right hand and presses his finger against the glass, writing the word HUNGRY in the frost, followed by a question mark.

I nod *yes*, and he holds his hand by his ear, joking that he can't hear me. I laugh and nod bigger. He races around the other edge of the glass, walking carefully on his skates along the carpet toward me.

"Why are you nodding like that? You look ridiculous," he teases.

"Shut up," I say through nervous laughter.

Andrew is probably the only real friend I've made here, and I only see him at our school for an hour a day, sometimes only entering and exiting the locker room. I don't even know him that well, but I know I would rather get to know him than waste time getting to know anyone else. There are girls I've met here, like

Melody. She's in most of my classes, and we like the same TV shows and music. I guess we're friends, too. We call each other, which is more than I do with Andrew. But I would...call Andrew. If I could.

"So, are you ready for lesson number two? Or do you want to eat something first?" he asks, pulling off various pads, but leaving his skates on his feet. I breathe slowly, blinking at them, not sure if I should break that promise to my mom or not. Of course, skating wasn't her real concern anyhow.

"My feet are kind of sore..." I begin my excuse.

"That's okay. Let's just eat, and maybe I'll show you a few more things around town," Andrew says, slipping his feet into his shoes. He almost looks relieved we're not skating. I smile and let myself relax into the bench while he packs his things into a large bag, then carries it over to the rental counter.

"You keep your stuff here?" I ask, noticing him startle when I speak behind him. I put my hand on his shoulder to reassure him, almost out of habit—a habit that doesn't exist, but feels like it should. When I touch him, his shoulders rise with his long breath, almost as if I've healed something.

"Oh, I borrow pads. They're expensive, and these fit fine." He pauses, almost like he wants to say more, but stops with his feet square to mine, his hands looped in his pockets, his eyes staring just above my own. He takes another deep breath, like the one he took when I touched his shoulder, then raises his right hand and sweeps a lock of hair from my forehead over my shoulder. When his eyes meet mine, he looks surprised that I'm watching, and he falters a step backward and rushes his hand back to his pocket before looking down and shuffling a few more steps away.

"So, lunch then? Yeah?" he asks.

"Sounds good. Do you...what...just eat here?" I look over at the menu on the wall of peanuts, fries, and soft pretzels.

Andrew lets out a short breath of a laugh. "No, I was thinking somewhere *a little* nicer than this. Come with me; I wanna show you something," he nods toward the door. We stop back by the bench where his stick and skates are and he carries them through the door, holding it open for me as I pass closely by him. I watch his chest as I do to see if he breathes deeply again, but he seems to be used to me. I'm the one who releases a sharp breath this round.

I follow Andrew into the parking lot, and he stops at the back of an older sports car, the black paint faded in many places, and the glass missing and replaced with cardboard in one of the side windows. He pops the trunk, tossing his skates and stick in the back, then turns to face me as he shuts it.

"What do you think?" he asks. The trunk creaks as he closes it. As I graze over the body of the car, I notice the various rusty places and a few deep dents. My face must be revealing my reaction. "I know; it needs some work for sure. But...it's all mine."

I follow him around to the passenger door, and he pushes in and up on the handle with both hands so he can open it for me. "The door handle...that's one of the many things that needs work," he shrugs with a semi-proud smile.

When I look down, I notice there are several rips in the seat. Andrew reaches in and drags a towel from his side, smoothing it out for me. I slide inside and let him shut the door for me, noting the loud pop just before it closes. He has to push on the door an extra time to be sure it's latched.

He pulls his handle the same way, and slides into his seat, which is perhaps more torn than my side, and the fact that it was more important to him that I was comfortable isn't lost on me. I reach my hand forward and run it along the dashboard, which is slick and black and shiny. I bet Andrew makes the rest of the car just as nice one day.

"It's pretty cool," I say, tilting my head to the side just in time to see him exhale and smile proudly.

"Thanks," he grins, turning his focus to his key and the ignition. The engine roars and the entire car rumbles. I look at his face again, and see a flash of thrill ignite his eyes.

"Well it *sounds* like everything's working," I say, not really knowing if the car sounds right at all. I don't know anything about cars, other than where to put the pump for gas. But I know this car sounds fast and loud, and I get a feeling Andrew likes that.

"Yeah, it's working," he chuckles before punching the gas once and squealing the tires while he backs out, kicking ten pounds of gravel up into the air behind us. I grab both sides of my bucket seat on instinct and hear my mother's warning to *be careful* echo in my ears.

"So...driving lessons from your brothers too I'm guessing?" I ask, my hand somehow now clutched to my chest, crinkling the fabric of my shirt. I don't even remember moving it.

"Sorry...I get carried away," he says, wincing.

"No...it's okay. You just surprised me. I wasn't expecting it," I say. He watches me for a few extra seconds, I think to judge whether or not I'm lying. Eventually, his eyes begin to relax, and he shifts the gear, pulling out of the lot slowly.

"Okay, well how about I take it slow and the next time I want to speed things up I give you a sign," he smirks. My body flushes, because I get the sense he might be talking about *other* things.

"Okay," I whisper, forcing my hands to remain still on my legs, not to pick at one another and give away how tense he makes me.

"But to answer your question," he says, pulling my attention to him again. He's looking at the roadway, so I feel safe to stare at him while he talks. "My brothers would never teach me how to drive. Owen wouldn't let me touch his truck. I had to get his friends to teach me. And his best friend was all about drag racing, so when Owen left us alone, he sort of let me go crazy."

"How nice of him," I say, not masking my sarcasm.

Andrew glances at me with a short laugh. "Yeah, I guess it wasn't safe or whatever, but...I don't know...life is what it is, and you can only control like...this much of it," he says, holding his thumb and index finger out toward me measuring less than an inch. "Sometimes I just want to feel a little more of everything, you know?"

He glances at me again, and I can't seem to smile back at him, as much as I want to. I can't because I know *exactly* what he means. I want to feel more, but I'm on pause—not allowed to really feel anything until I'm cleared and told it's okay to do so.

I'm feeling things now. And I intend on keeping all of that secret.

"Maybe that sounds crazy. God, you probably think I'm nuts," he says as he runs his hand over his face and through the blowing wild strands of his hair.

"You're not nuts," I say, and notice his jaw twitch at my response, his lips tight in a straight line. He clears his throat and leans to the side to roll up his window. We stop at a light in the center of town, and the loud clicking of the blinker fills the dead air, and eventually Andrew and I both laugh.

"Goddamn that's loud, right?" he says, leaning toward me and looking at the gear shaft as if somehow he can control the sound from there. He glances back up, now inches closer to me, and his breath falters again. "So maybe that goes on the list of things to fix."

"No, don't," I smile. He flinches and squints, sitting back comfortably as he turns and pulls into a diner parking lot. "If you fix it, then it won't make that sound anymore, and now it's sort of our thing. We'll always be able to laugh at the loud blinker noise."

His bottom lip sucked into his mouth, he nods as he pulls into a spot and shifts into park, tapping both hands along the black rubber of the steering wheel.

"Well then that's settled," he says, grinning as he pulls the keys from the ignition. "The clicking noise stays."

I nod in agreement, then reach to my door handle.

"Hang on, wait for me," Andrew says, springing from his seat and jogging around the front of the car. He's wearing the same gray jeans and black shirt he wore Friday night, and I'm glad. He looks nice like this. With a jerk of the handle, he has my door open, and I step out and make a silent wish to feel his hand along my back, the way a guy walks a girl from the car when they go on a date in the movies. I get to the restaurant door without ever feeling it, though.

Andrew raises two fingers, and a waitress shows us to a booth in the back corner of the restaurant, our feet touching underneath as we climb into our seats. I move my right foot out of the way, but I leave my left foot in place against his, almost like a test to see what he'll do. He doesn't move either.

35

We both flip open the menu, and I wonder if he's reading without reading like I am. My eyes are passing over the words, but my attention is on the outer edge of my left foot, the one lodged against the inside of his right one. It's such a stupid touch, but in some small way, it feels like I'm holding his hand.

"So it's a...Camaro?" I ask. I looked at the logo on the way into the restaurant.

Andrew chuckles, his eyes still on his menu, his foot still against mine.

"Yeah, it's a seventy-six," he says. I have no idea what that means, but I nod and smile as if I do. He reads me quickly though and laughs again as he flattens his menu. "There's a guy down our old street who has a backyard that's just...like...*filled* with these classic old cars. I used to go visit him with Owen, and we'd sit in them and pretend we were driving around. This one was always my favorite though. Anyhow...he stopped by my apartment just before we left to visit my brother and said he was getting rid of a few. He sold it to my mom for five hundred bucks. I'm getting a job this summer to pay her back."

I might not know anything about cars, but I understand dreams. I get wanting things, and I can imagine how it must feel to finally have something in your hands you want so badly.

"It's a great car," I say, my smile soft. He looks into my eyes for a few seconds before shaking his head and picking his menu back up.

"It's shit right now. But...it will be a great car. I promise," he says, and there isn't a doubt in my mind that it will be.

We both order sandwiches and sodas when the waitress comes, and with our menus gone, I feel a little more exposed— and much more aware of the weird footsie standoff happening under the table.

"Delaware," Andrew finally says, breaking a long rut of silence. "Tell me about it. What's your story, Emma Burke?"

When he says my name, his lips take care of every syllable. I wonder if he says every name like this, or just mine.

"Well..." I start, pausing to tuck my right leg over my left, shifting my weight, but never moving the foot against Andrew's.

I glance up to catch his smirk when I do, and I know he's playing the same game I am. "You saw my little brother, right?"

Andrew nods, and I swear his smile has stretched to cover more of his face.

"His name's Cole. He's three. It's just us, and my parents. My mom's a telemarketer..."

"Wait," Andrew interrupts, looking up and holding his question while our waitress delivers our plates and drinks. When she leaves, he leans forward, elbows on either side of his plate. "Your mom is a real-life telemarketer?"

My eyes wide, I nod, not sure what makes that so interesting.

"Man, that's like the suckiest job! Do people hang up on her all day? Oh...I bet she gets cussed out all the time. Or...do people prank her?"

"I have no idea," I giggle.

"Sorry, I just...I've always wondered who does that job. Every time someone calls us, I wonder how bad it is on the other end. I mean, though...I'm sure your mom is a really nice person," he stops abruptly, then sucks in his bottom lip.

"Okay...anyhow..." I start again, but he holds up his hand to stop me.

"One more question, and that's it. I swear," he says, and I laugh. "What does she sell?"

"Uh...she does surveys, I think. For things like commercials people remember and different food chains," I say, realizing I don't really pay attention to the words my mother says when she's on the phone all day. I just know she gets to work at home because of it, and *that*...has come in handy.

"Okay, I don't think I've answered one of those. Just...ya know. Wanted to make sure I didn't get one of her calls," he says, his lip ticked up on one side. "I'm not real nice to telemarketers. But I'll change that; I swear."

He crosses his chest with his finger then picks up a fry from his plate, chewing it whole.

"Okay, well...you'll love this then. My dad's a dogcatcher," I say, covering my eyes with both hands. When I let my fingers fall open so I can peek at him, he's squeezing his eyes shut.

"I know...he's like Cruella de Vil kinda evil. Except he's not," I begin to defend my dad.

"Uhm...dogcatcher . I saw *Lady and the Tramp* when I was a kid. That shit messed me up, and it's the reason we still don't have a dog. If I accidentally let it loose, your meanie dad will haul it away and lock it up in the rain somewhere," he says, shaking his head.

"So...that's not how it works—and *dogcatcher* really is more like *stray-dog finder.* He always finds a home for animals, and usually he gets called on to deal with strange animal situations for animal control," I explain. Andrew keeps staring at me with one brow quirked.

"Hmmmm, okay, but I'm starting to wonder about you, Delaware. You better want to be something happy when you grow up," he says through a full mouth.

"Surgeon." My answer is one word, and it's definitive. I've known what I want to be since the day I understood who the person was that did that job. I want to save people. I want to be their last hope. Because I will never quit.

"Oh yeah sure, surgeon. Like *those* are good people," Andrew kids. I pick up one of my fries and throw it at him. He catches it against his chest and drops it on his plate, then taps his foot into mine twice, reminding me it's there.

He doesn't move it, though.

We're quiet while we're eating. A group of seniors I recognize from my school spill into the diner loudly, interrupting the awkward quiet. It distracts both of us, and we smirk at each other when one of the girls laughs—her cackle comes out almost sounding like a dolphin's call. I hold a fist to my mouth to keep myself from laughing; Andrew stuffs more fries in his and looks out the window, knowing if we make eye contact again, we'll both lose it.

After a few seconds, we glance at each other, exchanging a silent look that says we both think that chick should do her best not to laugh out loud—ever again.

The group settles down, but after a few minutes, their whispers are what catch our attention the second time. I notice Andrew glancing up from his plate, beyond my shoulder, then back down to his food. His movement is repetitive, and each time he looks at the group behind me, his scowl grows a little.

His reaction forces me to pay attention, too. Eventually, I hear one of the girls speak a little too loudly, mentioning James and Owen, and then I hear one of the guys in the group say something about betting "he'll end up shooting himself just like his brother did or becoming some hardcore junkie."

They're talking about Andrew—or his brother, Owen. It doesn't matter which one, because I get the sense that Andrew and his brother are so close that if you cut one the other bleeds.

Everything that follows happens in milliseconds—my eyes zero in on Andrew's hand, the contraction of his muscles as he grips his fork. Then, I see the flex of his jaw and the strain in his neck followed by the cold shadow consuming his eyes. The hurt he's feeling is there—I see it—but there's anger and hate brewing, too.

I sense his conflict—ignore the wave of familiar ridicule being spun behind me or stand up to it and become one more reason for people to talk. His eyes watering, Andrew has been at this crossroads before. I have a feeling he's been here a lot. And I also think I'm the thing keeping his feet tethered to this side of the line this time.

When our eyes finally meet, Andrew almost looks as if he's apologizing to me, sorry that I am witnessing any of this. It's more than being embarrassed; it's being ashamed. That one look from him breaks me and resolves me all at once.

I smile and hold up a finger, my shift in mood halting him for long enough—the few seconds I need to slide out of our booth. I hear his feet shuffle behind me, and I turn to see him starting to step out behind me, but I smile bigger and hold a hand up with a wink. "Just give me a sec," I say.

Andrew looks uneasy. I feel uneasy. But I also feel right about this, so I keep walking toward the group of seven strangers until I'm leaning over the counter next to the stools they're gathered around at the other end of the restaurant. I purposely brush the arm of one of the girls to get her attention, and she apologizes and steps from her seat to give me room, assuming I'm trying to reach for salt, or napkins, or any of the other tiny things piled in a basket near them.

"Oh, no. I just heard you all and thought I'd come over to join in. You're talking about the Harpers, right?" I say, glancing from one set of eyes to another, an interested smile on my face feigning that I also want in on this *oh-so-fun* gossip fest. They all look uncomfortable, and the girl closest to me—the one who moved out of my way—keeps looking over my shoulder toward Andrew, as if she's trying to clue me in that I should keep my voice down.

"Oh, I know, you're totally right. I should be quiet, huh?" I whisper. "I bet he can hear me."

I leave my eyes on hers for an uncomfortable amount of time. There's a flash of guilt in them when I say it out loud, publicly acknowledging that we heard everything. And normally, I'd stop there; she'll learn a lesson from this, and probably not gossip about the Harpers except in the privacy of her own home for at least a month. But that look on Andrew's face sticks with me, so I take things just a little farther.

"You know, I hear there's a foster home around here that takes care of kids who lost their parents to horrible accidents or illness. Maybe when we're done here, we can go make fun of them for a while, tease them about how they're going to die in car crashes too one day. Or...or...wait! Even better...let's make one of those viral videos where we wake people up in the middle of the night and remind them that their loved one is dead. That would be awesome...no?"

A can see a chill fall over them all, and the guy who was talking the most five minutes before, swallows hard. We all hear it. I step closer to him, letting my fake smile fall back into the hard line my mouth wants to make. "Or, if you'd rather, you can just keep being assholes over here, and I'll go back over there and try and ignore you," I say, pleased at the regretful feelings I've nurtured. "Your call."

I reach to the counter, grabbing a bottle of ketchup, then spin on my heels and walk back to Andrew, who's still sitting with his legs stretched out underneath the booth, munching on his fries one at a time. He doesn't look up at me when I sit back into the booth, and he never glances up when I twist the cap off the ketchup, pouring a small amount on the corner of my plate.

When I'm done, I move the bottle on the table until it clinks against his plate, and I let my hand rest flat on the space between us. After a few seconds, the group I'd just left leaves the restaurant. Neither of us turns to look—the only confirmation, the small chime of the cluster of bells tethered to the door. Once we hear the sound of their cars pulling from the lot just outside, Andrew reaches up, sliding the bottle out of the way, and takes my fingers into his hand, squeezing just hard and long enough to let me feel him.

That's when I finally smile for real.

We finish our meals, and Andrew pulls a twenty from his wallet, not letting me chip in for my half. I follow him to his car and wait while he lifts the handle, then move into my seat.

He attempts to slide over the hood of his car, but his skid stops midway, so he pushes down the front and walks to his door, reaching into the backseat to grab a beanie for his head, sliding it on and pulling it over his eyes, playing up his humiliation.

"Massive fail," he says, poking fun of his bombed attempt on the hood.

"Oh, I just assumed that's how that was supposed to go," I say, pretending to be impressed.

"Uh yeah...I mean, bitchin'..." he says, puffing out the collar of his shirt and shrugging with a sniff before breaking into a short laugh.

"Wow, I was willing to fake it until you said *bitchin'*," I say, unable to help but smile so hard my cheeks hurt.

"Fuck," he says, his head slung forward, his eyes down. "Ruined by my own lame vernacular."

"*Bitchin'* will kill you every time," I say with a short tisk and headshake.

He turns the engine over, but looks at me from the side, his eyes moving in quick motions from mine to my mouth and back again. He chuckles to himself before looking up into the rearview mirror and shifting the car into reverse. "I'm pretty sure you can say anything and own it," he says.

I don't answer, and I watch his cheeks turn just a little redder. I fight grinning at his compliment, pushing my lips together tight, but losing the battle and smiling anyhow.

Andrew picks up where our tour left off the time before, driving me through various neighborhoods and streets, pointing out places he and his brothers used to sled, places where he got into fights, and then down his street, stopping in front of his old house.

It's a simple two story, the color dark brown with brick, the yard neat but simple, and a few trees towering in the front, their branches growing bare for the winter.

"You miss living here?" I ask.

He leans forward on his steering wheel, folding his arms and resting his head on top. "Sometimes," he sighs. "But...I don't know. Never mind."

"No, tell me," I say, for some reason not wanting him to feel he can't tell me things.

He leans back in his seat, his gaze still out the window, on the dull porch light shining in the front. "This house wasn't full of happy memories. At least, not for me," he says, his eyes lost to the light now, and I can tell he's letting it pop in and out of focus.

"Your brother James?" I ask. I pull my sleeves down over my knuckles and bite on the fabric, hoping that question was okay to ask.

"Yeah, that's most of it," he says. "James died here."

I heard the story—both from the gossipy tale my neighbor told my parents and through the whispers spoken in the diner tonight—but hearing Andrew say the words, even though he didn't offer any details, made the pain of it all palpable. His brother was an addict, and when he got caught up in something with the police, he ended up shooting himself in the driveway. When I heard the story, I couldn't imagine it was true. But as Andrew mentions James now, I can tell just by the look in his eyes that it is. And it's awful. And I wish I'd done more to those assholes in the restaurant who thought his pain was funny.

"But I didn't really have much of a life here. I mean...I had my brother's life, my brother's friends. And we lived next door to Owen's girlfriend. But, it was all Owen. None of it was really *me*."

42

His head falls to the side, and I reach up cautiously and let my finger run along the ridge of one of the gauges in his ear. It's not very big, but it's edgier than anything I would ever have the courage to do. I envy him for it.

"I met you while I lived in my apartment," he says, his eyes still on my hand next to his face. I pull it away, back into my lap, nervous about what he may say next. Everything inside of me wants Andrew Harper to like me—*like that*. Everything inside wants him to kiss me—*like that*. And it's also the last thing I want, because then my parents will freak out, and they'll ruin this perfect friendship. I think I might like kissing him. But *I know* I like sitting next to him in his car.

"So being my friend is a good memory?" I say, leading him, and regretting it the second a shade of disappointment paints his eyes. He hides it as best he can, breathing deeply and adjusting his posture in his seat before shifting the car and pulling back out on the roadway.

"Yeah, Delaware. Being your friend is a pretty damn great memory," he says.

Before the sun kisses the horizon, Andrew pulls up in front of my house, and as I expected, both of my parents are waiting on the front porch for me to come home. Andrew puts the car in park, and skips around to my side to open the door for me. I silently curse his broken door, because now that he's out of the car, my parents are going to want to meet him. They're already walking toward us when I step up to the curb.

"Home before sunset, just like I promised," I say through gritted teeth only my mom can see. She ignores my nonverbal plea, though, and shifts her focus right to Andrew.

"Yes, I see. Thank you, Andrew, for bringing Emma home," my mom says, reaching out a hand for him to take. This is a test, to see what he does. But Andrew does nothing but act like himself. He stutters a bit, then responds with a few *of courses* while he repeatedly shakes my mother's hand before awkwardly reaching for my father's.

He calls them both Mr. and Mrs. Burke, saying their names at least a dozen times, and when he's not looking, they're taking turns surveying his car for danger, then memorizing his piercings and the way he's dressed. I'm sure in their mind he looks to be everything the nosey neighbor warned about—the youngest in a brood of hoodlum troublemakers—but I'm hopeful that his bumbling speech and clumsiness in front of them cancels most of it out.

Before I realize it, he's made his way back to the driver's side, and when he gets in the car and revs the engine, I realize I've managed not to get his number for a second time. I regret that the moment he drives away.

I regret it more when my parents begin to pick him apart as we walk back up to the house.

I regret it most, though, when I shut my bedroom door on them and curl up in front of my window and wait for the sun to go down—for one more day to tick off my calendar, for the waiting to be over.

I should tell him. It would be nice to tell someone.

Maybe after our trip to Chicago.

Chapter 4

Andrew

I'm pretty sure Emma's parents don't like me. I don't think they dislike me, but I got the strong sense they were working through a lot of Harper-shit to drill down to the real me. And I think they still think the real me isn't far off from the stories they've heard.

I didn't help things by acting like an idiot. At least I wasn't threatening.

Of course, now I can't find Emma. I drove by her house every morning this week, and their cars were always gone. I looked for her in PE every day, but she was missing from the line of girls racing up the steps or out from the locker room. After my morning drive-by on Friday, when I got a strange look from the woman who lives across the street, I finally broke down and asked Dwayne where Emma was. He checked with the office for me and said her parents signed her out for the week.

I know she isn't gone because of me. But there's also that fucked-up little voice in the back of my head that's working real hard at convincing me that *yeah*, she's gone because of me. I creeped her out. Her parents hate me. She's moved back to Delaware—fleeing the entire state of Illinois because Andrew Harper is bad news.

The only thing that's made me feel better is skating, and I've been extra rough with the guys who've shown up to scrimmage this week. One of them finally had enough, and checked me back, then took his elbow to my chin hard, cracking my lip open.

I've been sitting on the other side of the glass, spitting, for the last fifteen minutes. Chris, the dude who popped me in the face, stopped by to apologize. I flipped him off.

"Look at baby Harper," a voice calls from behind me. I twist in my seat, wincing at the deep bruise Chris apparently left on my ribs. I'm able to shift enough to see my brother's friend House in my periphery. House is kind of an asshole, but he's harmless. And he was glued to Owen for most of my life; when he moved away, it was kind of like losing another brother.

"Dude, what are you doing in town?" I say, standing, but holding the washcloth to my mouth while I slap House's hand with my free one.

"Yo, Indiana sucks worse than this shithole," he says, spitting his tobacco into a cup he's carrying. That cup—it's fuckin' disgusting.

"Yeah, well, I could have told you that. If you want change, you need to go to the city, or some place like Vegas or California, man," I say, testing the bloodstain on the rag I've been holding to my mouth. The blood is less, so I toss the cloth on top of my borrowed equipment on the floor.

"Your lip's all fucked up, dude. What happened?" he says, reaching his hand toward my face as if to touch it. I smack his hand away, but he does it again. He keeps doing it until I punch his arm. "Look at that, baby Harper's growing up, and he's feisty."

"Dude, whatever," I roll my eyes and bend down to pick up my things to return to the counter. "It's nothing. I just took a jab to the face."

"You Harpers, always getting hit in your pretty-boy faces," he says, pulling himself up to sit on the counter while I hand my things over to Gary and toss the bloody cloth into the trash.

"Whatever, man," I say, stepping toward the door and encouraging House to follow. He isn't quiet, and people are already starting to watch us suspiciously. House—he's like a warning siren for a shit-storm of trouble.

He follows me out to the parking lot, to my car, and when he whistles, my chest feels a little fuller. There are few people who will recognize this car—my brother and House are at the top of that list.

"Damn, that old man finally sold it. Or...wait, did you lift this shit?" he says, stepping back with his hands in the air.

"Fuck off. Mom bought it, but I have to pay her back," I say, cracking open the door, not even minding the sound it makes.

"You are the good son," he teases, pushing me out of the way and sitting in the driver's seat. "Ohhhhhh, baby Harp. This shit is fast, yo? Hey...you got time? I'm dying to see it open up."

I glance at my phone as if I have anywhere to be. It's not quite lunchtime on Saturday, and the girl I'm stalking is nowhere to be found, so I look back up at him and let my grin grow slowly.

"Yeah haaa haaa," he says, slapping at the top of the steering wheel. He reaches for the keys, but I only open the door as wide as it will go. He gets out with a chuckle, then jukes toward me like he wants to grab my keys. I don't flinch, because House has been doing shit like that to me for years. Maybe I see him coming now, or maybe I'm just so used to it I don't juke for anyone any more. I think the latter might be the case, and I also think that's maybe why I let Chris punch me with his elbow about twenty minutes ago.

House gets into the passenger side, and I buckle up and wait for him to do the same. He rolls his eyes at me, but he does it anyhow. I look around the lot, and when I confirm it's empty, I fishtail backward from my spot until I hit the roadway, then I punch it and feel the tires grip after a few seconds of burnt rubber and smoke. The back end slides for the first hundred yards, but I straighten everything out—careful not to punch the gas until we hit the edge of town.

House leans forward, and we both glance in all directions, checking for cops. It's winter, so the landscape is pretty clear. In the summer, the asshole cops hide behind the corn. I crack my knuckles as a joke, and House laughs, his cackle growing more maniacal as I hit the gas hard and climb the car up to ninety in a few seconds. The roar echoes everywhere; I try to take the car up over a hundred, but it starts to feel loose, so I back off.

I flip around at the edge of the woods and push it just as fast on the way back toward town, slowing down to the speed limit when we start to see other cars. House has turned the radio up, and he's rolled down his window. I can tell he's happy. It's nice having him here, too. He and I—we used to do this a lot.

I drive him back to the Ice Palace lot and pull up next to his truck. He gets out, but pauses at my door, knocking on the window. I roll it down.

"Hey, a few of us are getting together for a little party at Sasha's. Mostly guys you know. Anyhow, if you wanna come, just hit me up," he says. I nod, and think about forgetting his invitation immediately—just like I used to. But then I realize, Owen's gone. And I was invited.

"Hey! House!" I shout out the window just before he climbs into his pickup. He turns and flips me off, because that's his thing. "I'm in. What time?"

"Show up around five. And bring fuckin' pizza!" he yells, half chuckling.

Maybe I'm the guy bringing the pizza, but House wouldn't invite me if he didn't want me there. He's always been an extension of Owen, and I think I'll always be a kid brother in his eyes because of that closeness.

One fucked up family. But it's mine.

I spend a few hours wrapping up some reading on existentialism for an essay due next week, then I rush out of the apartment around four, giving myself enough time to pick up pizza and avoid my mom coming home from work. I leave a note for her and Dwayne that I'll be out late, knowing if I say I'm with House that she will call. I just say I'm meeting with a few of the hockey guys instead.

On my way to pick up food, I swing by Emma's house, and everything about it is as quiet and shut down as it has been all week. Her family has disappeared, but there are a few lights on inside. It's always the same ones, which makes me think maybe they've just taken off for a family trip or a vacation. A little weird in early October, but maybe that's a thing normal families do. I wouldn't know. We've never taken a trip anywhere, other than a drive for the day up to Wisconsin for some water slides. And that trip was all Owen's doing.

I stop by the pizza joint next, pick up the four large ones House ordered, and head to Sasha's.

I've been here a few times, but never for long. Usually, I was tagging along with Owen while he talked to someone about something or made plans with House. He never let me stay. But tonight, I pull up on my own, in my own car—invited.

"Douchebag!" House shouts the second I walk through the door.

"You owe me fuckin' money, yo!" I say, sliding the pizzas on the counter seconds before a dozen people I don't recognize flip open the lids and start taking away slices. House walks into the kitchen and throws a wadded up ten-dollar bill at me. I look at it in my hand and then furrow my brow at him.

"It's all I got now. I'll hit you up with the rest later," he says, already devouring a slice.

"Right you will," I say, stuffing the money into my wallet and knowing it's all I'm going to get. House confirms it with his full-mouthed laugh.

I grab a slice and follow him to the sunken living room, taking a seat in one of the large beanbag chairs. The lights are low, and there's a group of people playing pool at a table in a room near the back of the house.

Everything in here is either really expensive or a piece of trash. It's weird. I know Sasha's parents have money—they own a lot of land, and they've sold most of it. They farm this small plot, and they don't even do their own farming.

They're never around, but I heard Sasha and her friends are staying here for college, driving to Northwestern for school. The result—this farmhouse has become a five-bedroom dorm without any supervision.

"Hey, baby Harp..." House nudges me with a red plastic cup in his hand. I take it from him and smell it; it isn't beer. "Just drink it."

I take a small sip and start to cough instantly while House leans forward and lets out a belly laugh. "Welcome to your first taste of Jack, baby Harp. Don't tell your brother I gave it to you; he'll kick my ass," he says, holding his cup out to click cheers with mine, urging me to drink the rest along with him.

I do.

And I drink one more after that.

I've been drunk on beer before. Owen was always more lenient about that. But never the hard stuff. This buzz...it's different.

I like it.

I stop after two, though, and manage to discard a third shot of whiskey, knowing any more will probably have me throwing up. The living room has become the hub for the party, and Sasha has set herself next to me, her legs draped across my lap from one side of the beanbag to the other. I can tell she's lit, and House keeps raising an eyebrow at me.

"You look a lot like your brother, you know?" she says, taking a long, slow drink of whatever's in her cup. Sasha was always *the* girl—the red-hot one who every guy wanted to sleep with and many had. She always liked Owen, though. They had a fling, but I don't think she could ever call my brother hers.

Right now, she's looking at me with eyes that say she's willing to accept the consolation—even if it's three years younger.

"Well, we're related," I say, laying my hands on her knees, feeling the temptation of how smooth they are sting my fingertips. I leave them there for a few seconds and slide them out an inch at a time, moving up her thigh and down her shin simultaneously, like I'm playing an instrument. She bites her bottom lip when I do, letting it slowly slide from her teeth, and I can completely understand why every other dude in the room wants to trade spots with me right now.

"You're the cuter one," she teases me. I keep my eyes on her legs, knowing if I look to the right, into her eyes, they'll be waiting to seduce me. But then...

Sasha isn't Emma.

I'm buzzed, but that thought floats on repeat in my head. Emma. I can't stop thinking about Emma.

"Well, I'm younger, so I guess that makes me cuter," I say, lips tight in a semi-smile, hiding my inner struggle to do the right thing. Sliding my hands under her legs gingerly, I let myself hesitate for one extra second before lifting her legs from my lap and pushing myself to my feet.

I move to the stools on the other side of the room, taking a seat next to House, who is shaking his head at me.

"Dude, you might be the first virgin I've ever seen say no to that," he laughs lightly.

"Yeah," I sigh.

"Here," he says, handing me a joint he's been smoking for the last few minutes. I look at it in his hand, then look to Sasha

50

who has now let her legs fall open; I can see the black lace of her underwear peaking out through the middle. I turn back to the joint and pinch it between my fingers, bringing it to my lips. Drunk and high is still probably a better choice. Of course, the smart thing probably would have been to choose neither, but I blew that with the second shot of whiskey.

I spend the next three hours intensely watching two guys play a made-up game on the pool table—rolling the striped balls at the solids. There don't seem to be any rules, or fuck—maybe there are rules. Whatever, it's fascinating. I watch it until I realize exactly how boring it is, and when I glance at my watch, it's ten o'clock at night and somehow five hours of my life have passed and I missed it.

I walk through the house to find a bathroom and stumble into a room where House seems to have filled whatever need Sasha had, and I feel a little tinge of regret that I didn't give in. Her shirt is off, and her bare tits are staring at me. She's clearly comfortable with her body, because she stands up from her straddling position on House, her lace underwear the only thing on, and steps toward me. House slaps her ass as she walks away, his drunken laugh a soundtrack to her strut.

"Bathroom," I stutter, somehow. She giggles and moves close enough to touch my chest with her index finger, dragging it slowly down my T-shirt and stomach until she runs it along my now-hard cock.

"Down the hall one more door," she smiles, pressing her palm flat against my jeans and pausing as I pulse. "Or you can stay…"

"I'm good," I breathe, aware of every sensation happening under the zipper of my jeans. I leave the room and hear her laughter briefly behind the door, but I keep my resolve, putting one foot in front of the next until I get to the bathroom where I take the most painful piss of my entire life—then spend about five minutes running water over my face.

I quickly pass the room on my way back down the hall, not wanting to hear any sounds that might act as a siren and call me in.

51

Grabbing a bottle of water from the fridge, I twist the cap and drink about half of it before fishing my keys from my pocket. In a house full of people, I'm still alone, and I wonder if this is how Owen felt when he would come to these parties.

I step out front and spend a half an hour throwing rocks from Sasha's driveway into the thick forest abutting her property—listening to each rock fall through the cracked branches and onto the bed of dried brush and leaves. The first snow hasn't happened yet, but it's coming. I can see my breath.

My breath.

I cup my hands and smell as best I can. I'm sure I stink of whiskey. Or maybe not. I only had a couple shots hours ago, though, and I feel fine. Maybe a little bit of a headache, but fine otherwise.

I climb into my car and turn the engine on, letting the heat seep into my sweatshirt and reach my skin. My knuckles are red from being cold, so I hold my hands over the vent for a few minutes, letting my bones thaw.

When I glance to the empty seat next to me, I think of Emma. Shutting my eyes, I let my head fall back against the seat and imagine her there. I'm interrupted by the sound of my car door flying open, and I'm startled when House climbs in, laughing hysterically and talking a million-words-a-minute.

"Fucker, get out of my car," I push at him.

"Yo...yo...no, listen," he says, speaking through laughter. He's drunk. And stoned. I've seen him like this a hundred times, and it's always a pain in the ass. "I'm hungry. Like, really hungry. Take me to get a burger, dude. Come on."

"Go make a sandwich, and get the fuck out of my car," I say, gripping the wheel, intent on not taking House *anywhere*.

"Awwww, come on man. Here, here...I'll give you some shit," he says, pulling a sad-ass bag of weed from his pocket, giggling as he fumbles with it.

"Dude!" I roll my eyes.

"Fucker. You suck," he says, reaching over the console and smacking my face hard enough that it stings and I'm sure it's pink.

I lunge at him, but he's too fast, and is already out of the car walking back toward the house. I am pretty sure I'm okay not getting invited to another one of these parties.

With a deep breath, I look back at the wheel and then to the once-again empty seat, trying to get back to the place I was—imagining Emma there. When it doesn't work, I push the car into drive and do the next best thing, heading to her house.

I expect the same empty driveway, the lack of cars in the street, the single light shining through the upstairs window. But when I pull around the corner, everything about the Burke house is full and lived in. I'm fumbling with my seatbelt before I even stop the car; I shove the gear into park, and turn the engine off the second I pull behind the small car along the street.

I get to the middle of the brick walkway when I realize I have no clue what I'm doing. It's almost midnight, and I'm sure everyone in the house is asleep, and I barely know Emma—let alone her family, but she's in there.

Knowing I can't knock on the door, I step backward along the walkway and look up to the brightly lit windows over the front door. I make my way to the other side of the street, my eyes straining to figure out what room I'm looking at. I can see two ceiling fans spinning, and the tops of some bookcases, and I'm sure I'm looking at a loft space.

Jogging back across the street, I slow when I come to the corner of the house, and I walk cautiously over the wood chips and mulch along the trail in the side yard. There's another light on near the rear of her home, so I move to that area, stepping back just enough to let me see pink drapes along either side of a small bay window and then a knee.

Her knee.

I know it's her leg. I've stared at it in PE shorts and pretended to grip it with my hand in my car. I've memorized the fantasy of that leg, and I would know it anywhere. She's sitting in her window, and I'm overcome with a sense of urgency to talk to her.

Looking around the ground in front of me, I bend to pick up a few wood chips then toss them at the base of her window. They're not heavy enough, and they fall back to the ground after a few feet. I move a little farther away from her window, and finally find some stones nestled in the tufts of dead grass around her lawn. I toss my first one gently, not wanting to make too loud of a noise, but it barely grazes the side of the house. I wait, and her leg doesn't move.

Fuck.

I hold my arm up and take a deep breath before launching my second attempt. This one pings directly off her window, and her leg jumps back fast. I scared her. Shit! I scared her. I hold my breath, waiting for her face to appear. But it doesn't. She's not looking for the noise. I panic and look for another rock, finding a small one and throwing it quickly without much aim. It ricochets off the side of the house, but close enough to her window that she has to know.

Come on, Emma. Look out your goddamned window.

I look for another rock, but hear the sound of her window sliding open.

"Andrew?" she says in a loud whisper. "What the hell are you doing?"

I smile and let the small stones I've just found fall from my fingers. I stretch my arms to either side of me and almost laugh.

"I have no idea," I grin. "Come down."

She pauses and looks at me for a few seconds, her hair blowing along either side of her face as she leans out the window. I am kissing this girl tonight. I am kissing her, and I don't care if she hits me because of it. I'm tasting those lips, and I will savor every second I get of it before she smacks me across the face.

"Hang on," she says, pulling her window shut again. Her light stays on, so I'm not sure whether to look at her window or wait for her at the front door. Finally, I hear the sound of her door opening, so I jog over to her the porch. She locks the door behind her and ushers me to follow her closer to my car along the street.

"Oh my god, what are you doing here?" she asks, her eyes lit up, glowing silver. She's smiling. She's smiling because she's happy to see me.

I...make her happy.

"I missed you," I admit. Those words hit my chest the second they leave my lips, and I feel both free and terrified at the same time. My hands go deep into my pockets on instinct, and my legs feel numb.

And then her lip ticks up on one side.

"I missed you, too," she says, her voice soft, not wanting to wake anyone. "Let's get out of here."

I don't hesitate, running to the passenger door and working it open so she can get inside. The sight of her *actually* in my passenger seat is so much better than the version I had going on in my head. I close the door and run to my side, getting in quickly and shutting the door carefully. I know the engine is going to make a loud sound, so I wince when I crank it, but pull away slowly, hoping I didn't disturb her parents.

"I hope I don't get you in any trouble," I say, looking in the rearview mirror, as if I could tell by looking in the one-inch reflection if her parents were awake and catching her escape.

"Me too," she giggles.

She's wearing this plaid shirt with long sleeves, and it's big on her, like it's her father's. Her legs are in a pair of tight black jeans, her feet wearing the pink Converse that I use to track her in PE. She's holding her hands over the vent in front of her, warming them, and I wish I didn't have to drive this car so I could reach over and warm them within my own.

I drive until we get to a forest preserve, pulling off into the parking lot, not really knowing what I'm doing. I have no plan. I just had to see her. And when she told me to go, I went.

"So..." I say, then let my breath fall into a nervous laugh. I'm gripping the steering wheel for strength, knowing I can't just kiss her now, but god do I want to.

"So," she says, pulling her seatbelt off and turning sideways in her seat. She pulls her knees up into her body, her feet flat along the center console. She looks cramped and uncomfortable.

I stare at her shoes for a few seconds, thinking of my life a few hours ago, when an older girl wanted to hook up with me and draped her legs over my lap without invitation. This scene— it's a million times sexier, maybe because I have to work for it.

With timid hands, I reach to the heel of one shoe, my eyes moving to hers briefly before coming back to her foot. She's watching me, but she isn't stopping me. I cup the back of one shoe in my hand and lift her foot from the console and pull it toward me. I let my hand move from her shoe to the back of her leg, my fingers shaking nervously, as if I could break her leg if I were to drop it.

Emma gives in easily, giving me complete control, her muscles relaxing, and I move first one leg then the other to my lap. She eases into the side of her door slowly, her hands clinging to one another in her own lap. I let out a short breath when the weight of her sinks into me, and I rest my hands along the soft denim over her legs, sliding them up and stopping at her knee. That knee. I squeeze it once, and she twitches with a giggle.

"Ticklish," she smirks.

"Good to know," I say, my head tilted to the side, my eyes unable to look away from her.

There are so many things I want to know, so many little facts I need to memorize about this girl. But I can't take my eyes from her lips; I know I can't kiss them yet, so I look back down at my hands, letting them run down the length of her leg to her ankles. Her ankles to her knees—that's my line.

"What brought you to Woodstock?" I ask, rapping my fingers a few times along her legs to work out more of my nerves. "I hear it's the hot bed for dog-catching and telemarketing careers, but..."

She lets out a breathy laugh, then stretches her hands out flat along her thighs. I watch her move, wishing I could touch her there.

"Sort of a family thing. We...we needed to be closer to Chicago," she says with a lopsided smile and a shrug.

"Woodstock is so not Chicago," I chuckle, thinking about the ways my hometown is so small compared to the city. There are things I love about being here. The smallness is comforting at times. But the older I get, the more I sense how suffocating it is too.

"No," she laughs. "But it's also not Delaware."

"Good point," I say.

"What's your favorite food?" I ask. She tilts her head and offers a suspicious smile.

"Pancakes."

I nod, then look out to the blackness in front of me to think of another question.

"Have you ever had a pet?" I ask after a few seconds of silence.

"Lots of them. But never very long. I told you...my dad is always rescuing things," she laughs.

"I've never had a pet. I always wanted a dog," I say, leaning my head back again and looking at her.

"They're a lot of work," she shrugs.

"Yeah, but I think I'd be okay with that. I'm good at working hard. And I don't want a small one; I want one of those big breeds, like a mastiff," I say, lifting my hands and measuring a wide distance with my arms in front of me.

"You know that means their poop is bigger."

"The bigger the better, baby," I joke.

It grows silent again, and I flit my gaze from her to my hands a few times, my stomach twitching nervously.

"Do you like the Excel Program?" she asks.

I suck in my bottom lip and shrug. I never know how to answer that question. It's like asking someone if they like being really smart. "It's all right," I say.

"I bet it's amazing," she says, looking to the side, her hair falling over her shoulder slowly, like an avalanche. "You get to go to a college, hang out with professors and learn things like philosophy and culture."

"It's not *that* amazing," I say. "And I still have to do calculus, and language arts and shit."

"Whatever. It's amazing, and you know it," she says, lifting her foot and nudging my chest with it. I grab hold of her leg and hug it. It seemed like a good idea when I spontaneously did it, but then it got weird instantly.

I made it weird.

We're both quiet and staring at her leg that I'm now hugging, and I start to laugh at the absurdity. I rock it side to side, like it's an infant, and she gives into laughter too. She kicks at me with her other leg, so I tug on her and pull her closer to me, holding on tight and moving her into me as if I'm pulling in the length of a rope—until she's in my lap. Her legs curled up against my door, her body in front of me, and her hands pressed on the ceiling, her laughter fills ever inch of space inside my car.

Her sound fades as her eyes open and her gaze meets mine.

Inches. There are inches in life. Inches that make the difference between a race, that determine your height or pants size, that might mean you make it to the train on time.

I'm living in inches right now, inches and breaths.

Beautiful inches.

"I like you, Emma," I say. My heartbeat fills my throat; I swallow and feel the heat take over my chest and arms and hands.

She doesn't answer with words, instead letting her lashes sweep shut while I take in the dusting of freckles along her cheeks. Her lips part with a shallow breath, her bottom one trembling.

"Andrew," she breathes out my name. It's a whisper. Like I'm a secret.

Maybe I am.

I move my hand to her cheek, and she lets her weight fall into my palm, her eyes closing again briefly.

"I want to know everything about you, Emma Burke," I say, sweeping hair away from the one side of her face, leaving my other hand flush against her cheek, my thumbs over those very mesmerizing freckles.

"I'm not very interesting," she says, her voice tiny and unsure. I can see so much of her nerves in the slight tremors on her lips, the way her hands are now quaking with her grip on my sleeves along my biceps. Her eyes, they tell me so much of her story too.

"You liar," I smirk. She flinches at first, looking hurt. "You are incredibly interesting."

I let my head fall forward to meet hers, and her eyes close as she hums.

"You're a lot of other things, too. Like beautiful, and spirited, and funny, and smart," I say.

58

"You don't know that I'm smart," she lets out with a laugh, her lips almost brushing mine when she speaks.

"Yeah, I kinda do. I saw your transcripts," I admit.

She slaps her hands flat against my chest and leans back, trying to decide if I'm kidding. I grin with half my mouth and shrug.

"I'm tight with the front office, and I was worried about you missing class last week. I was going to get your work for you," I say, now my own nerves kicking in. I sound like a lunatic stalker.

Thankfully, Emma thinks differently, her head falling to the side again, her hands retracing their path along my arms.

"That's sweet," she sighs. "I got my work. It was a planned trip. With my family."

"I figured," I say, not able to pull my eyes away from hers. "You have really pretty eyes."

She lets her head fall forward against mine as she lets out an embarrassed laugh.

"I'm serious," I say. "Don't let that make you uncomfortable. I mean...it's almost selfish not to take that compliment. Think of all the people walking around with really hideous eyes."

She laughs harder, and her grip on my arms gets tighter.

"You're really funny, Andrew," she says. I move my hands back to their rightful spot on either side of her face.

"And maybe a little cute? Maybe...just a little?" I squint. I'm teasing her, and I'm begging her. I want this girl to be *the* girl— my girl. The one I take to things and experience everything with.

"I'd have to say...." She pauses, her eyes taking in various features along my face, like she's evaluating me, but her grin betrays her, breaking into her cheeks until we're staring into each other's eyes again. "Yeah...you're pretty cute, Andrew."

I blush. I can feel it, my cheeks warming, my mouth unable to keep a straight face. Every part of me is smiling.

"I'm gonna go ahead and kiss you now," I say, my lips practically tingling to the point they almost feel numb.

Emma pinches her lips closed tight in a tiny smile, as her eyes close again. Her head held in my hands, I move her the few fractions of an inch left between us until I feel the tickle of her breath and her bottom lip between mine. She lets out another breath, and I suck her lip, tasting it with my tongue, holding her here, in this perfect place, this perfect moment, until I'm sure I'll never forget it.

Then I move to her top lip, doing just the same. Tugging it into my mouth and holding it lightly with my teeth until she whimpers. My hands find their way into her hair, and she turns so more of her body is facing me, her hands sliding around my neck and back, pulling our bodies closer together.

When her tongue finally brushes against my lower lip, I know that I'm gone. I will never be the same after tonight. I've kissed girls, been fixed up on dates of younger siblings of people my brother knew, and I've had crushes.

Emma Burke is different from anything else.

She's what I'm supposed to have. She's what my first kiss should have been. And she's the only kiss I ever want to remember. I kiss her harder, letting my tongue explore the inside of her mouth, letting my hands move down her back until I grab her hips and ass, pulling her into my lap to straddle me. I kiss her and touch her and memorize every frame of us, erasing everything that I ever knew of what a girl was supposed to feel like before.

We kiss like this for nearly an hour, the windows of my car frosting up with our breath. I touch her skin, letting my hands roam under her shirt, feeling her back and shoulders until I know it's okay to feel more.

I touch her breasts, letting my fingers find every curve, my thumbs grazing her nipples and my mouth watering with the want for more. But I know that this is as far as Emma Burke wants me to go. And I'm okay with that, because this girl has me, every part of me. She owns it all, and I am willing to wait for every new touch, knowing that it will feel just the same, just as perfect as this one does.

She is what I will look forward to.

When I look at the dashboard finally, I realize it's nearly two in the morning, and at some point, both Emma and I need to return home. I don't want her parents to worry, so I sigh as I stare into her eyes one last time.

I reach into my pocket finally, looking for my keys, but don't feel them. I check the other pocket and then let my hands start to search the sides of the seat when I don't feel them there either. I'm about to slide my hand between the seat and the console when Emma starts to giggle.

"You," I point at her. She dangles my keys from her thumb, fumbling with the door handle and finally racing from my car as I lunge at her. I get out of my side and race after her, catching her only a few steps away, pulling her into my arms and lifting her in front of me. She kicks her feet up into the air as I raise her, her entire body rumbling with the vibration of her laugh.

"Girl, you are going to make your parents hate me if I don't get you home before they notice you're gone," I say, reaching for the keys as she pulls them into her chest.

"I know. We can go, but..." she looks at the keys in her hand then up to me. "Can I drive? I know, I know...it's your car and she's some Camaro or something, but..."

"I don't know," I say, feeling a little bit like an asshole over the fact that I don't want her to drive my car.

"It's...it's okay. It was a dumb idea, never mind," she says, handing my keys back to me. I take them and follow her back to the car, but I grab her fingertips just as we get to the front of the car, pulling her into me.

"Here," I say, closing her hand around the keys while I kiss her one last time.

"Really?" Her voice is almost a squeal, and I can tell how excited she is. I nod *yes*, then move to the passenger door, climbing inside. Emma slides in excitedly next to me, pushing the key in quickly and turning the engine before we've even buckled up.

"Whoa," I say, grabbing my belt and buckling fast.

"Oh, right. Sorry..." she says, biting her lip. "I was anxious, and I didn't want you to change your mind."

"It's okay, just...take it easy. This car has some kick, all right?"

She nods and buckles her belt, checking all of the mirrors and turning on the lights before moving the shift into reverse. The car rumbles as she backs out slowly, her lip firmly planted in her teeth now. I don't think she's letting go, and her concentration is my second-favorite expression she makes. My first, the one she makes right before I kiss her. She idles her way to the exit, turning slowly onto the main roadway, and she glances at me before she looks back to the road, scooting forward in her seat, clutching the wheel, and pressing on the gas.

We travel for about a mile, going maybe thirty miles per hour, and eventually I start to laugh.

"Don't make fun of me," she chides, reaching at me with one hand, but only for a second, returning her grip to the wheel.

"I'm sorry, you're just so damn cute," I say. "You're so nervous. It's a car, you just drive it."

"I drive my mom's Honda Civic. It's…like…*way* different. Trust me," she laughs nervously. She's constantly looking over her shoulder, then in both mirrors. We've made it maybe two of the ten miles we need to travel.

"I know, trust me. I drove my mom's boyfriend's Buick, remember?"

She glances at me and smiles, then looks back to the road, relaxing a little more into her seat, the gas flowing a little heavier as our speed finally climbs up to forty-five.

"I loved that car, too," she says, blushing for a different reason now.

"You know I tried to be your partner for square dancing first, right?" I say, taking in her profile. I love the slope of her nose and the high roundness of her cheeks.

"You faker. I'm the one who picked you!" she huffs. It's cute that she wants credit for such a simple thing.

"Yeah…you did," I say, knowing the truth. I picked her the second I saw her legs stretched out in the hallway. I think maybe I chose her once in one of my dreams.

Our calm shifts into chaos in a blink.

Emma screams as she jerks the wheel to the right, sliding the car into the rough brush along the side of the road. We skid, fishtailing a few times before coming to a hard stop that sends both of us forward, our bodies held fast by the pull of our safety belts. Her forehead slams into the steering column, cutting her just above her eyebrow.

62

"Emma, Emma," I say her name over and over, my veins coursing with adrenaline, my body numb with panic and fear. She looks at me, and blinks; her tears are instant.

"Oh my god, Andrew! Oh my god, oh my god, oh my god!"

She's panting; she's breathing so hard. She's fighting to free herself from her seatbelt, and I'm only making it worse by getting my hands tangled with hers. I finally hold her hands still, and my other hand rushes to her face, moving her hair to the side.

"Emma, you're bleeding," I say, trying to keep my voice calm.

She touches her fingers to the place on her head where mine are, then pulls them in front of her to see the red on her hand.

This only makes her cry harder and begin to shake.

"I hit something. Andrew, I hit someone," she shouts. Her body is shaking, and her eyes look terrified.

I felt it too. Just before she jerked the wheel, something hit the front of the car. I wasn't watching the road. I was watching Emma.

Emma was watching me.

We didn't see it.

"It's okay," I say. "You hear me? It's okay."

I reach for the passenger door and she grabs for me.

"No, Andrew. No! Don't leave!"

I hold her hand, bringing her fingers to my mouth. Her cut is dripping blood into her eye now, so I reach into the glove box for a napkin and put it in her hand.

"Hold this right here," I say, guiding her hand and pressing firmly on her gash. "Leave it there, and keep the pressure on. I'll be right back."

She nods, but I can already see her hand starting to slide down and grow weaker. I push on it again, and she follows my lead, pressing harder.

I step from the door and move to the front, seeing the large dent in the bumper. The headlight is busted too, and there's blood on the glass. My stomach drops, but I don't let my face show any of it.

Watching her watch me through the back window, I hold up a finger, signaling I'll be right back. I step into the roadway, keeping my face still, no sign of the terror ruling my body. When I turn back to the road, I see a large mass lying on the asphalt—my only relief, it's moving.

The moaning hits my ears when I'm ten feet away; I realize it's an older man and his dog. I rush to his side—his head is bleeding onto the pavement.

"Sir, can you hear me. Sir?" I shout. I touch his neck, looking over him again, and he rolls to his side and the extent of the cuts and injuries to his abdomen and face hits me.

"Sir, I'm going to call for help," I say, standing and fumbling my phone from my pocket. My eyes are seeing things in scenes—in flashes, really. This man lying on the ground, his injuries, his dog whimpering at his side flat against the road—they are all scenes from a nightmare—then I look to the car, nearly one hundred yards away, and my eyes lock onto Emma's...I realize this nightmare, it's just beginning.

The emergency operator answers instantly, and I give our approximate location along the dark rural road. The temperature feels about twenty degrees colder than before, my breath thicker, and the air damp with mist.

I pull my sweatshirt from my body, wrapping it around the man's head, resting it easily on the pavement and promising him I'll come back. He seems to be fading in and out of consciousness. I reach for his small dog, and it growls at me, so I leave it where it is and jog back to the car, where Emma is now rocking in the driver's seat, her eyes wide and full of tears.

"He's going to be okay. Emma, listen to me." I cup her face in my hands, turning her to face me. I feel badly because I'm being a little forceful, but she's slipping into a real state of panic, and I don't think that's going to help.

"Andrew, this is going to ruin everything," she says.

I shake my head *no*. She's just panicking, and I understand that. But the man is going to get help; he'll be okay. My car—it's just a dent. These things, they're not forever nightmares.

No.

"You don't understand," she says, her voice more forceful, her worry showing in her eyes in a different way. There's something about the way she's looking at me that says something more, something she can't seem to verbalize. "Andrew...I can't. This...oh my god. Andrew—"

Her shaking begins again, so I cradle her to my chest tightly, looking out the window that is hazing over with dew from outside.

"They are going to take everything away," she whispers against me, her eyes open, staring into emptiness. Nothing I say seems to bring her out of this trance. I know I need to get back out to the roadway, to the man lying there in far worse shape than either of us, but I can't leave her here, without hope. There's an absolute look of fear on her face, and the more seconds that pass, the more dire her expression becomes.

"Come with me," I say, stepping out of the passenger side and moving quickly to the driver's door, opening it and pulling on her arm. She shakes her head *no*, so I reach in and lift her into my arms, carrying her to the passenger side, where I place her in the seat I just left.

"What are you doing? Andrew...no..."

"Shhhhhhhh," I interrupt her protest, holding her head to mine as I kneel in front of her. "Listen to me. You. Were not driving. Tonight—you never touched the keys. This car, you never drove it. Not once—ever. I was driving. Do you understand?"

"Andrew...I can't let you..." I look up and see lights reflecting in the distance, an ambulance and fire truck on the way. Police will not be far behind.

I leave her in the seat and rush over to the ignition, pulling the key out and wiping it with my shirt then shoving the keys into my pocket. I run back around the front of the car to her, and hold her in place as she tries to step out from the car.

"Emma, I'm going to be fine. He's hurt, and we didn't do anything but have a horrible accident. He was walking on a dark road at night. I didn't see him step into the roadway, and I hit him with the front end of the car. I called for help right away, and you hit your head on the dashboard." I repeat myself three times, and she shakes her head and mutters *no* the entire time. I see the police cars trailing behind the medical help, and I know I only have seconds to get her on board with my story.

"Emma, I drove this car tonight," I say with more force, my teeth gritting. She needs to embrace this—she needs to let me lie. "I'm going to say this to them, and I need you to back up everything I say. I *need* you to!"

She gives me a slight nod, her eyes never once blinking, and her gaze looking over my shoulder at the emergency personnel now rushing in all directions.

"Sir, are you all right?"

There's a flashlight in both of our faces, and I stand to talk to the firefighter at my car.

"She hit her head on the dash. I think there's a cut," I say, and he flashes his light on her immediately. I move out of the way and let him work on cleaning up Emma as I step away to the man on the road. By the time I get there, three men and a woman are working on him, checking vitals and stripping away his bloodied clothing. My sweatshirt has been tossed into a biohazard bag along with the man's shirt. His injuries don't look life threatening, but I can tell he's not fully aware of what's happening.

"Is he going to be okay?" I ask, getting a variety of short responses—the gist always to let them work and they don't know enough yet.

I step away to give them room and move toward my car, where two firefighters are now working on Emma, walking her to the side of the car and checking her for more injuries. Two police officers have also started circling my car, and I notice them ask her a few questions.

Come on, Emma. Lie for me, baby. Please...just this once—tell a lie.

She shakes her head no, then her eyes flit up to me—our gazes lock, and I know she's done as I asked. She looks so ashamed, but I nod and close my eyes, so thankful she followed through. Whatever has her terrified of this—whatever she thinks this will ruin—is in the past with that one little lie.

I walk slowly toward the car, and as I get to the front, where the damage is, the second officer moves from my back seat leaving the door open.

"Is this your car, sir?" he asks.

"Yes," I nod.

"Were you driving this vehicle tonight?"

Yes, this is what I was hoping for. I'll explain everything; there will be some processing. Insurance is going to suck, but the man...he's going to be okay. I know it. I'll be fine. Emma will be fine.

"Yes, I was. It was dark, and he stepped into the roadway after that bend, and—"

"Place your hands on the roof of the car, please," the other officer says. I do as he asks, and open my mouth to finish my version of what happened, when I feel him kick my feet farther apart as his hands pat down the front, sides, and back of my body.

"I'm going to put these cuffs on you, sir, and they're going to feel a little uncomfortable, but if you don't resist, it won't hurt," he says, jerking one arm behind my body, then the second.

The cuffs are more of a giant zip-tie, really, and he pulls them tight, then leads me backward a few steps, pointing me so I'm looking at his partner.

"Is this your marijuana, Andrew?" the officer says. I look at the bag, the same small fucking bag of weed House dangled at me as payment to buy him a cheeseburger, and I feel overwhelmed with the need to throw up.

"That's not mine," I say, realizing how typical every word I just said sounds. That's what everyone says. And it's never the truth—except this once. This isn't the lie I'm telling. But it's the only one they're interested in.

"Have you been drinking or have you taken any drugs tonight?"

Shit.

I glance to Emma, who is now a hundred yards away near the fire truck, and I look back to my officer, knowing I'm fucked. I nod *yes*.

"Andrew, I'm placing you under arrest. You have the right to remain silent. Anything you say, can be..."

I hear his voice. It's a droning sound, and I know every word he's uttering. I know the law, the way it works, what happened, and I can see every single frame of this moment and how the universe has lined up to destroy me. I'll call my mom. She'll find a way to fix this. She'll call Owen.

My heart is beating so fast I think it might stop from exhaustion at any moment—the rhythm hurting my chest from the inside. I look up as the officer presses down on my neck, lowering me into the backseat of the squad car, and Emma's eyes lock on mine.

"No!" she shouts, and I see her pulling away from the medics trying to help her, the woman holding her arm and keeping her still. "No, Andrew!"

I can't hear her second scream, because the door is shut on me. I only see her lips moving, her arms jerking and her legs fighting to get to me. She's trying to get them to stop, and she's probably trying to take my place, but it doesn't matter. I don't want her to, either. She needs to stay with them, to wait for her parents, to go home and to be safe.

She doesn't need to be afraid. She is not going to lose anything. She can't and she won't. And I'll be okay.

I'll be okay.

Chapter 5

One month later

Emma,

I'm sorry that this has to be a letter. It's the only thing I'm allowed to do. I wanted to call you, but there really wasn't an opportunity. I didn't know where to call, either. All this time, and I still never asked you for your phone number. I'm such a jerk.

I'm sure you heard. Dwayne, I mean Mr. Chessman said he would let you know. I hope you didn't get in any trouble. And I hope whatever you were afraid of losing is still with you, or still yours. I hope one day you'll explain.

I'm not proud of some of those things you've probably learned. But I had to explain, and I know you'll believe me. I'm not a druggie. That weed wasn't mine, either. It was my brother's friend's. He was visiting me, and he dropped it. Not that it matters. It sounds so cliché, and I laugh even now about how perfect it all is. Not a funny laugh. Nothing funny about this. But, I'll still be okay.

I did smoke a little. It was a stupid move, I know. But I was trying to feel less alone. Maybe I wanted to fit in. Fuck, if I'm honest, peer pressure is a thing. It's real. And I missed you. You had been gone for a week, and there was a part of me that thought maybe you'd never come back. I think maybe I thought I'd imagined you, too. Only, if I imagined you, I'd close my eyes now and you'd be here. Believe me, I've tried.

Anyhow, none of that matters, and I own that bad decision. I fell to peer pressure, and it kicked my ass. My mom kicked my ass, too. Owen—he won't talk to me. Which hurts. But I know that won't be forever. I'm sending him a letter, too.

They won't let me make any phone calls for at least three months. My schedule here is very...rigid. It's not military school, but I imagine it's not far off. At least my classes aren't boring. They aren't quite college-level, but the work keeps me busy. I have duties every morning until seven, and I'm in class until four. We have counseling at five, and then sometimes they give us recreation. I call this place juvie, but I guess that's not really accurate. It's more of a reform school, part of the bargain I got. Lake Crest Boys Academy.

I should be able to start back with the Excel Program in a few months. This isn't forever, and I'm okay. That's what I'm really writing about. I've been talking about you to someone here. She's a counselor, sort of, though, I'm not really sure how qualified she is. Don't worry, I don't tell her everything. Just...that you were with me, during the accident. She mentioned that you probably feel guilty about this, and I don't want that.
I'm okay, Emma. I'll be okay. And I'll be home soon.

I miss you.

Andrew

Two months later

Dear Emma,

Did you get your gift? I made you something for Christmas. I get to go home for the holiday, but I don't have a lot of time. It's not even a full day, really. I want to visit. I hope you know that. But, I may not be allowed.

I miss hockey. I know that probably sounds selfish, but I do miss it. I'm honest with you. And as much as I miss my family, my boring routine and that shitty apartment, I miss kicking someone's teeth in on the ice more.

70

They have basketball here. Owen would love it. Me...not so much. I suck to the point where I'm literally the last one picked during rec time.

A lot of these guys are real assholes. And a lot of them actually did some bad shit, but nothing really bad. Petty theft, fights, drugs—things like that. I mean, it's reform school. They call it boy's academy. I guess that makes it sound better.

Oh hey, I got a letter from Owen, by the way. They let me get mail. I'd love to hear from you. Please write if you have time. I get phone privileges next week for being "good." I've already been offered twenty bucks to make a call for someone who doesn't get them. I'm thinking of taking him up on it.

Anyhow, I guess I just hope you're okay.

Andrew

Seven Months Later

Emma,

I get to come home next week.

I'm not even sure why I'm writing this to you, because I know I will have the choice to see you in person next week.

I say "choice" because...you know why I say choice. I think you know what I'll choose. I'm sure you're hoping for it.

This letter, I think it needs to be the last one I write. I didn't keep track, but I know I sent you more than twenty. Whatever the number is, it's the same number you never sent back.

It's spring, and the weather is warm. I've worked ahead of my class here, which really wasn't very hard. They offered to let me into the Excel Program again, although I'm on probation. My mom has forgiven me, for the most part, and Dwayne comes to visit every weekend. Even Owen came last week.

Owen had a lot of questions about the accident. I think he knows things don't add up. That man on the road, he lives in one of the housing projects on the edge of town. He's in his sixties. My mom said he recovered, though, and they've settled with him. I don't ask for the details, because I'm sure Dwayne had to help with the costs. I don't like that. But I guess that's just money. I'm alive. I'll go back to where I was. And you...you'll be wherever you are.

Oh, and I never told anyone. I never will.

Maybe I'll see you around.

I probably won't.

Andrew

One Year Later

Dear Emma,

This letter is for me. It isn't for you.
I resent you.
I blame you.
I hate you.

And when I sat in my car last week, just out of your view, and saw you dressed in that pink homecoming dress, your hair done up, probably from one of those fancy salons in the city, and saw you kiss that guy on your front porch... I thought about going back to that moment and taking it all back— letting you stay in that seat, letting you lose everything important to you.

72

I thought about it.
I want to want that for you.
But I can't. I'll never want that for you.
I'll always want you to be the one who gets to be okay.
And I hate you for that most of all.

You said that night ruined everything, and you were right. It ruined me. I will never be the same.

It ruined us—as if there ever was an us.

I can't stay here. I can't stay in this town because there's too much of you in it. I've seen you too many times. You never see me, but I see you. I see you fucking everywhere!

And I don't want to see you anymore.
I'm going to live with my uncle in Iowa.
It doesn't matter, because you'll never visit.
I'll never give you this letter.
It wasn't for you anyway.

This letter—it's the only thing I've done in a year for me. Just for me.
I'll never make the mistake of picking someone else again.

I pick me.

Me.

And you can go to hell.

Andrew

part two

Chapter 6

Andrew Harper, Age 21

"You're a fucking cocksucker, Harper," Trent says, slapping the back of my head as he passes behind me at the bar. I hit him hard today. He blew it last week, though, and that's my job—to get guys ready to take hits in the real games.

I get to play, but I'm more of an insurance guy—the one they send in to be distracting and cause trouble for the other guys, to shift the game to our advantage. It lands me in the box a lot, but we're surprisingly good at penalty kill. We come out stronger, and sometimes we need to feel the pressure to get things going.

"I wouldn't have to hit you so hard in practice if you weren't such a pussy during games, Metzger," I say, pulling my lips from the rim of my beer bottle just long enough to dish out a quick insult to my best friend.

"Fuck off, you're just bitter that girls like me more 'cuz I'm the sexy captain," he says in this fucking annoying-ass voice while he rubs his chest like he's a stripper. It's creepy.

"Yeah, you got me. Totally jealous of *all that,*" I deadpan, gesturing toward him.

I kid with him, but truth is Trenton Metzger is the most talented goddamned hockey player I've ever been on the ice with. He's the only reason people talk about Northern Tech hockey, and it's an honor to be on the roster with him.

Hell, it's an honor to be on any roster at all. I'm a partial-scholarship player; partial lots of things, really. After two years of busting my ass in junior college and proving myself in junior leagues, I managed to pull together enough of an academic and athletic resume to get my ass into Tech. My grades were never the issue. It was my stint at Lake Crest that gave people pause. The list of schools willing to hand out free money just so I would go there dried up fast even though I finished out high school in the Excel Program, my senior year in independent study—graduating early with shining academics. I was still accepted lots of places, I just couldn't pay for them.

What a fucking tease college is. *Hey, come to our university and have this awesome life we're showing you in these glossy pictures. Oh...what? You can't afford it? Here...here's a nice mug and calendar magnet of our football schedule instead.*

Luckily, I'm enough of an asset on the ice for NTU to pay for part of my last two years. Part. I get another small percentage in academic scholarships, but even then there's still a shitload I have to figure out on my own. My mom and step-dad Dwayne help, but they don't have much either. They gave me what little they made from combining households when they got married two years ago, and that little went right to what was left on my tuition tab my first semester. So I work the rest off with odd jobs. Right now, I have two. In the mornings, I work at a nearby elementary school. I get there early for the parents who have to drop their kids off before school actually starts. We play dodgeball for two hours, and the girls sit at the tables and color. It pays shit, but it's better than nothing.

My other gig is...different. But the pay is awesome—when it comes. I'm a fall guy. Basically, I spar with wannabe fighters for this dude Harley who manages up-and-coming boxers. He pays me ten bucks an hour to throw a few punches, but take way more than I throw. It builds up confidence in the guys he wants to move up and it keeps me aggressive on the ice. When he thinks his guys are almost ready, he sets up small fights at a few of the gyms in the city, and my job is to always go down, but not until we've gone at least three or four rounds.

This is where I make my tuition money.

Harley takes bets on the side—rolling money into the thousands with a network of bookies he knows. I get a cut—because *I'm* the one who gives him the lock. He's careful about running me too often, switching me up with two or three other guys who have the same deal, and he always loses a bet when he needs to make it look legit.

The fights are only on Sundays, so it never runs into practice or games. And it's rarely more than one a month. But one fight can land me a few grand in a night. It's money I need, and the first time I did it, I couldn't believe how many of my financial problems it helped make go away. But that's not what made me come back.

That feeling—the one of knowing my arms aren't going to move fast enough, that my instincts are going to be purposely numbed, is a rush. To know the hit is coming, and that I'm going to deny myself protection. When I get hit—gloves to the temple, chest, chin, ribs—it's like getting high. Everything that hurts gets centered on the pain, and my runaway thoughts and fears come to a grinding halt. Regret fades. The only thing that exists is getting my ass kicked, feeling my flesh sting and my body hum with pain.

Sometimes, I think that if I didn't do this—if I hadn't stumbled into Harley's gym one day and found my way into a ring with a boxer twice my size—that I would have turned to something else. My body can take the abuse, and my mind...it craves the distraction. It's the same way on the ice.

"All right, Harper. Who's the target tonight?" Trent leans over me, startling me out of my trance, grabbing my next beer and taking it for his own.

"Hey, dickhead," I say. He holds up a hand and orders another one, sliding it to me. "I'm pretty sure it's your turn this time."

His face falls and his complexion turns green. Trent and I have this game we play with one another. It started as a drunken dare a few months ago, when he goaded me into taking a girl home from Majerle's Pub. I'm not suave; I don't have great pick-up lines. I usually wait for girls to hit on me. I wait for *easy*. When Trent dared me, I came up with my own set-up—I stole a girl's wallet. I returned it to her later, pretending I'd found it. She was so grateful she spent the rest of the night sitting on my lap, her arms looped around my neck, her lips sucking on my skin, her hands soon finding their way in my pants.

That first girl taught me never to bring any of them to our apartment. I go to theirs now. It's easier to leave than it is to kick someone out.

"Fine, I'll go. But next time, I get to pick your girl," I say, tipping my beer back to drink what's left before leaving the bottle on the bar behind me and pointing at my friend.

"Dude, whatever. You know it's your turn anyway," he says.

"My choice next time," I remind him as I walk backward. I know it's his turn, and I also know he doesn't really like taking the dare. Trent's too nice, and he usually ends up dating the girl for weeks after. He doesn't like to be an asshole. Or maybe he just doesn't like people to say bad things about him. Maybe there's no difference between the two.

I couldn't give a shit what people say about me. Let 'em talk.

I make one pass through the crowded bar, letting my eyes roam over the dance floor and the tables that line the back wall on the way to the bathrooms. It's a Friday night, so there are lots of girls here. It's the middle of the semester, too, so they're all ready to party—no finals to worry about. There's one group that seems like an easy target, a blonde on the end who keeps trying to talk the others into dancing. I hover around the restrooms waiting for my shot, and when she finally drags the group of girls with her out to the dance floor, I walk back through the crowd, passing their table.

So easy.

Their wallets and purses are all piled in the center of the table except for a red bag looped over the back of a chair, the ID sticking out of the top. I drag my hand along the bottom of the table, and as I pass the red handbag I grab the small plastic card poking from it, tucking it into the sleeve around my palm. I glance up to make eye contact with Trent, and raise the corner of my mouth in a smirk.

"Dude, you are so slick at this. Seriously, if you flunk out of the engineering program you should just turn to a life of crime."

I slide into my stool and look away from him. I know he was just saying words, but the joke doesn't sit well with me. I have a chip on my shoulder. It's my fucking chip, and I earned it by giving up a year of my life for a series of bad decisions and shitty circumstances. Trent knows my story—mostly. He knows there was a girl, and he knows I got screwed over by both the girl and the law. But I'm not sure he knows exactly how fucked up it all left me. And he also doesn't know how many nights I walk that line with Harley, fixing bets that are illegal in the first place. Trent just thinks I like the workout boxing gives me.

"Well...let's see it? Who's the lucky lady?"

I pull my sleeve loose from around my wrist and let the card slide out, flipping it over while I drink what's left of my beer, and that's when karma slaps me like a bitch.

She's older. Of course she's older. She's twenty-one, too. But she looks...older. She also looks the same. Nobody looks good in an ID photo. Emma Burke looks like a dream. Her brown hair is just as I remember it, long waves around her bright pink cheeks, lips that stretch into this sensuous smile. I don't know if it's sensuous to anyone else, but to me, it sure as fuck is.

It's also cruel. I swear to god she's mocking me in her picture, her eyes shining through and looking at me, calling me stupid, telling me what a chump I am for thinking I was some sort of hero or something.

She's slapping me in the face for being good and decent to her.

Don't worry, Emma. I won't ever be good and decent to you again.

"Well?" Trent asks. I slide the card toward him, never looking down at it. He picks it up, holding it in his hand and reading her details while I choke down another beer and wonder how the hell I'm going to get out of this.

"Damn, Harp!" he says, his heavy pat on my back almost making my beer spill down into my lungs. I know what has him impressed; it's her eyes. I get it. They worked on me too. That's the first thing I recognized. And *like hell* am I putting myself in a position where I have to stare into them again. She'd probably hypnotize me right into prison—for good this time!

"It was your night anyhow; you take her," I say, letting my gaze drift off to the TV mounted above the bar. It's a commercial for toothpaste, and I'm so interested in it. So very interested. I'm ignoring everything—Trent, the brewing sensation in my gut, the heaviness of knowing Emma is in this room, breathing the same air I am.

I feel the card slide under my elbow, and I close my eyes.

"Awwww no you don't. You're not going to pussy out on me now. You know the deal." He's talking loudly. I know there's no way she can hear me, no way she'd know, but my body heats up at the thought of getting caught.

I take a slow, deep breath so Trent doesn't notice how tense I've become, then slide the card back into my palm, glancing at it before putting it in my back pocket as I stand. I toss a twenty on the bar and put my empty bottle on top of it.

"Whatevs, man. I'll play hero a little later; I've got some shit to take care of," I say, nodding goodbye.

"You're such a prick, making her wait," he chuckles.

If our friendship were a superhero, Trent would be Ironman, and I'd be Tony Stark. I think Trent is amused by my dick moves, because he's the good guy and could never pull them off. I used to be that way, too.

I don't respond. Yeah, I'm a prick. I'm a prick because what I really want to do is toss her ID in the trash on my way out. But I don't do that, because instead I'm the kind of prick that gives up a year of my life and any possible future because of a fucking crush on a high school cock tease. This gift—knowing where she is—feels like something I shouldn't waste, so I'm going to think of the perfect way to play it all.

I hit the exit and glance over to the group of girls on the dance floor again, and I wait for a few seconds until I see her body come into view. She looks like she's having the time of her life, arms over her head, eyes shut, smile on her face, sweat dripping down her body. She's the sexiest thing I've ever seen. There was a time when I imagined her like this, grown up—this is what I saw in my sixteen-year-old fantasies.

That hate I've worked so hard on burying comes right back, and my heart hardens as her eyes drift open and there's a short flash of recognition that crosses them. That's right, Delaware— it's me, and I see you.

I leave quickly, pretending not to notice her, knowing that she's still not sure about what she saw. I don't want to give her enough to be sure. I want to give her doubt and worry, and then I never want to see her again.

When I left the bar, I headed to the warehouse. Harley wasn't expecting me, but he let me work in, take a few rounds in the ring. Harley's only at the gym at night, and usually only on the weekdays. During the day, he's the perfect law student his rich parents think he is. He manages the warehouse space as a gym; it's in a building his grandfather owns. He told his dad he wanted to learn about running a business. Nobody in his family visits; they just take his word on things.

Harley is the kind of guy people trust.

I've run the numbers in my head, and I'm pretty confident Harley's making out better running his boxing scam. His father's a pretty powerful corporate attorney though, so there's an expectation of his life going one way. If things go south, I guess he'll be able to find his own loopholes and get his ass out of trouble.

The only guy boxing tonight is a dude they call Pitch Black. He got that name because he knocks people out cold. I've never sparred with him before; he's not one of the guys Harley needs to *fake* things with. He took it easy on me; I could tell. But he still fucked my face up pretty good. I've had the ice out for an hour, and I'm just putting it back in the freezer when Trent walks in, sliding his keys on the counter behind me.

"Dude, do not tell me you blew that chick off just to get your fix at the gym." He's leaning back against the counter with his arms crossed.

"I had a guy who wanted to work on some things with me," I lie.

"Yeah, like seeing how many stitches he could rack up on your face?"

"Fuck off; it's not that bad," I say. He reaches at me, poking my tender jaw, and I wince and slap his hand off me in one motion.

"Right...not bad at all," he says, judgment oozing from his tone.

I sigh and open our pantry, grabbing a handful of almonds from an open tin. Then I shut the door and ignore my friend, knowing he's going to ask me about the girl and the ID and my plans. I thought going to the warehouse would help me gain perspective. I was wrong.

"Look," he starts as he kicks his shoes off and empties his pockets onto the counter. He leaves his shit in piles—drives me fucking nuts, and it's not just because I'm in a bad mood.

Maybe it is. Whatever. I stare at his crap until he waves a hand to get my attention back to his face.

"Drew, man...if you weren't really in the mood to hit on some chick, you shouldn't have taken her ID. That girl is going to be freaked out and worried when she can't find it, so at least just get it back to her."

My gaze has drifted away from him again, back to his pile of stuff.

"Why can't you dump your crap in your room? That's what I do when I come home. I go to my room, put my things in there, and *then* I come out here."

Trent cocks an eyebrow at me, staring for a few seconds, then moves back to the kitchen, scooping up his wallet, keys, and change and holds it up so I can see him and acknowledge it.

"Don't forget your shoes," I add.

He laughs once. Not a funny laugh. He's pissed. I'm being an asshole. He can fuck off. He doesn't have *her* ID in his back pocket.

Trent bends down and grabs his shoes, pointing one toward me as he goes to his room.

"Sometimes you're a real dick, Harper," he says. He lets his door slam closed behind him.

I turn my attention to the TV in front of the sofa and hold the remote up, turning on some bad teen soap opera and cranking the volume up to an obnoxious level. Might as well let this being-a-dick thing really run its course.

Trent never came out of his room, and I finally fell asleep on the couch to some protein-supplement infomercial. I woke up when Trent let the front door slam shut loudly. We have practice in thirty minutes, morning skate before our game tonight. We usually ride together, because Trent has a car. Looks like I'll be walking today.

After a quick shower, I change into sweats and my long-sleeved tee and jog to the arena about two miles away. I shove

Trent's pads off the bench when I walk by his locker. He laughs, so I know he's over being pissed at me. I also know that I still have Emma's ID in my wallet.

Pre-game skate only lasts half an hour, so I can't put things off any longer. I want to. I want to be so busy I can never go to 407 Clark Street, which yeah...is less than three miles from my apartment. Usually, I have to look the girl up to find her address—her license normally from another state, but Emma's is right there on her license. She must be planning on living here for a while, or maybe she already has. How the hell I haven't seen her in the year I've attended this school is a miracle.

Then again, I get the feeling Emma and I probably run in different circles. I know her building. It's the big high-rise on Clark. Balconies, windows that look over the lake, a bellman at the front desk—a far cry from the rats and drug deals that go down out on the street in front of our apartment. It's not like *gangland* or anything, just cheap rent and a lot of college kids who like to get high.

When I'm done skating, I rush through changing and just hold up a hand with her license for Trent to see. He smirks, figuring I'm off to make good on my dare. I'm really going to take my penance. Lesson learned—I'm never playing *this* game again.

The wind from the lake has a cold bite to it, so I pull my hoodie from my bag and throw it on over my beanie. Maybe I'm also shielding myself. I get to the front of her building, and my heart starts to race wildly, my throat dry, but somehow my mouth so moist I feel like I'm going to throw up.

The doorman is helping a group of girls when I walk by quickly, and he glances at me, probably memorizing what I'm wearing, but he doesn't stop me when I pass. My hands are shaking in the elevator, and when I press the button for the ninth floor, I hold it down, afraid to fully commit.

Number 907.

I'm nine stories away from the girl who ruined my life.

My plan is pathetic. I'm not going to ring the bell. I'm not going to knock. I'm just going to slide the ID under her door, then get the fuck out of here. I thought about leaving it with the doorman. But I *have* to see. There's something that's pushing me forward, some part of me that just needs to get close, to know exactly where she lives, what her door looks like.

When the elevator dings and the doors slide open, I pause briefly, considering riding it back down and going with the other plan—leaving her license at the front desk. But the hallway is quiet, and that silence coaxes me through the doors that fall closed behind me.

Breath held, I glance back down at her picture in my hand, the sharp edges of her license digging into my skin as my hand closes on it, squeezing it so hard I bend it a little. Signs on the wall guide me down the hallway to the right, so I walk by a few doors until I get to her number, slowing down before I'm fully in front of the frame. I don't want her to see me here—not through a crack in the door, not through a peephole.

There's nothing special about her door at all. There's only the number on the outside. No welcome mats or seasonal décor plastered on the doorknob or frame like a few of her neighbors. It's just a door, and it looks just like any other door.

Emma is just any other girl, I remind myself.

I laugh lightly at how ridiculous I'm being and how nervous I am for no reason. She'll never even know, and I can go back to living a life without her, now knowing a few places to avoid.

Bending down, I slip her license from the pocket in the front of my hoodie, and hold it between my thumb and finger, sliding it along the carpet until it meets the bottom edge of her door. When I see it fits, I flick it hard with my finger, satisfied when it disappears underneath.

"Uhm, excuse me?"

The voice behind me scares me enough that I jump forward and press my hand flat on Emma's door to catch my balance. I know it isn't her; I'm pretty sure I'd still know her voice. But it's someone. And I've now been seen—*here!* When I get to my feet and turn, I'm greeted by a girl with a laundry basket filled with towels, detergent, and fabric softener.

Not Emma.

All that matters.

"Sorry, I…" I stop, realizing I can't really make up an excuse, nor do I need to. "I found someone's license at the bar last night, so thought I'd just drop it off. I…I knew where the building was."

I slide my hood from my head when she starts looking at me suspiciously. I pull my beanie off too and run my hand through my hair, pushing it out of my face. I probably look a little rough, still bruised from a fight and sweaty from practice.

"Oh my god. Emma's!" Her eyes light up with realization. "Thank you so much! Oh my god, she's been totally freaked out over that! She's going to die. I have to call her. Thank you so much!"

"No problem. Really," I say, exchanging places with her in the hallway. Just hearing her say Emma's name does something, twists something deep inside. I was anxious to leave, but it's like there's a part of me that's been asleep for years, and hearing the word *Emma* woke it up. My mind is begging my feet to carry me away, but there's that other thing inside me that suddenly wants to stay.

The girl is balancing her basket and reaching for her keys. She drops them on the floor, and as I see her struggle to kneel down with the basket and pick them up again, an idea strikes me.

"Here, let me hold that," I say, bending and taking the basket from her. She smiles gratefully, fumbling with her keys, sorting through the dozen or so on her ring to find the right one. Why do chicks have so many keys? How many things do you seriously need to keep locked?

Finally finding the door key, her eyes flit up to me a few times as she nervously works it into the lock. The more jumpy she gets, the more I start to like my probably-very-bad idea. I like how it's making me feel.

Her door finally open, I follow her inside, reaching down to pick up Emma's license as we step over the threshold.

"Here, I slid it under the door," I say, stepping in a little closer than I need to. I want to see her reaction. Her mouth twists into the kind of smile she's trying to control. I can tell by the slight shiver in her lips. I step to the side, giving her some space, and notice the deep breath she lets out. I slide her basket onto the table right inside the door, glancing around to take in the full apartment.

So this is where Emma lives now.

"I like your place," I say, noticing she's still looking at me, still trying not to smile. She glances to the side of my face, examining my bruise. "Oh, I...I play hockey here. Game injury," I lie. She likes my excuse though, her smile losing its battle a little more.

When her back is turned, I look down the hallway and out on the patio that seems to run the width of their apartment. There's nothing in here that screams *Emma*—not that I'd know what that would be any more. It's a nice apartment. Not any bigger than mine, really, but the neighborhood's nicer, everything's newer. It's a good place for two girls to live alone.

"Hockey, huh?" the girl says. Interested. Yeah, that usually works. I nod down at my chest, to my NTU Hockey sweatshirt. "Oh..." she says, blushing when she looks back up and our eyes meet.

"That's where I came from. We had a light practice. There's a game tonight," I say, my pulse kicking in all the right places. It's a mix of adrenaline and fear of being caught. "You ever come out to the games?"

Or maybe you and your roommate? Does she know I'm here? Is she avoiding me? Dozens of questions race through my mind, but I keep everything calm on the outside.

"Oh, no. Emma and me don't get out much. We're both pre-med—total book nerds. Almost scalpel nerds, ha! We just moved in...maybe two months ago," she says. "Last night was rare for us. We hardly ever go out."

She doesn't ask me to leave, instead moving into the kitchen toward the fridge, so I give her a little space before following her steps. I don't want to make her nervous. But I also want to see how far I can go with this—what I can learn.

Scalpel. She's really becoming a surgeon. I almost smile at the thought of her living one of her dreams, but then my other feelings take over.

"So just the girl on that ID and you here?" I'm looking around for a sign of a boyfriend, but I'm not getting the vibe that one exists from this girl, for either of them.

My naïve host is wearing a sweatshirt and leggings, and she's already kicked her feet out of the boots she was wearing which means she's comfortable with me being here in her space. She's cute—short hair, cut to her shoulders, kind of brown, kind of blonde. She's small, like the sort of girl I could pick up easily over my shoulder, and what I can see of her body, looks pretty tight.

"Yeah, just Emma and me," she smirks, sliding an unopened can of cola toward me when she turns back. I pull the tab up, and the carbonation sprays over the counter. Pulling my sleeve forward on my hand, I wipe it away before peering back up at her to catch her lip in her teeth while she watches.

"And *you are?*" I tilt my head to the side, and I know the second her lip slides loose from her teeth that I've got her. She blushes—hard.

"Oh, right. Hi, I'm Lindsey." Her voice comes out in a nervous giggle. I stand and wipe the moisture of the soda from my hand, reaching across the counter to her.

"Nice to meet you. I'm Drew."

Her hand is cold when I shake it, so I bring my other hand up to cup it completely, rubbing them together to warm her up. She likes it. I can tell. Her entire hand is swallowed up between both of mine. It's almost sweet. Yet...I feel nothing.

"Thanks," she sighs, the smile she's been trying to manage growing a little more out of control. She's into me.

"So...I've gotta go, Lindsey...game tonight and all. But I was wondering if maybe you'd let me come back here sometime, say around dinnertime, so I could take you out?"

Her eyes grow wider, and I get the feeling she's not used to guys being so blunt. That's fine, because I'm not used to hitting on girls without some sort of pretense—like a missing phone or wallet. There just happens to be a bigger thirst I'm trying to quench right now, and Lindsey's really the only safe way for me to get at it.

Lindsey isn't really safe at all.

But I can't stop. Whatever I'm doing has my belly warm, and I feel more energized about the next minute, the next hour and the next day than I have in years.

This isn't flirting; it's strategy.

"I'd like that," she says, her eyes flitting once more. I could kiss her right now, and she'd let me. I think about it, letting my tongue lick my bottom lip at the thought. Oh how great it would be if Emma walked in right now, and my lips were on her roommate. My eyes haze a little, and her breath hitches, which gives me a satisfied grin. I don't give her what I know she wants, instead stepping back and watching her smile falter, replaced by disappointment. She stammers to get me to stay longer.

"Here...uhm...what's your number? I'll text you." She's opening her contacts screen on her phone when I take the device from her, letting my hands run into hers during the exchange. She giggles.

"There," I say, handing it back after I've typed my number in and sent myself a message with her name. "How about Wednesday at seven?"

"That's good," she says, following me back to the front door. My pulse is racing with adrenaline. I have no idea if Emma is coming upstairs, or if she's doing laundry too. I know that she's worried about her ID, and I know Lindsey will text her about it the minute I'm gone. She'll tell her all about the guy who brought it here then asked her out. I'll be this cute story they'll share. Then on Wednesday, I'll find out exactly what Emma's doing here, how long she plans to stay, and how long I have to think about her.

"Good. I'll text you, and we'll meet somewhere nearby," I say, stepping through her door, relief washing over me when I find the hallway still empty. There's a slight exhilaration that flies through my veins too. I'm playing with fire, and I like how it feels.

I wink at her before I turn to leave. When her door shuts, I take big strides toward the stairwell, deciding this is probably the best route to be sure I don't run into Emma. There's a part of me that feels lighter now that I don't have her license on me, like I've gotten rid of this massive obligation. Adding the roommate into the equation was a bigger risk—the entire thing completely happening on impulse—but it also excites me. I need to know more about Emma. It's curiosity, probably driven by the desire that she's suffering...in some way.

One date. With a cute girl. Harmless.

I'll learn secrets, get enough to satisfy things, enough to move on. Then, I'll let Lindsey down easy.

I rush by the front desk when I make it to the first floor, but I'm careful enough not to draw any more attention from the doorman, who's still talking with the group of girls from earlier. Once I've made it safely a block or two away, I pull my phone from my pocket and send Lindsey a text.

I'm really glad I found that license and ran into you.

I know exactly what my words are going to do to her. And when she sends me back a gushy smiley-faced emoticon, I know it worked. I send her one more message, just to cement everything in place.

Can't wait for Wednesday.

She writes back quickly that she can't either. Satisfied, and feeling a little proud of myself, I put my phone back in my pocket and decide to jog the rest of the way back to my apartment. I spend those few miles thinking about the perfect way to work in my questions about Emma. I think about that, and I think about how she looked on that dance floor last night, and in that picture on her ID.

I think about her eyes.

The ocean.

Lake Crest.

I think about the fact that her eyes have found their way back into my mind...uninvited.

Then I think about how good it felt asking out her roommate.

Chapter 7

Emma

"So...it's a little weird for you to be giving *my date* a present. I'm just sayin'," Lindsey shouts from the hallway bathroom. I'm in the kitchen, layering the last batch of oatmeal cookies over the sheet of wax paper I've cut to fit perfectly in the tin.

"I know, but seriously, that guy saved me from having to deal with the DMV and lines and mean people," I say, tucking a short thank you note under the lid before closing it. When she steps into the kitchen, I hand her my gift. "Here...you can just tell him your roommate is a nut, but she's grateful. It'll be an icebreaker—seriously, you could spend an hour on the topic of your crazy roommate alone."

"Don't I know it," Lindsey says, her mouth twisted in a one-sided smile.

"You didn't have to agree so quickly," I laugh, turning back to our oven to shut everything off.

I don't have many domestic skills. My laundry remains in the basket when its both dirty and clean, dishes are only done in our apartment because of Lindsey, and forget about vacuuming. I don't really like cooking, either. But baking—that's different. When I bake, I get to eat the ingredients along the way. It's not like I can sample pieces of a casserole while I'm throwing in corn and meat and crap, but chocolate chip cookies? *Oh yeah.* Oatmeal are my favorites though—it's the brown sugar. I could eat that stuff by the spoonful.

"Okay, enough about you. How do I look?" she asks, spinning slowly. She's put a lot of thought into this date—blew out her hair, bought new lip gloss and I'm pretty sure she got a manicure. It's sweet. She doesn't go out much, even less than I do, really. It's part of being a medical student. And I know it's only going to get worse next year. Lindsey's studying general surgery, I'm cardiothoracic. I've only ticked off three years, so only...seven left.

"You look like a total hottie," I smile.

"Eeeek, thank you," she squeals, before running into the bathroom one more time to check her makeup, and dashing out the door in a cloud of Victoria Secret body spray.

I shake my head, smiling at my friend, then move back into the kitchen to finish cleaning up. I run right into my tin of cookies, which stares back at me, forgotten in the midst of my friend's excitement. I snicker quietly to myself, grabbing the tin after I finish mopping up the stray grains of sugar from the counter. I climb into the worn part of the sofa, the spot my roommate and I both refer to as *my corner,* raise the remote, and begin my big night out.

It's the first night in weeks I haven't been swallowed up completely with biology homework. I intend on watching mindless television until I can't keep my eyes open, and it looks like I'll also be making myself sick on oatmeal cookies. Glad I baked my favorites.

I make it twenty minutes into one of those shows where two people take over decorating a couple's house when my phone buzzes with a text from Lindsey. I'm tempted to read it after I watch the big fight—the guy hates everything they're doing to the house, but the wife loves it. But my phone buzzes again right away, so I mute the TV, brush the few oatmeal crumbs from my lap, and lean forward to read my text.

Help! Please.

I panic at her first text, getting to my feet fast and moving to the front door for my shoes as I scroll to her next one.

Sorry. I didn't mean to make that sound that urgent. I just feel like an idiot. I don't think this guy is going to show up. I texted him...twice. Now I just feel stupid, and I'm sitting here at Mello's alone drinking wine like a loser.

I relax a little knowing Lindsey's not in trouble, but I move forward with my shoes, grab my keys, and put the lid back on the cookies so we have something to share when I get to her.

On my way.

She writes back fast: *You're the best!*

Mello's is one of those places we always wanted to try, but just haven't yet. We spent our first three years in the dorms, and decided it was easier to concentrate in a place of our own without freshmen running around screaming and hooking up with each other next door at all hours of the night. Lindsey's parents pay most of the rent, but I chip in with what little I earn in summer jobs and the money I get from home and financial aid.

It takes me five minutes to get to the restaurant, and I find my friend sitting near the wall by the front door the second I step inside. I brush by the host table, beelining toward her and sliding into the other side of the booth quickly so I can tuck my sweatpants and sneakers underneath.

"I didn't really dress for this," I whisper to her, pushing the tin of cookies on the table in front of us.

"I wasn't planning on making you my date," she shrugs, her lips a tight smile that I know is hiding her disappointment. She pops the lid from the tin and laughs to herself when she sees the top layer is missing. "You get hungry?"

"They're my favorite," I smile. "Good thing you forgot them."

"Yeah, sorry. I was just so nervous, I left without my key, too, so I would have had to call you or ring the doorbell like mad anyhow," she says.

Lindsey pushes half a cookie into her mouth before sighing and relaxing into the plush back of her seat.

"So he's a no-show?" I ask, breaking one of the cookies in half to nibble on.

"Looks like it," she sighs. "I texted him about ten minutes ago. And oh my god, Em, I sound like an idiot."

She hands me her phone, and I read her messages that at first asks if maybe she has the day and place wrong, noticing that he texted her right above that with the exact time and place for them to meet on Wednesday—*today*. Then she tried to fix it with a: *duh, I could have just read your last text. Okay, so I'm here. I'll just be here waiting.*

I cringe when I hand it back to her, and tilt the lid on my cookies a little higher, encouraging her to take one more to console herself.

"I know, right? So bad," she sighs, falling back into her cushion. "Do you want some of my wine? I got a whole bottle."

"Sure," I say, reaching for one of the upside down glasses at the end of the table. I pour a small glass, and hold it up to toast when Lindsey grabs my wrist, making me spill a drop or two on the sleeve of my favorite Tech sweatshirt. Damn.

"Oh shit! He's here!" she whispers excitedly, immediately brushing off the front of her dress, wiping the corners of her mouth and fidgeting in her seat. I'm blotting at the now-purple spots on my super-soft, I'll-never-find-one-like-this-again, white sweatshirt when Lindsey drops her uneaten half of a cookie back into the stash to hide what we were doing. She's making me nervous now, too.

"Oh...crap...uh...I'll go," I rush, grabbing my cookies and lid and chugging my glass of wine quickly while I try to exit the booth gracefully. I don't realize what's happening—what has happened, what this would feel like or the fact that I could feel anything like this at all—until I stand and stumble forward, letting my hand land flat in the center of his chest.

I'm sixteen the second our eyes meet.

I'm sixteen again, and I'm right back at the kitchen table with my parents, and they're telling me how right they were, everyone was, about Andrew Harper.

I'm sixteen, and I'm looking at the aftereffect of my lies—my omissions.

I kept my mouth shut.

And Andrew did too.

Now here we are, five years later, in a wine bar where he's meeting my best friend for a date. Their first date. And he's looking at me like I might be the worst human on the planet. But then, he also looks at me like he misses me. And a little like he hates me, then as if he doesn't know me at all. It's all in there, in that space behind his eyes. They're swirling—his emotions.

My heart has never hurt like this. I've thought I saw him so many times. I never thought it was real.

I feel like I've been kicked in the chest, my lungs are burning, and my mouth is trying to remember how to gasp for air, all of me too stunned to actually just breathe. By the time my lungs function again, I suck in air so fast it chokes me, and I start to cough. I realize my hand is still on his chest when he looks down at it, his brows raised. I pull it away quickly, balling it into a fist, because for those few seconds I had my palm on him, I swear I felt his heartbeat. It's like I want to catch it and put it away for later.

"Emma, this is your big hero," my friend says behind me. "Drew, this is Emma."

The irony that she calls him that strikes fast, and I laugh once, but quickly cover my mouth because a part of me also feels like crying. I'm unable to close my mouth under my palm. That anxiety that plagued me for months after our accident comes roaring back into my being. It never truly left. The scar—the memory of that night, of him being driven away from me, the feeling in my gut at what he was doing...for me—it creeps in at night, invades my dreams, and surprises me in quiet moments. That sharp stab—it's always really there.

What can I possibly say to him? That question etches itself into my mind all hours of the night, while I lie in bed and look out my window wishing he'd just show up, stand outside and throw a rock up to wake me. If he did, what would I say?

What can I say now?

Thank you? Thank you for taking the fall for me, for my carelessness? You may have saved my life. But then...why were you high? And...how could you? You drove like that; you could have killed me. Did I ever really know you at all?

Did I?

"It's nice to meet you, Emma. I'm glad I was able to get your license back to you. I bet that had you worried," he says, holding his hand out for me to shake, his eyes directing me toward it, to shake it. It's the same smile from our youth, but...then it's not.

"Yeah, uh...nice to meet you too," I stammer, my voice awkward and meek. I take his lead, playing this as if we're strangers, but I know he recognizes me. I feel my friend's hand on my shoulder, and I jump, turning to her just in time to see her holding the tin of cookies. *Oh god, she's giving him the fucking cookies!*

"She was so grateful, she baked you cookies," Lindsey laughs. I smile at her through gritted teeth, my brow pulled forward and my mouth aching from forcing a smile. She shakes her head at me, unsure why I look so desperate. "We...uh...well, sort of ate a few while I was waiting."

Andrew takes the tin in his hand, and I'm glued to his face again, waiting for his reaction. This whole scene is a morbid type of irony, and I'm not sure I'll ever be able to taste an oatmeal cookie again without associating it with everything I'm experiencing right now.

Here he sacrificed so much, and I'm giving him cookies.

He holds the tip of his tongue between his teeth as his mouth slides into that familiar smile, the one I was so smitten with as a teenager. It dimples his cheeks exactly as it always did, but those cheeks are now covered in stubble, and maybe a small scar on the right side. I bet there's a story that goes along with it. I bet there are a lot of scars and stories we both have to share.

"I love cookies," he says finally, his lips closing into a tight smile. His amber eyes burn through me, into me, and for that brief second, it's like I can see his *him*. "I bet I'll *really* love your cookies, Emma," he smirks, his eyes haze, and I notice a difference in his tone and demeanor. He gives me a look that is meant just for me, and he slips it in right when Lindsey isn't watching.

Andrew Harper has no intention of sharing secrets with me ever again.

I swallow hard enough that I fear the couple sitting at the next table can hear it. I'm showing my nerves, and it makes Andrew chuckle a little. He sets the cookie tin down on the table, then steps closer to Lindsey, tucking her hair behind one ear and kissing her lightly on the cheek.

I hate it.

"I'm sorry I'm late. I just saw your text," he says, giving her all of his attention, along with the gentle smile that still shows up in my memories. He pulls his knitted hat from his head, sliding his other hand through his hair. It's longer, but the same. He's still wearing black gauges, but even those somehow look older— harder. "We weren't supposed to practice today, but this weekend is gonna be tough, so we worked out this afternoon. Set me behind a little, but I thought I'd still be on time."

"Oh, it's okay. Emma came to keep me company," she says, turning the attention back to me. I can't look at either of them. I don't know why he's pretending we don't know each other, yet I'm oddly grateful for it.

"Oh…uhm…yeah," I smile and chew at the inside of my mouth, my face heating up and my legs starting to feel weak. I put my hand flat on the tabletop, knowing it won't do much to keep me from passing out, but maybe it will at least stabilize me long enough for the feeling to pass.

"She was afraid you were going to stand me up," Lindsey blushes.

Andrew chuckles, and I look at my fingers, how they're touching the tabletop, my knuckles turning white. His voice—it's deeper.

"Oh, I always show up when I make a promise to someone. It's kind of a thing with me," he says. That statement—that was for me, and when I glance at him quickly, I feel the burn of it.

"Well, I'll let you two have your night. I've got a couch waiting for me," I say, pulling my purse close around my body and tucking the soiled ends of my sleeve into my hand.

"Thanks, Em," Lindsey calls out as I leave. I wave to the side without turning, but I know they're both watching me leave.

I focus my attention on my feet, my steps, and the stains on my shirt all the way back up to our apartment, and when I get through the door, I rush to the bathroom and throw up.

I slide down to the floor with my back against the wall and tug the towel from the shower bar into my lap, shaking it out to cover my body so I can curl up into the corner. The tears come from a place I never thought I'd see again. All these years, I've always thought of Andrew, but not since those first few months did I cry for him.

I'm not even sure why I'm crying, but every time I convince myself to stop, my breath catches and my lip quivers and I can't hold it together.

He was gone.

Gone!

And now he's here.

After an hour, I manage to calm myself enough to move into my room, to my bed, where I pull my covers up to my chin so I can throw my ruined shirt on the floor. When I squeeze my eyes shut, Andrew is all I see. Sometimes, it's the young version, the innocent one. Other times, it's tonight—the smile, the hard line, his eyes.

My entire body is throbbing with the beat of my heart, and my chest hurts so much I start to count along with every thump.

"Emmmmm? Are you in your room?" Lindsey calls from the doorway. All I can do is leave my arm over my face, blocking my view of anything, while I lie here in bed and pray she's come home alone.

Please have hated him. Please, god. Please, please, please.

"There you are," she says, opening my door completely, but thankfully leaving my light off. "Are you sick?"

"Migraine," I answer. My head hurts like it does when I get them, but this...it's way worse than a migraine. My migraines go away eventually. I fear this is just beginning.

"Oh, damn. You haven't had one of those for a long time. I'm sorry, Em. You need me to get you anything?"

Lindsey is the kindest, sweetest girl I've ever known. She's a true friend, and I'm so lucky that I found her. She's been my rock through pre-med, through mountains of academic stress, through life's growing pains—through my mother's death. And all I can think of is how much I resent her for spending the night getting to know *him.*

"No, I'm okay. Just a little tired. It hit me as soon as I got home," I say, my voice breaking with a cry. I clear my throat to mask it.

"Here, let me get you a washcloth at least," she says, stepping out of my room and into our bathroom. I breathe heavy, trying to clear out everything else while she's gone, and I manage to smile at her when she steps back into my room.

"Thanks," I say as she presses the cool cloth to my forehead. It soothes me some, reminding me that I'm alive, that I'm here where I always wanted to be—reminding me of what's important. I can feel this coldness, and that is a blessing.

"I'm sorry you're sick," she says, and I can sense the girlfriend part of her begging for me. She's happy, and she wants to share.

I slide the rag down to cover my eyes and pinch the bridge of my nose, feeling the force of my grip tighten as I speak.

"Did you have a nice time?" I ask.

Her sigh crushes me. I feel the bed shake as she sits next to me, taking over pressing the cloth on my head, as she shares. "Oh my god, Em. He's like so...gah! I don't even know. He just...he's so fucking sexy!"

She laughs, and I let my mouth smile even though my eyes tear.

"Yes, he's pretty good looking," I swallow, turning from her to roll to my side. When she flinches I hold my hand up. "Just trying a different position, to see if that helps," I say, wanting to hide my face from her, knowing I won't be able to plaster the smile on the entire time.

"He's a hockey player. For Tech? He said he isn't very good, but he gets to play." She sounds so excited when she talks about him. She sounds exactly like I did when I lay in bed next to my mom after skating with Andrew the first time and told her about this cute boy who plays hockey who isn't anything like the neighbor said he was. She sounds so happy.

"That's cool," I manage to eek out.

"I know, isn't it? I'm going to watch him play Friday. They're home. Oh my god, he was just so...so real, you know? Like a normal, real guy," she pauses, pulling her feet up on the bed now and kicking her shoes off. I feel her weight slide down next to me and her arm come up to sweep under her neck on the pillow.

"Yeah..." I start, my eyes fluttering to a close again. "Normal. That's...that's great, Linds."

So terribly, awfully, nightmarishly great.

"You know, it's true what they say," she says through a yawn. I let out a short breath and laugh in response—no clue where she could be taking this conversation. I can't believe this night is happening to me. "You know. About not looking?"

"Sorry, I'm lost," I respond, not able to sound enthused any more. My eyes are staring at the numbers on my clock, watching the dot count seconds, waiting for this to be over.

"The good ones always show up when you stop looking for them," she says, my mind finishing before her words enough to let a single tear slide from my eye to my pillow.

"Yeah," I say, biting my lip and drawing as much air as I can get through my nose. "It's true. They always come...right...when you...stop looking."

"Thanks for losing your license," she says, reaching her hand over to grasp my arm once and give it a squeeze. I want her to leave. I want to be alone. I want to cry.

But I can't do any of that. I'm hell bent on pretending that the past isn't real, just like Andrew. Maybe that's how it hurts him less. And if it works for him, maybe it will work for me, too.

"You're welcome," I whisper, playing the part of a liar. That's what I am, after all—a liar.

Lindsey yawns again, and soon her breathing starts to fall into a regular pattern. She's on her way to dreams, and I'm sure they'll be wonderful. She deserves them, but I'm jealous all the same.

It's nine at night, and we're both usually exhausted. It comes with our schedule, with the amount of extra everything we both put in just to be med students. Lindsey is an amazing friend—an amazing girl.

And she found him.

Maybe...maybe I give him this.

Chapter 8

Andrew

"Kind of an early night for you...for a date night...no?" Trent says to me the second I step through the door. His crap is piled on the counter again. I just laugh this time and ignore it. I'm not in the mood to be pissed off at my friend for no reason. I'm too pissed at myself.

"Yeah, I guess," I shrug, passing through the kitchen and grabbing each of us a beer, then handing him one.

I sit on the opposite end of the couch and kick my feet up on the coffee table. He's watching a bunch of guys debate on ESPN over the latest drug scandal in baseball. Actually, right now he's watching me. I can see his face pointed in my direction, his bottle tipping my way so his eyes stay on me. He's waiting for me to open up. Trent...he's a *feelings* kind of guy. We are one of those sets of opposite-types of friends—his feelings are complimented by my complete lack there of.

"License girl not what you expect?"

I keep my breathing normal, stifling my desire to huff and sigh. I shake my head as if I didn't hear him. "Huh, sorry. Was lost in the show," I say. There's a commercial on right now, and he looks at me in a way that says *bullshit.*

"License girl?" he asks again, shit-eating grin and all. He senses there's something off with me about this.

I shrug and turn my attention forward again, taking a short drink from my beer. "It was her roommate I went out with. She's the one that answered the door the other day. She's cute. Just...I don't know," I let the rest of my words linger, never finishing.

We watch about ten more minutes of TV. The entire time, all I see are Emma's eyes—her goddamned heartbreaking eyes.

I don't know what I expected, how I thought any of this would go. I know I wasn't expecting to see her though, and maybe that was stupid. It's clear that Lindsey is her best friend. And unless I planned on ditching Lindsey and never calling her again, changing my number and avoiding her at all costs, there wasn't much of a chance that I would never see Emma.

I knew it was her the second I stepped into the restaurant. Her hair color is unmistakable. I'm sure to anyone else, there's nothing about it that's unique or rare. But I can see it. It's familiar. It's part of me.

I know how it feels in my hands.

My first reaction was anger. That's what urged me forward. Something inside got excited at the idea of messing with her, making her feel uncomfortable and out of place. Fuck—if I'm being honest with myself, I *wanted* to see her cry.

And then she looked at me.

I didn't want to make her cry any more. But it was there. She looked sick, and shocked. And the next ten minutes were this pendulum of hate and pity, and I wanted to punish her and save her at the same time. I'm still swaying now.

"Dude, what are these?" Trent gets my attention from the kitchen. I stand up to see him lifting the lid off the cookies.

"Oh, yeah. The chick whose license it was made me cookies. I had one; they're good. Go ahead," I say, walking toward him.

Of course she made cookies. And then I made the cookies into something sinister. I taunted her, twisted the guilt knife I imagined in her gut, and it felt good and terrible all at once. I couldn't stop, though. I just couldn't stop.

"Oh shit, these are good," Trent says, inhaling the rest of the cookie he started and picking up another one. "Oh...hey. I think there's a note in here for you," he adds, crumbs falling from his mouth as he chews and slips a paper from the edge of the tin and begins to open it.

My chest seizes a little, and I reach for it quickly, taking the folded paper from his hand. He looks at me like I'm crazy for a second, but rolls his eyes eventually and just gives over to his second cookie. I unfold it and hold it in my hand in such a way that he can't read it. Trent knows the name Emma. He doesn't know she's *the* girl, but he knows she's one I don't care to see again. Apparently, I got really lit one night at a team party and made up an entire rap about her. It wasn't flattering. Trent isn't stupid, and I know he'd put this moment and that one together

103

quickly. I don't want to have to lie and say it's just a coincidence—so I graze over the words without really reading then shove the note into my pocket.

"What'd it say?"

Nosey fucker.

"Just thanks, you saved me, you're my hero, I want you, take me..." I make a joke out of it, and Trent flips me off then grabs another cookie.

"You going to study hall tomorrow?" he asks, and I'm unusually grateful for the change in subject—even if the new subject is also a pain in my ass. Part of being in the university's athletics department is making mandatory grade checks. It's never a problem for me, but everyone has to log so many hours a week at the study room near the athletic department whether they really need to go or not. I'm always making up my hours at the last minute, and I'm five behind for the month.

I sigh in response, looking up at the ceiling before leveling my gaze back at my friend.

"Dude, don't take it out on me. It's not my fault you're smart and don't need to sit in a library with the rest of us dumbshits," he says. "You better go tomorrow though. You know they're checking hours before the game Friday."

"Yeah, yeah. I'll go," I say over my shoulder. I leave Trent with the rest of the cookies and shut my bedroom door behind me. I pull Emma's note from my pocket the second I'm alone, sitting on my bed and flattening out the paper against my leg. She wrote a lot. Maybe it's a lot. I wouldn't know—this would be the first letter I've ever gotten from her.

Dear Drew,

Thank you for being the kind of guy who pays attention to lost things. You have no idea the trouble you saved me. I made you these cookies because they're my favorite. It was the least I could do. I'm glad you met Lindsey. She's a great girl, and I think you'll like her a lot (do not tell her I said that ;-))

Anyhow. Really, thank you again. I think that's the nicest thing anyone has ever done for me—and here I was a complete stranger.

Enjoy the cookies.

~ Emma

I read the letter six times, each time flipping it over, expecting more, expecting...I don't know...a joke maybe? What the fuck? This...*this* is the nicest thing anyone's ever done for her? A complete stranger?

After my last read, I crumple the note and throw it on my desk, then grab my jacket and keys. I pace a few times, my hand twitching and wanting to hit something, my body craving adrenaline. By the time I step from my room, I must look like an amped up bull given the way Trent reacts to me.

"What the hell's wrong with you?" he asks, sitting up a little straighter on the sofa, squaring his legs as if he's considering tackling me or holding me down.

"Nothing, just...just some shit I found out," I say, not wanting to give him more.

"Owen? Your ma?" he asks, one eyebrow up. Trent hears me argue with my mom over not visiting enough, over making sure I'm following rules, driving safe—she and I argue over everything. She thinks I'm a fuck up and that I'm going to blow it now that I've climbed back this far. And Owen just calls to echo everything she says. I take a deep breath and remind myself to act rational.

"Sort of," I say, simultaneously thinking of the number of lies I've told my friend in the last two days. I'll never be able to keep up, so I stick with half answers that never satisfy, but at least aren't totally wrong.

"Wanna go shoot some pool?" Trent asks. I don't make eye contact and do my best to think if that would help. What I'd really like to do is find Pitch Black and go a few rounds with him, but Harley usually likes to schedule fights on Wednesdays, so I'm pretty sure the gym is closed.

I grip the back of my neck and stare at Trent's feet for a beat before nodding. He doesn't pause at all, just moves to the door, leaving the TV on in the room behind us. He slips on his shoes and the sweatshirt he left hanging on the back of a nearby stool. He locks up as I start down the walkway to the main road.

We live on the first floor of a two-story building. No need for elevators. No doorman greeting me as I come and go. No one doing amazingly nice things for me that would make me want to bake them cookies. I fume over the words in Emma's note the entire way, sometimes talking to myself. Trent can sense I'm pissed, so he doesn't question me. He's used to seeing me get worked up over a bad game or a weekend with my mom and stepdad. Usually, I'm frustrated at having to defend myself, prove that I've grown up. The only sound he makes tonight is the occasional huff of breath in his hands to keep them warm. Winter is coming in Northern Illinois.

Majerle's is warm, and I don't waste any time ordering up two shots of Jack and commandeering a pool table in the back corner. This is a common scene for Trent and me—honestly, this is what we do for dinner most nights during the off-season. Trent is easy going, and I like to look for trouble. He keeps me in line—usually—and Majerle's accommodates us both nicely. I rack quickly and toss a stick to Trent. He grabs it in the air.

"I'll break," I say, positioning myself and bending forward to line up my stick without waiting to hear his answer.

"Do you have to be a bossy fuck, too?"

I lean forward with my hands on the edge of the table, my stick leaning against it too, between my palms. I've gotten myself so worked up that I've lost sight of reason—and being reasonable. I let my head sling forward more as I exhale, then tilt my head up to look at my friend leaning against the wall across from me.

"Sorry," I sigh.

"You know you're miserable when you get like this?" He picks up the white ball in front of me, tossing it in his hand a few times before motioning for me to step to the side.

"I know," I say, taking two steps back.

"Okay, as long as you know," he says, leaving his eyes on mine for a few seconds, like he's waiting to see if I'll explode some more or actually calm the fuck down this time. I hold up a thumb and nod, mouthing *I'm good.*

"You wanna tell me what this is all about?" he says, leaning forward and lining up his break. He slides his stick twice before sending balls in all directions on the table, sinking both a stripe and a solid. He works his second shot, sinking a solid again. "You're stripes."

Our waitress drops off two shots, and I take mine fast, setting the glass back on her tray before she's more than a step away. I hold up my fingers for two more, and Trent tells her to make it only one.

"Pussy," I call him.

"I have a test in the morning. And then we're going to the tutoring lab. You show up hung over, and I guarantee you that'll be worse than telling coach you're two hours short on your time," Trent says.

I keep my eyes level with his, reach for his shot on the tray, and drink it.

"Two more," I tell the girl. She smiles at me uncomfortably and heads back to the bar.

"Fuck," Trent breathes, shaking his head in disappointment.

I sit back on my stool while he works most of his balls from the table, missing with only two left. I take over and sink three before missing—just in time for my next two shots to arrive. Trent reaches for one of them.

"Hey, hands off, bitch!" I say, smacking the top of his hand. He flips me off and drinks it down, leaving me with only one to grab and follow suit. "Two more!" I shout, holding up two fingers.

"What are you doing?"

"Drinking." I don't look at him, instead circling the table like an animal.

Nicest thing anyone has ever done for me.

Is she fucking serious? I bet someone lent her a penny once when she was short. Is that guy higher on the list, too? I guess I shouldn't complain, at least she thanked me for returning her missing ID.

Emma wouldn't have had to go to a place like Lake Crest.

"Are you going to shoot or what?" Trent asks. I'm irritating him. Good. Melissa, our waitress—whose name I got from the nametag pressed against her tits—has brought more Jack. I think I'll drink these two first.

I grip the first glass between my finger and thumb. Trent takes my stick from my hand when I do.

"Andrew," he says, leveling me with the kind of look I should only get from my father. If I had one. I have Dwayne. Fuck Dwayne. And fuck Owen.

I push his chest so hard he stumbles backward, knocking over one of the high-top tables. The bar isn't crowded, but the dozen or so people around us get quiet, and one of the security guys walks over.

"It's fine," I say, raising my hand up. "Go on, get back to the front door with your stupid tight black T-shirt and flashlight, like that really helps you spot fake IDs."

Trent's face falls into a look of disgust, and he sighs, shaking his head and tossing both of our sticks on the pool table before walking away.

"Come on," the bouncer says, his arms folded in front of his body as he steps into my personal space. "You're done for the night, kid."

I hate being called *kid*. I haven't been a kid in years, since I ran after an ice cream truck with a crumpled dollar bill. I spit on the floor, and for a brief second, I consider taking a swing at him. Luckily, I'm not drunk enough for that yet. This place—it's my favorite bar. Trent and I come here after games and tough practices. I'd hate myself more than I already do if I fucked that up, too.

"Yeah, yeah," I say, pulling my beanie from my back pocket and sliding it on my head. I toss two twenties on the pool table, then shove my hands into my jacket pockets when I leave, stopping a few steps from the bar's front door. Trent didn't wait for me; he's already a block away. I let him go, because if I caught up with him I'd only keep being an asshole, and he didn't do anything wrong.

He's right. I don't know what I'm doing. I'm lost. I was barely with it before, but then I saw her. Now I'm done.

I lean to the side and spit again before looking up into the eyes of the dickhead who kicked me out. I thrust my chest toward him, juking him with my arms out wide. He doesn't flinch.

"Fuck this place," I say...to no one.

I walk the long way home, circling through campus, by the lake. A few students are out running, and others are walking quickly from the library in the center of campus out to cars or to their dorms. I bet they're walking fast because they're afraid of me. I pause at a bench that's shadowed by the only tree around that seems to still have its leaves. I sit down and pull my phone out to check the time. I notice a few texts from Owen.

Are you making it to mom's and Dwayne's for dinner Sunday?

He sent it only a few minutes ago, so I respond.

Yeah. I'll be there.

I don't want to go. But I don't want to hear the mountain of shit I'll get for not going more. He writes back a minute later.

Good. Mom's really freaking out because Kens and I are going to Germany. Try not to be an asshole, K?

Yep.

I lean my head forward into my hand, my arm rested on my knee. Owen and his girlfriend are spending a year in Germany thanks to some offer my brother got to play basketball there. His girlfriend Kensi plays...like...a dozen instruments or something. She got into some master's program over there to study with the national symphony. They've lived together in the city since graduation—Owen coaches at some prep school and Kens plays in an orchestra. I think they'll probably end up getting married, which is good because I like Kensi; she's good to my brother and my mom. Better than I am.

Kensi visited me at Lake Crest. I can't even count how many times she came to see me—sometimes with Owen, sometimes on her own. When I got in my first fight there, she was the one I called. I was beaten by a guy twice my size and two years older than me. He was in Lake Crest for committing armed robbery; he drove the getaway car. When he asked me to write his term paper for recent American history, I said *no*. So he fucked me up when I rounded the corner after my shower in gym. My eye was swollen shut, and he cut me on my cheek and arm with a knife he wasn't supposed to have, but no one dared take away from him. I called Kensi so she'd come up with an excuse to keep my mom away for an extra week. She did.

Kensi made a lot of excuses for me.

That right there—that small thing that the girl, who will probably marry my brother, did for me, no questions asked—is *the nicest thing anyone's ever done for me.* Kensi wrote to me, too. She sent me clips from the college paper on Owen's games, and she took pictures and printed them out to make collages of things I missed—my car, my old house, the rink.

I gave up a year and a future, and Emma Burke couldn't be bothered to stamp a goddamned envelope.

Pulling my phone from my pocket, I scroll to the string of texts between Lindsey and me, and I send her one more.

Can't wait for Friday. Can I see you tomorrow? I'll come over. Oh, and don't tell your roommate, but her cookies made me sick. Had to throw them out.

Standing from the bench, I push my phone back into my pocket and stuff my hands into my jacket, walking back to my apartment feeling entitled to lots of things. First on that list is Emma Burke's roommate.

And I intend to have her.

Emma

I didn't sleep.

Lindsey did.

She slept right through the sound of her phone buzzing on the bed between us. She'd brought it in with her, never stopping in her happiness to leave things in the kitchen or her room. She came to take care of me, then left her phone there as she fell asleep. I know she didn't do it on purpose; she doesn't have a clue about any of it at all, about who Drew *really* is. But it still all feels so carefully played, as if she's working with him to make sure just the right everything finds my ears and eyes and insides.

...*her cookies made me sick.*

My body ached reading those words. They weren't for me, but yet...they have to be for me. I lay there and thought about the way he looked at me—and the way he looked.

I let Lindsey stay asleep in my bed. Sneaking out of my room to the shower, I slip into my workout clothes so I could head to the gym before my morning class. I packed a bag with everything I thought I'd need, the plan to stay away until I heard from Lindsey about a date—that he'd come, and they'd both be gone.

But that text never came. Not a word. Nothing—not even an excited text from my friend about how he wants to see her now, because he just can't wait.

I fought the urge to text her leading questions that would prompt answers about Andrew. We only shared labs on Mondays and Wednesdays, so I was on my own today, which made it harder to stretch things like lunch and studying into taking longer than they really needed to. By the time the sun was down, I was exhausted, running on maybe an hour of sleep in total. If they were going out, they'd be gone by now, and Lindsey would have let me know.

My backpack loaded down, I drag my tired legs to our apartment building, through the lobby, and to the elevator where I'm so exhausted I drop my bag from my shoulders during the ride and drag it along the floor as I exit and walk to our door.

It's a weird season here now—not quite the snowy winter I've grown to love, but not warm enough to wear single layers. Every hallway and classroom is pumped with heat, though, which makes me sticky and uncomfortable by the end of the day. I've hit my limit for today.

I listen before putting my key in the lock. It's quiet, which makes me think that maybe Lindsey left without telling me. My mind runs away with this thought, jumping to the conclusion that Andrew mentioned how he knows me—and my friend didn't want to hurt my feelings, so of course now they're off somewhere both talking about how they need to keep this a secret from me. I let these thoughts dance in my head until I open the door and see the both of them laughing, throwing strings of pasta at each other in our kitchen. Confronted with what's real, I actually wish the daydream in my head from seconds before were the truth. At least then, I wouldn't *really* know and see it all.

I'm too noisy, and they both turn to look at me, my clothes disheveled from being stuffed in my bag for the morning, my hair limp and stringy from my rushed shower, my back sweaty from carrying my heavy bag all day. Lindsey covers her mouth, hiding her giggle from whatever they were doing before—whatever was funny—but finally lets it go, laughing without abandon as she walks closer to me.

Andrew isn't laughing at all. She doesn't notice he's stopped. He's behind her, and all he's doing is staring.

"There you are!" she says, rushing at me with a spoon. "Here! Oh my god, taste this."

There's a red sauce in her spoon, but I look at it as if it's poison, my eyes flitting to Andrew for a second, but looking back to the spoon because he's still looking at me, not smiling, and if it is poison, I think it's still my better option.

"What...is it?" I ask, pulling my bag back up to my shoulder and adjusting the weight of it.

"It's marinara. Drew made it, and it's so freakin' good. You have to try." She holds the spoon to my lips, and I lean forward, letting her feed me like a child, my eyes glancing to Andrew— *Drew*—as I taste it. His mouth tugs up on one corner into a smirk, and I can't help but hear his voice in my head.

Her cookies made me sick.

"It's good," I say, my eyes on him the entire time. It's delicious, but *good* is polite. It won't make me sick, and it won't make me well. It's just a taste that somehow feels very much like the boy I knew...know.

"Made it from scratch," he smirks. Lindsey joins him in the kitchen again, and he takes the spoon back from her, but his gaze lingers on me. "Dinner's served in ten minutes," he adds, waiting for me to react. My stomach sinks.

112

I was gone the entire day. My body hurts, and all I want is a hot shower. I wanted to miss this, yet somehow, I timed it just right.

"Oh...it's okay, I'm not that hungry," I say, looking down to my feet. His stare—it hurts. And he won't stop.

"You sure? We made plenty. We didn't want to leave you out," he adds, turning back to tend to the stove. Lindsey's looking up at him with stars, hearts, and probably rainbow unicorns in her eyes; it makes my breath feel heavy.

"I'm sure, but...thank you," I say. His arm stops moving, no longer stirring the noodles in the water. Lindsey steps away, carrying a pile of bowls and plates to the small kitchen table by our window, and the second she leaves the room, he turns to face me, the mask gone.

"You're welcome, Emma," he says, his mouth a hard, flat line and his eyes cloudy with what I'm pretty sure is regret.

We stand in our little pocket of silence with our eyes locked for a few seconds, and it's like he's memorizing parts of me he's forgotten while I'm counting how many parts of him have changed—nearly all of him has as far as I can tell.

"Please join us," Lindsey startles me, her hands wrapping around my bicep. I jump, and she laughs. "Sorry. Really, though, I was about to text you to tell you he was here, and we made dinner. It'll be fun. We usually eat sandwiches or microwave meals, Drew. This is a big night out for Em and me. Ha...and we didn't even go out."

I manage to keep my attention on her, even though I can see Andrew standing in the same place behind her, his eyes never once leaving their hold on me.

"Please?" she begs, making tiny jumps on her toes as she slides her grip down to my fingertips. This is how a toddler begs for a toy. It's effective.

I breathe in slowly through my nose and nod a few times.

"Sure. I just need a minute," I say. I need several minutes. I need hours, maybe days. But minutes are better than nothing.

I carry my bag to my room and fall into my bed, crawling up to the pillow and pushing my face into the folds of the material. All I want is to stay here. I indulge in the coolness of my bed for a full minute, breathing in and out until I convince myself my anxiety isn't going anywhere.

I sit up and look at my reflection in the mirror above my dresser, my hair now knotted in twists and tufts around my head. Leaning forward, I grab my brush, holding my hair near the base of my head and tugging it through the long strands until I look a little less wild.

I kick off my old clothes, putting on a clean pair of jeans and the purple sweatshirt slung over the end of my bed—throwing it over my head without even thinking until I step back out into the living room and Andrew's eyes fall on me, registering the familiar shirt. His expression tells me he recalls the memory that goes along with it. I usually think of it, too. And I don't know why I didn't tonight. Maybe, my mind wanted to fool me into wearing it just to spite me, my subconscious in cahoots with the boy who built up the memory in the first place. I wore this sweatshirt when Andrew taught me how to ice-skate. It was new then, and I've thought about throwing it away or donating it so many times since. I could never seem to part with it, though.

"You look nice in purple," he says, stepping closer to me on his way to the dining area, his voice low enough Lindsey doesn't hear as she finishes setting the table for our awkward dinner-for-three. He doesn't linger, and he doesn't look at me, not directly anyhow. His eyes hover along my shoulder, tracing a line down to my fingertips, to my hand—the one he held when I was sixteen and unsteady on my feet.

When we were young, and nothing bad had happened.

My fingers tingle as a short burst of adrenaline runs through my body, and I flex my hand wanting to force the feeling away. I remind myself to breathe, repeating a mini version of my useless calming exercise from earlier, and I follow Andrew to the table, noticing his hand down along his side, flexing just as mine did.

Our table is a circle, a small one, the space not made for anything large, meaning we're all technically sitting next to one another. I wish it were bigger. If it was, there would be more too look at. I hyper-focus on my spoonful of noodles, on the sauce I drizzle from the hot pan over them, on the salad I put in the bowl—I spend as many minutes as I can making my plate perfect, ignoring the laughter and banter between Lindsey and Andrew.

"Here, you didn't get enough," Andrew says to me after everyone's plate is full. He stands, and my eyes catch the frame of his body, the tight gray shirt he's wearing, how it clings to his waist, his stomach and the expanse of his chest underneath the thin fabric. I look up to see him watch me take him in, and his cheek dimples as he raises the corner of his lips, careful to keep his attention on my plate the rest of the time.

"Thank you," I say, and he chuckles.

"You're still welcome," he says, this time a little bite to his tone.

I drag my fork through the noodles, wrapping them around the prongs and lean forward to take my bites, doing my best to become small. I'm taking mental measurements of the amount of food on my plate, cross-referencing it with the amount of time it's taking me to swallow each and every forkful, and I grow discouraged. I feel like a child with a bowl of broccoli—no dog to feed it to.

"Oh, you missed it earlier, Em. I was telling Andrew about how we met—me and you?" I choke when Lindsey speaks, reaching for my glass of water while I wave them both off that I'm fine.

I'm fine—only that I met Lindsey in perhaps the worst way possible for this very moment. We met at driving school. It was the summer before our freshman year. I had run a red light near campus, trying to make it to the admissions office before a deadline. When the officer pulled me over, I had a panic attack—to the point that he had to help me lie down on the side of the road so I didn't collapse and crack open my head. He still gave me a ticket. Just the flash of his lights brought so many feelings back, but I never told Lindsey that. And I don't think Andrew's interested in that part now.

Lindsey was in my class for blowing a stop sign. We were the only two people in the class under fifty, and when we both found out we were going to Tech and would be freshmen pre-med, we decided to room together.

"Lemons out of lemonade," Lindsey said at the time.

It goes down like venom now.

"Yeah, Linds tells me you're quite the speed demon," Andrew says through a mouthful of food. He's remaining aloof, but I know better. I can see the truth in his eyes.

I open my mouth, partly to defend myself, and partly to explain, but the way he pauses—leaning with one arm along the back of his chair and his body to the side, so he can hold me hostage with the look on his face—makes me forget the words to say. Not that I had the right words ready. I don't. I never have.

"Hey, I didn't say that," Lindsey says, the laughter escaping her teasingly and sweet as she swats at his thigh with her hand. He catches it and holds it, his lips curling into a grin as he brings her hand up to his face so he can kiss the knuckles, his gaze shifting to me as he lowers her hand back down, never letting go.

I look down at my plate, admonished. I'm struck with an overwhelming sense of shame, but it's more than that, too. I'm hurt, and I'm jealous, and I don't understand what any of this is about. Why are we keeping our history a secret? Why am I allowing it?

"So, Lindsey says you two have lived together for three years now. And you're both...med students?" he asks.

I find myself spending too much time studying him, trying to find the next double meaning so I can be prepared for it. But he doesn't look up again, instead, going back to his dinner plate.

"She's my best friend," I say, smiling at her quickly, genuinely, but returning my attention back to the table in front of me. I don't know why those are the words I say. There's a part of me that wants to make sure he realizes what he's messing with, I guess—that he's being personal. Lindsey is personal.

"Med school is so hard, and it takes so long. It's just kind of nice to have someone by your side who gets it," Lindsey says. I smile at her again, catching Andrew's eyes as I look away. It's like he never really stops watching me.

"You two should open your own practice when you're done," he says, pushing his plate a few inches forward. He's done eating, I guess, though his plate is still full.

"I wish," Lindsey says, picking up a tomato from her salad with her fingers and popping it in her mouth. "But Emma here is all about cardiothoracic. She was hand-picked by the goddess of surgery herself."

"Linds," I say, my eyes begging her to stop from saying too much. Why I got into Tech, why I'm studying here with Miranda Wheaton, is a story I don't really want getting around. My being here looks like pity to the outsider—a lot of things in my life look like pity and charity. But it's not. I earned my spot here just like every other student.

But Andrew won't see it that way. He'll see it as selfish. He'll see it as selfish because he'll put it all together, see how it fits with that night and what I let him do for me. And then, quite possibly, he'll hate me even more.

Andrew grows quiet, his eyes studying both of us as we have our silent exchange. I can tell he's unsatisfied. To punctuate things, he pulls his hand—the one holding Lindsey's—up to rest on the tabletop, putting on a show of his fingers caressing against hers, his thumb teasing along the top of her hand and then around her wrist. I hate that I'm looking at it, but I can't look away.

I'm weak.

"So you're gonna be a surgeon, huh?"

The way he says it, it's both innocent and dripping with contempt all at once. I smile despite him, and nod *yes*. But my lips can't hold their form for long. I feel his leg slide forward, and I wish for it to be a coincidence, hoping he just doesn't realize how close he is to me. I say it isn't so over and over in my head until his foot comes to rest against the outside of mine, his shoe perfectly matched against my bare foot, my toes recoiling as he taps against them twice, a gentle reminder—a threat.

I back away from the table abruptly, my hands gripping the front of the table hard. Realizing how crazy I look, I tap the tabletop twice and grin at my friend before forcing a pleasant look to remain on my face as I answer Andrew's question.

"I am," I say, standing and pulling my plate into my arms. The food is delicious, but I wasn't hungry when I walked in; I'm certainly not hungry now.

"Is that so you can cut people's hearts out?"

My back is to him when he speaks, and I'm so glad, because I wouldn't be able to hide my reaction to his words. Lindsey has already interrupted, telling him he's being gross. She's laughing, and he laughs with her, apologizing for being graphic. He's playing along with her, like the words he said were just for morbid shock value. And they were—just not for the reason Lindsey thinks. I keep moving forward, one foot in front of the next as the tear falls down my cheek, thinning as it reaches my chin. I lean my head to the side, rubbing it dry along my shoulder.

"I'm still not feeling well, Linds. If it's all right with you, I'm going to lie down for a while," I say from the kitchen, pulling a sheet of foil from a drawer and covering my plate with no intention of eating it later. Two of my favorite things now ruined—pasta and oatmeal cookies.

"Okay," she says between flirtatious whispers and laughter.

I tuck my dish inside the fridge and walk to my room, closing the door behind me, and letting my hand rest on the handle—feeling like I need to hold it to keep the bad stuff out like they do in those zombie movies. After a few seconds, I loosen my grip and backpedal until my legs hit the edge of my bed, forcing me to sit.

I pull my sleeves low into my palm with my thumbs looped on the inside and bring my fists to my face, inhaling the fabric, searching for any trace of a scent from years ago. I know it's futile. I know it's gone; he's gone. I sent him away.

Another tear is threatening to come, so I run my sleeve along my eyes, wiping what's left away with my thumb. I move my thumb over my skin twice, imagining it's Andrew's thumb the second time. I bring my hands to my lap, and lock my fingers together, imagining one is his, before closing my eyes with a single laugh of pain. My hands look nothing like his and Lindsey's, and I'm being foolish.

The sound of the television comes on soon, and I pull my biology book into my lap as I scoot all the way to the back of my bed, sliding my laptop out to review our lab assignment in the morning. I read the same page for an hour, listening for clues on the other side of the door. I've kept the earbuds in my ears the entire time, never once playing any music. When Lindsey raps on my door and opens it, I fake startle, pulling them from my head as if I've been listening to music the entire time.

"Drew go home?" I ask quickly, realizing how anxious I sound about it, so I start to busy myself with papers and my backpack and my computer screen angle.

"Uhm..." Lindsey says.

I know.

I keep my eyes down so she can't see the truth, but I let my sigh fall out in a heavy breath.

"I asked him to stay...but he's such a gentleman, he wanted me to make sure it was okay with you," she says.

My body jerks with a slight laugh. Shaking my head, I lift my gaze to her as I swallow.

"What's that look for?" she asks.

I have a look. Of course I have a look. Why is he doing this?

"Emma Brooklyn Burke, I'm a grown woman; if I want to sleep with a guy after the second date, then I'm going to," she says, stepping to my door, gripping the side of it as she turns to face me. "I'll tell him you said it's fine."

She glares at me as she shuts it behind her hard.

Time stops for a full minute. I don't blink. I don't breathe. There isn't a sound to be heard, until the familiar click of her bedroom door across from mine.

I kick my things from my bed and let out a battle of grunts I try to keep quiet—my papers, computer, pens, and notecards all scattering around the foot of my bed into a mess below. The sensation doesn't satisfy me, so I rip my blankets away too, crawling up on my knees as my fists grab at the sheets, pillows, and mattress pad, tearing the corner as I yank so hard it pulls up the corner of my mattress.

I wad everything into a ball and push it on top of my papers, leaving me in the center of my empty bed, breathing hard and numb, not knowing how to feel. I feel angry—angry with Andrew, and angry that I feel anything at all.

He left. He's the one who left.

And now he's here. And he's gone. The boy he was...he's gone.

I scramble to my feet, cramming my papers and computer back into my bag, shoving and kicking my pile of blankets out of the way. Stuffing my feet into my shoes, I pull the purple sweatshirt from my body, switching it out for a Tech one hanging on a hook behind my door. I grab my headphones, keys, and phone, then grab the purple sweatshirt and carry it with me out the door, pausing in the kitchen to step on the trash lever and throw the fucking sweatshirt away.

I let the main door slam closed behind me, locking up with a hard twist of my wrist as I bang my bag against the hallway wall on my way to the elevator. When I get outside, I look up and see a light still on in Lindsey's window. After a few seconds, it goes out.

And all of my breath escapes me.

Chapter 9

Andrew Harper, Age 16

Dear Emma,

I'm losing myself. For the first two months, I swore that wouldn't happen. I said it every night before sleep; I woke up reminding myself of who I was.

I haven't done that in days now...maybe weeks.

I'm letting go, whether I want to or not. I don't care, and that scares me a little. Not caring? It's liberating. It's lonely.

There's a guy here; he's 18. His name's Kingston, but most of the "students" here call him King. They say he was in some gang or something; that he used to sell drugs. He has tats all over his fingers and the rumor is he drove a getaway car for his older brother during some armed robbery over in Rockford. I'm not sure if he was really all that tough before he showed up here, but he sort of took the lead. A lot of the other guys let him. They buy the stories—his self-made hype.

He doesn't like me.
I don't like him.

Apparently, he's not used to people telling him no. I tell him no a lot. Last week, when I told him no, he snuck into my room at night and put a pillow over my face. He's pulled shit with me before, tripping me at lunch and sucker punching me around corners. This time, though...I was ready. I stabbed him with a pen, dug it into his side and held it there. I thought that'd make him stop right away. But he just pushed the pillow into my face harder. The harder I fought, the stronger he was. And for a moment, I was losing.

I almost gave in. Just...let him take me. But something made me keep fighting.

I struggled enough to wake someone across the hall, and then the guard set the alarms off and another person pulled him from me. I lost my phone privileges for an extra month for stabbing him. I got extra therapy sessions too, to talk about my aggression. Fucker tried to kill me; pretty sure aggression was the only way to go with that.

King got a trip to the emergency room and an overnight at the hospital. Funny thing, it was phone day today, and I saw him making his calls. I guess a pen weighs more than a pillow in this fucked-up court of justice I'm stuck in.

I hate them all. They pretend like they're teaching us lessons, reforming us to become better men. We go to these sermons, and there's an old man who gives us these long stories that we're supposed to identify with and recognize our weaknesses so we can improve. Nobody listens. I tried to last week, but the longer he spoke, the more I focused on the lack of passion in his voice, the way he really didn't care if he made a difference, or if we changed—just as long as he got a paycheck.

I looked around at the room of these forgotten kids. That's why we're here, because we're still kids according to the state. Worth saving. Our offenses forgivable. I was a better person three months ago, before I got here. Whatever I am now, I'm not so sure it's good.

I've had a few fights. Nobody knows except my brother's girlfriend. She knows. She visits. She convinced everyone that she's family. She threw around stories about my grandfather. Everyone bought it. I like it when Kensi comes. Sometimes we just sit without talking. It's nice. And when I have things I need to hide, like bruises or...other things...Kensi helps. She doesn't like it; I can tell. But she understands.

I think she tells Owen. But I also don't think she tells him exactly how bad it is. I begged her not to.

My family can't see me this way. They won't like what I am becoming.

At first, the fights came out of nowhere—guys who have been here for months, or almost a year for some, would just kick me and beat the shit out of me to prove they could. The longer I've been here, the less initiating I get.

Thing is, though...the fights...they give me something to do. I've started instigating. I don't mean to, and every night, I tell myself I'm going to stop. But I can't. I don't do it without cause, really. Usually, someone newer than me is getting picked on, so I open my mouth and say shit to get people to stop. And when they turn their attention to me, every other thought and feeling I have goes away. It's nothing but fighting for survival in this place.

I guess I'm surviving.

When I fight, I forget about you. I didn't want to tell you that part, but now that I've written it...I think I'll leave it.

I hope you'll write back.

Andrew

Chapter 10

Emma

"Are you *sure* you can't come…just for the first period. Look…see what I just did there? I called it a period. I'm learning my hockey lingo," Lindsey says, holding her fist out for me to pound. I do it slowly, my lips in a tight smile as we touch. This faking and pretending thing…I'm not sure how long I can keep it up.

"Yeah, they should totally let you in the booth to call the game," I tease, pushing myself to be light and funny despite how sick I really feel. She scrunches her face at me as she continues putting on her boots and wrapping her knit scarf around her neck. I haven't been able to make eye contact with her for longer than a few seconds at a time. Lindsey and I have never been big on swapping stories about our intimate moments. She's only slept with a few guys, and my list is still at *zero*, so I guess there isn't much to share. I hope we don't start with this one.

"Very funny," she says with a grunt as she finally gets her boot snug on her foot. "Seriously, though…I'm going to be sitting there alone. Can't you come for…like…just a little bit?"

I could come. I have some time before Miranda's presentation. But I managed to hide myself in the library on campus until the morning, and I snuck in here at five, exhausted enough that I didn't have to hear Andrew leave for his place. I know he was still here when I came home, because his wallet and keys were on the counter when I came in. I touched them. I wanted to flip his wallet open, look at it. But I didn't. I can't actively go see him play hockey—not now that I've done such a bang-up job of avoiding his face for almost a full afternoon. And seeing him on the ice? I just…I can't do that. I wouldn't be able to pretend anymore.

"I'm just really stressed. I'm introducing her, and they want the usual speech—you know…about *me?* Anyway, I really want to get there early. I'm so sorry; don't hate me," I say, biting my lip, my inner voice begging her not to guilt me anymore. I can't handle any more guilt.

"I get it," she sighs. I sigh in response when I turn away from her, about eleven hundred tons of pressure fleeing my shoulders all at once. "At least...tell me, how do I look?"

"You look nice," I smile at her, taking her full outfit in. She's dressed like she's ready for a ski trip. It's not *that* cold at the rink. But I don't want to burst her bubble. And there's probably also a part of me that likes that she won't have to borrow something warm from Andrew.

When Andrew left, I sort of got into hockey—Blackhawks mostly. My dad had always been a fan and was thrilled, and we went to a lot of games. I learned the basics from watching, and my dad taught me the nuances. It was our thing, even though I went in the beginning because it reminded me of Andrew. When my mom got sick, we had to put a stop to our trips. Neither of us ever wanted to leave her home alone for long—her body was weak, and the chemo...it wasn't working. I think we knew it wasn't working long before a doctor told us. We didn't want to miss any time with her, certainly not so we could sit in nosebleed seats at the United Center.

I haven't been back to a game since. It just doesn't feel right going without my dad. And I don't think going anywhere but to work and home feels right to him. She's been gone for two years, but it still feels like yesterday we put her in the ground and said *goodbye*.

I move to the kitchen while Lindsey finishes getting ready. There's a dinner being served at the presentation tonight. It's fish—salmon—which I guess most people think is delicious. It makes me gag. I pull the peanut butter from our cupboard, scraping it empty so I can overload a slice of bread to tide me over until the presentation's done. I flip open the trash lid to throw the jar away, then go back to spreading the peanut butter when a flash hits me; I flip the lid up again with my pinky finger. No purple. The trash is halfway full. I know it hasn't been taken out.

No purple.

I drop the knife and wipe my hands on a towel, then completely lift the lid, kicking the side of the can to move debris around just enough that I can see if my sweatshirt is buried.

It's not.

"Hey...uhm...Linds?" I call for my friend, prepping myself to ask her if she's seen my sweatshirt—if she's the one who saved it from the county dump or if *someone else* did—when I march by the front door and do a double take at the clothes hanging from the hooks nearby. Her jacket. My jacket from last night, which I know I hung there without seeing anything else. But this afternoon...there *is* something else. My sweatshirt is hung on the last hook.

I pull it free and smell it, noticing it doesn't smell like it's spent the night in the trash. It also doesn't smell like Andrew.

"Yeah?" Lindsey answers behind me. I grip my sweatshirt and take a quick breath before I turn to face her.

"My sweatshirt..." I start, waiting to see if she has a reaction to it, like an *oh yeah, I saved it for you* kind of reaction. She doesn't, which means...

"You know, I heard Andrew say he liked purple. He mentioned it—that it's a nice color—when I wore this. You should wear it," I say, the words just coming out one after the next before that little gatekeeper in my head has time to tell me to stop it, because this is a really bad idea. And it's mean. I'm using Lindsey.

She smiles and takes my sweatshirt into her hands, and my insides rush with conflict. She's taken it, though, so I walk the line on the other side—the one that's not being nice—and keep going.

"You know, I always loved this one. You should wear it more," she says, carrying it back to her room.

I love it too. That's why I wore it the first time I went out with Andrew. It's Roxy, and has little diamonds on the front that are both tough and feminine at the same time. That's what I wanted to be—tough and feminine. Not broken and frail and unable to do things like run, or skate, or date a boy. I should wear it more, especially now that my new go-to sweatshirt is

126

forever ruined with wine stains. Except now, it reminds me of *this* Andrew—*Drew*—which makes me love it less.

I hover in the kitchen, nibbling at my sandwich while Lindsey changes, and when she comes out in my shirt, I compliment her, ignoring the loud voice kicking me from the inside and telling me I shouldn't do this. I'm not being fair to Lindsey, and I'm stooping to Andrew's level. But I let her walk out the door anyway, and I sit quietly in my chair and finish my sandwich, playing out the scene that's about to happen in my head—she'll show up, he'll see her, and he'll think of me.

Part of being the prized student is being available to shine the spotlight on your benefactor at a moment's notice. Miranda Wheaton is winning an award, and she called me two days ago to ask if I would introduce her before her presentation and speech. She's kind—but there's also a very rigid thread that runs through her that's not to be messed with. When she asks, you say *yes*. That's the unspoken rule, and I learned it quickly when I backed out of something freshman year and found myself fighting to get back into her circle.

I'm special, and I still had to fight. There is no gray with Miranda Wheaton—everything is black and white. You are either *in* or you're *out*.

I need to stay *in*.

I also need to get the projector working. I'm sweating. I sweat when I panic. I'm panicking, too. Even though I'm not the one really getting an award, I *am* the one sitting up here on my knees in front of the small table, unplugging and replugging the same cord to the computer—expecting the screen to just randomly appear one of these times—despite the fact that I'm not doing anything different.

Come on. One, two, three...work!

I lean forward and rub my head. I should have worn my hair up. Right now, my heavy locks are only making me hotter. I twist my hair into a knot at the base of my neck, jabbing a pencil through the middle of the bun to secure it in place. I go back to the stubborn computer and punch a few buttons. Here I want to cut into people's bodies for a living—and I can't even get a PowerPoint to show up.

"Hey, mind if I maybe...just..."

A pair of very large, very masculine hands reaches in front of me, and when I look up I'm greeted with startling-blue eyes on a chiseled face and just enough of a beard to make me want to touch it...just once.

No, no...don't touch it, Emma!

"Sorry, didn't mean to scare you, but I was in the back...over there?" He nods over his shoulder, to the doorway where two other equally handsome men are leaning, watching me flail. I've been flailing in front of them for nearly an hour. On my knees. I think maybe I swore a few times, too. *Oh my god!* "You're...kind of struggling, huh?" he says. I blink at him, twisting my lips before I look back at the computer in front of us both. I pull the cord out and plug it in again.

"This is my only move," I say with a shrug, looking back up at him again. "That's all I've got." Yep, those are definitely blue eyes. Not blue-gray like mine. His are a better blue, like...sky maybe?

His laugh comes from somewhere deep inside his chest, under the tight silvery gray shirt and slightly darker gray tie that he's wearing on his chest like a superhero emblem. I laugh internally at my observation: my hero in a suit and tie.

"I think you just need to put it in...display mode...which is right..." His speech comes out in pieces while he crouches down next to me and opens a few windows, punches a few buttons, and *holy shit, Miranda's presentation is on the screen!*

"You're amazing," I say, standing on my feet and staring at the screen with wide eyes and an open mouth, working every second to avoid looking back at him with the same awe and amazement. I can tell from my periphery that he's smiling. I can also tell that his smile—it's *really* nice.

He chuckles, and I give in. I look, and my body flushes instantly.

"No, I just do a lot of presentations. It's more of a matter of knowing how to push the right buttons, not really being amazing," he smirks, taking a few steps back until he reaches the edge of the stage I'm on—we're on. This sexy, sexy man is talking about pushing buttons and I'm blushing in front of professors and doctors while on a stage.

"Oh...yeah, right," I say. My heart is beating the way it does when I chug uphill in a rollercoaster. I'm nervous, and my palms are sweating, and this hot guy with a beard just winked at me.

When he leaves the stage, I move my attention back to the computer—sorting through the slides to make sure they're in order and on the right one to start. I tug my purse out from under the table and pull the small note cards I've made out next. I sit against the back wall, in a seat in a line of chairs left there for the presenters for the night.

Dr. Miranda Wheaton saved my life.

Dr. Wheaton is more than a visionary.

It's an honor to study with her.

I mumble to myself the start of my few short paragraphs. I'm uncomfortable speaking in front of a crowd, but speaking about *this*...it amps up my anxiety about seven-thousand levels.

I understand why I need to, though. Or maybe not *need* to, but why people want to hear it. It's compelling. My story is the perfect illustration on why Dr. Wheaton is the best, why she deserves this award tonight, and why she'll continue to win hundreds more just as prestigious.

The crowd filters in, and after several minutes, the background is filled with nothing but non-stop chatter and the clanking of wine glasses. When I look up from my notes, I'm almost dizzied by the number of important people—sitting in chairs around tables with linens—looking at me.

I've never been nervous about the idea of cutting into someone. I'm not worried about the MCAT, and I'm actually looking forward to my first rotation through trauma. The idea of working in the moment—to save someone's life—it's the entire reason I made this my dream. But speaking to this room full of people?

I'm terrified.

"You look a little pale there, Emma. You feeling okay?" Miranda Wheaton's voice is somewhere between an angel and a sergeant in the military. Her tone is friendly and non-threatening, but there's a confidence underneath that is intimidating as hell. I wish more than anything I could mimic it. I'd like that ability in about six minutes when I step up to the mike.

"A lot of people here, huh?" I admit with a swallow as I look up at her and flip through the cards anxiously in my lap. She smiles and sits in the seat next to me, pulling her small pocketbook into her lap and flipping it open to check her lipstick in the mirror on the underside.

"They're all afraid they'll need me someday, so they figured they better show up," she jokes. I laugh lightly, mostly because she's probably right.

"I practiced a few times at home, and it's under a minute," I say, holding the cards up, hoping she doesn't want to see them. Christ, what would I do if she started editing them now?

She leans into me, her shoulder draped in a silk blouse, pressing against mine wrapped in polyester.

"You are going to do just fine. Honestly, you can get up there and tell four knock-knock jokes for all I care," she says. I smirk, but look back down at my cards, knowing the story on them is important to her, despite what she says. She claims she doesn't want the attention, but her office is immaculate, and the entire back wall is covered in awards, framed letters, and tokens from important people recognizing everything she gives.

Miranda does amazing things for people, and I was just one of them. But I'm the one...the one who has *the* story, and I've been urged by her, gently, enough times to share the story on her behalf to know she likes the credit that goes along with it. It's fine—she deserves it. I'm here because of her, and if it costs me a few uncomfortable minutes on a stage in front of Chicago's best doctors, then I can handle that.

As prepared as I am, I suddenly feel taken off guard when the dean of Tech's medical school begins to speak at the microphone. He doesn't share many details about me, just a teaser that I have a compelling story to tell—the whoosh of my pulse through my head drowning out the rest of what he says. I know it's my turn when he turns to face me, clapping, and I notice the rest of the crowd clapping as well.

130

I suddenly wish I had worn something prettier—something that would at least give them something to look at rather than the black pants and navy blue blouse with the thin gold necklace dangling between the pockets. I'm with it enough to remember the pencil in my hair, and I pull it out quickly, tucking my twist of hair to one side over my shoulder. I didn't even wear tall shoes. I'm in flats, because I was afraid I would have to walk up steps to the stage. Seems my youth and upbringing has worn off on me—always minimizing hazards.

I don't know why, but when I step to the podium, that thought rushes through me. That word—*hazards*. And then all I can think of is that day with Andrew, of skating, and the time I let go of his hand and stood on my own. The day I laughed at hazards, and begged my parents to let me just have this one thing—a day to be young on the ice with him. When I look back out over the crowd, my nerves feel in check. I place the cards flat in front of me, no longer feeling the urge to have to look at them. I know my story. I know it well.

"My name is Emma Burke, and I was born with a congenital heart defect. Usually," I pause, smiling at the thought I just had, "I have to really dumb it down for people when I explain it to them. But this isn't that kind of room, is it?"

I wait for a few seconds as the crowd gives in and laughs, a sense of comfort settling into my chest. I glance back at Miranda, who smiles in support, nodding—acknowledging all she and I have been through together.

"I was diagnosed with hypoplastic left heart syndrome. For those of you who are here with your medical-jargon-loving dates and aren't quite sure what that means—basically, I was born with half a heart. One side worked...and the other was more than just lazy."

I get a few more chuckles from making fun of my stupid infant diagnosis. It owes me a few laughs—it's stolen enough over the years.

"By the time I was eight, I had three surgeries. Yep..." I say, pausing, lips pulled together in an accepting smile. "All the big ones. You know...Norwood, Glenn, Fontan...Larry, Moe, Curley..."

131

The audience gives in completely now, their laughter the kind that people passing by outside could hear. I glance up and into the eyes of my new friend, the one with the sexy tie and touchable beard. He's smiling and laughing, too. For some reason, that makes me feel even more comfortable.

"Things were going well. I had a forever-good excuse to get out of running laps in PE. I had to get some exercise, but never anything like running. I could do less vigorous things, like simple tumbling or dancing. I'm horribly uncoordinated, so trust me— dancing was not too much for my young heart to handle."

Out of nowhere, my arm chills at the memory of Andrew's elbow looped through mine; my mind hums the sound of the fiddle that played over and over for that glorious week we had square dancing. Even as I stare back into the smiling eyes of my new friendly face across the room, my memory is pulling up the dimples and messy hair of the boy I met when I needed someone most. I don't think of the him I know now, but rather then— when he was...everything.

"For a long time, I was surviving and beating odds. Then the fatigue got worse," I say to a nodding audience. They don't know my story personally, but they all know how my story goes. Stories like mine—they have fuzzy endings, no spoilers that tell me exactly how my life's going to play out. I've always been of the mindset that my life is what I make of it—even if I have half a heart.

That's what got me here.

"I was a status two. Not sick enough to get the first heart out of the gate. Not even sick enough to get the tenth, really. And my parents, brother, and I spent a year getting called into Philadelphia, from our home in Delaware, for false hope and rejections. All for a surgery and post-op treatment that we couldn't afford in the first place."

"I got scared—plain and simple," I shrug. "I was fifteen at the time, almost sixteen, and looking at a black hole. I couldn't get excited for things like driving or prom or the Friday-night football game. My girlfriends were all growing up, getting boyfriends, figuring out who they were, but I *knew* who I was. I was too busy being both frightened and hopeful of moving from status two to status one. That fear consumed me, and it could have paralyzed me. Instead...I wrote a letter."

"I don't know how many letters Dr. Miranda Wheaton gets. All these years, I've never actually asked her," I say, turning to face my saving grace, my brow pinched as I shake my head at her in question.

She raises her shoulders as she smiles and whispers, "It's a lot." I laugh to myself, turning back to my podium.

"She says *a lot,*" I say, garnering a few chuckles from the crowd. "Well, I don't know what it was that convinced her to open mine, read it, and then fly all the way to Delaware to meet with me and my parents in person, but I'm sure I'll never be able to repeat the magic of those words in my letter again. I hope I never have to."

"I was Dr. Wheaton's twenty-first donated surgery. As she said when she met with my family months before it actually happened—the wait for a new heart would still be long. And there would still be false starts. But Chicago was where I needed to be.

"So we moved. And I homeschooled for the first few months in the city while my parents looked for work, and a suburb we could afford. I spent those early weeks waiting for the call—for a heart—at home. But part of being a status-twoer, is not being sick enough *not* to want to leave your house—or, if you're a teenager, to be somewhere with friends. So I went to school, and life...it went on—the safety net of hope that Dr. Wheaton swore would come there to catch me when I fell.

"On November first of my sophomore year of high school, that net...it worked," I smile, no longer registering the fact that I'm in front of anyone at all. "There was a heart, and it wasn't right for anyone above me. But it was perfect for *me.* I was pulled from school, and in surgery in less than three hours."

"Dr. Wheaton is sitting up here next to me tonight, thanks to her generosity. I don't take it lightly, and I hope one day I get to stand at the operating table with her, assisting and learning, as we give a gift like this," I say, my hand clutched against my heart—my second heart, "to someone else. It is an honor, distinguished guests, to present to you Miranda Wheaton...this year's recipient of the S. Holden Taft Award."

The applause erupts quickly as everyone gets to their feet. Dr. Wheaton hugs me as we exchange spots. When I get to my seat, the enormity of everything catches up to me, and breathing begins to feel difficult.

It's a panic attack. I know them. I don't have them often, only when I let myself really stop and think about...well...my life. Usually, I'm just working hard, studying, applying for something—pushing. Always pushing. It's when I stop that I realize—*holy shit, I'm alive.*

I'm sitting in a chair at the end of the row, so as Dr. Wheaton begins her talk, I excuse myself to the small curtained area to the side of the stage, and around to the wall behind the rows of dinner tables. There's a water station, and my hand is shaking as I guzzle cup after cup.

"You probably need to breathe more than you need to drink," he says. My IT guy is also my emergency medic. So far, he's getting all the hero roles, and I'm only technically-inept and skittish. I should be more embarrassed, but I'm to overwhelmed, so I nod in agreement, handing the small paper cup to him and raising my arms above my head to open up my lungs.

"Breathe in until she looks to the left," he whispers, now leaning against the wall next to me. I glance from him back up to Miranda, noticing that he's right—she has a pattern to her speech. She starts at one side of the room, then switches topics, takes a breath and moves to the other.

I breathe with her on every turn—in several seconds, out several more. Eventually, this routine becomes kind of funny, and it makes me giggle. I breathe through it though, still feeling flutters in my belly from nerves. Unless...the flutters are from something else.

"When I had to give my first dissertation...this is how she told me to deal with the room," he whispers next to me. "Divide it in half to make the crowd smaller. Thing is, I gave my dissertation to a table of seven people. Not a lot to divide, and frankly...I would have given anything for it to have been more crowded or noisier."

134

I look at him, still breathing, but now on my own.

"When it's a small room like that, you can totally hear when someone writes something down. Screws with your head," he smirks. He's playing it cool as if we're just two people who like to stand off to the side—as if this is where we're supposed to be.

I turn my head to watch the end of Miranda's speech. She touches on the topic of me once more—at the end—when she lets everyone know about how I wrote her a second letter, after my surgery, telling her I had every intention of walking in her footsteps. She makes a joke of it, of how I was right, and it didn't live up to the first one I wrote. But then she talks about how I beat out more than seven hundred other applicants for her mentorship, and my smile slips, because I'm sure everyone's thinking about how I probably didn't deserve the slot, that she picked me because she felt bad, or she thought I had a great story. Sometimes I let that doubt eat at me, and I feel a little inadequate. It gets a lot of applause today, though, and most of the room turns to look at me, so I plaster the smile back in place.

"Just keep breathing," my mystery friend whispers from behind his hand as he pretends to run it over his beard. When the dean takes over at the podium again and begins recognizing others in the audience, my friend nudges me to get my attention, then nods over his shoulder, toward the double doors to the right of us. I follow him out quietly, and allow myself to sigh loudly, my lips flapping and making a motorcycle sound.

"Wow, you were really holding a lot of that in, huh?" he chuckles.

"I guess I was," I say, feeling the threat of my chest tightening again now that we're out in the hallway alone. I look down at my hands, which are clutching my purse hard, my knuckles white. I breathe out a short laugh and relax my hold.

"I'm Graham, by the way," he says, his palm out, waiting for mine, which is clammy, and I'm embarrassed to touch him, but I do anyhow. When our hands meet, I notice more than I probably should just from shaking someone's hand—like the fact that there's a callus at the base of his fingers, and his nails are kept short, and his palms are unusually warm for the coldness of the room.

"Hi, Graham. I'm...Emma," I start, squinting my eyes as I cut myself off with a shake of my head. "You know that already though, I guess."

"Yeah, I got that from your speech," he chuckles, leaning into me enough that his arm brushes against mine. "Which...nice job, by the way. I think you might have stolen her thunder."

"Thanks," I say, my face flushing and my lips twitching with the pressure to smile. The doors next to us push open before I can say anything else, and the crowd begins to exit a few people at a time, many stopping to congratulate me along the way. I'm not sure why—I didn't win the award. I'm gracious anyhow, though, and Graham stands next to me the entire time.

"Well...what did you think?" Dr. Wheaton says as she steps through the doors last. Her eyes flit from me to Graham and back again. I open my mouth to speak, but before I can, Graham responds.

"It was better than your last speech. You still do the side-to-side thing, you know," he says, his hands comfortably hung from his thumbs in his pants pockets, his head tilted at her in a friendly way. Something in his eyes is off, though, like while they may be familiar with each other—he's also challenging her, maybe even baiting her a little.

"Graham, when you've been doing it one way as long as I have, you don't change," she answers, her mouth twisted, almost as if she's scolding him.

"Yet you can learn the latest surgical techniques and master them," he chuckles, nodding before turning his head away. "Funny what old dogs *can* learn."

There's a flash of displeasure that crosses her face, but the consummate professional, she quickly masks it, her deep red lips smiling.

"For now. Until I teach someone else," she says, directing the focus to me. I feel her eyes on me, and my head starts swimming with a little bit of fear and pride all at once.

"Better her than me," he says, tossing a laugh out, still looking away from her.

"So how do you two know each other?" Miranda asks. I feel my stomach drop, suddenly nervous as my brain slowly starts to put their relationship together. Standing next to one another, it's painfully clear—but apart, I guess my nerves blinded me.

"I just met her tonight, but…" Graham says, leaning toward me again, his elbow jutting out just enough to touch my arm. I catch Miranda's eyes as they see it, and I can't tell if the expression on her face is one that approves or not. "I was gonna see if I could convince her to meet me for coffee tomorrow."

My eyes grow wide, and I feel like I've been thrown into some sort of sick and twisted test. I look to Dr. Wheaton, thinking I probably need her approval, or that maybe she'll give me an out, telling him it's not appropriate.

"Just make sure my son picks up the tab," she says, bending toward my ear.

"Oh, yeah…right," I giggle. It's not a cool giggle, but a messy, nervous one, that turns into a choking kind of cough that leads me to have to excuse myself as she says goodbye to her son—her hot son…the one that just asked me out…in front of her…after having an awkward pissing match with her in front of me on top of it all. I'm really not sure if coffee with Graham is a good idea or not, but I'm not sure I have a choice in the matter now.

I spend longer than I need at the drinking fountain, until she's walking out the main door with the dean and a few of her colleagues, leaving me with Graham, who's somehow still calm and confident-looking. I don't think his hands left his pockets once.

"So…coffee?"

The way he sucks in his top lip and raises his eyebrows is, well—it's adorable, even if his clear need for dominance is a little off-putting. And it also seems to have rendered my tongue useless, because more than a few seconds have passed without an answer from me, and he's starting to bunch his brow. And now he's looking at me like maybe I'm a little off.

Maybe…maybe I am a little off?

"Oh, yeah. I mean, yes. Sure. I'd love to," I stammer. Graham slips his hand from his pocket with his phone, holding it up and ready to type.

"What's your number? I'll text you early in the afternoon, and we'll find a good time."

I pause awkwardly-long again due to the inner-dialogue I have with myself, trying to decide if this is a good idea or a bad one. Eventually, I rattle off my number, my pulse speeding up as he types into his phone.

"Well...Emma," he says, reaching for my hand again. I give it to him, and this time his touch is a little more familiar, and a little...more. His fingers wrap around my wrist, and when I look up at him, I notice the twitch in his lips as he watches his hold on me. "I'll see you tomorrow."

"Sounds gerd...I mean, good. *Gerd*...is just on my mind I guess...medical awards dinner and all. Oh god." I shut my eyes as he laughs. I open them as I start to take a step toward the door. "I swear, tomorrow I'll be back at the top of my game. Public speaking does a number on me."

"I look forward to seeing the top of your game," he chuckles.

I raise a hand and spin to face the double glass doors, actively thinking about pushing them open, not running into them, not tripping, and walking quickly, but not too quickly away. This is why I don't date. Thinking of all of this, trying not to look like a jackass for a solid minute—it's too hard. Give me advanced chem and bio, instead.

My giddiness lasts only a few minutes, and soon I'm walking back to my apartment, dreading the fact that I have a date with someone.

Handsome as he may be, Graham is not Andrew.

These butterflies are not the same.

Andrew

I don't think I've ever spent the night in a girl's bed without getting something out of it. Even in Iowa, when I hooked up with girls my senior year or at junior college, I never stayed at a chick's place without at least a hand job.

I could have had anything I wanted last night—anything...but Emma. That's the problem. This whole thing—coming back to their apartment again, hooking up with Lindsey—it was always really about Emma.

Punishing Emma—*seeing* Emma.

138

I guess in a way, I'm getting something out of this, but it doesn't feel as good as I thought it would. There must be a shred of decency left inside me, because I made out with Lindsey until my lips were raw last night, and then we just went to sleep. In her bed. Fucking spooning like we were two kids sneaking off at camp. I bet she thinks I'm this big gentleman—either that, or an enormous pussy. She kept giving me these little signs, small tugs of her shirt, little exposures of her skin that signaled it was all clear for me to keep on moving.

But I couldn't do it.

I started stroking her hair, putting her to sleep. I panicked, like I was babysitting an infant, and just trying to put it to sleep, the whole time feeling sick as fuck to my stomach. I lay there awake holding her, wishing she were Emma. Emma—who I hate. I hate Emma. I can't even talk myself out of hating her. Yet...I keep fantasizing about touching her instead of Lindsey. That's the only way I can make my affection feel like it's real. My head gets cloudier with every minute that passes in this scenario I've trapped myself in.

I left their apartment when the sun came up, not able to take it any more. Lindsey woke up just enough to see I was leaving, but I kissed her back to bed and slipped out her door. I should have kept walking, but my eyes caught the sleeve of Emma's shirt hanging from the side of the trashcan. It's like she put it there to surrender—the only flag she has to wave.

It smelled like her. She still smells the same.

I should have left it in the trashcan where she put it. But I didn't want her to surrender. I wanted her to keep playing, to have to hold on to this stupid piece of material that I now know reminds us both of before. I want her to have to look at it, too—even if she never wears it again.

If she surrenders, I win.

Then what?

I'm kind of impressed that she sent her roommate to me wearing it. Up until now, she's been just taking my comments and dismissing them, even when I can tell they get to her. She's been going along with this pretense that we don't know each other. I have been giving her nothing but shit, and she's just been taking it.

Until now.

"Didn't your roommate wear that yesterday?" I say in an offhanded manner as I step out into the hallway from the locker room where Lindsey's been waiting for me. I saw her in the sweatshirt during the goddamned game, and it was the only thing I could concentrate on. I blew a major play. All I want in the world is for her to take it off, to get rid of it. I feel a little bad about my comment, though, because I see her face fall as she looks down and pulls the bottom of the sweatshirt out to look at it.

Shit...this part of my plan doesn't feel good. Lindsey isn't the one I mean to be provoking.

"Oh, I...yeah, I guess she did. I just like it, so she said I could borrow it," she says. I can tell she's lying because she's embarrassed. Emma probably fed her some bullshit to make her feel pretty in that sweatshirt just so she'd wear it here, and I just crapped all over her. She pulls it off and folds it over her arm, though, and I smile to myself at how easy it was to take away Emma's power.

Lindsey's still pouting a little when I turn around. I grab my equipment bag and jerk it up higher on my shoulder, then lean into her, kissing her neck. "I like you better in your things," I say, which makes her blush. She's already forgotten about the sweatshirt.

"Harper, you still have to talk with coach. He's pissed, dude," Trent says as he comes out of the locker room, his eyes quickly noticing my date. He smirks and winks at me in front of her, which irritates me. He's doing that eyebrow waggle too, which is only going to make Lindsey think I talk about her to Trent. I don't. In fact, Trent doesn't even know her name.

"I have a 4.0. There is literally nothing for me to study, so why should I waste time sitting there in the study lab," I sigh, ready to get back to the fact that I blew my study hall hours, which I don't need, and coach wants to bench me for it. Some system—the guy with the highest GPA gets the smack down, but Tony Agaluta, our goalie who's flunking basic algebra, gets

140

stickers on his goddamned helmet because he shows up at four o'clock every day for tutoring—*and still fails!*

"I don't make the rules, Harp. And neither does coach," Trent says. Sometimes I want to punch my friend. He's like Dudley-Do-Right, even when he's being logical.

"Well, unless he's planning on sitting me tomorrow, which fuck it if he is, I'm pretty sure our talk can wait until then," I say, repositioning my heavy bag on my arm.

Trent rolls his eyes, but then turns his attention back to Lindsey. Lindsey is his type. I should just give her to him, rid myself of this entire dumb fucking idea I had.

"Hey, I'm Trent," he says, shaking her hand.

"Hey, I'm Trent," I repeat, mocking him. He doesn't turn to look at me when he reaches to the side and punches me in the right peck. "Ow...fuck nut!"

"You must be Emma?" Trent asks. Fucker did that on purpose.

I'd feel bad about the look on Lindsey's face right now except I'm pretty sure the look on mine is worse. He called her *Emma*, which means somewhere along the way he noticed that name. He saw her license once, briefly, but I didn't think he memorized it. And I get enough from the quick glance he shoots me to know that he's trying to make this a teachable moment.

Not in the mood, Trent. I'm so far in on a bad idea there's really no way to get out now. Quit making it worse.

"She's...my roommate," Lindsey says, her voice half of the volume it was before.

"He knows that. He's just a really shitty listener. This is Lindsey, Trent. And thanks for paying attention to me when I talk." I lay it on super thick, and Lindsey eats it up. Trent's eyes become slits, and I know I've only made him more curious. Just one more thing I'll think about atoning for...or not. Might as well embrace this piece-of-shit guy I've become.

"Right, my mistake," Trent says. What he really means is *"What are you up to, you asshole?"* I put my arm around Lindsey and lead her out ahead of him. This conversation between them—it's done.

Trent heads to his car, and probably to Majerle's, which is where I'd planned on going with Lindsey after the game, but now I just want to get her back to her apartment so I can go through with everything I chickened out on last night. She seems all right with it, too, her fingers hooked onto mine over her shoulder as we walk the six blocks to her apartment.

My back is killing me from carrying my gear. I normally dump it in Trent's car, or drop it off at home before we go out, but those weren't options tonight. Maybe I'll somehow work a back rub out of this.

I feel a charge when we get to her front door, and I know why it's there. It's there because I anticipated this—the look on Emma's face the second I walk in behind Lindsey. In a second, her eyes go from Lindsey's to mine, and down to the sweatshirt folded over her purse.

There's that disappointment I was banking on. I grin, and she catches it before quickly looking away.

Lindsey dumps her purse on the table as we walk in, and I take advantage of it, picking up the sweatshirt and twisting it in my hands to make it even smaller. Emma watches the entire time, her cheek caught between her teeth while she rethinks her decision to send her friend out in it in the first place.

That's right, Emma. This bothers you more than it bothers me.

"How was the awards dinner?" Lindsey asks from behind Emma as she opens the fridge to pull out a beer for each of us.

"It was good."

I don't think Emma even registered her answer. She's too busy staring at the sweatshirt—her eyes never blinking as she watches my hands work the fabric as I step closer to her.

"Here," I whisper, handing it to her. She takes the other side, and for a second we're both holding on, like a tug of war. Her eyes flash to mine, and I notice she stops breathing. I should stop here, but something happens when she looks at me, and I step in a little closer, close enough that I know she can feel my breath. "Are we done now?"

I let go of my grip, but I keep my eyes locked with hers. For a brief moment, she looks wounded, and I start to smile.

"I met someone," she says. She's speaking to Lindsey, but as the left side of her mouth starts to rise, her eyes haze, and something stronger steps in place of the girl who was letting me walk all over her a second ago.

You think I care that you met someone, Emma Burke? Go ahead—make me care.

"Oh yeah?" Lindsey moves into my side, handing me a beer. I put my arm around her and let my hand cup her shoulder. Emma's eyes move to it, so I loosen my grip and drag my fingers along her arm suggestively, just to see if Emma's gaze follows. It does, and I take a very satisfied, long drink, not bothering to hide the smile on my lips behind the bottle.

"Yeah," Emma says, her voice weak again. I almost feel like I'm putting her in a trance, her eyes are tracing every single stroke of my fingers along her friend's arm. "He's a grad student," she continues, telling her roommate about some boy who thought she was cute and asked her out on a date. I couldn't care less. She says something about how he saved her, came to her rescue and got the projector working. She's gushing over some guy who knew how to click a goddamned mouse, and she's calling *him* her savior. The more she talks, the more I feel every scar on my body all at once—the burn marks, the stab wounds, the broken bones that never healed quite right—abuse I took so Emma Burke didn't have to experience anything sad.

Something in me snaps.

I know it's crossing the line when I do it, and I know that it's going to start something that won't end in spooning tonight. That's why I came here, though...isn't it? Emma keeps talking, but her eyes are constantly checking my hands. Every pass of my fingers over Lindsey's shoulder and down her bicep moves closer to her breast, until finally, I let my thumb drag slowly along the curve of her tit, taking extra time when I feel the hard peak underneath her thin bra and shirt—and Lindsey, bless her fucking little heart, actually hums in pleasure.

"I'm seeing him tomorrow, so I'll let you know...you know...if it's something..." Emma cuts her story short, suddenly a lot less sure of herself. She sucks in her bottom lip as she flits her eyes to me quickly before looking down and then back up to her friend, who is now absolutely dying for me to touch her more.

That's right, Emma. Nobody cares that you met a boy and he's your fucking hero.

"Yeah, that's awesome. I'm so excited for you," Lindsey says, nothing about her focused on Emma. Lindsey is my puppet right now, and I'm pretty sure she didn't hear anything past the part where Emma said she met someone. Everything after that was about my hand on her breast, and how fast my dick will be inside her next.

"Anyhow, I think I'll turn in," Emma says, faking a yawn. "That speech, it's always hard, ya know..." I roll my eyes at her sad performance, then run my hand down Lindsey's arm to find her fingers waiting to tug my hand and body to her bed.

"Yeah, us too," Lindsey says at the feel of my grip. I follow her down the hall as we leave Emma alone in the kitchen behind us. I don't care that she's alone. I don't care that she knows where I'm going, and I don't care that she's met some guy who wants to buy her coffee.

I don't care about Emma Burke.

I step into Lindsey's room, and she pauses at the doorway, hanging out of it to look down the hallway to her friend. That's guilt she's feeling. She needs to let that go.

"She's okay," I say, coming up behind her, breathing into her, reminding her. My fingers find her stomach, and I tug her shirt from her jeans and let my hand find her bare skin.

"Yeah, you're probably right," she says, part of her giving into me, but part of her still out there in the hallway. I can tell. I kiss her neck, moving my hand through her hair, wrapping it around my fingers. She sighs, letting her weight fall into me. I turn her to face me and lift her into my arms, my hands grabbing her ass as I walk us backward. We just need to get to her bed. She'll forget everything there.

I'll forget everything there.

"Goodnight."

Lindsey's door is still open; Emma pauses on the other side of the hall and speaks, her profile outlined by the faint light spilling from her room, which means she can see just as much of us. I knew the door was open; I wanted her to see. I timed that kiss just right. I hoped she'd walk by, but another piece of me wants to take that last kiss back.

Lindsey's mouth tightens up and eventually falls away from mine.

"Goodnight," she says back to her friend, her forehead sliding along my shoulder until her face is tucked against my chest.

Fuck, I'm an asshole.

"I'm sorry."

Lindsey is apologizing to me. The irony.

"It's fine...really," I say, looking over her form as Emma's door closes behind her. Emma never looks back again. She's seen enough. Maybe I have, too.

"Something's with her, tonight. I think it was the speech. I...I probably should have talked to her more, or maybe gone with her. *Gah*...I'm so sorry, I just feel bad now. You probably think I'm nuts." Lindsey looks up at me with her mouth caught between an apology and a frown—waiting for me to tell her it's okay. I pull her in against me for a hug, mostly because I can't handle looking in her eyes anymore. I don't like the reflection in them.

"You know what? I'm gonna go ahead and go," I say, my lips tight now, too. I'm not looking at Lindsey though. I'm looking beyond her. I realize it a little late, and she catches me. When my eyes drift back down to hers, there's a hint of suspicion in them. "Why don't you and your roommate have a night—do that girl-talk thing, huh?"

Her misgivings about my motivation seem to melt, and her hands squeeze my arms in thanks. The puppy-dog grin she looks up at me with seals it. I hug her again, but my eyes stay on the shut door across the hallway.

Lindsey follows me through their kitchen and living room, where I grab my gear and pull it back up on my shoulder, leaving this apartment one more time without satisfaction.

"I'll call you tomorrow," she says as I back out of her door.

I hold up a few fingers and start my steps toward the elevator bank, but remember that tomorrow's Sunday, and

Harley told me to keep my evening open in case he could line something up. I could really use the stars to align for a fight—financially and emotionally—I take a few quick paces back to her door, catching it before she closes it completely.

"You know what? Actually, I've got some family things tomorrow, and I'm not sure how late I'm going to be. I'll just text you when I get home?" She looks down, and I can tell she's trying to decide if she wants to believe the line of bullshit I'm giving her. Part of me wants her to call me on it, and part of me also thinks maybe that's what I need—a good fight to distract me, to let me feel something other than angry and alone.

"Sure," she says. It's a pained response, but for now, I'll take it. I'm tired; I'm also not in the mood for a breakup. And a breakup would mean no more Emma...and I'm not so sure I'm ready for that either.

"Great," I smile, leaning in to kiss her lips lightly, just to leave her feeling something better than how I'm sure my blow-off just did. I really do have family shit to deal with tomorrow; I really only stretched the truth some.

The doorman is starting to recognize me, and he smiles and waves as I pass by this time. It's the hockey gear, and my Tech sweatshirt and hat. It works on girls and doormen, it seems.

As long as everything felt like it took at Lindsey and Emma's, I end up walking through my apartment door forty-five minutes behind Trent. He didn't go to the bar, and I have a strange feeling that he was waiting for me—probably sitting here stewing in his own self-righteousness and whatever-the-fuck he thinks he has all figured out. He's sitting on the couch, his feet up, beer in his hand, and the TV on a replay of some NASCAR race. He hates racing, so I know he's just posturing.

I walk behind the sofa with my gear, hell bent on not stopping or taking his bait.

"You're in over your head, Harper. What are you doing?" he asks, and mother fuck! I stop. I stop because he knows more than I thought he did. And since he has the bad shit all figured out, maybe he can help me wrap my head around what the hell is wrong with me—and why I'm still so angry.

I reach over the sofa and take the half-empty beer from his hand, claiming it for my own. I drop my gear behind the sofa and walk the rest of the way around the couch, sitting on the corner of the coffee table across from him.

My eyes are on his chin for the longest time. It's like when you're a kid and you know you're wrong, and you're about to get your ass chewed, but you just don't want to give in to the adult and take your licks. I don't want to have to face his goddamned honest face, so I keep my eyes on his chin and take a long sip from the beer I commandeered, draining it almost completely.

"I don't know, Trent. She was there. It was her, and I don't know, but I can't fucking stop," I say.

"Drew...who the hell is Emma?" He says her name, and my chest flips inside out, my heart running through an irregular rhythm of several fast beats followed by nothing at all.

"I've told you," I lie.

"No, Drew. Not the drunken version you tell when you think you're being honest. I mean the *real* story," he says. I give in and look up the inch it takes to meet his eyes, and I hold his gaze while I wait for my heart to begin working again. I don't talk about Emma. It started as a promise I made to myself that night, and then it grew into a rule I made to protect myself. I'm not so sure what would happen if I broke it now.

"There was a girl," I say, letting my eyes wander over to the TV, which he's conveniently muted. There's a pile-up of cars in the race, one is on fire, and I can't help but find some kind of sick humor in the many ways that scene mirrors my own life. "I got screwed over by the law..." I start, my eyes moving back to his, the recognition in his expression already there. He knows the story. And now he's filling in the details.

"Harp..." He shakes his head, literally biting his tongue, his hand rubbing the back of his neck, as if this is somehow stressful for him. I'm about to tell him to drop the empathy act when there's a soft knock at our door.

It's probably one of the guys, wondering why we're not celebrating at Majerle's. I use it as an excuse to get out of our conversation, and as Trent moves to the door, I walk into our kitchen to get each of us another beer. When I come out, she's standing in the doorway, and Trent is rubbing his chin.

"Over your head," he says under his breath as he trades spots with me near the door. He takes one of the beers from my hand and pauses to make sure my eyes meet his, get the warning in them, before he moves back to his spot on the couch.

"What are you doing here?" I don't even waste time with being nice. I'm so pissed she's at my door. It means she knows where I live, and she doesn't get to know things about me. That's not how this works.

"Why are you doing this, Andrew?"

I hear Trent scoff behind me, and it pisses me off that he's hearing any of this. I slide my beer on the small shelf nearby and grab my jacket from the hook on the back of the door, motioning for her to get the hell out of my way. She takes a step back as I move outside with her and hand her my jacket. She looks at it like I just handed her a slab of meat.

"It's forty degrees out here, and your teeth are chattering. Just put the damn thing on," I say, walking down the path toward the road. Our street is filled with cars nestled up next to meters, and graffiti mars the sidewalks. It's a far cry from the tree-lined cobblestone walkway that leads to Emma's front door. I live in the real world.

Emma joins me near the roadway, but she's still holding my jacket in her hands. I nod at her hands to put it on, and she scowls.

"Seriously, don't make this a thing. It's a twenty-dollar winter coat from Target. Just wear it for five minutes for fuck sake."

She takes in a sharp breath before shoving one arm into a sleeve. "I don't even know who the hell you are anymore," she mumbles.

"Isn't that the point? We pretend we don't know each other?" I move in close, and she takes a step back. She wants to keep distance between us, which only makes me want to shatter her comfort more. I advance again, this time a little aggressively as my chest rumbles with light laughter. She doesn't move this time, instead her shoulders sagging as she lets out a slow breath.

"Is that the point? Why is that the point, Andrew? What are you doing? Do you *want* me to pretend I don't know you? I mean…I thought that's what you wanted. I thought you really liked Lindsey. But then you keep doing things and saying things and you're so—"

"So what, Emma?" I challenge her, waiting for her to say it. Her toes are matched with mine, and I feel her shoe against the tips of my own. My lip curls, unable to stop from grinning when I tap my foot against hers softly. Her eyes wince, just a little, but enough that I see it. She's drowning in the fog of my breath, and I exhale once hard just to erase her. She backs down, her eyes falling to both of our feet as she takes a step back.

"Go on, Emma," I say, moving toward her again. "What am I? Am I mean? Am I…angry? Am I the kind of guy who returns a girl's license to her so she doesn't have to worry? Does that make me your hero?"

She nods, but then shakes her head, bringing her hands up to the side of her face. Her eyes are threatening tears, and I know I have her on the brink.

"Or am I the guy who tells a lie for you, and then sits back while your life is perfect and mine is a fucking nightmare, and you can't even bother the common decency of saying *thanks*?"

Her body grows rigid at that last one, and her face finds mine, her eyes wide and red, the water pooling in them, ready to fall to the ground in front of her. My hands out to my sides, I shake my head at a loss. I tried to make sense of it so many nights I lay awake at Lake Crest. I even tried to understand why she didn't care after I moved to Iowa. I think about it every time my feet touch the ice, every time a fist lands on my face, and when I look at the scars I got for her.

"Come on, Emma. Tell me…what am I?"

Her breath falters, and the tears finally release down her cheeks as her bottom lip quivers with her cry and her gaze falls to the ground.

"You're different, Andrew," she says. I laugh her answer off, looking up at the sky, knowing she'd say something like that. I'm different. No shit, I'm different. You would be too.

"I…" she continues, stopping to sniffle once. I fold my arms and tilt my head to the side to watch her. I look at her with contempt, but I enjoy the view—of her struggling. I might as well enjoy the show.

"I used to just not know where you went…"

My brow pinches as she pauses to take a slow breath to steady herself. *Where I went?* She pulls my jacket from her body, folding it in half and handing it back to me. I look down at it, no intention of taking it from her. She's being ridiculous. It's cold outside, and her body is shaking.

"Just keep the jacket, Emma," I protest. I'm not loud now.

"No. I don't want it," she says, her eyes meeting mine and leveling me with her temporary strength as she drops the coat at my feet. She swallows hard, as if this hurts. "You asked me who you are, Andrew. But I think maybe I never really knew. Whoever I met when I was a kid, that boy…he's gone. I don't know where he went. And I think maybe he never existed."

I look down at my jacket, then back up to Emma, her arms hugging her body, her long hair wild in the night wind. She's wearing a long-sleeved white shirt that's thin enough the wind forces it against her skin, showing every curve of her body. My eyes scan lower to her jeans and the Converse on her feet, so much of her still *that* girl, still trapped in the past.

"Why did you come here? Was it just to tell me some poetic shit that I already know?" I ask.

Her eyes soften into pity as she begins to take a step back in the direction of her apartment. It's late, and freezing, and I'm pretty sure she followed me here by foot. I shouldn't let her walk home alone. But then again, she shouldn't have come here in the first place, so kind of her fault.

"I hope you really like Lindsey…" she says. My mouth flinches because I don't want to accept her statement. I don't want to *deal* with her statement.

I bend down and grab my jacket, slinging it over one shoulder as I salute her with my other hand.

"Have a safe walk home, Emma. Maybe next time you drop by, you'll start being honest with yourself," I say over my shoulder, as angry with her as I was before her impromptu visit, but maybe now for other reasons.

"I won't be back," she says. "In fact, I plan on never seeing you again." She turns and walks away with purpose, back to where she came from, her stride fast, confident, and maybe...free.

"Fuck!" I yell when I'm sure she can no longer hear me. I tug on the sleeve of the jacket in my hands, ripping a seam in the middle.

When I come inside, Trent is just where I left him, but I'm no longer in the mood to deal with his psycho-babble-shit, so I throw my jacket onto the coffee table and walk right by him into my room, slamming the door behind me.

"This is one of those bad ideas, Harper," he says through my door a few seconds later. "We all have them, but you went ahead and put it into action. Just...stop now."

"Shut the fuck up, Trenton. I don't need you to tell me things I already know," I say, pulling my pillow up over my face and ears. It won't matter; I can't drown out the voice in my head. Turns out, I can't drown out Trent, either.

"I kinda think you do, Harp. Otherwise you wouldn't make such shitty decisions," he says.

I open my mouth to swear at him again, but I decide against it, sighing instead. I smack my hand on the base of the lamp next to my bed, turning out my light, then I flip to my side to plug my phone into it's charger—setting my alarm to make sure I'm up in time to drive to Woodstock and endure more criticism and advice from my family.

I used to just not know where you went.

It's that one thing she said that drums in my head when I close my eyes. It was in there, with all of those other things she said. But it's that one thing that hit my ears as if she were assaulting me with her words. That one phrase, it felt important, and I was too angry to stop and acknowledge it, to question it further.

One question, really.

Don't you know, Emma? Don't you know where I went?

151

Chapter 11

Emma Burke, Age 16

"I'm scared," I say under the comfort of my mom's hand on my forehead. I won't admit this in front of my dad. As strong as he is, I'm his weakness. My mom—she's the one who can handle life's imperfect parts, but my dad, he doesn't like to know I have nightmares or misgivings or regrets.

"It's okay to be scared," she says, her smile soft. "But..." she scoots in closer to me on the bed, moving the long tubes and cords out of our way, "it's also okay to be hopeful. And excited. And driven, or curious, or the millions of other things you get to feel now."

Her eyes are teary, but I know it's not because she's scared. She's happy. We've all waited for this day for so long. I'm getting a new heart. In an hour, I will be taken through those doors I've envisioned in my head, put to sleep, cut open—and a miracle will happen.

I will be a miracle.

A few nurses come in to take vitals and check on me. My mom steps out of the way, but she keeps her hand on mine as they work around us. I'm glad. The moment she lets go, I know the trembling will start.

I'm scared. But I'm hopeful too.

I'll be able to do so many things—things I always dreamt of. I'll be able to skate again. Maybe...maybe I'll find Andrew?

"Hey, Mom?" I tug on her hand, and she leans down to give me attention while the nurses finish their prep work.

"Have you heard from Andrew's mom yet? Dad said he found her number and left her a message. Have you...did he...or did they ever call back?"

It's been six weeks since Andrew was taken away in the back of a squad car. The officers that drove me home after the accident told my parents very little. But they said enough. Andrew was taken in for possession and driving under the influence. None of what they said made sense with the Andrew I knew—or the Andrew I was with all night. He wasn't acting weird, and I didn't smell any alcohol or see any drugs or smell marijuana. But maybe you can't see those things?

I guess he couldn't see my problems either. My heart was broken, but in Andrew's mind, it pumped blood and beat just as his own.

I waited to hear from him. I waited for nearly a week, figuring he was probably in trouble for the accident and for the possession charge. From what I could figure out online, he likely got some community service. And he probably lost his license until he's eighteen. He's a minor, so I can't find his court-hearing record online. But he said he would be okay, and he knew what he was doing. He promised, and that's the only reason I let him do what he did.

Every night, I expected to hear him below my window. I'd sit there and look out at the long roadway leading up to my house, waiting to see him. Maybe he'd walk, or maybe he'd drive even though he wasn't supposed to.

He never came.

"Mom?" She's paying attention to a conversation with a group of nurses, but shakes her head and looks back at me.

"Sorry, I was trying to see when they were taking you," she smiles.

"Andrew?" I remind her.

Her smile stays in place, but even though her mouth doesn't move, the meaning of her smile—it changes.

"Did Dad talk to him? Is he okay?" I try to sit up, but my mom holds my arm and shakes her head and chuckles at me.

"Honey, no, nothing like that," she says. I liked it better when I was excited, when I thought my dad saw Andrew. "He heard from his mom. And he's going to live somewhere else for a while. With a relative, I think. He has some things he needs to work through. Drugs...Em, whatever he has going on, it's serious."

I swallow and watch her face for a clue that she has more to say. She brushes a few pieces of my hair back and straightens my eyebrow by running her finger along it—a doting thing she's done since I was a kid. And after a few seconds, I realize that's all the information she has.

Andrew left. No goodbye or letter or stone at my window. Just some secondhand hint that he has a drug problem and "things to work through," and I just can't quite buy the full story. There's something missing, something I'm not being told.

But if Andrew really wanted me to know, he'd tell me.

"Well hello, Emma," Dr. Wheaton says, practically glowing like an angel as she passes through my room door. She's in scrubs; I like this look even more than the white coat she wears normally or the business suits she has for our monthly meetings at her office in the city. Everything else goes silent the moment she arrives. The chaos stops—no more Andrew, or machines beeping, and the sound of privacy curtain rings dragging open and bed guardrails flipping up. It's all gone. All I see is Dr. Miranda Wheaton's smile, the same one that made me a promise six months ago that this day would come.

It's here.

My heart—it's here.

Chapter 12

Andrew

The potatoes are good. If nothing else, my mother's garlic mashed potatoes are so goddamned good, I've been able to drown myself in helping after helping, which has somehow kept much of the conversation off me.

Not entirely—just *mostly.* There was that brief moment when I came in and Mom was finishing up in the kitchen where she went through the list of things I need to pay for this month; the bill for spring tuition is due, and my insurance is apparently going up...again. Not that I ever get to drive. My car has been sitting in the apartment storage garage since the accident, the damage to the wheel well just enough to throw the alignment to shit. It's fixable, but just like everything else in my life, it costs money.

"I hate you; I hope you know," Kensi whispers in my ear, leaning into me while my mom, Dwayne and Owen talk about Germany more. I stop eating, my fork stuck in my mouth as I turn my head sideways and look at her, taken off guard by those words.

"Wha?" I say, mouth stuffed full like a chipmunk.

Her serious face breaks slowly into a smile.

"If I ate like you did, my ass would be so fat. It's not fair, and I hate you for it," she says.

"Oh," I grin, laughing with my full mouth. I swallow my last bite, stand, and pick up my plate and hers to take them to the kitchen. She follows me, and I hear Owen's steps coming behind her. I'm too full to eat any more, so I guess I should take his last lecture before he leaves the country. I ready myself for a litany of reminders not to fuck up, be good to Mom, and never trust House, but the lecture doesn't come. Instead, he leans silent on the counter opposite me as I rinse the dishes and slip them into the dishwasher.

I pick up the towel, sensing he's still staring at me, and finally give in. "What is it?" I sigh.

He chuckles, his arms crossed over his chest, finally nodding his head to follow him outside. I narrow my eyes, but toss the towel on the counter behind me and move toward the door, pausing for Owen to slip on his jacket. Kensi follows us both out the door, and I notice she's shivering by the time we step down the stairs and begin to head toward the parking lot. Today's the coldest it's been this fall.

"Here," I say, pulling my sweatshirt from over my head and tossing it to her.

"Thanks," she smiles, putting it on without hesitating. I shove my hands in my pockets to keep warm in just my black T-shirt.

"Why do you always have to make me look like a dick in front of my girlfriend?" Owen says, pulling his jacket off and handing it to Kensi. She laughs and shrugs it away.

"I don't need it now. I'm good in Andrew's sweatshirt," she teases.

"Seriously? He's all skinny and shit. My jacket's warmer." I think he might actually have hurt feelings over this. He doesn't sound like he's joking, and I think...shit...I think he might be pissed. I look at Kensi, and we both purse our lips, trying to remain composed. It doesn't last long as I practically spit out the laugh I'm holding in.

"You're such a pussy, O. I haven't been skinny in four years. In fact, I'm pretty sure I could kick your ass without working up a sweat now—so don't distract from the fact that I'm a bigger gentleman to your girlfriend with some false illusion that I'm still just a kid. I haven't been a kid for a long time now. Maybe you're just an insensitive dick who needs to pay more attention to her," I say. My words somehow fell into bitterness. I'm not sure how or why, but it's too late now. Nobody quite knows how to respond, either. We're all standing in the parking lot caught in the cone-of-awkward-silence I just plopped on top of us.

Owen looks down at his jacket in his hand, then glances sideways to Kensi, who shrugs at him. He lets out a breath of a laugh, then looks back up to me, pointing at me while he puts his jacket back on.

"You are going to take that shit back in about fifteen seconds," he says, his mouth in a hard line.

I shake my head and whisper, "Whatever." It's easier than apologizing.

Owen walks to my mom and Dwayne's storage garage and punches in the code, and I step forward to stand next to Kensi while the door lifts. I feel better standing next to her, especially when I've done something wrong. And I did—do something wrong. My brother didn't deserve any of that. I'm just in a mood; one I can't shake. That's not an excuse to shit on him, though.

"Insensitive dick, huh?" he says, tossing a key at me as he gestures toward my car with his other hand. I let my eyes move from his to the keys in my hand, and it clicks with me instantly. I practically trip over myself as I step to the driver's side front tire—to the side of the car, the bumper, the front door, the paint—it's perfect.

"Shit, O!" I run my fingers along the side of the car as I kneel down. "Turns out *I'm* the insensitive dick. When...how? This must have cost a fortune!"

"It wasn't cheap," Owen says. Kensi moves to stand behind me, putting her hand on my shoulder as I stay crouched down, looking at my reflection in the black sheen of the paint. It looks better than it did before Emma and I wrecked it.

Before Emma wrecked it.

I force that thought away, instead wanting to focus on the good things happening right now. I look up at Kensi, and she nudges her head sideways toward my brother, raising her eyebrows. That selfless fucker did this for me.

Damn.

I stand slowly, leaving my gaze on what is probably my most prized possession for a little longer before turning my focus to my brother. Owen simply smiles, raising his shoulders, his hands never leaving the pockets of his jacket while he owns his good deed.

"O, I...I'm sorry," I say. There's quiet between us for a few long seconds, and I let it take us over so I can stand still for once in my life and appreciate what I have—appreciate my brother.

"It's no sweat. You deserve something nice; I'm still proud of you," he says. "Just as proud as I've always been. Maybe...maybe a little more, even."

I pinch my brow and gaze down at the keys, my keys, in my hand. I haven't held these keys with an intention of using them in years. Tonight, I'm driving home on my own. No cab for me.

"Why a *little more?*" I ask, curious how anyone could be proud of me lately.

"Because when shit got hard, you found another gear. It isn't easy," he says, his eyes zeroing in on mine. Owen and I never really talk about James. In fact, we never really *have* talked about our late brother—about what happened, about James's addiction and suicide. But we don't have to say words—the scar is there for both of us, different but the same, and we can see it in each other's eyes. James was hurting, in his own way, and Owen and I are hell bent on never letting each other feel that helpless. We lost James, and the loss is going to stop there.

I move to Owen and reach for his hand, gripping it when he puts his palm out for me to shake. When our hands meet, I move closer to hug him firmly, feeling the tightness I've been carrying around in my chest release just a little, simply from holding my brother close.

"Thanks, O. So much," I say over his shoulder, my voice hoarse. His hand on my back brings me peace. "I'm gonna miss you."

"Me too, bro. Me, too," he says, patting me hard on the back a few times before we both let go for good.

"I'll pay you back," I say, looking back to my keys again, still a little stunned that my car, my baby, is back and running and beautiful again. Owen starts to chuckle.

"I don't want you to pay me back, but there's one thing you can do," he says, pulling Kensi into his side, hugging her and moving his hand up and down her still-cold arms. I shrug at him with a questioning look. "You can quit hitting on my girlfriend with your *oh, I'm a gentleman, here take my shirt and...oh...did you see my abs?* move."

I smirk as he mocks me, then start to laugh hard when the words he just said finally hit me.

"Dude...my abs? Really? Jealous much?" I look to Kensi, who's laughing too. Owen's eyebrows are raised, but he's not laughing like we are—so we both try our best to stop. "Got it. Okay. No more abs or winter-wear for Kensi. Done. Kens?"

She looks at me.

"You're gonna need to start bringing your own jacket to things and opening your own car doors and junk, 'cuz...well...you know he's not going to do any of it," I say, laughing halfway through as I needle my brother for the last time until he comes back from Europe in a year. He steps forward and pushes me off balance, but his right cheek rises with his grin.

Today was the first in a long time that everything in me felt right. It was certainly the first in many trips home that I returned to my apartment without feeling like a failure. Mom was easy on me—minus the few reminders about financial responsibilities—and Dwayne was...Dwayne. He's always neutral, which I suppose I can't blame him for. He has to be on our mom's side, but Owen and I make difficult enemies. He really can't win.

I think what really made the world shift for me today though was the feeling of driving myself back home—in my car. I was careful, always right at the speed limit, several lengths away from the cars in front of or behind me. Nothing was going to touch my car. No scratches, no dings. Not even the threat of a hard break to throw the alignment out of whack.

She sang for me on the highway as I drove home in the late afternoon sun. The engine purred with every mile, the rumble of the road below me, and the angry tires still with plenty of tread, gripped the road. One day soon—when I'm comfortable again—I'm going to take her out in the country and open her up.

For now, though, I think I'll just enjoy driving her with the same amount of zeal that my grandfather would have behind the wheel.

Nice and easy.

Trent is leaving, locking up our front door as I pull up to park along the sidewalk, revving the engine until he can't help but turn around.

I leave the motor running and step out to look at him over the top of the car, my hands flat on the surface, loving it like it's a woman.

"Please say you did not steal that," he says, rolling a basketball from one hand to the other as he steps closer, admiring. This car demands attention, and I can tell it's won over Trent's heart just as it does every person with a penis.

"Ha ha, very funny. O fixed it up for me. Where you headed? I'll give you a ride," I say, twirling the keys like a teenager who just got his license. I might as well be.

Trent's mouth quirks into a half grin, his eyes still on the shape of the car.

"Yeah, a'right. I'm going to shoot at the rec center. You wanna come?" He opens the door, letting out a soft whistle as he feels the weight of it as it swings wide. The car still needs some fixes—the interior is still a little rough and it could use an upgrade on the air conditioning and stereo system, but the body and the engine are levels beyond what I ever thought I would get them to.

I slide in and shut my door as Trent climbs in.

"I'm not up for shooting, but I'll drive. I'll take us to practice tomorrow too," I say, pulling out slowly on our small side road.

"Fuck that shit, you'll drive us everywhere from now on," he says, looking in his side mirror. "Though...are you always going to drive like a fucking old woman?"

"Yes," I say quickly, glancing to him, but only for a second. Eyes back on the road. "Yes I am."

He chuckles, and I look both ways at the stop sign, checking my mirror for a sign of anyone behind us before I rev the engine once more and let the tires squeal just enough to give us a good jump off the line. I cut us off when I hit forty and back it down quickly to senior-citizen pace, but the thrill I feel from punching the gas, just a tiny bit, lets me know this careful habit—it won't last forever.

"Hey, so that Harley dude from the gym stopped by earlier, said he tried calling you, but couldn't get through," Trent says. I pull my phone out and slide it on my lap, not looking until we hit the red light before the main road to campus. My phone was low when I left for my mom's this morning; it must have died in the middle of the day.

"Did he say anything?"

My mind goes right to the list of bills I have due and the pathetic double-digit dollar amount I have in the bank right now. I don't get paid for the before-school program until Friday, and even then, five hours of morning coloring with five-year-olds isn't going to make a dent in my tuition bill. I'm not due to fight for him until later this month, but the thought that maybe he could use me a little earlier has me driving faster so I can say *yes* before he asks someone else.

"Nah. He just told me to tell you to stop by when you got home. He's a weird dude," Trent says. "He seems young to own a gym."

"Yeah, but it's not a very nice gym," I say.

Trent's never been. I'm pretty sure if he saw the sketchy warehouse set-up I spend time in, he'd start to question my sanity more than he does now. As scary as the gym is though, Harley is just the opposite. He comes off as a preppy young businessman from money, and that's because that's exactly what he is—on the outside. But he's also connected, with people who help him make things happen, people who make large bets with him, and sometimes, for him—and the money always flows. If there's ever a kink in the system, Harley makes sure it's taken care of. He might dress like a lawyer, but he's built like a fighter.

And when I do him a favor, I *always* get paid.

"Nice gym or not, junior Wall Street freaks me out a little," he says as I pull up to the drop-off for the rec center on campus. Trent steps out onto the lighted walkway, girls in yoga pants and tank tops walk along behind him with mats rolled under their arms. I laugh to myself at how different this gym is from the one I'm about to drive to.

"I'll be okay, *Mom*," I yell through the open window.

Trent rolls his eyes, then starts dribbling as he turns and heads toward the building. As a new group of girls passes the car, I wait to see if they notice, glance my direction, take in the ride, and wonder about the driver. Only one of them does though, and not for long. Their attention is focused on my roommate about twenty feet ahead of them. As nice as my car is, it's still nothing compared to the Captain America of hockey.

I leave Trent to be worshiped by sorority girls and head to the vacant row of buildings on the south side of town, circling Harley's gym twice until I find a spot that doesn't put my car right on the corner where some asshole could rear-end it. The sun is still up, but barely. I'm hoping Harley hasn't left yet. I don't know who he's rolling out for rounds tonight, but I'm sure he's leaving with someone soon.

The lights are on in the space, which gives me hope. I pound my palm on the rolling door when I hear voices, and after a few seconds, I see three pairs of feet appear underneath as it lifts. Music is playing in the background, the low thump of the stereo offset by the slapping sounds of gloves hitting hands.

"You finally check your damn messages?" Harley says. He's dressed in his dark gray suit, like he always does for fight nights, his hair slicked back and his glasses tinted. He says it makes him look older, and I think he thinks it makes him look tougher. I always thought it just made him look like a pansy asshole. Honestly, the version of him I see at the gym—the one that walks around with his shirt off and lifts fifty-pound dumbbells, tossing them around the joint like they're water bottles—is a shitload more intimidating. But Harley's also never been screwed out of money, so maybe he knows some shit I don't.

"Phone died, and I was at my ma's. Sorry," I answer, holding my phone up for proof. He slaps my hand.

"Put that shit away. I believe you," he says, turning to face the guy standing in the ring working out with Bill, one of Harley's head trainers. "Danny, he's here. You can go ahead and bail. I'll hit you with something in two weeks. Take care of that fuckin' hand."

The dude boxing in the ring is bald and looks a few years older than me, but we're about the same size. He pulls the tape from his hand, twisting it into a ball that he throws in the trash, and nods at Harley in response. Bill comes over to look at me, leaning on the ropes with both arms.

"I don't know, dude. You think we can roll him out there?" Bill asks.

162

Harley looks at him, his back to me still, and the silence means he must be making one of his faces at Bill, the kind that says *shut the fuck up* without the use of words. Bill leans forward and spits on the concrete floor, then looks at me.

"All right, boss. You know best," he says, his grin either crooked from getting punched by Danny a few minutes earlier or because he's snickering at me.

"Roll who out where?" I ask, ignoring Bill and hoping like hell this means payday for me.

"Pitch has a fight tonight. It's kind of a big one, and I need it to look good, but I need Pitch to *feel* good—like he can kill in his next fight, 'cuz that one will be real. He's been off, so I need to get him right again. Danny usually works with him, and he was going to go tonight, but that asshole hurt his hand doing some goddamned house project for his wife or whatever. You're close to the right weight, and you've handled Pitch before," he says, tossing a pair of shorts my way along with a backpack.

"If by handled you mean let him knock my front teeth loose and deviate my septum," I say. I need money, but fuck—Pitch could honestly kill me if he tried hard enough.

"Funny septum joke. I like it. Look, it's late and I just sent Danny home. Are you in or are you going to fuck me over? Because if you're going to fuck me over, you can just get out of here and find a new place to work out your juvenile-aggression shit or whatever it is you do when you come here."

I swallow hard, and I know he sees it. I can't cut myself loose from Harley—I need both the money and the pain, and I think he knows it. I nod and sit on the folding chair to pull out my gear from the backpack.

"Where's this thing at?" I ask, my tongue in my cheek as I check the gloves, tape and mouth guard to make sure everything looks ready, wishing there was armor buried in that bag, too, for the massive stomach shots Pitch always likes to land.

"It's by Cicero, just down the street from Union. You can ride with us," he says.

"I'm good. I got a car," I say, wrapping my wrists and hands early, cutting the tape with my teeth.

"Well look who finally grew up and got himself a license," Harley teases.

"I've had a license, asshole. My car's just back from the dead finally. And I have work and practice in the morning, so I wanna head home right after we're done," I say, looking up to notice Harley and Bill have already made it to the back door to leave, not bothering to listen to me—not really giving a shit, more likely.

"We'll pull around; you can follow us," Bill says as the door shuts behind them.

"Oh, you're welcome, Harley. Always happy to help out. I'm sure I'll love getting my ass kicked for thirty minutes in front of an angry, drunken crowd. This all sounds super," I whisper, chuckling to myself as I grab the rest of my things and walk back through the sliding door, pulling it down behind me and tugging up to make sure it's locked.

Actually, I'll probably like it more than I'm willing to admit. And I know if it's a Pitch fight, the pay is going to be pretty damn sweet too.

I toss my bag in the passenger seat and get in, pulling out as soon as I see Bill's black Tahoe in front of me. I follow them down Lakeshore for the twenty minutes it takes to get to our highway, then manage to find their car again on Roosevelt after losing them in traffic. We stop near sixteenth, where the roads are packed with BMWs and Porsches parked illegally. I'm not sure who else is on the card, but if Pitch is going, I have a feeling a lot of these people are here for him. I hope they've come to drop some cash, and I hope like hell I can make it four rounds.

I find a spot near the exit reserved for the crew and Bill holds up a badge when one of the club owners tries to give me grief for parking there. He nods and waves me forward to join them.

"Thanks," I say.

"Sweet ride. I'd park that shit somewhere close, too," Bill says.

The back rooms are swelling with people, half of them women all waiting to get with one of the fighters for the night. They drag their hands over my body as I pass through the narrow, crowded spaces behind Harley and Bill until we slip into a training room near the main hallway to the ring. Most of the fights I've done have been in front of dozens—maybe a hundred people at the most. The crowd I hear through the brick and concrete walls sounds like it reaches close to a thousand.

"All right, here's the deal," Harley says, already running through texts and numbers on his phone. "You need to make it to four. You understand? Four."

I nod. Shit, I hope I'm standing after four. My heart is pounding with the force of a boxer trying to break out from inside, and my body is drenched with sweat already. How ironic. I keep my game face on though and get to work, changing and prepping myself for whatever I'm about to step into.

"You go four, and we're looking at eight K for the night, you feel me?" I don't react on the outside much, just nodding that I hear him. Inside is a different story, because eight thousand dollars is about four times the amount I normally make at one of these. That also probably means my face is about to take four times the force from Pitch's fist.

Tuition. Paid.

Insurance for six months. Paid.

Three months rent. Paid.

Shit, maybe with the money I make from coloring with kindergarteners in the mornings, I can take Lindsey out for a real date, like dinner and a movie or something.

Or...not take Lindsey on a date.

Not take Lindsey anywhere, and just disappear because I can't take Emma somewhere. I don't want to take Emma anywhere, but I also can't let go now that I've found her. *Fuck!* I've managed to go the entire day without thinking about my problem—I'm stringing along a really nice girl I have absolutely no interest in. Of course, it all comes racing into my head now—minutes before I'm about to intentionally thrust myself into mayhem.

A good time for a distraction.

I pull my phone out and click it to check the time, but am greeted by nothing but a blank screen. Still dead. No music, nothing to read—only my fucked-up thoughts left to keep me company while I stand in a yellow-painted brick room that's big enough to house a training table and a locker, but nothing else. The room starts to feel smaller with every minute that passes, and my heart begins to race more, sweat threatening to drip from my brow as my eyes dart from corner to corner, my ears perked and waiting for the knock to come. I need out. This room—it looks like Lake Crest.

I need out. I need out now!

I lie back and hold a towel over my eyes, the weight of my arm closing over one ear and blocking out any other light.

"You like getting hit, boy?" he says. *"You like the way it feels? I'll hit you again. I'll hit you so hard you'll fuckin' cry yourself to sleep for a month, wishing you had a mommy and a daddy who gave a shit and didn't send you to a place like this with a guy like me. I'll set you straight. I bet you'll never try shit like that with me again! When I give you a job, you do it!"*

The voice in my head feels real, and I fling the towel away from my eyes and sit up swiftly, looking around at the bare walls. It's only a memory, but the fact that it was real once—that a man who was supposed to protect me did exactly the opposite—is enough to bring it back to life as I sit here waiting in this tiny yellow room.

The pound on the door comes seconds later, and I race to my feet, welcoming the escape.

"You ready?" Bill asks. His expression is worried, which isn't one he usually makes at me. I respect it, but I also can't let it get in my head, so I hold my gloves out for him to pound and then push them into my temples and chest a few times to prime myself for Pitch's worst.

I wait behind the crowd, behind Bill, while a blonde woman reads the cards in the center of the ring, announcing Pitch to a deafening sound of screams and the thunder of feet pounding bleachers. I tell myself the louder they are, the more money they'll drop, and I breathe deeply as she announces me, Pitch's opponent.

"And fighting in his sixteenth match, the Irish blood running restless through his veins, Andrew *Wicked Boy* Harper!" She lets the echo of my last name drag on loudly through the mike, and I

166

focus on her lips and the noise they make rather than the heavy *boos* and threats from the crowd around me. *Wicked Boy* Harper was Harley's idea—he gave me that name the first time I fought for him. He said the word came to him the first time he saw me spar in the ring. I just kept getting up, asking for more.

Wicked. Poisoned. Empty.

My eyes meet Pitch's as I step into the ring, and his lip ticks up with the only hint of recognition I'm going to get for the night.

That's right. It's me. Go easy, but get us paid.

I move to the corner and let Bill shout things at me that won't matter. He makes me drink water, checks my tape and gloves, then stands with me and squeezes my head in his hands, bringing his head against mine, the foul smell of his breath only mildly better than the view of the nicotine-stained toothpick dangling from his cracked lips as he mutters a prayer.

Too late, Bill—I'm beyond salvation, and Pitch is the only one who can control how much pain I get tonight.

The bell sounds, and I turn to face my penance, to earn my stay and forget my life. Pitch swings hard, and I dodge. He swings again, and I dodge. And then we dance.

I spend most of the first round moving with him, faking and stepping at all the right times, working from my memory of our sparring last week. I catch the smirk on his lip more than a few times, and I also note the nodding approval from Harley in the crowd when I let a few jabs land in my side near the end of the round.

His punches come full force. There's nothing pretend about them, even if he's going easy. The announcer says he's toying with me—I'm the mouse. That's fine, as long as this mouse gets to eat some cheese later tonight with all of his teeth in his mouth.

We spend the second round doing much of the same, but this time his fists find new spots on my body, and when the first hook lands squarely on my right cheekbone—my body is instantly flooded with the chemistry I'm constantly seeking. The sting is immediate; the bruising deep, and the pain is so good. I smirk as my head slings to the side, my mouth guard slipping from my lips. I suck it back in place, spitting blood out on the mat before grinning back at my opponent.

"Come on, Pitch! Yeah, baby. Yeah!" I shout, my gloves pounding my chest then hitting together.

My feet feel lighter, yet my head feels heavier. Everything is turning on itself around me, but Pitch is still locked in. I swing at him a few times, landing blows to his right ribs, where I know he can take it.

The bell rings, and I move over to Bill in the corner. He holds something from a stick against my right cheek and eyebrow, slowing down the blood that wants to spill.

Let it spill! Let me bleed!

"Come on, hurry up! Get me back out there!" I shout at him. He shakes his head, ignoring me. I push at him to get out of my way, but he leans into me with all his weight, which is twice mine.

"You're a crazy little punk, and I get that you need this, but just do me a favor and let me save you from getting killed, huh?" he speaks through gritted teeth.

"Whatever," I say, looking past him to Pitch, who smiles at me. He wants more too. He's having fun with this, and I'm forgetting everything. It's exactly what I need.

The bell rings, and I brush Bill away and rush back to the center where I find Pitch waiting, his fist opening up the wounds Bill just spent seconds trying to secure. I laugh as I stumble back on my feet, losing my balance enough to catch a glimpse of Harley, whose lip is between his teeth under his angry eyes.

I gotcha, Harley. I know this is only three. I'll stay on my feet. I just want to feel it a little more. Let me go, let me spar.

I come at Pitch with everything I've got. My swings are sloppy; he blocks most of them, but I'm wild and aggressive. A few shots land on his chin and head with enough power that he stumbles back a step or two. The crowd actually turns for a second, cheering for me. My breath, as stuttered as it comes, is mixed with a rush of adrenaline and fear and pride.

I'm too lost in this feeling of glory to see his next swing, and soon I'm caught in the ropes, his fists taking turns moving from my right side to my left, my skin red from punches and my bones begging to break.

But I'm still breathing.

I'm still feeling.

The bell sounds, and I falter back to the stool, where Bill goes to work quickly, my view of him skewed now from the swelling happening around my eye.

"You've never been hit like this," he says. He won't make eye contact with me, and it pisses me off.

"I'm fine!" I shout, spitting in the bucket he is holding under my chin.

"Yeah..." he says, pulling my chin up with his monster hand, the roughness of his calluses scraping my face so I'm forced to look him in the eye. "You're fine, huh? Then go out there and you end this. This is it. No more rounds for you, no matter how fucked up you are and how much you think you can take, you got it?"

Four rounds. I knew the gig. I got it. I stare at him without answering, though, because he's pissing me off. He growls at me, pushing my face from his view with disgust.

The bell rings, and I find Pitch once again ready for me in the center, his feet still nimble, his arms still up at his sides, everything about him fresh. I'm a bloody mess, and it makes me start to laugh.

"You're a crazy motherfucker, you know that?" Pitch pushes back a step, bouncing, as he stares at me.

"Oh, I'm crazy. And I can take anything you've got. Bring it, big man," I slur, my smile big as his fist elevates then rushes forward, landing squarely on my nose.

Oh fuck! Oh yes!

His swings don't stop. The pain keeps coming. I feel every single shot, as if time slows down just so I can take in the sensation of the leather of his glove pushing deep inside my gut, my chest, my face. Nothing else matters. Nothing else exists. I bleed. I land. The ref counts, and Bill drags my torn and broken body to the corner amidst the roar of the crowd around me; they're celebrating my fall, my failure.

They love me for it, and I'm drunk on my self-loathing.

"I'll do my best, kid, but I think you're gonna need to make a trip to the emergency room for some of this," Bill says, his face somber. Bill's disappointed too.

"I'm fine," I growl.

He laughs once, but his face remains serious.

"I said I'm fine!" I repeat, my face square with his. His eyes stay on mine, and we both breathe while they announce Pitch as the winner and people rush the ring to congratulate him, to touch him. I'm lost in the corner with Bill and my pain and nothing else.

"Okay, kid. But I don't like putting you back together. If this were my call, this wouldn't have been you tonight," he says, pressing a wet towel on my face. I grab it from him and stand.

"Well it's not your call. It's mine. And Harley's. And we say I'm fine," I say, spitting once more at his feet as I climb through the ropes and out to the back rooms where Harley is waiting for me.

The envelope exchange is fast, and unlike Bill, Harley hardly spends time looking at my face. The bruising and blood disgusts him, and I think I scare him a little. It's fine; I scare myself.

I don't count the money until I get outside and to my car, but before the rest of the crowd starts to spill into the streets, I pull the envelope from my backpack and leaf through the hundred dollar bills, counting twice and getting eighty-four each time. My lips can't fight against smiling no matter how badly it hurts my face to do so. The laughter comes when I hit the highway, pressing the pedal down with ease, crawling the car up to ninety-five as I weave into the flow of traffic, passing anything in my way.

The rush will carry me home.

And when I come down, I'll be at my next destination. I'll be at *her* house, and she can bring the pain back all over again.

Emma

Graham has been the perfect gentleman. His mother would be proud. Or, I think she would be. It's still hard to say—I'm not clear about their relationship.

I didn't let Lindsey know I was leaving to meet him. I didn't want to deal with expectations. I brushed her attempt to talk off last night, telling her I was just stressed after the awards dinner.

170

I told her I was walking to the store and back—instead, going to Andrew's to confront him. I wanted to see him without the veil, to see if he would be the same if it were just us.

Turns out he was worse.

He's so broken, and I don't know why. I let that consume me, and it was starting to push me into depression when Graham called and asked if I wanted to meet for a quick dinner. I jumped at his offer, wanting to find something else—anything else—that would mesmerize me for a while.

Graham has been ideal, what women are supposed to want—at least what I *think* women are supposed to want, all beardy and strong and masculine—but my mind hasn't abandoned its thoughts of Andrew once all evening. His messy hair, pierced ears, half-shaven face with eyes that have this way of boxing me in and suffocating me.

"So what's it like studying with my mom?" he asks as we walk from the small café two blocks away from my apartment. He offered to walk me home, and I allowed it.

"She's…I don't know…kind of tough I guess?" I say, glancing to his smiling face then back down to the walkway in front of me.

"She's mean, huh?" he laughs. "It's okay; you can say it to me. I mean hell, the woman raised me. She tells my dad what to do, too. That's the whole reason I went into psychology. I wanted a practice and specialty she knew nothing about. I had eighteen years of that woman knowing what's best, telling me what to do, but never really caring enough to stick around and watch me succeed at her plan. She just laid out new orders for me to follow, new expectations. I'm done with it."

"I bet she still knows a few things about your world," I smile, not really comfortable complaining about Miranda to Graham, or hearing his complaints—which seem to be plentiful.

Graham chuckles, holding his hand out in front of me to stop me from stepping in the road as we reach the intersection. A delivery truck races by, kicking my pulse up as it passes.

"Thanks," I say, embarrassed and looking down.

He bends his elbow out to the side, nudging me until I look up at him again. "Don't mention it," he says, leaving his arm out for me to take. I slide my fingers under his bicep and let him lead.

He layers his other hand over mine, and I notice that when I loosen my hold, he tightens his. I think it's because he's still worried about me stepping off the curb, but there's also something overly-possessive about the way his touch feels. If I weren't this close to home, I'm not sure how okay I would be with it. "And no, my mom doesn't do psychology," he continues, lowering his head, picking up my gaze and bringing my eyes back up to his. "My mom thinks it's a shit practice, actually. But we're past that argument. I'm too far in now anyhow."

"How many more years do you have?" All I can think of while we walk is how different his arm feels. There's heat that goes along with his skin, and his muscles are bigger than Andrew's. Or maybe they're not. I haven't touched Andrew in years, and the version of him in my life now is definitely not a teenaged boy.

"Probably four more if I want to really be something. Which I do. I want to be the doctor who solves things, with papers published in journals and all that. You see, Mom and I both have that in common," he says, and I squint at him, my brow pinched as I try to follow his suggestion. "You know, awards and accolades—Wheatons love the attention."

I smile as he chuckles, and I feel relief that he recognizes this about his mom as well.

"Well, at least you all earn it...the awards, I mean?" I say. He acknowledges with a quick nod and smile, but his expression quickly fades as he turns his head from me.

"I plan on earning it," he says, his focus on the long sidewalk in front of us, his mouth in a tight straight line. "Mom...she gets awards because people have just gotten used to giving them to her at this point."

I breathe in slowly through my nose, glancing at him carefully, turning away before he looks down at me. I don't respond to his criticism of the woman who saved my life. It's clear that he's privy to a side of her I don't know, though, and I'm pretty sure I don't want to delve into it—not now, anyhow.

My nerves make themselves present as we get closer to my apartment. Graham has been a gentleman, but I'm also not sure if that lasts all the way up to my front door. His hold on me is still rigid and unforgiving; the few tests I've tried to relax my muscles haven't induced the same response from him. I'm not inviting him in, and my extremely-limited dating experience hasn't taught me how to navigate this next step yet.

Karma seems to have sent me assistance, though, as the moment we get to the front of my building, a voice calls my name from the ground. Andrew is sitting with his back against the wall, his hood pulled forward over his head. He looks drunk on his feet as he slowly gets himself to a stand, but when I see his face I realize it's more than that making him shaky.

"Jesus, Andrew! What happened?" I pull away from Graham again, but he puts a hand over my chest, wanting to step in front of me. I wave him off, whispering that it's all right, then reach up to touch the side of Andrew's hoodie; he jerks away. I hold my palm flat, then move to touch the material again, pulling it back just enough so I can see the cuts and bruises on his face in the light. His eyes aren't on me at all, though. He's staring at Graham behind me.

"I got in a fight," he says, a low rumbling laugh brewing in his chest, but never fully escaping his lips. His smirk never pulls into anything more, and his gaze can't seem to leave Graham.

"Yeah, I can tell. Andrew, you need to see a doctor," I say.

"That's why I'm here," he says, shifting his eyes to me, but only for a second.

"Em, you need me to call someone?" Graham asks, his hand flat on my back as he lets me know he's right there behind me.

"She's fine. Who are you?" Andrew's voice is louder this time, but his face is just as hard. As beaten as he is, his eyes are still clear and threatening.

I look down, closing my eyes and wishing to rewind time. I'm just not sure how far back I should go. Maybe...maybe all the way before Andrew.

Graham reaches around me, his gesture protective, as he holds his hand out for Andrew. "I'm Graham Wheaton, a friend of Emma's," he says.

Andrew looks at his hand in front of me, his mouth seesawing back and forth as his eyebrows rise, then slowly his mouth slides into a smile. Never full, and never friendly.

"Graham," he repeats his name, finally closing the distance and shaking, his muscles flexing to show exactly how little Graham intimidates him. I'm shocked he's not pissing on him, just to really show what a man he is. "You're the guy with the PowerPoint. A real hero, I hear," he says, every word double-edged with meaning—he's being affable as far as Graham is concerned, but I know better. He's mocking me. His eyes move to mine, and my stomach sinks.

Graham chuckles. "Yeah, I guess that's me," he says.

I feel Andrew's gaze as he steps closer to me. The amount of testosterone radiating around starting to suffocate me, and I need to extradite myself from it all.

"Graham, I had a really nice time. I'm okay, really. I think I need to help Andrew out, until my roommate gets home, but I'll text you tomorrow. If that's okay?"

My face is in no way a reflection of how I'm feeling. On the outside, I smile and look grateful for his protection, not worried at all over the guy standing—*bleeding*—next to me. Inside, I'm repeating swear words and praying that my roommate comes home early from her spin class. Glancing at my watch, I realize her class has just started, so that chance—it's really slim.

Graham's holding his position, keeping his eyes on Andrew, his head cocked slightly to one side. When Andrew notices, he mimics him, just before he leans forward and spits a bloody mess at his feet on the sidewalk in front of us all.

"She's fine, Graham," Andrew says with a small nod of his head.

Graham still doesn't move, but he turns his face to look at me, his eyebrows raised. "You sure?"

I roll my eyes and sigh, glancing from Andrew and back again. "I'm fine. He isn't here for me. But I can't leave him out here waiting. *I'll text you,*" I say, repeating my words from earlier, maybe also wanting to rub in the fact that I'll be talking to Graham again, seeing him again, making more plans with him.

Graham is worth a second look. And maybe if I can go out with him without a mountain of anxiety dangling over me, I'll end up liking him more.

Leaving his eyes on Andrew, Graham reaches to my chin and tilts my cheek toward his lips, kissing the side of my face lightly, the whiskers of his beard tickling me and making me smile.

I watch Graham step backward, his hands pushed in the pockets of his gray jeans, his sweater curled up around his neck, everything about him right out of the pages of an Abercrombie catalogue. He even smelled nice all night. I should have told him that.

I should like Graham. I should *feel* something.

But I also feel like maybe, just then, he was marking me—laying claim on his territory. And that makes me feel uneasy.

"So guys with beards...that's what does it for you, huh?" Andrew says, not letting my mind stray too far. I turn back to him, Graham's image still in my mind, a comical contrast from the rough, beaten mess standing before me now.

"You're an asshole," I say, shaking my head and stepping past him, pushing the glass doors open and greeting Sam at the front desk.

"Good evening, Miss Burke. Saved a copy of the paper for you; thought you'd like to see it today," Sam says, as I stop to gather my mail and then pull the paper from him.

I smile politely and whisper, "Thanks," but I leave the paper rolled. It's a copy of the Tech Campus News, and I know why he saved it for me. I saw the reporters there last night, taking pictures. No need to see a reminder of what I look like when I'm being open and honest. I'll just put it in the box in my closet with the others.

"What's so special about the paper? More stories about how your PowerPoint hero came to the rescue?" Andrew says behind me as we both step into the elevator. The doors close on us, and instantly the space feels small. I don't answer him, but I feel him—I feel him watching me from four feet away, his arms folded over his chest, his hood draped over his face, his body smelling as if he's stumbled in from some alley.

We reach my floor, and I step out, not inviting him. If he wants my help, he'll just have to show himself in. I unlock my door, toss my mail and keys and purse on the table and walk down the hallway to our bathroom. I hear the door close a few seconds later, and soon Andrew steps into the frame, stopping with his hands gripping either side of the wall, his head slung forward. His knuckles are covered in blood, and his legs are spackled with red. He's wearing black shorts that drape below his knees.

"Why were you fighting?" I ask, pulling the alcohol from the cabinet and the bag of cotton and gauze from underneath our sink. I step to him, and notice his grip tighten on the wood as I move into his view, his lip twitches on one side—he sneers like a stray dog not ready to trust the hand about to feed it.

"I fight for money," he says, his mouth now a hard line, his brow still shadowed by his sweatshirt. I reach up to move it, but freeze the second his eyes meet mine, the swelling on his brow, the blood on his cheek nothing compared to the broken look in his eyes.

"So this wasn't like some pissing contest in a bar or you trying to act like a big shot on the ice?" I ask, dabbing the cotton again, ignoring what I saw in his eyes. I wish for that look to go away—it makes me weak.

"I fight to forget about things," he says, leaning forward just enough that his breath tickles my neck. I swear I feel his lips against my skin. Maybe I imagine it.

Maybe I want it to be real.

My breath hitches, but only once. I look down at the bottle in my hands, inhaling once more, deeply, the scent a mix of the alcohol fumes and him, then I pour some solution on one of the pads, moving it to his face. He's playing me, and I don't like it. I expect him to jerk when I touch him; his cuts are deep, and the alcohol is bound to burn at first. He doesn't flinch. My eyes move from his wounds to his gaze—off and on as I work to clean him up. His expression never changes. It's hard. His eyes hazed as he watches me. He's trying to intimidate me.

"What are you trying to forget about, Andrew?" I speak softly; something about him feels like I could set it off at any moment. I push his hood back just then, and my hand finds his hair as I do. The movement is natural, and I don't know why my fingers act as they do. It's muscle memory, from one night and years of dreams. I push a few strands back, letting my fingers touch his scalp—touch him. He's still so familiar. The feeling of him rushes through me, and it burns.

He doesn't answer me. His eyes watch me as I work to clean out the deep cuts on his face—one on his eyebrow definitely in need of sutures.

"I'm going to have to stitch this one," I say, touching it once more with the cloth. He shrugs with one shoulder. "Unless you'd rather wait and have someone else. Lindsey will be home in an hour."

"You can sew me up." His answer comes fast, the words crisp and short. His tongue lingers between his teeth as his mouth curves to smile, as if everything he says means something else, too.

"Where else are you hurt?" I ask, treating him like a patient. Andrew is no different from one of the people I talk to at the clinic when we volunteer and fill out charts. This...is just a clinic visit.

Andrew is just a patient.

Just a patient.

His face forms a response to my question, but slowly, his lips curl ever so slightly more on the side, and his eyes close just as slowly. He laughs, the kind of laugh that seems like it comes from somewhere else—from memories, from the past, from loss maybe. What begins as smug body language meant to dominate me gives way before my eyes to confession.

"Everywhere, Emma. I. Hurt. Everywhere."

My breath stops, and I wait as his eyes look down at his hands, as he turns them to see his palms, to look at the scrapes and cuts on his fingers. He snickers to himself again, but stops quickly, looking at me as he stands in front of me, our bodies maybe a foot apart, maybe less. He grabs the bottom of his sweatshirt and pulls it up over his head, all of him overshadowing me, his skin and muscles bare before me.

I don't look at first, but when I do I see the dark purple bruising that's taking over his sides and ribs. That's not what I'm supposed to see, though. That's not why he pulled his shirt from his body, why he's standing here with his sweatshirt lying on the floor at his feet. That's not why his breathing has changed, or why he sounds like a frightened boy, each exhale short and desperate. The largest scar is maybe three inches long, and it starts an inch to the right of his belly button. Others are smaller, but clustered, and they look like burns. The lines are faint enough I know they've been there for a while.

This is something that's been with him for years.

"How long have you been fighting?" I ask, my arms no longer able to hold the open alcohol still enough not to shake drops on the floor. I set it down on the sink, leaving my hand on the counter to brace myself, my arm shaking with my own weight and need for balance.

"You see my scars there, Emma?" he asks, stepping closer. I try to move back, but I'm in a corner, the bathroom small, and my back already against the sink.

"I do. Andrew, how long have you been fighting?"

I answer him and repeat my question fast, thinking it will make him pause. It doesn't. He keeps moving forward, his eyes down on his own skin, and the closer he comes, the faster my lungs fight for air. When he reaches for my right hand, the one now gripping the corner of the counter so hard that my knuckles are white, I refuse to let go. Andrew leaves his hands on mine, though, waiting for me to surrender. I eventually loosen my grip, and he picks my hand up in his, his touch tender, slow, sweet. My lip quivers at the memory, but I hold it in. He places it on the line of four small circles on his side, holding it there against his bare skin, his eyes unflinching as he watches his hand cover my hand as it covers his wounds.

"This isn't from fighting, Emma. These scars...they're from surviving," he says. His body shakes under my touch.

He never looks up. Several seconds pass in silence, and the tiny room begins to stink of the opened alcohol bottle. I look over his face, his arms and hands and body—so much of him covered in bruises. It's like he was stolen—taken by someone, tortured, and returned half the boy he was—only to grow into a man with holes and broken pieces.

"What happened to you?" My voice cracks when I ask, my eyes still on the look of his hand on mine.

His hand. On mine.

"You have no idea, do you?"

I feel my brow pull in tight, my stomach binding as my mind begins to run through the thousand of possible things that means. I shake my head, my eyes moving up his body, gazing along his long torso, his golden skin, his curved muscles and neck and chin—his face so much older, but still the same. His eyes the ones I waited for, the only ones that ever looked at me that way before a kiss. Even if I didn't realize it, I was waiting for him. I was in love with Andrew Harper the first time he held my hand. I've just been waiting to see him again to fully fall. I can't fall now. Not when he's...like this. But I fear I may not have control over any of that—over...*feeling.*

"I'm afraid, Andrew," I tell him. When his chest fills with a deep breath and his head drops to the side, I know he understands.

"You have no idea..." he says, this time not asking a question.

His hand lets go of its hold on me, but I leave my hold on him a little longer, noticing his eyes close again as I do. When he opens them, he keeps his gaze down and away, his thoughts lost somewhere else entirely.

I let my hand slip away carefully, like a child trying to balance two cards in a pyramid. I watch him for a sign, waiting for him to say something more. I don't know what to ask. I don't know what I don't know. But I'm starting to think it's a lot—and it might mean the difference between the man standing here in front of me, and the boy I once thought I loved.

"I should stitch you up," I say quietly, my lip pinned between my teeth to keep me from saying more. A shift happened just now—I hold the power. I can feel it. I'm not sure I want it, or am ready for it. Andrew only nods, his movement small, his eyes still at the corner of the room.

I slide the small drawer at the edge of the counter open and pull out the medic box from our hours at the clinic. Tech believes in teaching the basics early, so all pre-med students are trained medics before they begin their four years of med school. I've stitched maybe a dozen lacerations. I'm a better sewer than Lindsey. But I wish...oh how I wish it were her hands doing this now.

179

I flex my fingers, rubbing the tips against my palms, working the nerves through them. I pull the thread and needle out, readying it before preparing the alcohol and tape and gauze.

"I'll need you to sit," I say, expecting Andrew to use this, to take my request and turn it into a challenge, to defy me just for the sake of watching me suffer. Instead, he nods with the same lethargy he's had since I touched him, his legs moving to the edge of the bathtub where he sits, holding on to the side, his eyes still lost.

I'm careful with every movement at first. And when I finally puncture his skin, I move my hands swiftly, repeating to myself that this is only a patient, that this is just like the other times, and that I can move smoothly. My hands work fast, closing the wound on his brow before the shaking settles in. I don't feel it until I bring the scissors up to cut, and I have to pause before finally slicing the ends of the thread away.

"The place was called Lake Crest," he says. I wait for more, but his silence indicates that he wants a response from me. I don't know what Lake Crest is, where it is, what it means, but I want more—I think I *need* more. Even if it terrifies me.

"Okay," I say, my voice quiet, unthreatening. I cut a small square of padding and two strips of tape to cover Andrew's stitches. He remains on the tub, his hands still clutching— holding on. I'm delicate with my touch, but the tape doesn't stick, so I run my finger softly along each strip against his face. When I look to his eyes again, they capture mine.

"Lake Crest is a place they send boys who need to be broken...when they fuck up and do something wrong. It's run by the state, and a guy named Nick Meyers. The first time Nick choked me, it was because I refused to kiss his feet...*actually* kiss his feet. He held my windpipe in his hands while security stood behind me with a Taser, just in case I decided to fight back."

Oh my god!

"The second time, I decided to try. The volts sent me to my knees."

My eyes close involuntarily.

"Some of the boys did him favors. That's how it worked there. You were either on top, on the bottom, or invisible. Favors put you on top. I tried real hard to be invisible, but they wouldn't let me. The ones who did him favors would leave the campus late at night, coming back with large envelopes—sometimes coming back with stab wounds and beaten faces."

"Nick kept after me. He didn't like that I said *no*, that I wouldn't bend to his needs. I was a threat to his secrets, because I saw more than the others. I paid attention. Money passed through his hands like water, and I saw it all. I didn't want any part of it. I only wanted to survive. And there were so many things to endure. So many factions, gangs within gangs, groups you needed to be *in* with and *out* with. I only wanted to be left alone."

His eyes find mine again, but his words pause, his jaw working back and forth while he thinks. I think he's trying to protect me from knowing too much after knowing nothing at all.

"I wrote you letters. Dozens."

His eyes penetrate me. Mine grow wide, my stomach becomes sick as I clutch the sink again, letting my legs have their way this time as I slide down to sit on the floor, my world spinning.

"You never wrote back. Not once."

No!

His voice sounds angry, but only at first. It breaks quickly; the realization squelching years' worth of hate and doubt caused by some unknown force. I never knew. I would have written. I would have traded him, saved him—*loved him*. I needed him. My heart was broken.

And I needed him.

He needed me.

He needed me...*more!*

"One day, I said *yes*." He looks down again, running his thumb over the long scar on his belly.

"He did that?" I ask, my words crackling from my chest, my eyes barely able to look at the long line that slices through him.

Andrew nods.

"I said *yes* just so I could get out, so I could find you. I had to know why you weren't writing, where you were...if you were okay. I never collected what was due to him that night. I never had any intention of meeting his people at all. He found out before I could make it to the bus station to buy a ticket with the money I'd hidden under a loose tile on my floor. You were a forty-minute bus ride away—but I never got to see you. At least not then. I had to continue to live off of your memory. He took me into his office as soon as we got back to campus, hitting me until I could no longer stand. And when the guard pulled my arm over his shoulder to carry me on my weak legs back to my room, he told them to wait for one more second so *he could give me something to make sure I'd never forget.* The knife was small, but sharp; more of a razor. I bled for days—just deep enough so it would heal on its own...*in time.*"

It's all too much. His story—*his life!*

"Andrew," I whisper, my lips dry, my mouth drier. My throat aches, and my heart hurts as it never has before.

"You didn't know," he says, his mouth half open, his eyes back to the lost place. I shake my head to confirm his assumption. He notices. "All this time...you...you didn't know."

"I would have come. I swear, Andrew...if I knew what had happened to you...I would have made them..." I'm breathless with my words, my plea cut short before I can tell him I would have made them stop, would have confessed the truth.

"Em? You home?"

Lindsey's shout and clamor through the front door rocks me like thunder, and I stumble to my feet, clearing the counter of the remains of my work on Andrew. I look to him, expecting him to be just as frozen, just as stunned and worried about what to say, what to do. Instead, he's already standing, pulling his sweatshirt back over his body as he moves toward the sink to wash his hands.

I watch him.

"Oh! Damn! You scared me—" Lindsey jumps when she sees me in the bathroom, stuttering when she sees Andrew in here, too. Her eyes dart between us.

"I was helping him. He needed...stitches," I say, looking for a sign from him, waiting for his eyes to look up to see me in the mirror. He turns the sink off, dries his hands then leans into her, never looking at me at all.

182

"I had a bit of a fight. Hockey thing. I'm okay. Emma stitched me up," he lies, kissing the top of her head.

My eyes sting with jealous tears as his mouth touches her hair.

"Oh my god, are you okay?" Lindsey says, quickly working her hands to appraise his wounds on her own. He flinches and steps away, but not far.

"Sorry, sore. But I'm okay. I promise. I just promised I'd come by. I didn't want you to worry. I'm going to go home, clean up, and maybe knock myself out for the night," he chuckles.

"Sure, yeah. I mean...you can stay..." She's still taking all of him in.

"Thanks, but I'll be better company tomorrow," he says, touching the side of her face gently. His touch is tender. His performance is flawless. His instant hold on me is painful—but it's real. And I hate Lindsey right now. I hate her so much.

She walks him to the door, and I start to follow behind, but my legs only carry me a few steps before they stop, like I've reached my limit—this is as far as I get to go on this journey.

They say a few things to one another, half whispering, and she begins to close the door as he leaves. His hand grabs the edge, though, and his gaze looks over her right to where I am, his eyes saying we have more to say—both of us.

We do. I do. *I have scars, too, Andrew. They aren't evil like yours. Mine are miracles. But you need to know.*

"Thanks for the stitches, Emma." His voice is calm, his mouth a faint smile—all of it...*fake.*

The door closes, and Lindsey begins speaking. I nod and respond, but I never once hear a single word. I pretend. I keep on pretending.

And when Graham sends me a text just to make sure everything is okay, I tell him it is, pretending for his sake too.

Because the lie is so much happier than the truth, and I only know a sliver of it.

Chapter 13

Andrew

I got sent home from work this morning. Seems the school doesn't really want the people showing up to hang out with little kids in the morning to look like they just got the shit kicked out of them. I told them it was a hockey fight. It got me a pat on the back from the principal and a promise that he'd have to come watch me play sometime.

I still got sent home though. Whatever. I had eight grand in my pocket and could afford losing out on the ten dollars I'd get from coloring princess posters and playing kickball this morning.

Trent was asleep by the time I returned last night, and I always leave well before he's awake. So far, I've managed not to have to deal with any of the shit on my body or in my brain. But hooray for busted lip and swollen eye! I got sent home early, and Trent is sitting on the sofa slurping the milk from his cereal, eying me, ready to make me work.

"Dude. You look like hell," he says in between slurps. The bowl finally empty, he slides it in front of him on the coffee table. He's going to just leave it there. I know it. I stare at it until he rolls his eyes, stands, and carries the bowl into the kitchen.

"You're like a fuckin' chick sometimes, you know that?" He actually rinses it and puts it in the dishwasher, which makes me proud. If I'm like a chick, he's like a Labrador. Only, Labs learn faster.

"Let me get this straight: You're calling me a woman because I don't want to live like a homeless man in shit and filth?"

His sigh in response is overexaggerated, and it makes me laugh.

"You're trying to distract from the point...and hey...*shit and filth?* Come on, it's a dirty bowl. Hardly a crack house," he says, collapsing back into his spot on the sofa, staring up at me, hands folded on his chest.

The shrink is in.

I rub my hand over my chin, and it hurts like hell. Trent chuckles at me.

"Do you want me to ask questions? Or...do you just want to tell me why in the hell you look like this?"

I hold his stare for a few seconds, because shit...maybe I want the ease of just saying *yes* or *no* to his questions. I shrug, shaking my head, and take the chair opposite him, turning it backward and laying my arms over the back, my forehead resting on them so I can shut my eyes. I'm exhausted.

"Did Emma do this to you? Or that Harley dude?" he asks.

"Neither of them *did* anything to me, ass monkey," I say, not bothering to look up.

"Okay," he says, his pause long and quiet and...why isn't he talking? I glance up to find him staring at me, his brow pulled forward, his mouth a hard line.

"Coach isn't going to like this," he says.

"Whatever. It's not like I'm you," I shrug.

Dick thing for me to say, but it's true. I'm the guy people expect to show up looking like this. Trenton is the face of the team. I'm just the guy who the crowd loves seeing get thrown in the box.

"Look, I can sit here and play twenty questions and never get close to what's actually going on with you. How about you try this friendship thing out and maybe trust me with some shit, huh?" He leans forward, resting his elbows on his knees. I laugh and look away, but I can feel him looking. I turn back to see his face serious, so I lower my gaze, maybe a little ashamed.

Digging into my pocket, I pull out the envelope from my fight, holding it in front of me for a second before finally tossing it on the table between us. Trent watches it land in front of him, glances to me again, then looks back to it, pulling it in his hands. His eyes react when he opens the fold and sees how many hundreds are stuffed inside. He closes it quickly, tossing it back on the table before running his hands over his face. He can't seem to bring his eyes to me now, and I know it's because he's thinking the worst.

"I need to know. Did you do something...illegal to end up with this?" What he means—is *am I selling drugs.*

"No...not...not really," I shake my head. It's not really legal, but my end...well it gets sketchy. I'm just doing a job. I get offered a fight and a purse. I do my thing; I go home with money. I'm not hurting anyone.

"Not really...as in you are just like...what...a middle man?" Trent's voice grows louder, and he's rubbing his hands together nervously. I can sense his temper, his patience waning.

I pull my face up to really look at him, my hands gripping the back of the chair. "Do I *look* like a middle man?" I say, arms out, my beaten body as evidence. "I fight sometimes. For money. Harley...he pays me," I say.

Trent flinches, not expecting that answer.

"So you're, what...like a boxer? Are you any good?"

"I can take a punch," I say. "That's why he books me. I'm like a practice fight for his real guys."

"So you get paid to get the shit beat out of you?"

I nod slowly, letting my eyes drift back to the table, to the stack of cash peaking out from the yellow envelope.

"Yep," I say, chewing at the inside of my mouth.

"Wow," he says quietly. Slowly. He leans forward again and picks up the envelope, really flipping through this time. His eyes flash as the number he's counting grows higher. "So...the worse shape you're in, the bigger the payday? Is that how this works?"

He chuckles, handing me my money. I lean back and stuff it back into my pocket.

"Nah. Last night was sort of special. I fought a guy that's sort of a big deal. Paid my tuition," I say.

"That guy...he gave you that?" he asks, pointing to my crusty brow, the dark stitches sticking out. I touch it, and immediately think of Emma. I nod in response.

"Does Harley just stitch you up then?" he asks.

I purse my lips, tilting my head to the side.

"I...uh...I had *Emma* do this," I say, finger back on her handy work.

Trent starts to laugh slowly, standing as it grows to a full belly laugh, the kind that makes him start to cough. He walks into the kitchen and pulls a bottle of water from the fridge, guzzling half of it before finally calming himself down enough. My life is funny to him.

"Emma," he repeats. I just nod.

"Not...what was her name?" He's being an ass now.

"Her name is Lindsey. You know her name. Stop," I say, standing, done with my little session. I flip the chair around and walk toward my room.

"A'right, a'right. I'm sorry. You're right. I'm helping, listening—go on, give me the story behind that part. Emma...you said she's the girl. This is *the* girl? The one who you went to that group home for or whatever?"

"It wasn't a group home. It was more like a reform school. And yeah...same Emma," I say, folding my arms, protecting my heart. "Long story short, I took the fall for her, then I never heard from her again."

"Oh that shit ain't cool," Trent pipes in. At least he's on my side for this. I hold up a hand to spare him.

"Yeah, that's sort of what I always thought, except..." I pause, shutting my eyes for a beat, picturing her face as I told her, as she filled in the gaps, as her heart broke hearing my pain. "Turns out she never knew. She thought I was just gone. I don't know where, but just...gone. Not in some shit-hole wannabe prison getting the shit kicked out of me on a daily basis."

"Oh...damn, bro," Trent says, leaning forward to lean on the counter across from me.

"Yep," I say, mouth tight. "Damn. Or damned. Whatever."

I walk away and leave my friend with the synopsis of my hell. I toss my envelope on my bed along with my keys and whatever other crap I've collected in my pocket. I look around at the blankness of my room, the walls and dresser top void of anything personal. I don't have anything personal. I've kept my life sterile. I don't even have a favorite...*anything!*

Except my car. I have that back.

And maybe I sort of have Emma back too. If I want her...

Do I want her?

Can I forgive her?

Is there really something to forgive anymore?

Letting go is proving harder than it should be. Or maybe it's as difficult as I wanted it to be. I spent years building up the walls and anger—turning them into weapons against the *Emmas* of the world so I'd never fall victim to one again. To find out I did it all in vain—I just don't know if I'm ready to believe that either. I don't know what to believe. I've held on to that sourness, that poison, for so long that my insides aren't sure what to do without it there.

I could fill it, though. I could fill it with her, with what we were supposed to be before that night ruined everything.

But would she even have me? Like this. What I am now? A hollow version of the boy my brother and mom spent years trying to protect to keep me whole and light and hopeful. One night was all it took to make my heart dark. One night, and a year of having my bones broken, my skin burned, my spirit shattered by an evil man and a group of boys just as damaged as I am.

She didn't know. She said she didn't know. Then she said she would have...what? Stopped me? Would I have let her? It's easy to say that now. Sorry is a word. Actions...those are harder.

But maybe...maybe if she showed me something, a piece of who she was. Maybe if I knew she really cared.

"Hey. Let's go hit the ice," Trent says behind me, snapping me out of my self-pity and dangerous self-diagnosis. He's holding my stick and my gear bag. His face is erased of everything I just told him. I stare at the stick in his grip, laughing lightly to myself. I just got my face tore up in a boxing ring and I want to make everything better by crashing my teammates into glass.

"I'll drive," I say, grabbing my bag from him and passing him in the hallway, my keys pressed in my palm.

"Hey, maybe I can take it for a test run sometime? You know...just up to the arena or whatever..." I stop at the door and laugh, then look at him over my shoulder, my lip raised. He already feels stupid for asking.

"No fucking way in hell," I say, and I swing the door wide enough for him to follow me out, admiring my car on the road. In this mountain of shit I'm sinking in, that car makes me smile.

Maybe I'll get Emma in it just once...for old time's sake. Just to see how she looks here, in our past, in what we almost were. Maybe I can try *us* on.

I drive away a little faster, and I notice Trent's smirk as I peel out.

Emma

I don't know how I knew he'd be here. I just knew. I had to find a way to see him alone—without Lindsey. I need to know more. He needs to know more. And this need—it isn't about my friend. Even though she's precisely the reason I shouldn't be here.

I've compounded this sham of Andrew and I not knowing one another to the point that there's no escaping losing her friendship if it blows up now. No matter how I look at it, I've lied.

I lied to the girl who helped me bury my mother.

I suck in a deep breath, letting the cold harden my lungs—maybe my heart a little, too, just so I can hide it from the guilt brought on by thinking of Lindsey.

The Tech arena is colder than the one back home. It's nicer here, too. The rink is surrounded by stands, different from the few bleachers that press up to the glass in Woodstock. I see his name on the marquee by the door. It isn't one of the ones up top. It isn't even in the middle. But it's the first one I see.

I hear him before I see him, his voice carrying across the ice, his laughter—*his laughter.* I pause and take a seat in the front row on the opposite end, just so I can watch as he slides back and forth effortlessly, his stick working against his teammates, the ease with which he steals the puck away, the speed he shows when he chases—when he leads.

That vision right there, the man I'm looking at out there on this ice—that's *my* Andrew. He rushes once more, the puck loose and coming toward me, and he stops hard right in front of me, his face looks up, his eyes finding mine at the last second. He's breathing hard, and at first, it's because he's out of breath. But then he stops and stares at me a while longer, still breathing rapidly. That...that's because of *us.*

189

"Hey, Trent! Give me a sec, 'kay?" he yells to his friend still skating on the other end with a few of the guys. Trent nods and begins lining up pucks on the ice to take shots over and over again.

I follow Andrew along the other side of the glass toward the opening. He's wearing a dark beanie and his team jersey with a dark knit shirt underneath. Even the way he's dressed reminds me of the boy he was, the man he should be.

"Hey," I say. All this time, the walk here, the time thinking about coming here this morning, the hours awake last night, and the best I can come up with is *hey.*

"Hey," he says back, making me laugh. He grins, dimples denting both cheeks as he lowers his head and looks down at his skates. He's a solid foot taller than me right now.

"How'd you know I'd be here?" he asks, looking at me sideways, his lip curled on one side of his mouth. I like him better like this—happy. Or at least *not* angry. He isn't being mean.

"You used to go to the rink at home...you know...when you were stressed, or whatever," I say, my bottom lip tucked in my teeth, my face flushing from his closeness. I'm assuming he's stressed. I'm stressed. Last night, what he told me—that was a hell of a lot of stress-inducing crap, surely.

"Yeah," he says, leaning against the opening from the ice. "Some things don't change, I guess."

His gaze lingers on me after he says this, his smile subtle...special. Different. I wish I knew what he was thinking.

"I was hoping...maybe...we could talk a little? I...I don't know. I just...last night? I have so many questions. And I thought..." I'm stammering, my stomach all twisted and my confidence suddenly nonexistent. I'm afraid he thinks I'm being silly, that I'm being a child. That I got all the answers I deserve and that's where it all ends.

"I'd like that," he breaks into my thoughts, dipping his head lower to force my gaze back up to his. "I would *really* like that," he repeats, and this time he's wearing a real smile, a full one.

"It doesn't have to be now. You have practice, and your friend is here..."

"Nonsense," he laughs, cutting me off. "Yo, Trent! You know Emma, right?"

His friend holds a hand up to wave. I wave back, still blushing.

"I'm gonna take off so we can go talk. You okay with that?" he yells over the ice.

"I think that's the first smart thing you've done in a week," his friend yells back.

"Real nice, Trent. Real nice," Andrew laughs, his hand finding the back of his neck as he shakes his head, but peers up at me. This is his version of embarrassed. I remember it, too.

"Give me a few minutes, and I'll meet you by the front doors," he says. His eyes stay on me, and his mouth is in this forever-quirked smile, small enough to erase, but there.

I nod and walk to the front lobby where I came in and spend a few minutes looking over the plaques and trophies and clippings in the case along the wall. There's only two photos of Andrew in the bunch—one the team photo, and another a clip of him from the school paper, the picture of his face looking busted and bruised, just like last night. The headline reads HARPER THE BRUIN'S BRUISER. It makes me smile.

"That was after the opener, against Southern. I spent a lot of time in the box," he shrugs.

"I bet it makes the other team think twice about being aggressive," I say, giving him an excuse for being rough on the ice. He seems embarrassed by it, but smiles sheepishly when I say that.

"Yeah, that's sort of my job. I'm like the guy they put in the basketball game just to foul out," he chuckles.

I don't look at him, but I catch his eyes in the reflection in the glass in front of us. It feels easier to look at him this way, even when he's looking back.

"So, you hungry? I skipped breakfast," he says.

"Uhm, yeah...I could eat," I say, my chest suddenly feeling tighter.

"Come on," he says, nodding toward the front door. I look away from his reflection, to the real him, and I follow him out, walking a few steps behind, watching his form. His body is still bruised, but the swelling in his face is gone. His shoulders are broader, his T-shirt clinging to his back, his jeans loose around his waist. His feet are in flip-flops, sliding along the ground.

"We can go somewhere close. I don't want you to have to carry your bag far," I say.

He chuckles.

"Nah, let's go get pancakes at Estos," he says. Estos is far, maybe a half an hour away, which means I'll be with him for most of the morning, alone, away from my roommate, who's sort of dating him, I think...

"Oh no, it's okay, close is fine," I say, fumbling to make an excuse, to stay near home base, to keep the option of backing out of this crazy idea if I want to. I stop talking, though, when I notice his car parked in the lot. Suddenly breathing becomes hard, and that night comes crashing over me—the lights flashing, the man on the road, my hands numb, my eyes burning, my future gone.

My lips open with a gasp, and I suck in a hard breath.

"My heart..." I say, my words almost a whisper, my voice cracking and stopping before I say too much.

"Huh?" he asks, turning and seeing me. He drops his bag and reaches for my hand when he fully takes me in. "Shit. Shit, shit, shit...I'm so sorry, Emma. I thought you'd like to see it, my car, all fixed up. I just got it back, and I was excited. I didn't even think about what...I...I just didn't think."

I look down, my fingertips in his palm, his other hand on my arm. It's a cautious touch, but he did it so fast—on instinct.

He's always acting on instinct...for me.

"I'm...I'm okay," I pant. "It's weird, I haven't panicked like that in a while. I'm fine, really," I stammer, my mind catching up to the words I said, the admission that I once panicked. Five years ago, the panic came often, hitting me when I least expected it—sparked by seeing a fire truck race by, from riding in a car through the woods or sometimes a nightmare. I'm not sure when it began to fade, but one look at his car brought those feelings screaming back to the surface.

Andrew keeps his fingers loosely tangled with mine, and his eyes move down to where our hands are touching as he peels his hold away one finger at a time. I feel sadder with each finger that leaves my hand. Everything gets colder. It feels like...loss.

"Okay, if you're sure." His voice is quiet, and his face is wearing a mix of disappointment and worry.

"Yeah, I'm good." I push my lips together and force a smile, begging my stomach to stop clenching.

I move to the passenger side and pause, looking to him before I tug on the handle.

"Owen...he had it fixed," he smiles.

I grin back, then glance down at the handle again, still swimming in memories. Some of them, though...are good.

"So you mean I don't get you opening the door for me like a gentleman anymore," I smirk. I'm flirting. I shouldn't be flirting. It's my nerves.

Andrew stops at his door, pulling it open but leaning over the top of the car, both hands flat on the surface as he stares at me, one eyebrow raised.

"I will open doors for you anytime, Emma Burke," he says, the left side of his lip raised as he chews at the inside of his cheek. His eyes are soft, and smiling with his lips, then he taps the roof of the car once and climbs in. I do as well.

Andrew is flirting back. I swallow hard.

Inside the car is almost worse than outside. While the gashes, poor paint and other exterior things are all gone from the outside, covered in a fresh coat of slick, racing black and polish, the inside is still the same—still packed with memories everywhere I look. I focus intently on my seatbelt, on pulling it tight, on the vents in front of me. I tuck my purse between my feet and squeeze, focusing on the feel of my muscles pushing against it. I focus on anything I can that isn't the feel of my legs on Andrew's lap, my lips on his, his hands around my waist—and the crash.

"Are you sure? We could walk," he says, the keys perched at the ignition, his hand gripping the wheel, his head tilted to the side, eyes bruised, but looking so full of hope.

"I'm okay," I exhale, letting my body relax a little. I glance to the side of his face, then smile bigger. "And you still have holes in your ears."

His head falls forward on the wheel, and he laughs hard as he turns the engine over. "Yes, Emma. Yes, I do," he says, continuing to laugh as he looks over his shoulder and pulls us out onto the road.

He drives slowly, always five miles slower than the limit, and he doesn't speak. He's being careful and cautious for me. He doesn't have to say so; I know he is. The first ten minutes in the car with him is nothing but silence, even the radio on a gentle hum. Looking at it, I doubt it can go any louder. I laugh to myself because I doubt Andrew even likes the slow rock music that's playing. My mind is racing with all of the questions I still have, but I don't know how to start them.

Every now and then, he glances to me, then back to the road. Each look is full of an *almost*—a question, an answer. Finally, one comes.

"Where..." he starts, but stops, his tongue held between his teeth as his eyes squint into the distance ahead. "Damn, I don't know why it's so hard to talk to you. It's hard, though. Is it hard for you?"

He glances at me, swallows once, then looks back to the road. I suck in my bottom lip, nodding. "Yeah, it is," I admit. "But maybe, now that we've said it, it won't be so hard?"

He chuckles, flexing his hands along the steering wheel, moving them to the top then around the sides, lengthening his arms into a stretch. I imagine his arms around me again, then just as quickly work to force that vision out of my head. "I'm pretty sure it's still hard to talk to you, Emma," he sighs.

I feel sad when he says this. We used to talk. That was our one thing—or at least it was on his end. He could talk to me, and I listened, never judging. He told me about his father, about James. I regret that I kept so much from him.

"You said *where*. Where what? Ask me, Andrew. Let's get through this...whatever it is," I say.

He smiles, glancing over his shoulder a few times as we merge onto the highway toward the next town over. "I'm not ready for *where*. That's a big question. I need to work up to it. How about...how about I start with a *who*," he says, the right corner of his mouth twisted with his pause, still unsure.

"Okay, who. Go for it," I say, just happy we're talking more easily.

"Who's the guy who walked you home the other day?" he asks. My chest constricts a little, like someone just jumped out from a corner to scare me. I'm not sure why, because Graham isn't really anything...yet. He's my mentor's son, which I guess makes him...complicated.

"He's just a guy," I answer. The lamest reply possible, and it takes Andrew all of half a second to call me on it.

"Just. A. Guy." He laughs once, the sharp belly kind, then clicks the blinker to exit the highway, the sign for Estos standing above a hill. "Okay. We'll go with that for now. I'll let you have that one."

I sigh lightly, watching out the window as we pull in to a space near the door. Andrew cuts the engine, but sits still, watching families and old couples walk in and out of the restaurant.

"There really isn't much more to say," I say, feeling defensive. I can't really explain who Graham is without connecting him to how we met.

Andrew nods, then steps out of the car, leaving the door open, his feet on the pavement outside, but his body still inside with me.

"Where do you think I went?" he asks, his back to me. Everything about him is suddenly deflated, his shoulders lowered, his head sunken. "You said you didn't know where I went. You didn't know about Lake Crest. Where...where was I in your world?"

"Iowa," I answer quickly.

His body rises with a silent laugh, his shoulders raising once, but dropping back into sadness.

"Iowa," he repeats, standing slowly, turning and leaning into the car. "Come on. Let's go eat."

His door closes, and I take this small moment in his car alone to *gasp*, letting my body make a small sound, a short cry, so I don't do it in front of him. Then I get out and step around the car, joining him at the front door to the restaurant. He steps in front of me, pulling the door open, his head tilted to the side as I step through.

"Just a guy, huh?" He smirks. We look at each other, his hand finding my back as he guides me inside and I pass him, his touch gentle, but purposeful. I let him. I relish it. And I know I won't be able to let it go.

The hostess guides us to a booth in the back of the restaurant. It's away from the front windows, away from the view of his car. I'm glad. Looking at it is hard.

The waitress takes our order quickly. We both order a short stack and a coffee. When she walks away, Andrew sets his eyes on me squarely, his head leaning slightly to one side. I look back into his eyes, holding on as long as I can. It feels like a game of chicken, and eventually I lose, moving my attention to the rolled up silverware and napkin in front of me. I unravel it and move my knife and fork to the side, unfolding my napkin and spreading it on my lap. When I glance down at my hands, I realize just how badly they're shaking. Then Andrew's foot finds mine under the table, his shoe tapping into mine. It makes me laugh.

"There she is," he says. I let out one more breathy laugh, and it mixes with a cry. I choke it down quickly, before he can see.

I rub my hands on my cheeks, thankful when the waitress comes to quickly fill our coffee mugs. I thank her and go to work adding creams and sugars to my cup.

"Wow," Andrew chuckles. "That might be the unhealthiest cup of coffee I've ever seen."

I nod in agreement.

"I'm a little high strung," I shrug, blowing over the top of the liquid before attempting a sip. It's hot, so I set the cup in front of me to let it cool.

"Yeah, I'm sure the seven packs of sugar and liquid fat will totally help calm you down," he jokes.

"Feed the beast," I say with a shake of my head.

He chuckles at me, then pulls his arms up to rest his elbows on the table, leaning his face into one hand. His eyes haven't left me once in the last five minutes.

"I was in Iowa," he says finally. My eyes lower and my brow pinches as I try to understand. "Not at first, but after...when I got out of Lake Crest. I moved to Iowa with my uncle."

Every new piece he shares from his life fills these missing gaps in my world of Andrew Harper. Some of the things he says erase what I thought, strike out the story I'd believed and replace it with something sadder. He's careful when he shares, too—like he's testing me a little each time to see how I react. I think he's wondering if I care. He has no idea how much I do.

I care. I care, and it feels so dangerous to let myself, like caring about him could topple over so many other things that lay in the balance. This is how it's always been with us—our feelings on a teeter-totter.

"When did you move there? To Iowa?" I ask, hoping he says it was only a few weeks after the accident, that he wasn't at Lake Crest for long. I don't want my parents to have lied to me.

"Junior year," he says. His eyes are hard, almost stoic. His foot slides away, and I'm tempted to chase it. Instead, I bring my legs up to the booth, folding them under me.

A test.

"So you were at Lake Crest...for a year?" My eyes sting, but I hold in my cry. My mind races through memories of my mom, how she told me my dad went to look for Andrew, how they were told he was with family in another state. So. Many. Lies.

"Ten months, really. I came home at the end of spring, sophomore year," he says, pulling one of my empty sugar packets from the center of the table and folding the small paper into a fan pattern.

"Sophomore year," I repeat. He was home. And he never came to see me. My parents lied. And Andrew gave up too quickly. I shudder in the booth, and I know he sees it. His eyes flinch and his gaze lowers as he continues to study me; he's waiting to see if I'm pretending. "Why didn't you visit me? Before you left."

He shrugs quickly and pushes the small folded paper off to the side, running his palms over the table, clearing the few grains of sugar away that had spilled out.

"You'd moved on," he says, his eyes moving up to meet mine briefly. I gaze at him, my forehead low, not understanding. His teeth hold on to his top lip for a second. "You never wrote back," he finally adds.

I breathe in hard, holding my words while our waitress delivers our breakfasts. When she leaves, I let myself move beyond that silent barrier that's been making everything this morning so difficult, that wall that's been keeping us both from saying things.

"I never got your letters. Not once. I didn't know, Andrew. I didn't know. If I had known…"

He shakes his head, turning his attention to his pancakes, pouring syrup, cutting vigorously, stuffing a bite in his mouth. "It wouldn't have mattered," he shrugs.

How can he say that? It would have mattered. I wondered about him, worried about him, wanted to see his face for so long. I wanted his hand in mine when I was scared. I wanted him there—in the hospital when they cut me open.

Feeling brave, I reach over to his side of the table and put my hand on his, stopping him from lifting another bite.

"It would have," I say, staring at him, begging him to look back at me. He keeps his eyes trained on his plate in front of him, his muscles flexed and his arm still beneath the weight of my hand. I don't know why he's so against believing me.

"I drove by your house," he says, his lips paused open. His eyes finally move up to meet mine. "At the start of our junior year. You were getting ready for some dance, your parents were taking pictures. You were wearing this really nice dress. You had a date—some guy who looked like the kind of guy you *should* be going to a dance with. I'm just a fuck up."

"Don't say that," I swallow.

Our eyes remain on one another.

"Why not?" he asks.

"Because…" I start, not knowing how to explain everything Andrew has been in my life. He vanished, but the mark he left was a forever kind. His sacrifice for me so big, he has no idea how enormous. And now that I know what he went through…

"How many times did you write to me?" I ask instead.

198

He shakes his head and goes back to his breakfast, shrugging once.

"How many?" I repeat. My voice is more forceful the second time, and maybe a bit desperate.

His lips purse and he puts down his fork, pulling his napkin from the table to wipe his lips. "I don't know. Twenty maybe. Maybe more."

I gasp, pushing my plate away, holding my napkin to my mouth to hide my reaction from him.

He sighs, closing his eyes for a second, then he slides from the booth, stepping around to my side where he moves in next to me. My breathing stops with the feel of his body next to mine. And then his arm reaches around me, and everything strong inside collapses as I give in and lean into him to cry.

"I didn't know," I say again. It's all I have to give. I didn't know. He must hate me.

Andrew doesn't respond, but the feel of his hand as it cups my shoulder then slides up to reach into my hair, his fingers on the side of my head, threading my hair and sliding it from my instant-tear-strewn face, is enough.

"I didn't know," I whisper once more.

The waitress comes after a few minutes, and Andrew reaches into his pocket, pulling out his wallet and sliding a twenty on the table. His arm never leaves its hold around me.

"We're good. Keep the change," he says.

She walks away, and he remains in the spot next to me, his breathing slow and regular, his hand tender against me.

"Come on. Let me get you home," he finally says, his head leaning against mine as he speaks. I nod slowly. When his arm leaves from my body, the air rushes around me. The feel left behind can only be described as sickness.

I feel sick.

Andrew stands at the end of our table, waiting while I slide from the booth to follow behind him.

"Thanks for the breakfast," I say.

He laughs lightly.

"You didn't eat a thing. And you didn't even get to enjoy your fatty-ass coffee," he says. When I glance up at him, his crooked smile is waiting for me. "I think I owe you one."

I smirk back, but start to feel the sting of tears again. Andrew steps in to halt them.

"Come on," he says, running his hand down my arm until he finds my fingers, grasping them tightly. He squeezes just to let me know he's not letting go, then walks with me next to him, guiding me through the restaurant and back to his car, where he walks to my side to open the door.

"Thought maybe this was one of those times I should open the door for you," he says. My breath stutters from my body, almost feeling painful. I slide into my seat and let him close the door for me. I watch him rush around to his side, then wait while he starts the engine, buckles his belt and pulls away from the restaurant.

I'm lost in a world of *what-ifs* and other questions for most of the ride home, and I hardly realize how far we've travelled when Andrew wakes me from my trance.

"Who told you I was in Iowa?" he asks nervously. He's worried about upsetting me more. All this time—these years he must have thought the worst of me—and he's worried about how *I* feel now.

"My mom. She said my dad asked your family…" I drift off at the memory. I was in a hospital bed, terrified, wanting everything that ever made me feel secure to be in that room with me as doctors cracked open my chest. The realization of it all weighs on my shoulders, my head feels heavy and my body feels numb. "They lied…my parents…they lied."

I glance at Andrew, and his hands flex as they grip the steering wheel, his jaw tightening as he swallows. He looks to me, but only briefly before turning back to the road.

"Are your parents still there? In that house? I…haven't driven by since the last time I saw you." His eyes rake over me once again, and I wonder what he must have seen. I remember that day—it was homecoming our junior year. My mother had bought me a pink dress that showed my bare shoulders, but covered my chest completely. I had been worried about people

200

seeing my scar. It was the most expensive dress I'd ever owned, but she didn't care about the price tag. She wanted me to experience something normal and not have to worry about what people saw. I found out about her cancer the day after the dance.

"My dad lives in Woodstock still. He put the house up for sale...after my mom died. But it's not an easy sale. He's still there," I say.

Andrew sinks deep into his seat, his hands running down the wheel to rest at the bottom. He glances out his side window and sighs. "I'm sorry," he says. "I didn't know."

"There's no way you could have," I say.

The bridge between us is so small and fragile. I hate to say anything more for fear that it will wash it all away. For so long, he was gone. And then he was only a wound—something that left me feeling hopeless. Maybe something I also tried to forget. I didn't mean to. I think I just *had* to forget him, or at least hide him from my heart. It wasn't right—and my heart, it knew he was there all along anyhow. The guilt over what he'd done for me, it was always tempting me, begging me to feel. All it took was seeing him to bring it back to life. And now that I know...*now that I know!* Right now, thanks to our words, secrets finding the surface—Andrew feels close; I can't lose him, even what little of him I have.

I'll take what little I have, whatever he'll give.

We pull up in front of my building, and my shoulders sag from the weight of everything else I wish I had the courage to say. I want more time—more mornings like this one. I want to travel back five years ago and fix things. I want to have known the truth then, to have gotten to decide for myself. And I want Lindsey not to be tangled in with our story. She is, and because she is, I'm slightly paralyzed. But my heart...it's still reeling after his words. And at the very least, there are some things he deserves to know...things he deserves to hear.

"Thank you for the ride," I say, grabbing my purse, clutching it to my chest. *Be brave, Emma. Be brave.* My heart is pounding underneath my grip. I close my eyes tightly, willing myself to get one thing out—to be raw and honest just once. "And thank you for what you did for me, Andrew—that night, for taking my place. You saved my life. You'll never know, and I'm so sorry that I didn't know, and I'm so angry right now that I can't even think clearly. But...just...you were always my angel. Just please know that. There hasn't been a night that's passed that I haven't wished for you to show up at my window just so I could tell you that," I say, my words falling out fast, my lips quivering, my hands shaking, my body sweating and flushed.

Somewhere in the middle of everything, I start to cry. My cheeks burn with embarrassment, and I blow air out through my lips, trying to regain my center, my world tilting just from the way he looks sitting there. I want him to look at me. I want him to tell me it's okay, that what he went through wasn't so bad. But he can't, because *that* would be a lie. Nothing is okay. None of what happened is all right—and Andrew is ruined because of it...because of me! My selfishness ruined him. My broken heart broke his—and I have to live with that.

"I just need you to know that one thing," I speak, my voice strained as I try to hold the meltdown that is seconds away at bay. "And I'm sorry if I didn't say it well or if I sound crazy right now. I think maybe I might be a little." I laugh and cry at the same time, my eyes falling closed. I'm losing it—cracking up. "I can't even look at you, I'm so embarrassed and scared, but...okay. Yeah. Just...you." I pause, breathing in deeply, looking down into my own hands that are clinging to each other. "Andrew, everything would have been different. I swear."

I glance up at him once before I pull the door handle and push the door open. His eyes are intent on his knuckles, and his grip in front of him is tight, his hands wringing on the leather of his steering wheel. He nods once slowly, but doesn't turn to face me.

I don't know if this is still him testing me, to see how far I'll go, how many speeches I'll make. I don't have anything left, though. This was all I had. And the fact that it might not be enough, that Andrew will still hate me, resent me—it feels so unbelievably unfair. Yet when I think of what he went through, it doesn't seem my punishment is harsh enough.

My feet are shaky on the ground as I step from his car, and I walk around the back because I can't bare the thought of him seeing me pass in front of him. I'm afraid I might fall. My face feels red, and the only thing I can think about is how I'm going to get the courage to ask my father why he lied to me, why Mom lied. My legs are tingling with energy, and I feel like I do when I dream—when my limbs want to run, but somehow they just can't.

One foot in front of the next, I watch the ground before me, not realizing that Andrew hasn't pulled away. I don't look back, and I don't see him coming, but his hand soon glides up my back, startling me. I gasp as I turn quickly, dropping my purse at my feet, my phone sliding from it, my lipstick rolling down the walkway into the dead grass, my medicine rolling next to it. I move on instinct to pick everything up, but Andrew's hands find my face quickly, his thumbs on my cheeks, his palms cupping my face. Soon his forehead is on mine, and he's breathing hard.

"Andrew," I whisper, my hands clutching the sides of his shirt. My eyes flutter closed as our heads rest together. He licks his lips once, grimacing from pain, his bruises still apparent and his wounds still fresh. His mouth opens in a hard breath.

"It was always you," he says, his body shuddering as he rocks us side to side, his thumbs tracing my cheeks softly until one finds my lips. I let out a sharp breath at his touch, as the pad of his thumb slides over my bottom lip. Surely he can feel it shaking. My entire body is pulsing, the sound of my heartbeat loud in my ears, filling my head, drowning all reason. "It was worth it...for you."

His head tilts up just enough that his lips graze mine, our touch almost a tickle as his bottom lip passes over mine, his breath slow against me as his forehead rests heavy. "Emma," he breathes, his whisper against my mouth. "So long...I wanted...I waited."

My eyes flutter open then drift closed again, something awakening in me from his touch. My body rushes with heat as he steps in closer to me, his hold on me firmer, his breathing more steady.

Years begin to dissolve, and my heartbeat feels strong and steady.

Then music begins to play at my feet. It's Lindsey's ringtone—alarms sounding off, calling off mistakes, stopping accidents. This is my chance to stop hurting people, to *not* make things worse. I step back and Andrew's grip tightens, his body feeling panicked. We both look down and see her name.

I kneel down, and Andrew steps back a pace, his hands falling to his sides, his eyes wide.

I hold my ringing phone in my hand, then look up at him, his sad eyes saying everything that's in mine.

"Hey," I answer the phone, never breaking my gaze at Andrew, who keeps his eyes on mine as well.

"Hey, I'm at the library. I need to finish up a research project, but I'm starving. Wanted to see if you wanted to grab lunch before our lab?" Lindsey's voice is in one world, and I'm in another. Those worlds are so far apart, and one will destroy the other if I let them collide.

"Sure," I say. My eyes stay on Andrew's, my hands wishing they could touch him again, but my head knows they can't. The dull ache starts to creep in slowly. "I'll meet you at the library in half an hour."

Lindsey and I say goodbye, and I push my phone into my purse quickly, no longer able to look up and see Andrew's face. I reach for my lipstick, but before I can grab the rest of my things, he kneels down and takes my pills into his hands. My initial instinct is to grab them back, but my fingers recoil before I do. A few seconds pass, and I know he's reading the long name, wondering what it's for. Eventually he passes the bottle to me, and I stuff it into my purse before zipping it closed.

"Thanks," I say without looking at him. I won't give any hint that that bottle is anything significant, even though when I finally stand and meet his stare, I know the question is just perched on his lips. He doesn't ask it though.

This is one secret I'm not ready to share today. There are too many things, and Andrew's heart has been broken enough without having to add the weight of my story—of what he missed while he was busy being tortured at Lake Crest—to his heavy load of things to bear.

"Lindsey...she's in my lab and wants to meet," I say quietly. He nods. He knows. "Andrew...I..."

He holds up a hand, shaking his head, his lips a deeply unhappy smile.

"It's okay. She's your friend, and I'm..." he pauses, chuckling to himself, "I'm not in the place I should be."

He pulls his keys from one pocket and his beanie from another, tugging his hat over his head and opening his palm for one more wave goodbye as he falls back on his heels, turning to leave. "I'll see you again soon, Emma. There's too much to talk about—me and you?"

I watch him go, wanting to race to him, wrap myself around him, kiss him like I really want to. But I stay in my place, remaining in the lie we've built on Lindsey's behalf, regretting every second of it, and now taking it as my punishment just as I'm sure Andrew is.

His engine fires up, the sound hitting that familiar nerve, but this time I'm able to stop the feeling before it numbs me. I wait to watch him pull away, and he lowers his window, looking ahead, breathing—thinking. Then he leans out the window, urging me to take a few steps closer so I can hear him.

"I said I wasn't in the place I should be," he says over the low idle of his car, licking his lips once, pulling his bottom lip in, chuckling to himself and looking down into his lap. He shakes his head slowly, then peers out the window again, his eyes square on mine, his heart talking to mine now. "What I meant to say was I'm not with the person I should be."

There's an emptiness and fullness that settles over us at the same time—a feeling of hope and hopelessness. We wade in it, breathe it in together, and I want to run back to him, to tell him the rest of my story, to climb back into his car and let him drive us away, not caring if it hurts Lindsey. But my feet stay where they are, and Andrew's hand pats the side of his car, his fingers drumming along the shiny black surface and the gleam of the chrome stripe.

He drives away, and long after he's out of sight, I wait.

I wait for him to come back.

I think I've always been waiting.

205

Chapter 14

Andrew

I should have kissed her anyway. I should have stayed. I should have picked her up in my arms and carried her into her goddamned apartment.

Instead, I drove away, headed right to Harley's gym, and convinced him I was fine, good enough to stand in the ring for an hour with some new guy. This time, though, I hit back. I hit back more than I normally do. I hit back with the force of all of the shit I was feeling. I took out my frustration with Emma, with her parents and the lies they clearly told, with her lack of trying to find out the truth sooner. Was it her job to find out the truth? Would I have if I were in her position?

There's still this part of me that can't help but feel like I was busy thinking about her while she forgot about me completely—while I lost a year of my life and most of my soul.

I took it all out in the middle of Harley's gym on some guy named Taylor. Some frat boy who cleaned up during the campus fight night and thought maybe he'd make a go of it, get himself some sponsors and really try and fight. I'm pretty sure I broke his nose.

Harley was pissed at first, and before I left, I thought he was walking over to tell me to quit showing my crazy face in his gym. Instead, he pulled up a stool and sat silently while I unwrapped my knuckles and packed up my bag, sliding his chair away right before I left, his back to me as he grumbled "that dude isn't ready. Good work, tonight."

Good work. Ha!

I left feeling just as confused and frustrated. I spent the night ignoring the three—*she sent three!*—texts from Lindsey. And then I laid awake, getting to my feet and moving to the door, with every intention of driving to Emma's apartment, before talking myself out of it and throwing my ass back in bed.

The problem is it's not just Emma's apartment. It's Lindsey's, too. I've made things messy. But I haven't slept with Lindsey. I mean...I've *slept* with Lindsey. But that hardly counts. That can't count. Not now that things with Emma are...well, they're different.

I didn't think my hate could give way so easily. I'd spent so many years harboring it, carving it into this delicate weapon to guard myself from ever dreaming again. It turned into vengeance when I saw her in the bar. There was only one thing that could have made a difference, and that was Emma not knowing where I'd been. I don't know why her parents lied to her, and I hold them accountable. My anger—it's shifted in their direction. And I'm a son-of-a-bitch for hating her mom now that she's gone. But I do. I don't know what their motives were, but I'm sure it had to do with everything they thought I was, and the one thing they thought I wasn't—good enough for their daughter.

Sleep might have helped me find reason today. Only, I didn't get any. I spent my morning workout just as pent-up, and now I'm laying here on this bench, rubbing my eyes raw, my cheekbones still bruised and tender from the beating they took two days ago, my heart bruised from the one it took yesterday.

"Better sit up, Harp. Coach is coming," Trent says, throwing his wet towel on my chest. I don't even fight back, letting it drench my shirt and make me feel as miserable on the outside as I do in.

"Your ass better not be hung over," Coach Bishop says, pushing my legs from the bench as he walks by, knocking me off balance. He's the only one on the team who can legitimately kick my ass, even at my scrappiest. I stumble from my resting place and follow him through the lockers to his office, throwing the towel over Trent's shoulders as I pass him.

"Fuck ass!" he yells, shrugging it from his now-wet shirt and shoulders.

"You started it," I chuckle.

"What are you, fucking twelve?" Coach grunts as I turn my attention back to him in his office. "Go on, close the goddamn door."

I do as he says and take my seat. Bishop is one of the country's best college hockey coaches. His NHL career was mediocre, a starter for the Stars and Sharks for a few years, but traded around the country year after year until he finally gave up. He slid into the job at Tech as a favor owed to him by a friend, but he's stayed for a decade thanks to his two hundred wins and forty-six losses.

"What's with your face?" he asks, pulling the toothpick from his lips and using it to point at me. He has this permanent scowl and crinkle around his eyes that makes him look like Popeye.

"Had a little fight. It won't happen again." I'm a fucking liar. Eight grand an hour, it sure as shit better happen again.

He stares at me for a few hard seconds, then leans back in his chair, slowly pulling his feet up on his desk. I'm holding my hands on my kneecaps, my posture straighter than it ever is anywhere else—I'm like a child waiting for my suspension from the principal.

"Don't get yourself hurt. I need your ass on the ice. You're starting," he says.

My shock is a little delayed because at first I start to stand, expecting to leave with my tail between my legs, but then his words register, and I fall back into my seat.

"Starting," I repeat. I don't ask. I know one thing—you don't ask Bishop questions. I just need clarification. I'm not questioning.

"You get punched in your goddamned ears? Yes. Starting," he says. "Your numbers are better than Gilbert, so I need you to spend more time out there on the puck. I need you to keep it out of Northwestern's control next week, and out of Penn's after that. You get that puck, and you get it to Metzger, and we will win it all this year. Now, you think you can do that? Or do you want to go back to spending your time in some stink-ass back alley with a mugger or whatever fuckin' piece-of-shit lie you told me about those bruises on your face?"

I blink for a second.

"No sir. I got it. Get the puck to Trent. Done," I say, standing before I say anything else stupid. "And you're right. I did lie. It was a *big* fight. But you should see the other guy."

I wait for him to laugh. He doesn't. I said something stupid, so I leave before I continue making it worse.

Trent's waiting for me by my locker, so I let him stew in curiosity while I throw my sweatshirt on and pack up my gear. I glance at him, but keep my face hard, letting him believe I got my ass chewed out as he follows me out of the rink, out to the parking lot and finally to the back of my car.

"Well, how bad? Did he suspend you? Please say he didn't suspend you," he asks. I unlock my trunk and throw my bag inside with a thud, closing the trunk and holding my excitement in for a few more seconds while I sigh and turn to face him.

"Do you prefer working a shot based on our offense or would you rather have more breakaways?" I ask. His face is blank at first, and his expression starts out as *what-the-fuck,* then suddenly it hits him.

"You asshole!" he punches my chest.

"Starting, at least through Penn," I smile.

"Hell yes, you are!" Trent slaps my hand, gripping it at our shoulders before he bumps into me. We both walk around our sides and get into the car. I pause before I start it, my mind flashing to Emma for a second, then back to the good news I got this morning. My heart feels lighter, and things suddenly seem clearer. I keep it to myself as I pull away, but in that instant, I decide that tonight's the night I'm honest with Lindsey and go after what I really want, what I've always wanted.

Emma Burke.

It takes Trent and me a few extra minutes to find a spot in the main student lot. I would have just driven back home and left my car there, but Trent's class starts soon, and I didn't want him to be late.

"Dude, why so many people today? Is there some event I don't know about?" I ask, wondering if I missed the memo that the President was on campus today or something.

"It's homecoming. There's a lot of stuff going on along the main mall, like a carnival or some crap. They're giving away free food—people show up for that," he says.

I finally find a spot near the very back of the lot, next to a dumpster, and I make Trent get out while I back in so he can guide me. No way am I scratching my car less than a week since I've had it back. Once I'm in, we both grab our backpacks and start the long walk to the heart of campus, the smell of barbecue pork and burgers overcoming us the closer we get and guiding us in.

"You weren't kidding," I say when we see the line of tents along the main walkway. Beyond the food vendors, there's a stage with some third-rate, campus rock band playing Blink 182. It's slightly appalling, however, the crap band is out-douched by the more pathetic groupies screaming for them along the stage.

"Why don't chicks do that for us?" Trent asks, handing me a pork sandwich from the tent just to the left of him. I bite into it, talking through my full mouth, wiping the small dab of sauce that starts to slip down my chin.

"They don't scream for you? Wow, I mean, I make girls scream all the time...I just figured you did too—"

"You make girls scream, hmmm?" Her voice cuts in, and I choke on my bite while Trent grins. Fucker saw her coming.

"I'm Emma, by the way. I don't think we've ever formally met," she says, shaking Trent's hand. He looks at me as he does, his tongue tucked in the corner of his mouth with his eyebrows raised. By some miracle, he keeps his mouth shut, but he knows I'm gone when it comes to her. He probably knew the second he put the *who* and *where* together over the driver's license I lifted at the bar.

"Emma, nice to meet you. I've heard..." I cough to interrupt him, a warning that he doesn't break the man code—we don't talk about when we talk about chicks. It doesn't work. "I've heard *way* too much about you."

Asshole.

I pinch the bridge of my nose as Trent excuses himself to grab more of the handouts. I open one eye to the vision of Emma sucking in her bottom lip, her cheeks red. I nod slowly, shrugging to admit my guilt.

"Yeah, Trent's my Lindsey," I say with instant regret. Her face falls as she takes a step away; she thinks we're too close now that I've uttered Lindsey's name. Unlike Trent, Lindsey doesn't know the details. They're really nothing alike at all. God, I wish I thought before I spoke. I wish I thought before I acted!

Fuck, I wish I thought before I *thought!*

210

Emma's wearing a dark gray hoodie and tight jeans tucked into boots at her feet, nothing remarkable, yet instantly memorable to me. Her hair is down in waves, the shorter layers up front blowing over her face as she pulls them away, tucking strands behind her ear.

"You know how I first recognized you?" I ask in my haze from looking at her. I'm definitely not thinking now. No...now, I'm feeling.

She shakes her head in tiny movements, her cheeks rounding with a slight smile, her lips closed tight as she works to hold in the effects of my attention. I love her blush. "It was your eyes."

Her lashes lift as her eyes widen when I say this, the silver shining.

"I was obsessed with those eyes when I was sixteen," I say. "I could never forget them."

God, that felt good to say!

We stare at each other for a long moment, and Emma relents to the small giggle building in her chest before looking down at her feet. "Thank you," she says, her voice meek and beautiful. That's the same, too—the timber, the inflections...all of it.

I kick at her toe with my shoe. She kicks back.

"I always liked your shoes," she says, her face falling to the side, her hand coming up to hide her embarrassed look.

My head falls forward, and I stare at my feet, my black Chucks, the same shoes I've owned for years, just a newer pair. Maybe a little bigger.

"They really are my best attribute," I nod, joking. She laughs, her voice a little raspy, maybe sleepy, too, and swings her arm at me, brushing against mine.

"No," she says. I look up at her. I want to kiss her. Her smile fades from a playful one to a serious one—an *honest* one. "That's not your best attribute," she says, her eyes looking as if they're about to cry.

I ache to reach for her, to touch her cheek to stop the sadness from taking over that space around her eyes, when she takes a sharp step back, lengthening the distance between us.

"Graham. Hi," she says nervously.

Just a guy is here.

"Hey, I was looking for you," he says, his eyes making a dominant glance in my direction. I laugh and roll mine.

"We were just checking out the free food," she says, squinting her eyes closed and shaking her head when he looks away. She does this move sometimes when she's uncomfortable—like she's a genie trying to wish the situation away.

"Were you?" he chuckles. This smug ass wipe thinks I'm intimidated by him.

"Yeah," I answer, surprising Emma, her eyes widening fast, caution lights firing behind them. I'm going to ignore that sign. "It's nice...you know...to be able to just *take what you want?*"

The moment that passes between Emma's friend and me is short, but it's filled with threats and lots and lots of *fuck yous.*

"Emma?" He's talking to her, but looking at me. I hate this *just some guy.* "There's this dinner my mom's hosting, her chief of staff and a bunch of other surgeon-types are going to be there. She's fairly insistent that I go, but it won't be any fun on my own. I thought maybe you'd like to join me?"

This guy is so fucking arrogant. He's flaunting his credentials like a peacock. No way Emma falls for this.

"I'd love to," she answers, slicing through the middle of my thoughts, cutting off my immediate assumption that *just some guy* is in fact nobody. She's just made him *somebody.*

"Great," he grins, pushing his hands in his pockets and pivoting on the heels of his shoes in my direction, just to make sure I get a glimpse at his triumphant smile. All I notice are his shoes, though. Shoes that are so irritatingly preppy—all I can visualize is the way they would look underneath the pressure of my Chucks, scuff marks left behind in the shapes of honeycombs.

"Great," Emma finally says in return, her *great* far less enthused. I stare at her. I'm a little baffled over the fact that this is all happening in front of me, especially after the things we've talked about, the progress we made...thought we made.

"So I'll see you tomorrow. I'll come by...around eight," he says, backing away slowly. I notice he never leans in to kiss her cheek. He's not cocky enough to do that. That's probably a good thing, because my hand is flexed at my side, and I think if he did, I'd punch his fucking face in. Then I'd step on his shoes.

I keep my stare on Emma, and when she turns from watching Captain Douchebag saunter away, she meets my gaze, then immediately drops her focus to the ground.

"*Just some guy*, huh?" I laugh.

"His name's Graham, Andrew," she sighs. "And it's not a thing with us, it's just...it's complicated to explain," she shrugs, glancing around me. She can't even make eye contact with me now.

"The dude's named after a cracker, Emma. Seriously?" I look beyond her where I can still see him walking down the main path where he's met up with two other guys that look just like him. He isn't small. In fact, we're probably roughly the same size. He's just covered in so much...douchebaggery...it makes him look smaller. His pants are pink. What the fuck? "I thought we were past this...or that you wanted...shit, I don't know...what I wanted? I thought we..."

"Lindsey's here," she cuts me off. The expression on her face is blank at first then it's instantly replaced by the fakest of smiles. I can tell her expression is a lie, though—her eyes give her away. They're full of regret and wishes. "Whatever you were about to say...don't. Lindsey is here, walking toward us. She's my best friend, Andrew. You started this, and I don't think I can lose Lindsey because of it. She's been through so much with me, and I can't—"

"Hey, I've been looking for you," Lindsey says from behind me. She slides her arm around me, her fingers running over my stomach and chest as she hugs me from behind. Emma turns away, but not before the look of pain flashes over her face. I shut my eyes and breathe deeply.

"Hi, yeah...sorry. I've been crazy busy with practice and classes." Lie, lie, lie. I've been ignoring you, not dealing with the beast I created, running away from my consequences, while I pine after the love of my past and drown in the truth.

"It's okay. I was just worried...you know, about your bruises. Your eye looks better," she says, reaching to touch my cheekbone lightly. It takes all of my willpower not to turn away—not because it hurts, but because I don't want Lindsey touching it. I don't want Emma seeing Lindsey touch it.

"Yeah...I heal quickly," I say, all of my attention on Emma. I'm not even sure I said that last part out loud.

My trance is broken when a yellow Velcro strap slides along the ground, sticking to my leg. I bend down to pick it up as some guy from our student government waves his hands emphatically on the nearby stage, the microphone in his hand.

"And we have our second team of players. You," he shouts, pointing at me. I glance around and look back at him, pointing to myself as he nods. "It's a hundred-dollar bookstore card if you win the three-legged race. Get on up here with your partner."

"I'm good, dude," I say, not wanting to be part of some stupid spirit week activity. But Lindsey changes my mind. Lindsey, of all people, changes everything.

"Oh my god, no...you have to do this. Trust me. You and Emma—she is the freaking master at this. Remember, Em? Last year, at the pre-med picnic? Seriously, it's like she was born for this race. Everyone who was her partner won." Lindsey waves her hand at the stage, buying us time while she urges her friend to join me. If Lindsey only knew.

"I don't really feel up to it, Linds," Emma starts.

"I really could use a hundred bucks credit," I say just for guilt. Suddenly, I'm desperate for her to do this race with me, to come with me, to give me five more minutes of her time. Her eyes slide up to meet mine, and I say something entirely different to her with my look. I beg her. *Please, do this one stupid thing with me. I can't explain it, but I feel like this might be the turn.*

Emma glances back to her friend, who is literally jumping up and down while clapping. She sighs and reaches for the Velcro strap, taking it from me and walking toward the stage. I trail behind, ignoring Lindsey's touch on my back, her encouragement and cheer for me. All I see is the wild strands of Emma's hair twisting in the wind like the fingers of temptation calling me to them.

It's going to storm tonight. I can smell it in the air.

Emma

I hate spirit week. Whose idea was it to have field day anyhow? I'm finding out, then I'm going to sink their campaign when they run for student government again. I might run against them. My platform will be to do away with forced audience participation.

When I get to the chair at the starting line, I sit down, moving my leg as far away from the edge as I can so I don't have to feel him. I can't feel him. Why doesn't he get that? He started this—he's the one who decided to get to me through Lindsey. And she can't be hurt by whatever happens next. It doesn't matter what his reasons were, or what happened in our past.

It's hard to hold on to that promise to myself though when he's right here. I don't know what the scent is that he wears, but it's hypnotic, and it messes with my good sense. I'm convinced that's what makes me weak. It can't be my heart—I can't defeat it if that's the case.

"Okay, contestants, time to strap yourself to your partners," the guy orders through the microphone. Andrew chuckles from somewhere deep in his chest. I glance up and see Lindsey watching us from the other side of the main mall. She's waving and smiling.

Andrew bends down, his hand running down my jeans along my calf as he wraps the Velcro strap around both of our legs. The heat from his body rushes through me instantly followed by more of his scent, and I feel my stomach drop in a free fall. I shut my eyes and breathe out slowly, just trying to survive this, to make the right decision.

"Please...please stop," I breathe, my eyes closing as I slump back into my chair.

His hands freeze against me as his head falls forward.

"I haven't slept with her," he says, his hands moving again to fasten our strap. He remains leaning forward when he's done, not ready to look me in the eye. That's probably for the best because my eyes are wide—I was so *sure* they'd been intimate. Those thoughts, they're the ones that tortured me. To find out that they haven't been *as* intimate as I'd imagined...

"You have to know, Emma. If I'd only known you were in the dark...if you'd only known where I was. Things...they would have gone so differently. I won't even say *could have,* because damn Emma...I know they *would* have. I'm going to talk to Lindsey. I'll tell her everything. Just don't go to that dinner. Please."

His voice is broken. His spirit...broken. The sound of him is desperate, and I can't say it isn't anything different from the feelings within my own heart. But my best friend is staring at me, the smile on her face enormous. And it isn't even the fact that she thinks Andrew is her *one,* or that she has deep feelings for him. It's that she trusts this story we've given her, and if she finds out I was part of the lie, she will never smile at me like that again. And that smile—it's the one that kept my heart beating after I buried my mom.

"If you tell Lindsey the truth, I will never forgive you," I say, my chest burning as the words leave my mouth. How can the heart want two things that are so very far apart?

"Let's go, racers," the announcer calls.

Everyone stands but Andrew and me. I feel his stare burning the side of my face, but I keep my eyes fixed on my friend. I smile at her and raise my hand slowly, my fingers curling. She can't know anything is wrong.

"You have no idea how important she's been to me, Andrew. Do not betray me," I say, feeling his breath shudder from his body. His head slings forward and his hand comes to cup the back of his neck as he nods slowly. My lips hang open, the words right there, waiting to come out. I want to tell him *never mind*. I want to tell him it will be okay and Lindsey will understand. I want to tell him I'm wrong, that he wouldn't be betraying me at all. But I can't. Our time was a few short weeks when we were sixteen. That time—it's gone. And I have to let him go. He needs to let go too.

"Come on, let's go win a goddamned gift card," he says, placing his arm around my shoulder as we stand, our bodies tethered together, his fingers gentle along my shoulder.

We walk in sync to the starting line, and before the man blows the whistle to begin, Andrew's fingers curl just enough to

216

scratch against the fabric of my sweatshirt until his hand clutches the material into his fist before finally letting go.

He let go.

And I've never hurt more.

Chapter 15

Emma, Age 19

The truth is I was waiting for the phone call. I'd been waiting for nearly three years. From the moment both of my parents sat me down and told me Mom had pancreatic cancer, I'd been waiting for this call.

She hadn't been well for months. Her body just couldn't fight anymore. The rounds of chemo, the trials, the naturopathy—the prayers; eventually, cancer wins. All we can ask for is comfort and time.

My mother got three years. I should take comfort in that. My father should, too. And maybe one day we will. But for now, I want to be angry with the world.

"Em? You have to eat something," Lindsey says from the other side of my bedroom door. I've lived with her for a year. I've known her for only a little more. The way she's held me up since my dad called three weeks ago with the news that my mother died feels like more years should have been shared between us. She never signed up for this, and I've kept most of it to myself. Until...until the phone call that opened up my heart, split my body in two and took away that feeling of safety that comes along with knowing both of your parents are alive and well.

"I did," I lie, my throat sore and dry. I can't cry any more— but my mouth hangs open, wanting to. I want to all of the time.

"Em, I have been out there on that sofa all day. I'm binge-watching hot superhero movies. I'm on my fourth one, and you haven't left this room. I would have known. I'm four feet away from the refrigerator. I would have *seen* you eat," she says.

"You missed it; you were in the bathroom when I came out and made a sandwich." I'm smiling a little. It hurts. This is the first time I've smiled in a week. It feels...unnatural.

"I haven't peed once," she says.

"Now *you're* the one who's lying," I laugh. The sound of that hurts my chest.

"Ha, see! I knew you were lying," she says, pointing a finger at me as she opens my door. I let my smile remain so she can see it; she's earned this one. Hers falls though when she sees me. I know I look bad. And I'm sure...oh man, I'm pretty sure I smell bad. I haven't really *moved* a lot lately. I've gotten most of my homework through home study and got a medical withdrawal from my language class. I picked German. I think I'm switching to Spanish the next time around. There's one silver lining to this cloud of shit—I was failing German. "And for the record, I *wasn't* lying," Lindsey continues. "I really haven't peed in eight hours—two Chris Evans movies in a row. You know how I feel about Captain America."

She sits on the bed next to me with a bounce. She's let me wallow for the last couple weeks, but last night she gave me one hell of a speech.

"You can be sad," she said. "You can carry that around somewhere inside all the time. It's human, and you deserve to. But your mom would be mad to see you waste even a single day not living. She'd want to see you giving each day your best, even if you have to carry your sadness through it the whole damn way. Drag that sadness around; make it your bitch. But don't waste the good ones."

She was right. She's still right. She doesn't say anything when she sits next to me now, only stares at me, like a blinking contest. I lose. My eyes hurt from crying. Everything is so...dry.

"I'm getting up," I say, dragging my arm up my body so my finger can cross my heart with a promise. This is a tactical error on my part, because Lindsey sees my hand and grabs it, pulling me from my bed, one leg sliding to the floor, the other following in desperate fashion to find my balance before she drags me on my ass. She would, too—she's very strong for a petite thing.

"I'm hungry. And now I'm sad that there are no real superheroes in the world, so you, my friend, are getting in the shower. You have exactly seven minutes to get yourself presentable, and then we are going to my favorite restaurant and sitting by the window to watch hot frat boys walk by," she orders.

"I don't know, Linds. I'll get up, but I don't think I'm quite ready to go out," I say, dragging my feet toward our bathroom. She shoves a folded towel at my chest.

"I told you last night—you're done wasting days. We're going out. I want a superhero," she says, holding one hand on her hip, looking a little like one herself.

I sigh, then stick my tongue out at her, backing into the bathroom and kicking the door shut. I stare at the blankness of it for a second or two and I think of my mother.

"You know I love you, right?" I say to my friend, my best friend. Lindsey doesn't know this, but she *is* a superhero. She's also the second best friend I've had in my life. I've been close to exactly two people not related to me—and the first one disappeared without a trace.

Andrew Harper, where are you?

"I know. And I love you too. Now hurry your ass up; you're down to six minutes, and you know all the cute ones come out when it gets dark outside," she says. I grin at her words, stepping into the shower and turning the water on. I can tell she's sitting by the door. I also know that if I don't make it out of here in six minutes, she'll come in after me.

For the first time since I answered the phone and heard my father cry, I breathe.

220

Chapter 16

Andrew

I wonder if Emma would think I'm betraying her now?

The house still looks the same, only the yard is dead, weeds taking up most of the space along the stone walkway that leads to the door. The compact sedan out front is the same one her family owned when we were in high school. That was my only confirmation that her family still lived here.

Her family. It's...smaller now.

I didn't know her parents well, if at all. I never got the chance. For those first few weeks in Lake Crest, I daydreamed about getting to know them. I had these fantasies that her parents would surprise me with a visit while I was there. Once, I even thought I saw a couple that looked like them in the waiting room—at least, it looked like them from the back. I walked through, postured a little straighter, shirt tucked in so I would make a good impression. The couple turned out to be there to pick up their son.

Now I get to meet her father, to acquaint myself with him, like this. I turn off the engine and sit in my car for a few minutes, looking over the house, psyching myself up for this probably-horrible idea. I look down at my forearms and my eyes lock in on the burn mark on my right arm. It's five years old, but it burns just as it did when Nick Meyers pressed his cigar into me. It was also the hardest mark to hide from my mom. I roll the long sleeves of my plaid shirt down as I exit my car, wanting to hide my scars from Emma's dad. The bruising from my fight is fading, but he'll still notice. Not much I can do about that.

My heart thumps wildly as I step up her walkway, little doses of the familiar attacking me the closer I get to the door. I recognize the smell of the bushes that line her yard, even though many of them are dead. I'm overcome with the curve around her house, the way to her window, and the pebbles in the yard across the street that I used to get her attention. I can almost see *her* walking toward me.

I press the button before I can chicken out, and a small dog scurries toward the front door from the inside. The side window gives me a view of its paws against the windowsill on the other side. A light flicks *on* in the hallway, and I can see the shadow of a person walking toward the door.

I think I'm going to be sick. This...this was a bad idea.

"Can I help you?"

A boy stands in the now-open doorway in front of me. This must be Emma's brother, Cole. He's awkward and his face looks caught somewhere between youth and his teen years. Maybe he's ten?

"Hi," I say, allowing myself a deep breath and a pause before speaking. It's part of my new rule to think before I talk. I bring my hand up to scratch my face as the boy scrunches his eyes and closes his lips tight. He's thinking he just opened the door to a stranger. He kinda did—dumb shit.

"I'm a friend of your sister's," I say to relax him. It doesn't seem to help, though, and now he crosses his arms. "I was looking for your dad?" I'm not quite *ready* for his dad, but I think any more time alone with little brother, and he'll slam the door on my face.

"Hang on," he says, pursing his lips at me, and squinting for a second more. "Dad! Some guy's here. He's not selling anything!"

I chuckle to myself, but stay still at the doorway while Cole walks away leaving the door wide open. A few seconds later, his father steps around the corner. He recognizes me instantly—his feet almost skidding to a stop. His hair has grayed, and thinned. He has glasses on, pulled to the edge of his nose, and his body is thinner than I remember.

"Mr. Burke," I say. I work hard to keep my voice even, to keep my mouth in an almost smile, to keep my eyes non-threatening. He has to know why I'm here. And he has to think I'm pissed. I am pissed. But I also think the man in front of me has been through hell and back—he's wearing his depression like a coat.

"Why are you here?" he asks, his question more of a grumble really as he fumbles his glasses from his face, pushing them in his pocket. He steps outside, closing the door behind him, then guides me to an open chair next to a bench on the end of their wooden porch.

He picks up a pillow and slides it across the wood, clearing it of dirt and debris, then motions for me to sit. I'd rather stand. I feel stronger, more in charge when I stand. Nick Meyers always made me sit when I was called to his office. I give in to Emma's father, though, and he quickly sits across from me, his body heaving out a breath.

He's afraid.

"I'm sorry to just show up. Really...I...hmmmm," I pause, running my hand along my face with a small chuckle. "Look...Mr. Burke."

"You can call me Carl, Andrew," he says. His eyes are tired, maybe a little sad, too.

I acknowledge his attempt to be civil with a tight smile before I lean forward, my hands clasped in front of me as my elbows rest on my knees. I tried not to look like a punk today. Normal jeans, a gray shirt, plaid button-down and my black hat—I debated on the gauges, but I ultimately decided the big holes sagging in my ears would put him off more. He keeps glancing at them, though, so I'm not sure I was right.

"I came for some answers. Well...one answer, mainly," I say, my hands wringing in front of me. I twist the silver ring around my thumb nervously, and eventually it falls off, rolling along the crooked planks of wood between us, coming to rest against his work boot. He reaches down to pick it up, clasping it in his fist as he closes his eyes.

"You want to know why we lied," he says.

My lungs collapse, and I struggle to fill them again. I expected confrontation. I expected denial.

I didn't expect this!

I don't speak, but nod slowly, my eyes waiting for his to open. When they do, they seem even more lost than they were when he first spotted me at his doorway.

"Katherine, Emma's mother, had pancreatic cancer," he says. His eyes fall even more, but their color—the same gray in Emma's—begins to grow darker.

"I'm very sorry, sir. I heard," I say, bowing my head. It's hard to see his pain—it feels too familiar.

"Thank you. It's been a couple years, but losing Kate was hard," he says.

"I understand," I say back quickly. We both stare into each other's eyes for a moment, and I can tell he respects the connection we both share—for loss.

"I'm sorry about what you've been through, Andrew. With your father...and with James," he says. I can tell he means it.

"Thank you," I say.

Carl leans back, the wood of the bench creaking with his weight. He folds his hands at his chest as he studies me. I remain frozen, my thumbs locked together, folded over my clasped hands. I'm willing him to give me answers—I'm hoping it gives me some sort of clue.

"Come with me," he says, suddenly leaning forward and getting to his feet. I stand in response and follow him into his house, the screen door slamming closed behind us.

We wind through a formal living room and dining area that I doubt has been used since Emma's mother died. I doubt it's been cleaned since then, either, the rings of dust deep around coasters and lamps. I trail Carl to a small space in the back of the house that looks like a den, an old desk taking up the center, and boxes piled around the walls. The small dog comes into the room behind us, and when Carl sits in the chair, bending down to pull out a low drawer in the desk, the dog rushes over to him, jumping on his lap.

"Teddy, not now," he says, scooping him and dropping him on the floor. He glances up at me. "Hazard of the job," he smirks. I had forgotten—Emma's father is a dogcatcher.

I bend down, and Teddy scurries up to me, putting his front paws on my knees. I scratch at his chin.

"I always wanted a dog," I say, chuckling slightly.

"You want this one?" Carl says, I think only *half* kidding.

I rub my thumbs behind Teddy's ears, watching his tail wag, until Carl leans back again in his chair, a file folder in his hands. He lays it on the desk, flipping it open, nodding for me to look.

I move to his side as he rolls his chair out a little to make room for me. When I begin to slide out the clippings and photos, my stomach lurches. The first thing I notice is a photo that appears to have been printed out at home—Emma in a hospital gown. Her hair is just as it was the last time I saw her before Lake Crest, her eyes look happy—hopeful even—though maybe a little sunken in, and her mom is sitting on the edge of the hospital bed with her.

"Did Emma...donate bone marrow or something?" I feel insensitive asking the question, but I don't understand what I'm looking at, and the potential of what it might mean terrifies me to the point that I have to kneel next to the desk, no longer able to stand.

"No," Carl chuckles softly, picking the photo up and pulling his glasses out to study it closer. "No...this was the day Emma got her heart."

"Her...I'm sorry..." I stumble with my words.

"I didn't think she told you. She was funny like that. I think it was her age, wanting to prove how normal she was, what she could do. I get it...she just wanted people to treat her normal," he says.

"I'm sorry, Carl. I'm...I'm not following. Emma...she needed a heart? Was it the accident? Did something happen?" My mind is racing with dozens of questions. I understand getting cut and bleeding; I understand how burns and bruises heal. If this were mechanics, I would be able to get what Emma's father was saying, but this is Emma's world—medicine and biology and a broken body. I don't understand, and I can't help but feel like it's my fault, and that's why her parents never told her where I was.

My head is sweating, and I tug my hat off and run my hand through my hair, huffing for air. I fall back on my heels and land on my ass, bending my knees up and staring straight ahead.

"Andrew, it's okay. She's okay now, and no...this wasn't from the accident," he says. I barely register him, but nod in response.

"What...what was wrong with her?" I ask.

He sighs, sliding some photos around in the folder before pulling out a piece of paper and handing it to me. I read a few words along the top, something about New Hampshire Hospital, left ventricles, medications. It's dated the year before I met Emma.

"Emma was born with hypoplastic left heart syndrome. Basically, half of her heart worked, and the other half was broken. She had three surgeries before we turned to the transplant. That's when you met her—when she was waiting on the list. We moved here for a doctor. Dogcatchers and phone-bank workers—we're not exactly rolling in the dough," he says, his lip inching up on one side in a half smile. I reflect it with one of my own. I don't say it out loud, but turns out young men with juvenile records don't make a lot of dough either. I'm hopeful that will change, though.

"This doctor, Dr. Wheaton, she performed Emma's surgery for free. But we still had to wait for her to come up on the list," he says, his eyes wandering back to the folder. I slide the diagnosis sheet up, and he folds it in with the other papers. "Her heart finally came...about a month after that accident you two had."

He doesn't try to mask the disapproval in his voice, and I cower a little under it. I lower my gaze, but I don't acknowledge it any more. That accident has taken up too much of my life.

"While I was at Lake Crest," I say instead, wanting to talk about where *I* was, and why Emma couldn't know.

"Yes," he says, not even flinching.

His conviction causes me to look up, and our eyes lock again. We keep coming to the same civil standoff.

"I would have supported her...through that...her surgery? If I had known," I say, swallowing hard. "I wrote her letters. I would have written her every day, tried to call..."

I stop when I see his face fall, his lips pursed, a hint of regret perhaps shadowing his expression.

"You know I wrote her letters. You...you never gave them to her," I say, that sick feeling from when I stepped out of my car coming over me again in a wave. It's quiet for almost a full minute, the only sound the papers shuffling back into the folder, the drawer being pulled open and Carl's chair sliding back from the desk as he stands. I pull myself up to stand with him, following him back from the den toward the front of the house. He stops in the kitchen.

"Can I get you a water? I don't have much, but...I have water," he says.

I laugh once under my breath and look back to the room on one end of the hallway and the doorway to my car on the other. All of this—and I still don't have the answers I needed, the closure I needed—I'm still the fuck-up from that family everybody talks about.

"Sure, I'll take a water," I sigh. He reaches in and pulls out a small bottle, wiping the condensation away with a towel on the counter before handing it to me. I hold it up, clutched in my hand, and smile tightly before whispering a sarcastic "Thanks."

Carl pulls the top from his and guzzles about half down before setting the bottle on the counter behind him. I twist my cap off and move my bottle to my lips, my eyes meeting Carl's in between drinks. I shuffle my feet, readying myself for Carl to show me out.

"I couldn't lose them both," he says. I startle a little, not expecting any more answers from him. I lower my brow, but wait for him to give me more. "I knew Kate was sick when we moved here. We were hoping for a better prognosis, and had been seeing new doctors in the city. But their answers were all the same."

He relaxes into the counter behind him, his hands finding the edge and squeezing as he looks up to the ceiling. When his eyes fall back down to mine, they're red and glassy. "I couldn't lose them both, Andrew. And I was afraid if Emma stayed with you—"

"You were afraid I'd ruin her," I finish for him. My eyes shut with the realization, with my delivery of the sentence and final act of what went wrong between me and Emma Burke.

"It's not about your family, Andrew. I know what you're thinking, and don't. It isn't about that—it never was," he says.

My gut tells me he's lying.

"When we got the call to pick her up that night at the police station, our world was rocked. She was this close...*this close*...to having a fresh start, to having a chance," he says, his lips a hard

227

line, the rest of what he wants to say only a breath away. I stare into his eyes and dare him. "You were drunk, and you were high, Andrew. Drunk...and high!"

I roll my shoulders and take his condemnation. I nod slowly, my lips forcing themselves into a defensive smile and eventually a chuckle. I look down to the side as I reach into my pocket for my keys.

"Says the Woodstock Town Police report," I seethe.

"They convicted you, Andrew. A year in detention..."

"Ah...reform school," I correct smugly, holding one finger up. I shake my head at him, my insides feeling as if I've just gone a round in the ring. I open my mouth, but I'm smart enough to know that whatever I say next, if I speak right now, it won't be nice. So I close my lips instead and hold up my water to him. "I'm gonna take this with me, for the road, if that's okay?"

I turn and move to the door, not expecting his steps behind me. He's several paces back, and I know he's relieved to know I'm leaving. My thoughts dart to so many possibilities—racing one minute to the lost opportunities I had with Emma then quickly to everything she was probably told. The questions boil fast, and before I reach for the latch on the screen, I stop.

"I just need to know...did you tell Emma that I was drunk and high? Or did you keep that to yourself, too?" His face is ghost white, a mix of shame and indignant self-righteousness. "You know what? Never mind...I'll ask her myself."

I see him lurch toward me just before I close the door behind me. I don't know if he followed me. My pace was swift back to my car, and I never once glanced back at the broken house and broken man I was leaving.

I cashed in one more sick day for my trip to Emma's dad's this morning. But my face was already returning to normal. My only class today was mathematic theory, and I've already completed the practice work and reading, so I gave myself permission to skip that, too. I haven't missed one yet this semester, so it shouldn't raise any flags with coach. It's our off day, but I've been itching for the ice. Trent has a full schedule today, though, and he won't be home until well after five. My boiling blood won't wait that long, so after an hour pacing our apartment and throwing a racquetball against the wall to the point that one of our senior neighbors came over to ask me to "stop the partying," I head to Harley's gym.

The place is hopping for the middle of the day, so I work in with one of the regulars. I spend an hour not talking, only rushing my taped fists into another guy's gloves and chest. He pops me in the jaw a few times, but the familiar heat that usually accompanies it never comes. It seems I've been hit so much that I'm finally immune. Or maybe, I'm so angry that it's going to take more than what this featherweight can serve up to help me.

"Harp, I'm out," my partner says, slicing his glove in front of his face at his neck. He's calling it. I frown at him. "Dude, we've been going an hour. I come here for the workout, man. But I also have to get my ass to class."

I nod at him, my hard breathing catching up to me as I lean on the ropes. I pull the tape from one hand and reach my palm out to shake his, pulling the other hand free of tape as he grabs his bag and leaves the gym.

My heart rate feels faster than normal—spikes of adrenaline still pushing through it. I force myself to breathe long and deep, dropping my head into my hands so I can focus and really listen to my rhythm. What a simple thing—a heartbeat.

Emma's heart...it didn't do this. Or not...quite like this. I looked up her condition as soon as I got home. I read about the surgeries she probably had when she was young, and then I thought back to how her skin felt the only time I touched it. It was over her bra, and in a dark car—the stolen moments of two teens in lust. I never felt a scar.

My mind is lost in the past, and that's why I don't see him coming. But his words yank me right out of the puzzle I'm trying to solve, and they drop me into hostile territory.

"Nick Meyers said you were a fighter," he says. My head jerks up at the mention of his name, my hands forming fists instantly, my breathing picking up its pace, like an engine revving. Graham, Emma's *just some guy*, stands on the floor in front of me, two feet lower than the ring. He's wearing cut-off sweatpants and a tank top that squeezes his large frame.

"Nice to see you again, Graham," I practically choke on his name. "I didn't know they were letting assholes in here now."

He laughs at my response, but he doesn't think I'm funny. He doesn't think I'm funny at all. His eyes fall to his feet as he kicks at an old, dried piece of gum stuck to the floor.

"Harley, you're really letting this place fall to shit. You need to get an intern or something, someone to come through here and clean every once and a while," he shouts, then glances up at me, his eyes slits as they take me in. "Maybe this guy can be your intern."

Harley walks over slowly, and I study him, watching every nuance as I try to decide if he and Graham are friends. He never smiles, and when he stops in front of us both—equal distance between us—he folds his arms and frowns. I'm not sure what Graham is to Harley or how he knows him, but he isn't a friend. More than that—what does Graham have to do with Nick Meyers?

"I said I'd talk to him, Graham. Let the kid cool off. I'll catch up with you later, okay?" Harley grumbles.

Graham's smile slides wider as he nods.

"A'right," he says. I cough down a laugh when he speaks and Harley shoots me a look to keep my mouth shut. I can't help it—this dude sounds like a poser trying to talk all tough and shit. I'll give him this; he's bigger than me, and he looks like he knows how to throw a punch. But he also wore pink pants the last time I saw him.

"Hey, I'll say *hi* to Emma for you," he winks before walking away. My entire body flexes. Harley notices, and he holds his hand up to stop me.

Once Graham rounds the door, I turn my focus to Harley, who's staring back at me with equal intensity.

"You wanna tell me how you know Graham Wheaton?" he asks, chewing at the inside of his mouth. Harley looks like a Marine—what he lacks in height he makes up for in bulk. He's always been into fitness and boxing, and when you combine his build with his smarts, he's perfect for this business.

"I just met the guy. We don't...gel," I say.

"I can see that," he says, lifting the ropes for me to slide through. I climb out and turn a chair around, straddling it and resting my arms on the back.

"How do *you* know Graham Wheaton?" I ask, not liking the fact that this asshole has now ruined two things that make me happy—my gym, and Emma.

"He's my biggest investor. Well, his father is, at least. His dad's into real estate. We have a deal. He comes here to work out. He's got some skills," Harley says, downplaying that last part. I can tell he's not giving Graham the fighting credit he probably deserves, and I think it's because on a personal level, Harley likes me better.

"I see," I say, my insides still trying to process the name that Graham threw out to get at me. Could he really know Nick Meyers? Fuck me if that ghost from my past is an investor here, too.

"He wants to fight you," Harley says, and I spit out a spray of water as soon as his voice hits my ears.

"Shut the fuck up," I say.

"He's offering five grand. All you have to do is go down in four. That's five grand...just for you, Drew. This wouldn't be like Pitch. Graham's good, but he's not big like that—it would be fair, and you'd come out all right—and five grand richer. I won't be able to line something like that up for you again in months. He's looking at a small event in a week or two."

I stare at him while he speaks, trying to sort through the crazy shit coming out of his mouth.

"I don't know, Har," I say, looking down and kicking my foot. "That guy...I don't trust him."

"You don't have to," he says, holding up a check for me to see. "He gave me the deposit. I hold the money."

I breathe in slowly. Any other name on that check with that number and I'd be sold. But something about this feels *not* right. Even so, I would love to have an excuse to slam my fist through his face. I take the check in my hand, rub it between my fingers and look at it for several long seconds before I begin nodding.

"So, you're in?" Harley asks.

"Yeah, I'm in," I say, not liking the taste in my mouth.

Harley takes the check back with a nod. He never smiles. I don't think he has a good taste either. But he likes money, and I know that the five thousand that goes to my pocket isn't what he's in this for.

I leave the gym at three, knowing I have hours until Trent is home, and my feet carry me to Majerle's. I text him to join me, but I'm gone hours before he says he can make it. Chuck quit serving me after my fifth Jack, so I stumbled into the liquor store at the end of the block, leaving my car safe along the roadside outside the tavern.

And then I called Lindsey and told her I wanted to come over tonight so we could talk. I'm going to end the lies, and I'm going to punch *Graham cracker* in the face. And I'm also going to go home and drink. I'm going to drink a lot. In the middle of the day. Just like the fuck-up loser I am.

Emma

"We haven't had a girl's night in forever," Lindsey says, pouting a little. She just got off the phone with Andrew. He told her he was coming over, and she got excited. They haven't spent much time together over the last couple days. I know why, and it's killing me to know so much.

It's also killing me that he's coming here, to be with her. He's only doing that to hurt me. I can't let it hurt me. I'll leave early, meet Graham at the restaurant—whatever it takes to avoid him.

"I know. I miss my Emma-Lindsey time," I say, sinking down next to her on the sofa. I'm half dressed, a long, silky black shirt hanging over my underwear.

"You better finish getting dressed. Unless you're trying to get something going with this Graham guy," Lindsey teases. I stand and sigh, looking down at my bare legs and feet.

"You think I can go in jeans?" I joke.

"Uhm...to Polo's? No," she laughs. "I am pretty sure when the restaurant quits putting prices on the menu that they require their guests come in something a grade fancier than flip-flops and leggings."

"Ugh," I sigh. "Fine."

232

I stomp my feet playfully back to my room, returning to my closet, to the rows of boring formal wear and pantsuits. I pull out the silk pants and decide those will be good enough.

"Hey, Em?" Lindsey calls down the hall. "I forgot to give you something. Your dad...he came by. He left something for you. He said it was important."

"My dad came by? He knows my schedule," I say, my brow pulled in and my mouth twisted while I try to both figure out why my father came when I wasn't here and how to work the tight band of my pants over my hips. I haven't worn these in a year, and it seems my hips are not willing to work with me tonight. I discard them and reach for the cocktail dress I bought on sale over the summer and have never had a chance to wear.

"Yeah, I thought it was weird too. He said something about having to take your brother somewhere or something. I don't know. But he left this," she says as she enters my room. She tosses a large manila envelope on my bed as I spin to face her. I glance at it, but don't recognize it. It must be my mail from home. Sometimes I get magazines.

"What do you think?" I ask, bending down to pull on my silver strappy heals. These shoes make me taller than anyone in the room—always. I think the only person who could possibly stand taller than me in these shoes...is Andrew.

I huff and right my posture, shaking my curls from my shoulders, then spinning to one side so Lindsey can properly evaluate my outfit, a slender-fitting gray dress with a back that dips low. She smiles, but tilts her head to the side. She glances to my dresser top, her eyes lighting up when she spots a pin. "Here, let me just try something," she says, pulling the pin in her hand, opening it and taking a small strand of my hair between her fingers. She twists it into a tight line, pulling it to the back of my head where she fastens it in place. "There," she says, standing back with her arms crossed. "Now he can see your eyes."

My shoulders relax as I smile back at her. With a simple gesture, Lindsey has made me feel beautiful.

"Thanks," I say, taking one more deep breath.

"Relax," she says. "He already likes you."

I nod and keep my happy expression in place, never letting her know that what I'm really worried about is *me* liking *him.*

Lindsey retreats to her room, probably to get ready for Andrew's visit, and for a moment, I think about walking to her room and telling her everything. My feet never leave their comfortable roots in my carpet though. I tell myself that it's because I just don't want to ruin my friend's happiness. And that's definitely *part* of my reason. But I'm also scared. I'm afraid of how she'll react, afraid it will ruin something between us, and maybe…maybe a little afraid that it will solidify the path for Andrew and me. Lindsey and I wouldn't survive that. I'd have to pick. And my heart is so very selfish.

Graham will be here soon, so I look over my dress once more, making sure everything that *should* be hidden, is. This is a dinner with important people, so I decide to pull out the thin black sweater just to be safe. I look over myself once more in the mirror to see how the sweater lies in the back, and I catch a glimpse of the envelope on my bed behind me. I step over to it and lift it in one hand, a little surprised at how heavy it feels.

Sitting on my bed, I listen to the sound of our apartment. Nothing.

I pull the envelope into my lap and slide my finger along the poorly-sealed edge, reaching in. My fingers find a stack of thick-feeling paper, and when I pull what's inside out, my eyes catch up to what I think my soul already knew, and time stops. Even the handwriting cuts to the core, the way he took care to write my name, the look of his own name on paper. Every single envelope is sealed. Never opened.

"Your words went into oblivion," I whisper to myself, the tears pooling up quickly. I glance up to my door, my feet following my gaze to the lock on my door, and I click it, rushing back to the envelopes that were all meant for me—the words I should have read years ago.

These letters represent the gap in everything from my life before to now.

With a hard swallow, I tear into the one on top.

Emma,

I'm sorry that this has to be a letter. It's the only thing I'm allowed to do. I wanted to call you, but there really wasn't an opportunity. I didn't know where to call, either. All this time, and I still never asked you for your phone number. I'm such a jerk.

The past floods my insides, overtaking me completely. The envelopes still in my hand feel hot to touch, and I drop them on the bedspread beside me, spreading them out like a deck of cards, the one letter I began to read still on top.

He's sorry.

After what he did for me, the first thing he wrote me was *sorry*.

I slide one out from the middle, tugging the loosely-sealed edge open, and I pull the letter free. This one is only a single page. I notice that the letters are less thick the closer to the bottom of the spread-out stack I go.

Dear Emma,

Yeah. I'm writing again. I guess I'm a glutton for punishment. I wish I could tell you the things that I see here. I wish I could tell you the things I've been through. I'm so unbelievably alone. I thought I was lonely before I met you, but god what I wouldn't give to go back to that time. Not that I want to go back to life before you. Actually, I'd like to relive getting to know you again. Those few weeks were...well they meant a lot to me. I would probably skip the part where we get in the accident though—or at least I wouldn't go to my friend House's party. That was stupid.

I don't know what anyone's told you. But I'm counting on the fact that you know me—the real me. You know I'm not some drugged-out loser, right? I was at a party I shouldn't have gone to and tried some things that I shouldn't have tried. Everyone looks at me differently now, though. I'm afraid they look at me and see my brother James. I'm not James, Emma. I hope you know that.

I tear quickly into more letters, each one giving me another piece of Andrew's heart, a piece of his soul. He pours out feelings in some letters, talking about how afraid he is of Lake Crest, and in others he's almost resolved to what his life is there, offering me nothing at all, almost as if he's protecting me from what he's going through. The more I read, the sadder he becomes, and the less of Andrew I see. I pull one near the end, not ready—and maybe also not willing—to read his final letter.

Dear Emma,

I miss you.

I wanted to see what those words felt like. There are more words...other things to write, to say. Maybe one day I'll say them to you in person. Or maybe...I won't. I hope I'm not freaking you out, it's just that this place is so dark and heartless that I wanted to remind myself what light was like. You...you're my light.

I talked with my brother's girlfriend Kensi for a while tonight. She came to visit. I wasn't very good company at first, but then she asked me questions about you. She's offered to visit you for me, to bring you something. I thought about letting her bring you one of my hats or my sweatshirt. I don't know...I thought girls liked that sort of thing. But I'm too afraid you won't want it.
I'm afraid you won't want me.

I want to see you so badly it hurts.

You don't know this, but I tried—I tried to see you. This place has a way of keeping people on leashes though. I'm okay. Don't worry, I can take it. I promise you this place won't defeat me entirely. I'll come back to you, Emma. We'll start over, and I'll take you on a proper date. I'll hold your hand and buy you popcorn and kiss you in a dark movie theater. And I'll be your date for prom. And I'll spend my summer trying to make you laugh.

I'll come back to you if you'll have me. It's all I'm living for.

Please write soon.

Completely yours,

Andrew

I can barely see through the tears that stream down my face. My breath is stuttering, and my chest hurts. On instinct, I hold my palm flat over the center, over my scar, counting as I breathe in and breathe out.

One. Two. Three. Four. Five.

The calm that usually follows is short—the mixture of anger, regret, and heartbreak flooding me again and again.

Andrew was mine. I was his reason for everything. And when he needed me most, I wasn't there—because I never knew. And now...now that he's here...all I'm doing is pushing him away more. My skin turns red, and my body feels hot. My fist clenched, I bring my other arm down on the bed, slamming it hard enough to make the letters jump from the force. I slam my fist down again, then swipe the letters in all directions, sending them to the floor as I collapse onto my bed, my face deep in my sheets. I open my mouth wanting to scream, but I'm aware enough to know that I can't. Not here, not where anyone can hear me.

I scream inside, to myself, wishing I could turn back time.

"Em?" Lindsey knocks at my door. I push myself up, rushing to the floor to gather my letters, to protect them and save them.

"Just a second. I'm fixing something...on my dress," I breathe out in a panic, scooping the letters back into the envelope and tucking it into my backpack on my desk to hide them.

"It's okay. I just wanted you to know Andrew's here," she says. My eyes grow wide, and my body freezes, my fingers about to clutch my door. I pull my hand away and hold it against me.

Andrew's here. Just on the other side of this door. I can't see him—not now. I'm not ready. I want him. I don't want him with Lindsey. I'm greedy and selfish and these letters...his letters, they've completely swept away all reason. And it's going to hurt my best friend. I don't know what to do.

"Oh," I say, my mouth holding the *O* as I wait to think of what comes next. Nothing does.

"Are you leaving soon?"

She wants to be alone with him. I get that. And I have to leave to meet Graham and Miranda for dinner. I need to be there in twenty minutes, with my mentor and her son—whom I feel nothing for, who if it weren't for timing and circumstance, I probably wouldn't even like. This isn't how any of this should be. How can I look Graham in the face after reading what's in Andrew's heart? How can I live this lie knowing he once felt so much for me. He still does. I know it...I believe it.

"Yeah, just...just a sec," I choke out. I turn to the side where my backpack rests next to my purse, and I pull my purse into my hands, my eyes staying on the letters I want to carry with me too. I never want to leave them alone. I need to memorize them, feel them—no matter how badly they hurt to read.

Instead, I pull my mirror from my purse and check my face, powdering my cheeks and wiping away the blurred eyeliner from my cry seconds before. I can paint myself as much as I want—it will never erase how I feel right now. My heart is a steady rhythm, a warning that I should stay in this room, feign an illness. I can't go out there, I can't see him, and I cannot be anything with Graham.

"Emma?"

Lindsey sounds desperate. I should pull her in here, tell her everything, take the lashing she will give me—that I will deserve. I should.

"I'm ready," I say with the last breath that leaves my body in this room.

I push my door open and immediately meet Lindsey's eyes. They're wide. Why are they wide?

"I think he's drunk," she winces, pursing her lips and nodding her head down the hallway. I see part of his body, his legs leaning out as he leans against a wall in our kitchen. His dark jeans gather around his feet, his black shoes, his hands hanging from his thumbs looped in his pockets. I see enough to know that seeing the rest will break me open again.

"Oh," I say, just as I said before. I'm weak.

"It's okay," she says, shaking her head. "You have to go; you're going to be late. I'll sober him up. Who knows, maybe this will break the ice that he's had surrounding him lately."

Ice. Andrew's had...ice. Because of me.

Lindsey walks back down the hall, and I notice Andrew push off from the wall and sway on his feet, his expression meaningless—blank. His eyes haze as he paints her body with his gaze, but on his way back up, his focus is solely on me, and suddenly his expression changes. We're the same. We are hurting the same. And the way he looks right now—it's as desperate as I feel. Those words he wrote years ago, they're still so very relevant now; I see it in his eyes. I see it in his soul.

He remains several feet away from me, his fingers reaching for Lindsey's hand while he watches me pull my coat from the hook near the door.

"Call me if you need anything. We'll be up late," Lindsey says. The smile on her face makes everything hurt worse. I notice it, but only briefly. For the rest of the time, my eyes stay on Andrew.

"That's some guy," he says, his voice monotone and his eyes flat. "He can't even come to your door to pick you up."

"Andrew!" Lindsey chides him, grimacing. I can tell she's right—he is a little drunk. But I also think he's more sober than she realizes, too. I think this Andrew is on the other side of a binge, on his way out, coming through the pain, but bringing it with him. It never leaves him, really.

"It's okay," I smile at my friend. My eyes find him again, and when Lindsey turns away, I mouth, "I'm so sorry."

His face falls the second my lips send the message. I don't know why I said it, other than I had to—I need to say so much more. I need to read those letters.

I pull the door open and step into the hall, breathing deeply to survive one more night, to be a pleasant dinner guest, to impress my mentor and not to offend her son. I just need a personality for a few more hours, and then I can figure things out.

When I turn to lock the door behind me, Andrew is holding it open, just enough for my face to be square with his. His eyes hold mine hostage, drifting to my mouth then down my entire body. My scar burns on my chest even though he can't see it, and I clutch my purse to me tightly to cover it up even more.

"I have to go," I say.

"I'm telling Lindsey," he says, his lips parted and open, his teeth holding his tongue. His breathing is deep, his chest rising with the pressure of everything. He's not telling me this to tease me. He's telling me because it's what he plans to do, because he's determined. Those words are the gate to a whole hell of a lot he has to say. I can tell. And I wish our time were different; I wish it were right for him to say it and me to hear it. But it's not...it's just...not.

"Don't," I say, a small shake of my head.

"I have to, Emma. You know I do," he says, closing the door behind him. I place my hand on it and will myself to open it again, to come up with an excuse, to protest what he's about to do—to stop him from hurting my friend. But I hurt her too. And carrying this on any longer, that's not right either.

I back away slowly until I turn to the elevator, and I never look back again, washing away the thoughts of what Andrew could possibly be saying right now and reminding myself to be pleasant and not to screw up my relationship with Miranda Wheaton.

240

Chapter 17

Andrew

It seems that Lindsey was a high school all-star softball player. This would have been a good thing to know when she picked up the glass paperweight and hurled it at my face. I dodged it in time, but not fast enough for the follow-up of the metal photo frame. The sharp edge caught my chin, slicing it open deep enough that it bled huge droplets on her living room floor.

I deserved it.

I probably should have waited for Trent to show up at the bar, to help me work out my very loosely-planned plan. I also probably should have waited until I was *really* sober, not just the pretend *I think I'm sober* that I was when I told Lindsey "We need to talk."

My buzz was good, and it felt like my mind was clear finally—like I had the courage to do the difficult thing, the thing that Emma couldn't do. It was my fault that Lindsey was even involved in the first place.

However, she probably deserved a lucid version of me explaining things.

"I'm in love with Emma," was the first thing I said. I didn't open easy. No. I'd thought this through at the bar—again, probably not the best idea—and every time I played this out in my head, just stating the truth, and getting it out quickly, always felt right.

It was probably wrong.

Lindsey's first reaction was to laugh. She thought this was a joke. But then she realized she was laughing, while I was leaning against the wall, my hands deep in my pockets, sweating, my heart throbbing, my head aching, my mind remembering the look on Emma's face as the door closed behind her. My past would always be tangled with Emma Burke, and so would my heart.

Lindsey slapped me then. Hard. I nodded *yes*, almost wishing for more.

"I'm sorry," I said. My face still somber—brutally honest. I was sorry. I am sorry.

She hit me again, this time her palm cupped as it came at me. The force jerked my head to the side, and I took a few steps back. As much as I like a good battle in the ring, I was always completely sober for it. And it wasn't a woman whom I'd lied to kicking my ass. As much as my instincts balled my fists to fight back, my head knew better. I'd let her have this—she could take all she wanted.

"You...*love her*?" she'd asked. She didn't understand. I knew there was no way to explain this simply. All that mattered was protecting Emma—protect *her* relationship with Lindsey.

I told her that I'd loved her since we were kids; something tragic had happened between us, her parents had kept us apart, but I didn't know—so I had always blamed Emma. I tried to explain why Emma went along with my deception, that she wanted Lindsey to have me—but I belonged with Emma.

Have me. As if I'm a prize.

Lindsey's mind clearly had the same thought, because that's when she hurled the heavy glass globe at me, shattering it into thousands of pieces. She was a little manic—and my eyes went wide in surprise, my entire body flinching from it. I wasn't ready for her next blow.

She was kind enough to stitch me up. She tugged hard, and I'm pretty sure I caught her lip curled in a devil's smirk every time she stuck the needle through me. I think she gave me more stitches than necessary, and I can tell it's a sloppy job—also sure she did *that* on purpose. It's fine. I have plenty of scars. At least I provoked this one.

Lindsey cut the threads on my chin, then told me to get out. She yelled it three more times, throwing my phone and keys into the hallway behind me, my stuff ricocheting off my back. I glanced at Sam on my way out, holding up a hand as he shook his head and chuckled. He mumbled something about karma catching up to me. He has no idea.

Lindsey passed me as she left her building with a duffle bag, pausing long enough to tell me I was pathetic and to ask me to tell Emma to move out.

I started to protest, to defend Emma, but she only held up a hand and seethed "Don't." Lindsey's angry and hurt, and I get that. But I won't give up on making things right between the two of them. That's a promise I'm making to Emma.

I've been sitting out here on the stoop of her building ever since her roommate left. I've been waiting for hours—my hangover already seeping into every cell in my body. I was clearly not sober for any of that.

Trent texted me an hour ago, saying he came to meet me at Majerle's, but it looked like I left. I told him he had "no idea." He sent a question mark, so I told him I can no longer be left unattended. He sent a string of smart-ass remarks after that, which I never answered back. He's going to be disappointed in me when I see him, as it is—no need to start the lecture on a text string.

The ice pack Sam tossed to me an hour ago has completely melted. I don't know why he took pity on me, but the notion that the old man likes me feels nice. I get the feeling he and I might be a little alike—or at least we were when he was my age.

Most of the lights in Emma's building have gone dark. It's well past midnight, and the longer I sit here, the more my mind runs rampant with thoughts of her and that Graham dude doing things. I've fucked my life up so badly, it's bordering on a Shakespearean tragedy. But I'm done losing out in life. I'm done not going for what I want, for being on the shit end of people's opinions and what everyone else thinks is best.

I want Emma Burke. I always have. And I'm going to fight like hell to make her mine. I know a thing or two about fighting.

The quiet night air and the rasp of the crickets forms a constant hum that almost lulls me to sleep. The sudden rumble of the taxi pulling along her street jolts me awake though. And when Emma steps through the back door, tears pouring from her eyes, her face red and upset, her body convulsing with emotion, I'm rushed with adrenaline.

I sprint to her, and the closer I get, the worse I realize it is. Her cheek is bruised, her dress is torn, the strap on her purse is dangling by a thread.

I want to kill someone.

"Emma!" A breathy shout leaves my chest, and my legs feel like they want to fold under me. Someone hurt her—someone hurt her badly. Her lip quivering, she finally collapses against me, completely falling to pieces against my chest. I hold one arm around her, dig into my pocket, and fish out a crumpled twenty that I throw at the cab driver.

"That's not enough," he says, leaning out the window. I flinch toward him, and Emma startles. Thankfully, that move and the look on my face is enough.

"Mother fucker," he grumbles, twisting his steering wheel and pulling away fast.

Emma's still shaking in my arms, and I take this short moment to survey the rest of her. Scratches line her bare arms, and I realize just now that she's also barefoot.

"Did he do this to you?" I ask.

She's quiet, her eyes barely open, her tears still coming down like rain.

"Emma, did that Graham guy touch you?" I repeat. I'm trying so hard to keep my voice calm, but I know I sound like a lunatic.

I open my mouth to ask her again, but she finally nods slightly, stuffing her knuckles into her teeth as she lets out an enormous scream that echoes down the street. Sam hears from inside and rushes out to us.

"Miss Burke? Are you all right?"

He eyes me like a protective father, and I like him even more because of it.

"She's hurt, Sam. We need to call nine-one-one..." I start, but Emma interrupts.

"No!" she screams, clutching my shirt and twisting her head to look at me, shaking her head *no.* She begs, and I feel like I'm free falling, my stomach sick and my head not sure what's right or wrong right now.

Emma is all that matters.

"Miss Burke?" Sam asks again, his eyes flitting from her to me.

"No," she coughs out. "No...please don't call. I'm...I'm all right. It's a misunderstanding, and that...that would make things worse. Please...take me inside."

I breathe in slow, painful air, my lungs burning against the motion because home is the one place Emma needs to go, and I've gone and ruined that, too.

"I'm taking you home with me," I say, her eyes wide on mine. She's so frightened and in shock. "I don't want you to be alone, and we can't...we can't stay here."

I swallow hard, not wanting to give her details right now, not wanting to pile on her nightmare with more. She doesn't ask, but instead lets her head fall forward, nodding in agreement. She's letting me take control.

"Let's go inside and get some of your things," I glance to Sam, silently asking him to let me help with this. Our eyes meet, and I know he's in my corner.

Sam holds the door open for us, and I walk with her weight against me, my eyes meeting his once more. We follow Sam to the elevator, and he calls a car down for us to step inside. I nod to him once more as the doors slam to a close between us. Emma's breathing is steady, but every breath is deep and labored, almost like she's trying to self-soothe, but failing miserably.

"Emma," I hum her name, cradling her to me. She shivers when I speak, and I shut my eyes wishing I could do more, wishing we were past so many things so I could give her the love she needs right now.

I follow her into her apartment, pausing at the door to her bedroom as her body slips away from mine long enough to grab a small bag. She stuffs handfuls of clothing in, not really paying much attention. I step inside her room finally and push her hands down, holding them still.

"Go get your things in the bathroom. Let me do this. I'll do it right. I swear," I say, looking at the stack of thin shirts she's packed while the weather outside is in the low fifties. She shakes her head *okay* then moves to the bathroom.

245

I work quickly, grabbing a few sweaters from her closet, pulling jeans from shelves and emptying her underwear drawer without looking. I don't know what she wants or needs to be comfortable, so I take a little bit of everything; I can give her my things to stay warm, too.

Knowing Emma, I also grab her backpack, pulling the zipper fully open to slide the books strewn about her desk inside. I stop suddenly though at a familiar sight. My letters are scattered in her bag, some of them in a large envelope, others pushed far into the bag, bent and folded as if she hid them in a hurry. I listen for her in the bathroom and decide to brave a glance at the large envelope containing most of them.

Emma,
From Dad

My body rushes with a wave of panic, but the sound of Emma shutting the medicine cabinet across the hallway jolts me from the numbness that I want to swim in. My letters. Carl—he brought them to her. Emma—she read them. At least...some of them. I stuff her books on top quickly, knowing that when she can, she'll realize that I saw them.

"Here, make sure I got what you need," I say, distracting her with the other bag. Her eyes widen at the sight of her backpack, but I turn my attention away so she doesn't give it more thought than she can afford to now. "I'm getting us a ride."

She nods once, then lowers herself to sit on her bed, her overnight bag in her lap so she can stare into it. I don't think she's really looking at anything, but I feel pretty sure that I put enough of everything inside for her to be all right for a few days.

My phone rings in my ear while I watch her.

"Yo, what-up with the cryptic texts you jerk?" Trent asks, his laughter light. I need him to be serious now, and I also can't work through his logic and reason and the million ways that this is a bad idea and how so much of it is probably my fault.

"Trent, I need you. It's Emma. She's—" I glance to her and step into the hallway. "That fucker did something to her, hurt her, Trent. She's here, and Lindsey's gone. And I know I have a shit-ton to fill you in on, but Emma's hurt. I need you to come get us."

There's a brief silence.

"I'll be right there," he says. "Text me the address."

"Thank you, Trent. Jesus...just...thank you," I say, relaxing a little knowing he's coming. I hang up and send him the address to Emma's building then return my focus to Emma, who is still an ice statue on the edge of her bed.

"Trent's coming. Let's get you downstairs," I say, lowering enough to thread my arm around her and lift her gently along with me.

We take slow steps out of her apartment, and I take her key to lock up behind us. Sam greets us at the end of the hall, the elevator held open. I'm not sure if he did that to keep an eye on me or to help us move Emma smoothly downstairs. Right now, it doesn't really matter.

Trent pulls up outside within minutes, and one look at Emma stops any questions he's dying to ask me. He steps from the car, leaving the motor running, and opens the back door for Emma to step inside. I follow her, nodding *no* when he looks at me like it's a bad idea for me to be this close to her. Think what you want about me, dude—there's no way in hell I'm leaving her side tonight.

Trent pulls her two small bags into the front seat next to him, and minutes later we're unloading at our apartment. I tug Emma's arm gently as we exit the car, and she follows so I can guide her inside.

Her feet are still barefoot—*shit!* I forgot her shoes. I grimace to myself, but keep moving forward. My arm never leaves its cradle around her body. She fits against me so well, if only she weren't shivering. I guide her all the way into my room, and she doesn't protest. I pull out an extra-large Tech hockey shirt and lay it on the bed next to where she's sitting.

"Go ahead and change. I'll step outside and give you a minute," I say, my eyes studying her knees, too afraid to look up in her tear-filled eyes. She stopped sniffling during the drive, her eyes instead wide and stunned in one position. I'd give anything to read her thoughts so she wouldn't have to tell me what happened—I'd just know. My biggest fear is that what I'm imagining is exactly what happened—or not even close to as bad as it really was. Either way, when I get my shot, I'm going to hit that guy so hard that his tongue will choke him.

I shut the door behind me quietly, as if I'm trying not to wake her. I don't know why, but I just feel like too much noise will frighten her. She seems shell-shocked.

"She okay?" Trent whispers. He pulled a bottle of water from our fridge. I smile at him and nod *thanks.*

"I don't know," I say, shaking my head and looking back at the closed door behind me. "I don't know what he did, what happened, but this isn't my Emma…"

"Your Emma…" Trent repeats. His eyes are lecturing me subtly.

"She's always been mine," I say, my mouth working on automatic, primed to deliver nothing but the truth until I erase everything bad that's ever happened in Emma's life. My eyes dare Trent's. He turns his head a tick to the right, waiting for me to say more. When I don't, he nods once and holds up a single hand.

"All right then. I'll be awake for a bit taking care of some reading. If you need anything…"

"Thanks, man," I say, watching his door close with the same caution I shut mine. I smile at how much he understands without asking.

I knock lightly on my door and Emma's voice cracks out "Come in."

She's still wearing everything she was before, my shirt in her lap, her fingers kneading it like bread. Her eyes are lost in a trance. "My shoes…I…I don't know what happened to my shoes," she whispers. I look down to her feet as her toes curl.

I open my mouth to ask her if she needs more time alone, time to dress, but then I shut my lips, breathing slowly and silently through my nose.

"Here," I say, holding a hand out to her. She looks at it for several seconds before sliding her own into my grasp. I'm delicate with her fingers, but I can't help but let my thumb run over the top of her hand in a soothing way. That's all I do it for—

248

I want to soothe her. I want to fix things for her. I want to avenge her.

I crack open my door and glance toward Trent's. When I confirm his is still closed, I walk with her to our bathroom and shut the door behind us. I don't lock it because I have a strong feeling that doing something like that would spike her panic—she can't feel trapped tonight. I turn the shower on and set the shirt I brought in with us down on the sink.

"We need to get you cleaned up," I say, pulling one of my large towels from the cabinet behind the door. I unravel it and hold it up, covering her body from my view. "Can you step out of your dress on your own?"

She nods slightly again.

I watch the dirtied garment fall to the floor by her feet, and I swallow down my rage. Her underwear fall next, and I close my eyes for a second—I hide my wince because I hate that she wasn't wearing more than this. That asshole had his hands on too much of her. Yet I'm relieved she's wearing what she is still, that he didn't...

I lean my head toward the shower, then move the towel so she can step inside, shielded from my view. I drape the top over the top of the glass door, then sit on the toilet next to the shower while the water cascades over her body. I focus on the sound of the rain falling from the faucet for several minutes, the entire time wondering what I'm going to do next, how I'm going to make her better, when she breaks the silence, choking out a small cry.

"Don't leave me, Andrew. Stay in here. Are you still here?"

I stand to my feet fast and raise a hand over the towel, clutching the top.

"I'm right here, Emma. I'll be right here, and I'll go anywhere you tell me to," I say.

"Will you help me?" she asks.

"Emma..." I shut my eyes, my head falling forward onto the towel-covered glass.

"I trust you, Andrew. I...I just...I can't seem to get myself to move. Everything feels not right. And my heart is beating so fast..."

It's that part that gets me—Emma's heart beating fast. I'd give anything to be the man who gets to protect that heart. I want to hold it in my hands. And the fact that she trusts me— that's the first time I've felt like maybe I deserve to hold it.

I deserve her.

"Okay," I whisper.

I slide the towel out of the way but keep my eyes trained on her head, her wet hair clinging to her cheeks and neck. I don't dare look any further.

Reaching down with one hand, I pour a generous amount of shampoo into one hand and hold it up for her to see. There can't be any surprises.

She nods slowly, so I move my hand over her head, lathering her hair and letting the soap run down her body. I want to look at her injuries, but nothing else.

"Where are you hurt?" I ask, my jaw tight with the question. What I really want to ask is *where did that asshole hurt you?*

Her eyes glance down at herself, holding her arms out slowly until she raises her hands up one at a time in front of her face and between us. Her eyes are trained on her fingers at first, but then her focus changes to my eyes.

"I. Hurt. Everywhere."

My breath falls short and my stomach twists tightly as she breathes out the same words I spoke to her.

Her bruises—those are small and will fade quickly. But the marks we can't see—the invisible things Graham left behind— those are things that are hurting her right now.

"Emma..." I say, moving my hands from her hair to her fingers, clutching them and bringing them forward to me until I rest them on my chest. Her body is soaking, and the water is trailing down her arms and soaking my shirt. I don't care in the least.

"I'm so sorry, Emma," I say. I know they seem like empty words, but they're all I've got, and for me, they aren't empty. They're so full she has no idea—so full of love and care and a need to protect this girl.

"I know," she says, her lashes falling with the dew from the shower spray.

I hold her hands there and just watch her with her eyes closed. I let her stand still, because I think she needs this more than she needs anything else. I let the water wash the rest of the soap from her hair, and when enough time has passed, I turn off the spray and pull the towel down from the top of the shower to wrap it around her body.

I guide her with the same care as before out of the shower, and when I'm certain she can stand all right on her own, I pull the shirt into my hands and bunch it up to slip it over her head. She lets me, and I work it down her body until the towel falls and she pushes her hands through the arms. She hugs herself in it, and somehow it gives me peace to see her do this with something of mine.

She's staring at me now, which I guess is better than staring into nothingness. I only wish I knew what was going on in her head—I hope she knows I didn't look while she was naked, that I kept my promise.

I tug open my sink drawer and pull out the small brush inside. I hold it up for her, then move to pass it through her hair slowly. I'm careful with the tangles, and I don't comb any longer than I think I need to. I don't want to hurt her, and I can see the purple on her cheek—I know her head has to hurt.

I've had a bruise just like that. Someone *hit* me to give it to me.

With her hair brushed and her body cleaned, I take her hand and walk with her back to my room, closing the door when she steps inside. I pull back my blankets and tear away the top one, laying it on the floor.

"You're not sleeping up here?" she chokes out her question, and her body is shivering. I pause, looking at the thin blanket on the floor. I know it will be miserable, but I also know that tonight is not the night to be taking advantage of anyone.

"You can have my bed," I explain.

"You're leaving me alone?" she asks, her voice growing more panicked.

"I'll be right here. I'll even sit with my back against the bed until you fall asleep," I say, patting the place where I intend to sit. She nods slowly, then lowers herself to my bed. I pull the remaining blankets up over her, and she wraps her arms around them just as she did my shirt. My heart rushes again.

"I'm going to turn the light off. Unless...unless you need it," I say.

She looks over at the switch, her mouth perched open for a few seconds, considering. "Is there...maybe...some other light? Not so bright?"

My eyes squint while I think, and I turn to my desk, to my laptop, which I plug in so the battery doesn't die and flip open to my streaming videos, leaving it on *mute* so the only thing left behind is a small, blue hue cast about my room. I flip the switch and look to her.

"Is this enough?" I ask.

She nods, then pulls the blankets up tight to her chin.

I know she isn't going to sleep, so I pull my phone into my lap as I nestle next to the bed on the floor, prepared to read until morning if I have to. I won't leave her side.

I open up my reading app and scroll to the book I started a few months ago, before the semester started, and before I knew Emma was here. It's an overly complicated sci-fi fantasy with so many characters that I have to scroll back to the beginning to remind myself what the hell is happening. I'm not sure why I bother, because my eyes are just reading words—I'm retaining nothing.

Several minutes pass, and the bed behind me is still silent. I know she isn't sleeping though. I know, because I wouldn't sleep either. I didn't—for weeks—the first time someone jumped me at Lake Crest. I'd shut my eyes for quick rests, but my body never fell away completely. I was quick to wake at the smallest sound.

That's where Emma is now.

"Emma?" I whisper finally, just wanting to reassure her that I'm here.

A few seconds pass, and I think maybe I'm wrong, maybe she's asleep after all. Then I feel her weight shift on the bed, and soon her breath at the side of my face, her body so close to mine.

"I trust you, Andrew," she breathes. I don't look at her, her eyes are so near, her mouth...so near. I shut my eyes to avoid any temptation.

252

"Thank you, Emma. I'm sorry you can't trust others...I...I shouldn't say that. I'm just...God, I'm so sorry..." I ramble.

"I trust you," she says again. "Please...please come up here. Please hold me."

My lip quivers with this situation I'm in. My arms twitch to hold her, my instincts taking over and wanting to be the man she needs. But this isn't how I wanted to hold Emma Burke at all—this isn't the reason.

But it's what she needs. So I crawl up into the bed, lifting the cover, and I pull her into me, my breath exhaling in time with hers as I feel so much of what she's suffering from escape, if only for this moment.

"I've got you, Emma," I say, my lips falling to her head. I sweep her hair behind her ear and kiss her head again, this time letting my lips stay there while I speak. "I've got you, and I won't let go. I won't let go now, okay?"

She nods one more time, and even though she never fully falls asleep, she lets her body rest. And I know what a triumph that is.

Emma – Earlier that Evening

It's not like me to be afraid to talk. At least...not in small groups like this. That's one of the things Miranda likes about me—I speak my mind.

But there was a vibe at the table throughout our dinner. I felt it all night. Something's been...*off*. Miranda and Graham have traded snarky remarks, and from the small bits I have deciphered, I get the sense that she really doesn't approve of many of his choices, and that there's also a bit of resentment that runs rampant throughout their household. She's mentioned more than once that he shouldn't work so hard to take after his father, and there's a tone when she says that.

When the conversation veered toward Tech Med programs, Graham was completely cut out of the conversation, and that's when he started ordering drinks.

He's rowdy now, and I can feel my cheeks burning while he stands on the corner of Washburne and Racine shouting at cars that drive by, asking if anyone's an Uber Cab, his body teetering out into the roadway every so often, causing cars to honk. His mother left with the other deans and a man that seemed to be more than a friend, but clearly not her husband. She and Graham didn't bother to say goodbye to each other, and I can still feel the ice.

"I'll just call a cab," I say for the tenth time. He isn't listening to me.

Somehow, an actual cab drives by and responds to his waving. He grabs my hand firmly, the first time he's touched me all night, and his fingers feel rough and sweaty. I slide into the back seat next to him, and he lets go of my hand. I reach forward and touch his arm, trying to get his attention. I want to go home. But he ignores me, leaning forward, relaxing both arms over the front seat and talking to the driver.

When he sits back to rest next to me, he tugs his tie loose from his shirt, his right hand nervously tapping on his leg. He glances at me and does a double take. I think maybe my nervous look registers with him.

"Hey, I just wanted to stop by this place. A few of the guys invited us. We won't stay long. That okay?" He's asking, but not really. I nod and smile, and he leaves his glare on me a little longer than comfortable.

"So how well do you know that Andrew guy?" he asks. My guard goes up, and inside, I start to rewind everything I said tonight. Andrew has been the only thing on my mind—his letters, what he whispered when I left my apartment, the last week I've experienced with him. I've been checking my phone obsessively to see if Lindsey's texted me about their talk, but so far she hasn't. I'm pretty sure I haven't said anything about him aloud.

"I don't know. That's hard to say. I mean, we were friends in high school," I say, my answer purposely vague, not wanting to lie, but not wanting to divulge. Graham keeps his stare on me, the same look as before—it makes me shiver. His lip quirks up on one side, and he pulls a cigarette from a silver case he slides out of his back pocket.

I watch him light it, then glance to the windows around us, all of them up. I roll mine down for the sheer need of fresh air. The driver does the same.

"I didn't know you smoked," I say. I work hard to keep my face from souring. I get the sense Graham has had his fill of disapproval for tonight—I think maybe that's what his brashness is about.

He takes a long drag from his cigarette, holding the smoke in for a second or two, letting it swirl out around his teeth, rushing around his beard and filling most of the cab. That beard seemed so sexy when I first saw it, but now...I don't know.

"You know he has a record?" Graham asks me, his eyes back on mine, studying me and watching carefully for me to give something more away. I shrug and look out the window, wishing I were headed home rather than somewhere deep into the city.

"I heard something about that. He was a kid, though, so that stuff doesn't stay on your permanent record or anything," I say, still averting my eyes. I can feel him looking at me, and several seconds pass before he reacts to my response.

"Guess so. But shit like that still gets out..." he trails off.

I shut my eyes, but keep my face toward the window, not indulging him any more in this topic. I'm saved when the cab pulls abruptly next to some club named Primal. There's a line out the door, and the light strobing from the open doorways makes me dizzy. I dig my heels in as we step from the car, not wanting to go inside, but Graham simply tugs my arm a little harder.

My head rattles with the thumping of the music, and it takes us several minutes to slide through the packed bodies grinding along the main floor. We finally make it to a small tabletop against the wall in the back where two guys raise their hands and bump fists with Graham, half hugging him as he steps up close enough. They eye me over his shoulder, and the one closest to me smiles.

"I'm Brody," he says, reaching out his hand. "I sort of met you a couple weeks ago. I went with Graham to that dinner for his mom."

He looks familiar, and I'm honestly just thankful that he's kind. It's going to make however long I have to be here bearable.

"Nice to see you again. Emma," I shout into his ear. He nods and gives me a thumbs up, but I'm pretty sure he didn't hear a word I said.

"Whatcha drinking?" he asks.

"Water's fine," I say, looking around at the table loaded with drinks. Graham already seems to have one in his hand, and he glances at me, the same suspicious look he was giving me in the car.

When the waitress comes, my new friend Brody orders me a water, but Graham steps in, putting his hand on his friend's chest, his fingers splayed as he pushes Brody a little off balance.

"She'll have one of those vanilla pineapple things," he says. The waitress darts her eyes to me, and Graham morphs into his suave self, sliding his arm around me affectionately and leaning his head down to look me in the eyes. "It's sweet. You'll like it, I promise."

I nod *okay*, even though I don't really want it, and my inside self screams at me. Graham leaves his arm around me as he begins talking with his friends, and I do my best to ignore the possessive feel of it. It's nothing like the way Andrew's touch feels—nothing gentle or seductive or special. It's barbaric feeling, his arm heavy and hot, and even though I haven't tried to step out of his grasp, I can tell he wouldn't let me.

A guy brings our drinks over on a platter, and when he hands Graham his, I notice that Graham spends several long seconds looking at it while the waiter hands out everyone else's. I take mine, and after a tiny sip, slide it onto the table in front of me. I'm going to do my best to turn it into something that's forgotten.

Just as the waiter turns to leave, Graham grabs hold of his forearm, stopping him from leaving. The waiter regards his hand, then looks over Graham, I think trying to decide who would hit the other harder in a stand-off.

"I ordered a *full* drink, and you brought me this," Graham says, a slight slur to his drunken speech. He's still very confident sounding, but sloppy around the edges.

The waiter looks down at the drink in Graham's hand. It's maybe an inch and a half from being full, a sip short at the most.

"I'm not sure what you want me to do," the waiter says. I notice Graham's jaw twitch and his neck tense as he shoves the drink into the waiter's hand.

"I want you to go get me the right fucking drink!" he seethes. The waiter stares at him, blinking, I think a little stunned and waiting for everyone to laugh like this is a big joke. Only nobody does. I notice Graham's friends have all moved on and are talking with each other, ignoring this display, which makes me think this is probably normal behavior. "I mean...am I wrong?"

He looks to me for support, and I shake my head slightly, my palms instantly sweating. I want to leave. I want to leave right now.

He turns to one of his friends, nudging him on the arm and motioning to the drink, now held out between them by the waiter.

"Dude, that's crap, right? I ordered a full fucking drink, and this asshole brings me this. I'm not paying for that. Am I wrong?" His voice is carrying over most of our corner of the bar now, and several people are looking at us. I notice the waiter straighten his posture, rolling his back muscles, gearing up for whatever's next.

Graham's friend chuckles and laughs out *yeah* in response before returning to the conversation he was in before.

"I'll bring you a new one," the waiter finally says, muttering to himself as he turns away.

Graham's eyes drift hazily over to me, and his stare is intense and instantly causes my body to heat up and my back to sweat.

"Did that embarrass you?" he asks.

It takes me a moment to catch up to what he said; I'm too busy wondering if it's a joke, or if he's teasing. His mouth never cracks a smile, though.

"A little," I admit.

He holds his stare on me, then lets his eyes trail down my body in a way that makes me clench my knees together and flex my leg muscles, ready to kick and scream and run.

"It shouldn't embarrass you," he says.

I don't make eye contact. As I step closer to the table and run my finger along my drink as a distraction, I shrug and whisper "Maybe."

I can feel his stare on me, and it makes me mindful of every movement I make. I pull my small purse up to the tabletop and take out my compact, looking in the mirror even though I have no need. I clip it shut again, then move my phone to a place I can view it inside my purse. I slide the screen on and check the time, not quite midnight. I groan inwardly at the thought that I might be stuck here for a while.

My finger is poised over the contacts button when I feel Graham's breath at my neck.

"You calling that Harper dick?" he questions. There's a bite to his tone.

"I was checking the time and just making sure my roommate didn't need anything," I smile.

I pretend.

His heavy stare lands on me again, and somehow he feels bigger. His shirt is opened at the top, his tie now loose on both sides. It's funny how this look can be both sexy and repulsive—depending on who and when.

"You know I'm going to fight him?" he asks.

I pinch my brow, wondering what he means. Is he seriously challenging Andrew to a duel? I'm not sure who I'd bet on if he was. I know who my heart would pick.

"I was the Sigma national champ, last year. I'm trying to stay in fighting shape. It's my hobby, and when I found out Harper liked to box, I thought...well..." he says, his lips slightly curled into a grin.

"I don't really care for boxing," I say, wishing the liquid in my glass were water so I could drink it.

Graham's stare lingers a moment or two longer, then he steps past me to join his circle of friends at the next table, putting an arm around one of the guys. I turn so my back is to him, and I breathe out slowly, clutching my purse in my hands again, convincing them not to tremble. I glance around the bar, to the dozens of plush seating areas with well-dressed couples nestled close to each other, groups of women taking shots and laughing loudly, men running fingers up girls' legs, teasing them, flirting—fondling.

My head feels fuller with every beat of the music, and it's making it hard to see. I trace the walls of the interior, searching for anything that might get me through the next thirty minutes, my gut sinking, knowing it will probably be an hour. When I finally spot an open sofa, I move to it, my purse in my hands, my drink on the table behind me. I tuck myself into the corner cushions, then look over the other women sitting near me so I can emulate their behavior. All I want to do is fit in long enough to leave.

I settle on curling one leg under the other, then I pull my purse close, next to me and remove my phone, opening the text box. I think about texting Lindsey for a rescue, but then I remember Andrew—he's telling her.

I can't call Lindsey. She might not even come after he tells her everything.

My eyes fall to my lap and I slip my phone back into my purse. Graham finds me a few minutes later, and my stomach sinks when I see him hold a finger up to a friend and weave through the people to get closer to me. The heat of him next to me as he sits down close on the sofa repulses me.

"You want me to take you home?" he asks.

Yes! Yes, this is what I want. He's not a bad guy, and he gets it. Oh thank god.

I nod and apologize. "I'm just not feeling very well," I say.

He smiles, but briefly, knocking back the rest of his drink—the new one brought to him a few seconds ago from the waiter he badgered and bullied—then plunks his glass down on the small metal table in front of us.

"I'll take you home," he says.

I move my purse in front of me, looping the strap over my neck, relieved and ready to go. As I uncross my legs, I feel the eerie tickle of his finger sliding up my left thigh, stopping at the hem of my dress. My leg jerks in response. Graham chuckles, the sound escaping his throat raspy and dirty.

"Come on," he nudges over his shoulder, standing and pulling out his wallet. I notice several hundred dollar bills unfold before he gets to two twenties. He steps over to his friend and hands them to him, then reaches for my hand, tugging it completely into his grip. My instincts are screaming at me to fight against it. But I desperately want to leave, and right now, this seems like my only way home.

We get out front and Graham practically drags me to the corner, stopping abruptly, looking both ways, then dragging me behind him across the street. My foot jerks and I feel one of my heels break off, so I hop a few steps, his hand still grasping mine.

"My shoe!" I scream.

He looks down at my feet behind him, sighing heavily as I take my shoes off. His hand reaches for my arm when I do, and as soon as I'm able to walk, he drags me to the other side of the street.

"Cabs are easier to get over here," he grumbles.

We rush to the corner, a closed art gallery and several dark office lobbies lining the sidewalk. We pause by a metal trashcan, and I lean against it to lift my feet one at a time and look at their bottoms, inspecting for cuts. The blacktop has already stained them, and there's a pebble lodged in the skin of one. I pull it out with my fingers, and as I'm leaning forward I feel the snaking sensation of Graham's hand on my bare back. I arch myself away from him, straightening up quickly as I take a step away, leaving my broken shoes on the ground near the trashcan.

Graham holds both of his hands up innocently, his eyes still hazy and his mouth in a hard line. His right leg leans a little too far and he falters, but regains his balance quickly, his eyes on me the entire time. I look to the road, looking for a cab to call on my own, and in that second, he reaches for me again, this time his hand grasping around my side, his fingers sliding around my ribs, to my back, pulling up the material gathered around my lower back and causing my skirt to hike up several inches as he pulls me to him.

I shove my hands into his chest, forcing space between us, but I'm no match for his strength as I struggle against him. I feel his hand slide around my back completely, into the scooped curve of my dress, his fingers clawing at my ass. I bring my knee up, but he anticipates me and blocks my blow, turning enough to the side.

"Isn't this how your man Andrew likes it?" he huffs. His hold is rough, bruising my body everywhere he grips it, and I start to cry.

"Let go! Graham, let go of me!" I scream, my words muffled against his mouth as he forces a kiss on me, his beard scratching at my face and his breath hot. I push so hard that the strap on my purse breaks, and I feel my things fall to the sidewalk below us. I also feel Graham's other hand reach around me to force me even tighter into him. He tastes of old whiskey and stale smoke.

He growls as I shove against him hard, breaking his hold enough to get a foot of space from him, enough room to scream.

"Help me! Somebody!" My voice echoes, and I notice a few people across the street turn their attention toward us, but they move in slow motion—everything does. I can't tell if they're ignoring us, or coming to help, and soon Graham's hand is cupping my mouth. He's intoxicated and his fingers are messy, one of them at the part of my lips, so I open my mouth and grip what I can with my teeth, biting hard and fast. He rips his hand away, but flings his fist at me in an instant, his blow landing on my right cheek and sending my body to the ground on my knees.

"You bitch!" he yells, and I see him lunge at me from the corner of my eye. Before he reaches me, a pair of arms scoop under me and push me toward an open cab, and I notice one of Graham's friends holding him, pushing him backward several steps as the door closes on me. My belongings are thrown in next to me, and the cab driver looks over the seat mouthing something. I can't hear him—every noise a siren blaring in my ears, until finally I'm able to read his lips.

What's your address?

I manage to give him my building, and as the car begins to roll into traffic and Graham's figure fades from view, I start to cry harder, not stopping until the cab slows in front of my building and an angel is waiting for me on the curb.

Chapter 18

Emma

The light is dim, but it still feels too bright for my eyes. I hold my hand over my face, stretching my other arm and legs out, feeling the burn in my muscles and remembering the bruises on my skin. My fingers are cool over my eyes, and I leave them there until they warm.

I know where I am.

I'm glad I'm here.

I'm scared I'm here.

I wanted to be here, but never like this.

I pull my hand away and roll to the side. I felt Andrew leave the bed sometime early this morning. I thought about waking, but I didn't know what to say to him. I didn't want him to look at me—to see me like this. I feel weak and ashamed. And I feel alone.

Pulling in the heavy blue quilt to my body, I take in the scent on the material. It reminds me of young Andrew, and as I let my eyes look over the thinning fabric squares, I wonder to myself if he's had this blanket since high school. I smile at the thought of it—imagining him bringing pieces of home here to college with him. Then I wonder if he got to bring these same things to Lake Crest, and my smile fades.

There's a sound in the hallway, and I watch for movement under the door, wondering if Andrew's out there, if he'll come inside to check on me. Several minutes pass, though, so I finally leave the bed and shuffle slowly around his room to his dresser, pulling a few drawers open until I find one with a pair of sweatpants inside. I pull them on, rolling the top twice to keep them up on my waist. It feels good to dress in his things; it feels...safe. The clothes in my bag feel stiff—I don't want them.

I pause with my hand on his doorknob, closing my eyes and breathing in slowly as I twist and open his door out to the hallway. I see the bathroom across from me and wince at the thought of what Andrew did for me last night, what he could have seen. I know he didn't look though. As dazed as I was, I know because I watched him. I scoot across the hall to pee, then wash my hands and shut the light off behind me as I slide slowly down the rest of the hallway to the sound of the television blaring. There's a head leaning on the back of the sofa, and I recognize his roommate quickly, the crunch of the cereal as he scoops it from the bowl in his lap making me smile.

"Hi," I squeak. He jumps slightly, craning his neck to look at me, then moving fast to place his bowl onto the coffee table in front of him as his long legs maneuver around furniture into the kitchen.

"Emma, yeah. Hi...uh...Drew...he's...he's not back yet. Shit, uhm...you want breakfast?" he says, stumbling about the kitchen, opening cabinets and searching for something for me to eat. I'm not hungry. My stomach still feels sick.

"I'm okay. Thank you," I say.

He shuts all of the doors again, then leans against the counter, looking at me, his eyes scanning around the room.

"Can I get you something? I don't know, blanket maybe? Or...do you want to watch TV?" He rushes back into the living room and starts picking things up, turning the volume down on the program he was watching and glancing up at me every so often. It's sweet.

"Really, I'm okay. I...I was looking for Andrew," I say, my eyes falling, embarrassed about why I'm here, that I need someone—that I need *him*. I know I shouldn't be, but I feel so helpless.

"He's at work," he says.

"At...at that gym?" I ask, the thought of Andrew getting hit by someone squeezing my heart.

Trent chuckles lightly and looks at his feet, shaking his head. "No, his *real* job," he says. "He's at the elementary on Fourteenth. He's probably coloring right now."

My lips form a tight smile at the mental picture that paints.

"Coloring," I repeat.

Trent nods and laughs again. "Yep, Harper's one bad-ass colorer," he says.

Looking down, I let my smile grow slightly bigger. My feet are bare, and the chill hits them. I wiggle my toes.

"You need some shoes?" Trent asks. I laugh once to myself then look up at him, holding my arms out to show off my Andrew wardrobe.

"Andrew packed my bag, but he didn't include footwear," I shrug. "Seems I need a little of everything."

Trent nods, then holds up a finger and jogs back to his room. I wait in the middle of his living room, listening to the sounds of drawers sliding open and his closet door closing. He comes out with a pair of short socks and sport sandals.

"Here," he says, motioning to the sofa. "Have a seat."

I step around to the front, and he kneels in front of me, handing me the socks to put on. I slip them on quickly then put my feet on the floor so he can slide them into the sandals and adjust the Velcro so they don't come loose.

"You're like Prince Charming, only instead of a glass slipper, it's an old Adidas sandal," I laugh, holding my foot out and moving it to test to be sure the shoe doesn't fall away. Trent laughs with me.

"I guess so," he says. "Only, don't tell Drew that. He'll rip my head off if he hears you call *me* Prince Charming. That's his job."

I keep my eyes on him, and he glances up at me a few times, his lips in a tight smile, perhaps a little guilty for selling his friend's feelings out to me. I'm glad he did, though. And he's right—it is Andrew's job.

I head down the hall for a quick glance in the bathroom mirror then walk to Andrew's room to grab my broken purse and keys. Trent catches me before I leave completely, asking if I want a ride, but as much as I appreciate the gesture, I also want to go to Andrew alone. He seems okay with my "Thanks, but no thanks."

I leave their apartment, looking like a member of the Tech hockey team. It's still early, maybe not quite seven, and the traffic on the road is light. The fall weather is growing colder, and I notice my breath form a small cloud in front of me as I walk. I blow hard once just to test. I love it when the weather is like this.

I pass a few people walking their dogs, and I push my hair forward, wanting to hide the glaring bruise on my face. I don't know what drove me to leave the safety of his apartment this morning, only that I *had* to see him. I have to thank him, and it doesn't feel like it can wait. When I reach the school, I notice a few cars pull up to a main lot, parents stepping out and walking young kids up to a side building. I head to the open door, holding it as a woman walks out, her phone resting between her cheek and shoulder as she mouths *thanks* and passes me.

When I glance inside, I see Andrew's back to me; he's sitting on a long lunch-table bench with about a dozen six and seven-year-old girls gathered around him—all of them coloring. His hair is messy, tousled in varied directions, and he's wearing his black, long-sleeved shirt with gray jeans, the laces from his Converse shoes dangling off to the sides, waiting to trip him.

He looks like an innocent little boy in a man's body as his arm shakes from side to side with his coloring, his head leaning and his other hand twisting the paper in a slow circle so he can fill up something with the bright blue in his hand.

There's a tiny girl sitting next to him, her legs folded up as she sits sideways and watches him color. "Use pink next," she says, her voice high and precious. Her ponytails flop next to her face as she turns her head toward me and grins. She's missing two of her teeth on the top, but she's smiling like a supermodel. I hold a hand up and bunch my fingers in a wave. She waves back, then taps Andrew on the shoulder, scooting up on her heels to reach his ear. When she's done whispering, Andrew flips his body around quickly, his eyes wide on me.

"Sorry...Trent...he told me you were here," I say. His shocked look fades into a happy one, and he holds his crayon out for the young girl next to him to take.

"Kaitlyn, you mind finishing?" he asks. She pouts at first, but he brings both of his hands together in a begging motion and she finally sighs and begins coloring.

It takes him a few seconds to untangle his long legs from the bench that's clearly too small for him, then he looks over at the group of coloring girls until he reaches me.

"Just like you to have all the girls hovering around you," I tease.

He laughs, looking down and pushing his hands in his pockets, twisting one foot nervously as he nods in agreement, his eyes finally meeting mine. He squints the left one closed slightly, his right lip curling up—he's adorable. He's always been adorable.

"The boys all sleep in, so I don't get to play the boy things until the bell almost rings. They're lazy, I guess. The girls all get here right when I open up," he shrugs.

"I don't think they're lazy," I smile. "I think the girls just really like you."

He sucks in his bottom lip and nods to one side.

"Maybe," he grins. His gaze shifts from my eyes to the bruise on my right cheek, and I bring my hand up, sweeping hair back in the way to hide it. Andrew reaches to me slowly though, pausing to make sure it's okay that he approaches me. He's being cautious. He moves my hair back out of the way when I nod that it's okay, then leans his head to the side to look at my face, running the backs of his knuckles down my cheek slowly. It burns along my tender skin.

"It's not a very deep bruise," he says, tracing the skin one more time with his thumb. "I think it will start to fade quickly. It already looks better than it did."

His eyes come back to mine, and I notice the deep cut and stitches on his chin. This time it's my turn to assess the damage, and I run my finger along the rough edge of the threading then flit my eyes to his.

"You have another fight?" I ask, my gut twisting at the memory of what Graham said, that he plans on fighting Andrew. I wonder if that's true.

Andrew's brow lowers and he purses his lips.

"What?" I ask, worried that he may have done something else, that he might have hunted down Graham early this morning.

"Lindsey..." he starts, and I pinch my brow. "I...I told her the truth. And maybe I wasn't quite as...sensitive in my delivery as I should be?"

266

His face is bunched, not even hiding his shame, and my stomach sinks a little.

"So you did...tell her," I say. He said he would, and I had a feeling he would follow through. But that means Lindsey is probably angry with me.

"It's going to be okay, Emma. I promise," he says, cupping the side of my face with one hand. I stand there stiff, and I can see the hurt in his eyes as his hand slides away. "I told her it was all my fault, and I swear to god, I will make it right between you two."

"You don't have to. I'll...I'll talk to her," I say, looking down.

"Yeah...maybe not quite yet though?" he says, and when I look up, he's squinting one eye again. I exhale a deep breath and let my shoulders slump. "She wants you to move out."

I can't help the whimper that escapes me, and I bring my hands to cover my mouth. I stare at him, waiting for the part where he says he's kidding. But all I see is sympathy. He wears it well, and at least I have that—Andrew looking at me like he cares. Like he's deeply affected by my unhappiness.

"Emma...I'm sorry," Andrew says, shaking his head. He reaches for me, but pulls back again, instead putting his hands in his pockets. I hate that he's still so unsure with me. His touch—it would be so healing right now. But I understand his caution—it's out of respect. He's worried about what I've been through. "I'll fix this," he says, looking down at his feet. He repeats it again, this time more for himself.

I stare down along with him, not sure what to do now. I look at my hands, the way his shirt falls over my palms, and as upset as I am that I've lost Lindsey, my heart lurches that I have Andrew.

His foot kicks into mine, and I breathe out a small laugh before looking up at him, his lopsided grin saying he's sorry but he's happy he has me too.

"You look better in my things than I do," he smirks, unable to hold my gaze for long, his grin growing into an embarrassed one.

"I like the way you look in them," I say, biting my lip and flitting my eyes. This is the first time I've ever overtly flirted with him, and the thrill of it rushes my body. A few girls giggle behind

267

him, and Andrew turns to look, chuckling when he faces me again. This—it's all such a wonderful distraction from the scenes I keep replaying in my head.

He grabs his neck and rubs before raising one eyebrow and looking at me. "I think you might be right about my *girl crew*, and I'm not so sure they like you—I'm sort of their territory," he teases.

There's a long, comfortable silence between us, and my fingers tingle, wanting to touch him. I leave them wrapped in the comfort of his cotton sleeves though, and instead let the flurry of butterflies run around the inside of my body. It's nice to feel something different—I think this is joy. It's definitely anticipation.

"Move in with me," Andrew says, and the butterflies inside me all start running into each other, my heart speeding up and my hands forming tight fists as my nails dig into my own palms. My eyes must have given me away, because Andrew kicks his foot into mine again. "No, no...I just mean...you need somewhere to go, and I know Trent won't mind. Just until I get things worked out with you and Lindsey. We're close to campus, and I'd like..." he swallows hard. "I'd like to have you there, to know you're safe."

Our eyes hold onto each other, and our breathing falls into sync.

"Okay," I whisper, my lips tingling, not sure if they should smile or cry a little. "Okay," I nod again, maybe reassuring myself. "I'll grab some things this morning, while she's in class. I have class today, so I won't be at your house until late this afternoon. Is that...is that okay?"

"That's fine. Here," he says, reaching into his pocket and sliding a key from his ring. "I'm heading right to practice from here, and I'll just get in with Trent later and make a copy for myself."

"Don't you have class?" I ask.

Andrew shakes his head, laughing through a shrug. "I'll go tomorrow. It's fine. I've already done most of my work for the semester," he says.

"Nerd," I tease.

"Among many other things," he says, his smile a little sad.

"Many *good* things," I say. I hope my words make him smile, but he only breathes in deeply, shaking off my compliment.

"Maybe someday. I'm working on it," he says.

I want to tell him he's already there, and to thank him for taking care of me, but the doors burst open behind me and several boys come running, two of them grabbing onto Andrew's right arm when they reach him, climbing him like a jungle gym. A few of the parents are standing behind me, waiting to talk to him, so I just hold up his key and suck in my lower lip as I smile.

I take the long route to my apartment—my *old* apartment—and Lindsey is gone by the time I get there. I pull a few bags from under my bed and fill them with most of my clothes, thankful Andrew seemed to grab many of my necessities last night. When I glance at my desk, I realize my letters and backpack are also gone, and my body jolts with a shot of adrenaline. I panic at first that something happened—that during their talk, Lindsey discovered them, destroyed them, that they're gone. But my backpack is gone, which means Andrew must have seen them and brought that to his apartment too.

Andrew saw them.

I pause at that thought, not sure if it's good or bad. He wrote them for me, but now that we're both aware of the words he wrote—or at least many of the words he wrote—something deeply personal feels like it's settled in between us.

Lindsey will be gone for several hours—today is one of her longest, and though I used to wait desperately for her to get home so we could have dinner together, I'm grateful for the time now. I sit on my bed and pull my phone out of my purse, dialing on rote and in a trance. When my father answers on the other end, I'm not ready to speak—my mind still caught between being angry over the letters he kept from me and wanting to run to his familiar embrace after what Graham did. He waits me out, though.

"You get my package?" he finally asks. I nod even though he can't hear me.

"I'm sorry I didn't give it to you sooner," he says, and I hear him swallow, hear him thinking of ways to explain.

"Why?" I ask, a tear forming in the tender corner of my right eye. I pull the bottom of Andrew's shirt up to dry it.

"Your mom wanted to give them to you," he says, and knowing that makes me feel both grateful and terrible at once. "She made me save them. I threw the first one away, and she went out to the trash by the curb and pulled it from the bag."

My dad laughs, but it's a sad sound that comes out—one made of memories and repentances. "She told me it was a federal offense," he laughs through a cry. I join him, wiping away another tear, this one for that memory of my mom. "She said that any boy who took the time to write a letter, to mail it, with a stamp and everything, was worth rescuing. But I was so afraid of what might happen if Andrew wasn't worthy of you. I was afraid he would take you away—and not that he'd make you run away, but pull you away from us. His home life was so..."

"His brothers and mother and step-father—they're all really close and amazing dad. That isn't fair. That *wasn't* fair!" I shout, glad to be alone, free to be angry and feel.

"I know that now. But your mom...she was sick, and I just couldn't risk it. Oh god, Em...I'm so sorry. I was so scared, and I didn't want to lose you too..." My dad's words end with his crying, and I hear him let out heavy sobs, miles away from me, nowhere near me so I could hug him and assure him I was still here, even if I was angry with him. I got it.

I get it.

"I'm glad you didn't throw them away," I whisper as he grows quieter. "I'm glad...I'm glad Mom told you to keep them."

I listen to my father breathe, and I lay back on my bed that isn't really mine and wait for him to speak again. A few minutes pass before he finally does.

"Did he tell you that he came?" My eyes pop open, and I sit up straight.

"After Lake Crest? Yes..." I say, wondering if there's more to the story, if there are parts Andrew didn't tell me.

"Oh, no...not then. I didn't know...I didn't know he came then. I meant a couple days ago. He visited me, wanted to know why his letters never made it. He...he could have hit me he was so angry. I could tell," my father says. "But he didn't. He took everything in, everything I had to say, and as much as it wrecked him to know the truth, he respected me, and my bad decisions. I was wrong, Emma. And I'm sorry you didn't know about the letters before."

"I know now," I say in a faint voice. "I know now."

My eyes close at the thought of Andrew, at how much he cared for me then, and how much he must care for me now—even after so many wrong turns.

"Did he tell you why he went to Lake Crest?" I say, my eyes still closed, picturing everything that happened that night—picturing the resolve on Andrew's face when he told me to trade him places.

"I know, Emma. And even if he wasn't drunk or high at the time, it still...it still sticks with me that he was driving you around that way—" I cut my father off, before I lose the courage to tell the truth—the first time I've done so to anyone but Andrew.

"He wasn't driving, Dad. Andrew traded me places. I was the one who wrecked the car, and he..." I start to choke as the tears rush my face. "He took the fall for me, Dad. Andrew didn't want me to face any repercussions—and even though he didn't know it was my heart I was afraid of losing, he knew I was afraid of something. So he gave up a year of his life for me. A *year*, Dad."

"Emma..." my dad's breathing stutters as he tries to catch up to the truth, to soak in everything I just told him. "Emma?"

"I was driving. And that man stepped out in front of me, in the dark. And all I could think about was how any kind of misdemeanor or indiscretion would make Dr. Wheaton change her mind, would take me off the list. I was selfish, Dad!"

"Stop it!" my father yells on the other end. "Don't you dare think that, Emma Jane. Don't you ever call yourself selfish. You were scared, and it's okay to be afraid when you're sixteen and looking at the possibility of—"

"He lost so much, Dad..." I cry to my father. "So much..."

"He did," my dad agrees. If only my father knew how much Andrew truly lost—how much of himself was gone.

Another long silence passes while we both sit together on the phone, both of our thoughts consumed with Andrew Harper

271

I'm sure—both of us thinking of the good he has to offer, the good he gave, and how very ungrateful we were for it.

"Thank you for giving me the letters," I say finally, sitting and looking at my stuffed bags at my feet. I look around the room, and I think of my friend that I'm leaving behind, but when I look at the clothes I'm in, I think of the friend I'm running to, and I consider how my life seems to need to be in balance—to always give me something, but lose something else in return.

I will never give Andrew up again, though. But I want Lindsey, too.

I don't say it to my father aloud, but I think it: *I am selfish.*

Andrew

Somehow, I was on point today at practice. I have no idea how with the mess swimming in my head right now. I'm too distracted by everything to attend class, which was the first thing Coach brought up as I passed his office in the locker room. My mouth almost made it worse when my argument for him was that I didn't really *need* my advanced calculus classes, because I could build a working rocket out of the parts from his car right now—and ensure it had enough power to reach the stratosphere. He told me I was a smart ass and better show my face to my professors tomorrow. He's right, on both counts.

I've been waiting for Trent to ask about Emma, to want the details. He's doing that thing where he talks about everything *but* the elephant in the room, though. He even asked me about laundry, and if I'd done my load for the week or not. He's pushing me to let all of my baggage out, without prying— *directly*—and it's working. His goddamned method is working.

"Emma's moving in," I sigh as we pull into the only open space along the street by our apartment.

"Aha!" he exclaims, as if that...*that* is the thing he honestly expected me to say. He remains still, his hands on his knees; he sits proudly, like a fucking peacock in the passenger seat, then the meaning of what I said sinks in. He jerks to the side to look at me again. "Wait, what?"

I lean back in the seat and pull my hat from my head, tossing it on the dash, then run my hand through my hair, holding it between my fingers. I nod as I speak.

"Emma's moving in. Just...just for a few days. Lindsey's pissed," I say.

"Yeah, saw that coming," Trent says with a short laugh.

"Okay, no need to be a righteous asshole about it. You were right, bad idea, I'm a dick, got it," I say, glancing sideways at him before opening the car and slamming the door behind me. Trent follows suit and walks behind me up to our apartment door.

"Good, glad we're on the same page with all of that," he says. "So where, might I ask, will Emma be *staying* in our apartment?"

I sigh and let my head fall on our door as I wait for Trent to push his key in the lock. I shrug because I really hadn't thought about that yet. I was assuming she'd just stay with me, in my room, but maybe that's a little too presumptuous.

"Your ass can have the couch. No way am I giving up my room," Trent says.

"I know," I sigh and push through the door the second he unlocks it. I head straight to the kitchen and grab a beer, twisting the cap and gulping half of it down like water.

Trent sits on one of the stools at the counter and studies me for a few seconds. "What else?" he finally asks.

"What do you mean *what else*? Emma's moving in because I fucked up her living situation. What else is there?" I say, pulling the bottle up to my mouth. Trent lowers his brow at me when I do. "What?" I ask.

"Nothin' man. Just...slow it down. You got sloppy last night, and that's how you fucked things up in the first place," he says. I nod and slide the beer to the middle of the counter, then pull myself up to sit on the seat opposite of my friend.

"I fucked things up a long time ago. Last night was nothing—trust me," I say. I let my eyes focus on the beer, on the label and the gray color of the paper, the way it matches Emma's eyes. I can literally see her everywhere. I retrain my gaze to Trent, and he's studying me. "I love her. And it's so fucking bad. And it's messed me up...damn. Trent, I'm so messed up over it, I don't even know what to do."

"You tell her," he answers quickly.

I laugh in response, but he shakes his head and simply repeats his answer.

"Tell her what? Hey, I'm sorry I'm a loser who doesn't know how to have a real relationship; so instead, I steal chick's wallets—and love them and leave them? But really I'm not *that* broken, so maybe try me out?"

"Uh...no. You don't say that," he says, getting to his feet and grabbing my beer in his hand, finishing it. I raise an eyebrow at him, and he points a finger at me. "Hey, I don't do dumb shit after a beer or two. That's your thing."

"That Graham dude wants to fight me," I say, catching Trent off guard as he's about to toss the empty bottle in our recycle box. He pauses, pursing his lips before finally throwing the bottle away and moving back to his seat.

"So he, what...like challenged you to a duel at dawn or something?" he jokes.

I shake my head and let my gaze fall to my lap.

"No, or maybe, yeah. I...I don't know. It was before this whole thing happened, before last night. He knows Harley, and he's got some major bank."

"So you want to fight him for the money," Trent says, and I can hear his disapproval loud and clear. I fill my lungs and hold my breath, letting the air seep out slowly before looking my friend in the eyes.

"At first, yeah. It's a lot of money," I say.

"At first," he repeats me.

I nod.

"Now, I just want to beat the shit out of him for free," I say, my mouth hard, my breathing stopping, my eyes angry as I imagine the feel of my fist landing on him. I want to destroy him.

Trent doesn't respond, and eventually he slides from his seat and moves into our living room, picking up the remote and putting on ESPN, going right to his routine. I watch him for a few seconds, and I try to find the courage to ask him what he thinks I should do. But I already know—he doesn't think I belong in the ring with that guy, and he knows I won't be able to control myself when I face him. And I don't want Trent to tell me not to do it.

After a few minutes, I leave the kitchen and kick my shoes off by the front door, then grab my backpack from the table and start to carry it to my room.

"You should take her out on a real date. That's what you do. Buy her flowers, give her chocolate, or a teddy bear. Hell...do all three. You need all the help you can get," he says, stopping me before I reach my room. I turn my head back to look at him, and at first he keeps his attention on the TV, but eventually he faces me, giving me a slight shrug. "You asked me what you should do, and if you really love her, you should make that absolutely clear to her."

I chew at the inside of my mouth for a few seconds, considering what Trent said. Eventually, I nod in agreement, then make my way to my room so I can come up with something perfect for Emma—something I can do tonight, because I cannot let one more day go by where I'm anything but in love with this girl.

Chapter 19

Emma

I skipped Miranda's lecture today. I'm sure she'll text me. I've only missed once before, and it was because of a financial-aid meeting. She questioned my absence then, and it was easy to explain. Today's is a little more challenging. *"Oh, well, you see...your son got all grabby with me, then hit me when I fought back, and I want to hide this from you because I'm afraid you'll pick his side."*

Yeah—skipping was a good call.

I left my things at Andrew's this morning, and somehow, despite months of walking home in one direction, my legs managed to remember that today they lived somewhere else. The tickle in my tummy is constant the closer I get to his apartment, and I can't decide if it's because I'm excited, or because I'm anxious over Lindsey. I think maybe it's both.

I still feel selfish.

I'm about to push his key in the lock when the door suddenly opens in front of me, Andrew stepping through it and closing it behind his back. He's wearing a thin white T-shirt with skulls on the front over a black long-sleeved shirt, tight black jeans, and gray lace-up boots. His hair is combed back, and he smells almost edible. I swear his cologne is circling me for the kill. He pushes his hands into his pockets nervously, and shuffles his feet as he looks down at them while he talks.

"So I have plans. I mean, for me and you. I mean...shit. I'm already messing this up," he stammers. I suck in my bottom lip, trying not to smile or embarrass him. He looks me in the eyes and takes a deep breath, holding up a finger, stepping into his apartment and exiting it again just as he did before. "Let's try this again. Emma, I'd like to take you out tonight. On a date—a *real* date. And if this turns out to be corny or lame or if I gross you out or...whatever...then it's all Trent's fault. He told me I should show you how I feel. So, tonight, if you're willing to give me a shot, I'd like to start over. I'd like *us* to start over. And I'd like to treat you like you deserve to be treated...like I should have treated you all along. Whadaya say?"

My lip slides loose from my hold, and I can't stop the quick spread of my smile. Andrew smiles in return, nodding once and letting out a heavy breath. "Phew. Good. Okay then, before you go inside, I want you to know that I realize I might have gone a little overboard. But like I said—I didn't want there to be any question in your mind about my intentions here. I'm asking you on a date, and that date ends when you say goodnight. And then I will take my place on our *very* comfortable couch, giving you your privacy in my room for as long as you need it."

I open my mouth, my brow pinching with guilt; I hate the thought of pushing him out of his room, but Andrew holds a hand up quickly. "No questioning me. Not tonight. I'm too nervous about everything being perfect for you to question tonight, okay?"

"Okay," I say. Andrew closes his eyes, his smile once again relieved.

He pushes his door open, holding his arm out to direct me inside, where there are three gigantic boxes placed on the floor—wrapped in purple paper with white bows.

"Purple's my favorite color," I say.

"I know," he says in return. "Go on. Open them."

I look to him nervously, but move to the first box, excited to see what's inside. I tear away the tissue paper and pull off the lid to find two enormous Care Bears sitting inside. I lift them up and cradle each one on a hip, like they're children, and the silliness of them makes me giggle.

"Okay, so hear me out," Andrew starts, closing the door behind him and leaning against it. "That one there, the blue one? His name is Grumpy or Grouchy or..."

"Grumpy," I confirm for him, my mouth aching from my smile.

"Good, right. Well, Grumpy...that one's me. He's got this cloud that follows him around, and he's just generally blue and mopey and shit, and he doesn't really have any friends, other than this yellow bear here with the sunshine on it's stomach."

277

"Funshine Bear," I answer, looking over at the yellow bear on my other hip.

"Right...wait...Funshine? That's really his name?" Andrew asks. I nod *yes.*

"Wow, this is getting even lamer, and I'm really embarrassed," he says.

"Don't be," I say, catching his gaze before it falls. He squints one eye, questioning me. "So far, this is really sweet. Keep going."

He nods, his cheeks dented with the dimples of the smile he's trying to hide. The bashful boy from our youth is coming out to play, and it makes my heart soar to see.

"Okay, well *Funshine,* or as I called him, *Happiness...*this one's you. She's Grumpy's only friend in the world. And she's the only one that can make Grumpy forget about the damn cloud stuck on his body. He needs her. Without her, he's just not...well, without her there's just too much of the cloud," Andrew says, his mouth settling into a more serious smile. I notice how fast his chest is rising and falling, how hard he's breathing. He's scared.

I look at both of the bears and squeeze them to my body, then look back at him. "I love them. I'm keeping them with me all night," I say, and his lips slowly curl up again.

"Good," he nods, looking down. When he glances back up, he gestures to the second box. "Go on. Open it."

I tuck both bears under my left arm and move to the second box, working with one hand to unwrap it. I finally get the lid off the top and when I look down, I notice a pair of pink and white ice skates that look to be my size. I flash my eyes back to Andrew's, smiling.

"Holding your hand on the ice is the one memory I turned to when my cloud got really dark and heavy and hopeless. I'd like to take you skating tonight, at the rink, so I can hold your hand...if you'll let me?"

He's not breathing as hard as before, but he still sucks his bottom lip in, anxious for my answer. I nod *yes* quickly, then move to the third box. Before I can dig into the paper, though, Andrew places his hand on top, stopping me.

"This one comes at the end. It's...well...it's sort of important that I keep everything in order. When we get back from the rink,

I'll let you open it up," he says, his head leaned to the side, his eyes pleading.

"Okay," I say.

He's close enough that he could kiss me. I want him to. He never does, though. Instead, his eyes dance over me, following the curve of my face and line along my shoulders. For class, I changed into one of my turtlenecks and jeans, but I crave the warm feeling of being in his clothes again.

"You look nice," I say to him, my eyes moving to the top of his head, to the hair that's usually stuffed under a hat or twisted in all directions. He runs his hands through it, smoothing it back again, but messing it up just enough that a few strands fall forward over his brow, somehow making him even sexier.

"This is the best I've got," he says, arms outstretched. "I'm not really a suit-and-tie kind of guy."

It's my turn to let my eyes roam down him, his wide chest and thin waist, his arms filling the fabric of his shirt, his jeans tight around his muscular legs. I bite my lip on one side and smile through the other.

"I like this look better anyhow," I say, peering up at him.

His lips fall open with a breath, and I hold mine, thinking that maybe now he'll kiss me. But he closes his mouth quickly, smiling and taking a step back.

"We should get to the rink. I managed to find a half an hour that it's not being used, and the guy doing me a favor will be pissed if we're late," he says.

"Okay," I say softly, holding my bears tightly.

Andrew picks my backpack up from the floor and slings it over his shoulder, then tugs at the bears in my hand. I resist at first.

"You can't skate with these," he chuckles. "But...I'll put them with your things. You can have them back the second we get home."

Home.

How strange that he feels like home. And yet, how very not strange at all.

"Okay," I say again. I'm unable to do anything but agree with him. It's not that I owe him. It's that I *want* to go along with him. I meant what I said last night—I trust Andrew Harper...with my life.

I let him guide me back outside after he deposits my things in his room, and when he opens the door of his car for me, I force myself to keep my thoughts ahead—to focus on the future and possibilities rather than the past. Andrew's careful with me, taking my hand as I sit in the low bucket seat. He leans forward through the door as I buckle the belt, his head cocked to one side, silently asking me if I'm all right—the last ride in this car flooded me with painful memories.

I smile at him when my belt clicks, and his eyes skim down my body, down my legs, then back to my lips, and they quiver under the heat of his stare. Nothing about the way he's looking at me feels threatening or possessive; it's adoring, and it makes my palms sweat. Adored is exactly how I always wanted to feel, and I haven't felt it since he left my life five years ago.

He exhales slowly, backing away from the door and nudging it closed with the tips of his fingers, bringing both of his hands up to his mouth and closing his eyes as he continues to back away, shaking his head and smirking underneath it all.

When he gets into his seat, sliding in, buckling, and starting the engine, I question the soft chuckle and grin he's still wearing. He looks into his rearview mirror, almost like he's working extra hard not to look at me again. The tension causes my heart to speed up.

"What is it? Come on, Andrew...don't tease," I say.

His eyes shut; he laughs once again, his head falling forward, then his eyes open as he leans to the side, resting his head on his steering wheel.

"You have no idea how you bewitch me, Emma Burke," he says, his teeth dragging his bottom lip, his tongue caught in their snare next. "No idea."

His eyes wander around my face, and in that instant I see it—Andrew Harper is worshiping me. My heart drums louder, and I tuck my hands underneath my legs, holding my own breath.

The trip to the rink is short, and we spend those few minutes both blushing and taking small peeks at each other, like grade-schoolers who've passed notes back and forth and have just gotten thrown together in some playground tunnel. I don't know what to do or how to act—only that I know I want to leap onto his lap right now and never let go.

I stay put, and wait for Andrew to round the car to open my door for me on his insistence that I let him *play gentleman* for the night. He walks me up to the back door of the rink, and hands a guy a fifty-dollar bill before we slip inside. I wince at the amount of money, knowing how he earns it, and how little he has to throw away. But the slight smile he gives me keeps me from protesting. He's proud of this date—and I am going to love every second of it.

"Are we supposed to be here?" I ask, noticing most of the lights are off, minus three or four shining on the center of the ice.

"Define...*supposed to*," Andrew says, rolling his neck and grimacing at me.

I stop and watch him take a few steps in front of me, his body older, his legs longer, his look so very much the Prince Charming I've cast in my dreams. He was the original—the only.

"I don't think I should define it. I have a feeling the answer's *no* either way, so I'm just gonna go with the flow," I say, a little nervous that we're breaking a rule—a little excited by it, too.

"Probably for the best," he winks.

We slip through a small opening in the bleachers, and Andrew reaches for my hand, linking a few of his fingers with mine to guide me to my seat. When he stops, he doesn't let go of his slight hold, but turns to the side, his chin toward me and his breath tickling against my neck.

"Do you..." He stops, swallowing hard. "Do you need help with your skates?" I get the immediate sense that's not what he really wanted to ask. I know it's not what I wanted him to say.

I shake my head in tepid movements and take my skates from his other hand and sit to lace them. Andrew sits across from me, and when his skates are done, he slides his toe forward, knocking his blade into mine. We both look at it, then gaze up at each other, instantly breaking into laughter.

"I think you have a foot fetish," I tease as he reaches a hand out and helps me to stand.

Andrew shakes his head slightly as we scoot along the rubber floor out to the ice, his grip growing in strength. We switch to the icy floor and my skates begin to slide out from under me. His arm swiftly moves from my hand to around my body, steadying me on my wobbly legs, and he chuckles to himself.

"Emma, I don't have a foot obsession...I have a *you* obsession," he says, and my breath stops short, my ears working hard to make sure they heard that right, my heart secretly knowing they did.

Andrew leads me slowly to the other end of the rink, careful to keep us closer to the center of the ice, where the light reaches. We're far away from the wall, though, so my grip on him is a little more desperate, and I wonder if that, too, was maybe part of the plan.

"You're better on your feet this time," he smiles.

I giggle because just as he says it, my left leg sweeps out from under me, and I nearly fall on my ass. Andrew's hands are fast, though, and he saves me again, this time spinning me around so I'm facing him, his hands under my elbows and forehead against mine as we both stare at my awkward feet.

"Sorry," I say. It comes out in a breath, very little sound, because being in front of him like this brings me back to our last kiss—a feeling I want again so desperately.

I roll my head against him and shut my eyes, letting him guide me in a slow circle around the middle of the rink.

"Hey, it's our first dance," he says. I pull my head back a few inches and spare a glance at him, glad I did as the right side of his mouth is raised just enough to leave a dimple.

"It is," I say. "You would have been such a better date for prom."

His smile fades, and I kick myself for mentioning anything about those years that we missed.

"I would have taken you," he says, his words coming out a little somber. I feel his fingers move along my sides, almost as if they're grasping to hold onto me tighter—to keep me from going away. I dare myself to move in closer to him, to embrace him more, and his grasp tightens again to steady me. He wants me here, too.

"I didn't have a real prom date for my senior prom," I say.

"Liar," he challenges. I feel his body shake against me in quiet laughter. He thinks I pity him.

"No, really. I went with a few girlfriends. I don't even have a picture," I say, closing my eyes as I rest my head against his chest. "And that dance you saw me getting ready for— homecoming, junior year—was a guy who just wanted a date to make someone else jealous. He was the first guy I thought was really into me since you. He left with the other girl."

I feel the rhythm of his heart against my cheek, and I let myself imagine what our prom pictures would have looked like—what *Andrew* would have looked like, how he never would have let go of my hand the entire night.

"I'm really sorry, Emma," he says, his chin resting on top of my head now, all of him cradling me. "I really wish I was there."

We're moving in inches, my feet never leaving the ice, letting him do the work and gliding us in slow motion with no destination in mind. In his embrace, and out of his view, I let a single tear slide down my cheek, because I really wish he were there, too.

"You're here now," I say, my voice raspy and giving me away. He squeezes me tighter, and I shake with one more cry, bringing a hand up to wipe the tear from my cheek before he sees it.

"I am," he says softly. "I am."

I can feel him breathe, and I can feel the pause each time he opens his mouth, wanting to say something more.

"You can tell me anything," I say, finally. "Really. Anything, Andrew."

I feel him swallow hard.

"We don't have to talk about it...if you don't want to. But Graham..." My stomach revolts just hearing his name, and I clutch to Andrew a little harder. His hand finds the back of my head, stroking my hair and cradling me. "Did he...?"

I shake my head quickly, knowing what Andrew's worry is, and thankful that there was help and that I was able to fight just long enough, loud enough. "He only hit me. He tried—" I stop short before retelling everything.

Andrew whispers "*Shhh*," above my head and adjusts me in his cradle once more. "I'm sorry I wasn't there to stop him from hitting you, Emma. So very sorry," he says.

"Like I said...you're here now..." I say against him.

We sway in our hold on each other for the next fifteen minutes, until a bright light clicks on near the exit, and Andrew sighs, waving a hand to his friend who let us in. He never lets go of me for long, though, guiding me safely back to the bench and swiftly finding my hand again once our skates are off and we're walking to the car.

We drive back to his apartment in a rush, and I notice Andrew's left leg bouncing with his nerves. He grinds the gear on his car as he pulls into a space along his street, and I hold my lips in a tight line to hide my smirk.

I start to step out from his car on my own, but he tells me to wait, rushing around the front so he can open it for me. He doesn't grab my hand this time, though, instead, both of his hands tugging at the Tech University tag on his key chain, his fingers wrestling with the apartment key I returned to him after Trent made me a copy of his. He's nervous as we approach the door, and he drops his keys once in his attempt to unlock his apartment, finally opening the door and gesturing for me to step inside before him. He sets his things on a small table near his door then runs his hands through his hair, completely destroying the combed shape, returning his hair to his normal messy look. I secretly like it better this way.

His hands in his pockets, he steps forward a few paces, his posture nearly perfect and his shoulders raised high as his feet move nervously.

"My plan was to have you open the last box now," he says, shrugging toward it. I step in that direction, but he begins to talk again, so I stop. "I want you to open it. I do. And I'll let you. It's just...when I thought this whole evening out, I was...I don't know...really..."

"Oh god, were you drunk date-planning?" I tease.

"No!" he says, rolling his eyes. "I was just…I don't know…overly romanticizing things maybe? And now that we're here, and I'm standing here, and you're all beautiful, and you smell good, and you feel good, and I've held you, and—"

"Andrew…" I sigh, stepping closer to him, placing a hand on his arm, tugging his hand free from his pocket. I lace my fingers with his, pulling his hand to my lips, and pressing a soft kiss against the back of his hand—leaving my lips there as he watches with his mouth hung open.

"*Gah*! Emma," he says, his eyes scanning down the rest of my body now, the heat there this time—the desire and greed mixing with the amber color of his eyes. "You can open the last box," he says. "Just…if this seems really silly or childish when you see what's inside, just know that the sentiment is maybe the most adult thing I've ever done in my whole goddamned life."

My heart starts to race, and I have a small panic over what *could* be in that box. I glance from him to the box and back again a few times, moving my hands slowly to the paper and the lid, checking with him constantly for reassurance. I tear the paper away completely, and lift the lid, still turning to watch Andrew, to watch his reaction. With the lid off, I lean over the large box to look inside, seeing only a small paper folded at the bottom. Andrew nods toward it, urging me to pick it up and open it. I reach in, unfolding it to reveal a simple word written inside.

Me.

My brow pinches as I struggle to understand, but soon Andrew's hands are around mine, gripping the paper with me.

"Me," he says, reciting the word. "If you want me—you have *me*. Or…more clearly…I'm yours."

I blink, staring at his hands, listening to him hand over his heart, and my own beats louder than it ever has, its strength growing by the second, the thump echoing in my chest.

"God, Emma. I'm yours. I've *always* been yours. From the moment I saw the dark silk of your hair and the storm in your eyes, I was a lost cause…lost to you. I've been through hell, and I would go again. I would go willingly, and would charge through the gates if it meant it would keep you safe."

My lips part open with a tiny gasp, and my chest shudders at the beautiful honesty of his words—of his promise that I in no possible way deserve.

"Andrew, I never should have let you go to that place. I never should have let them take you away. I should have told the truth, defended you, taken your place…" I say, my eyes burning from the tears building somewhere deep and buried within me.

Andrew moves to me quickly, his hands finding my face, his thumbs erasing the tears as they fall and his eyes searing through mine. "That's the thing, though," he says. "I never would have let *you*. You get to come first. I don't have a choice, Emma, the universe wants you to be my reason for living. I'm a slave to its demand. And I will lo…" Andrew stops his speech suddenly, his body rigid and his eyes scared as hell as they stare back into me.

He shuts them; one small tear escapes, leaving a wet trail along the rough stubble of his face. Such a soft moment on something so hardened and masculine—a face still lightly bruised and battered from aggression cries for *me* now. His eyes are clear when he reopens them, and I fall into him completely.

"I will love you for always," he says, his voice void of any fear or apprehension. The only sign left that he's scared at all is the hard swallow that follows the most beautiful thing he could have ever said. He doesn't ask to love me. He tells me. He claims me. And though he doesn't say it, I am his too whether I want to be or not—Andrew Harper will spend his last breath defending my honor. I'm lost to this man. I was lost to the boy years ago— happily lost, and so in love in return.

I take the small note still clutched in my hand and bring it to my lips, kissing it and smiling to him.

"You're mine," I say, wanting to hear how it sounds, wanting to feel the way the words run off my tongue.

Andrew laughs lightly, nodding just enough. "Yeah…I am."

"I'm yours," I say, his eyes widening ever so subtly, giving away his excitement and hunger. "And I will love you more."

Andrew's jaw twitches as his gaze remains on me, on my eyes and my mouth and my body. I'm his—and I want to be taken. The air between us is almost thick enough to drown in—

our breath gone, and each the only thing the other needs to survive from this point forward.

His mouth mere inches from mine, his lips find mine within the second it takes me to blink. His hands again cradle my face, his body moving me in demanding steps backward through his living room and down the small hallway to his room until my back is flat against his closed door. The sudden stop gives him enough leverage to push the hardness of his body into me.

In one swift movement, his hands rush down my back, scooping me up and wrapping my legs around him as he maneuvers the door open behind me. He takes long, deliberate steps to his bed, his hands grabbing the bottom of my sweater and tugging it over my head as my body slides down his to sit at the end of his mattress.

He turns around, kicking the door closed, then faces me, pulling both of his shirts over his head quickly. My eyes take in his form, but they also gaze over his fading bruises and the few scars left on him from his time at Lake Crest. I slide toward him and run my hands along his hard chest and hot skin, my fingers grazing over every curve, contour, and mark left behind by those who tried to hurt him. I gaze up at him, my breath catching at the way he looks at me, at the love reflected in his eyes.

Leaning forward more, I keep my eyes on his as I kiss my way up his stomach and chest, taking care to be tender where I know he's still hurt. I trail kisses up the center of his chest, holding my lips longer over his heart as I climb to my knees to reach more of him.

Andrew moves two fingers to my chin, tilting my face toward his, then slides both of his hands deep into my hair, holding me there under the scrutiny of his gaze as I wrap my hands around his wrists.

"God, Emma, you have no idea how many nights I dreamt of looking at you just like this," he says, and for a moment, his smile seems lost—he seems worried.

"I'm yours," I repeat, needing to reassure him.

His eyes fall closed and he brings his forehead to rest against mine, his lips grazing lightly on mine with his breath until he sucks my bottom lip in between his and I feel the scratch of his teeth as he lets go.

"I will be the man who deserves you. I will, Emma. I promise," he says, his breaths shallow, almost panting. I nod *yes*, knowing he'll keep good on any promise to me—knowing he already deserves me, and I'm the one who has work to do.

Andrew slowly presses his weight into me, laying me back in his bed as he crawls over me with the grace of a tiger, his tongue licking his bottom lip and his hazed eyes raking over me with desire. When my head hits his pillow, his body cages me completely, his hands cupping my face gently at first, then growing stronger as he leans my head to one side, giving his mouth access to my neck and shoulder.

The sensation of his tongue drawing a line down my body makes me arch my back, and Andrew seizes the opportunity to sweep one arm behind me to hold me up, my breasts firm and barely concealed by the thin undershirt I'm wearing. Andrew's eyes find the hard peaks of my nipples quickly, and he bites through the fabric, his tongue soaking the material as he makes each of my breasts his, working them into painful submission through my clothes.

Lying me on my back again, he leans his head down and grabs the bottom of my undershirt with his teeth, and I hold my breath, bringing my knuckles to my mouth as he slowly drags the bottom of my shirt up and over my breasts. The cold air makes the ache in my nipples sweeter, but I'm also paralyzed over the display of my scar. My mark isn't subtle—there's no way around being cut open three times, and I notice the moment the evidence of my transplant hits Andrew's eyes. His breathing is steady, and as much as his body is still in a lustful trance, he's also seeing a glimpse of our past—of reasons why and excuses and selfish requests.

"Your father told me," he breathes, his eyes never leaving my scar. I can't tell if he's afraid of it or disgusted by it, and I part my lips with a worried breath as he speaks. Just as the sound leaves me, his eyes close and he leans down, kissing the dark pink of the center of my scar, the deep line that draws nearly the length of where my ribs meet. "I went to see him, to find out *why*..." Andrew swallows, his lips dusting against my body as he speaks, his strong arms holding him above me. "I just needed answers—why you didn't write, why they lied to you. He told me. And as much as I wish you were the one who told me, I also understand why you didn't. You were afraid of dying, Emma. And your father was afraid of you dying, too. I..." Andrew's voice breaks, and his eyes finally lift to mine. "I would have feared losing you, too. So I don't blame him, Em...for keeping my letters from you, for lying about where I was, for telling you to forget about me. I don't blame him. I would have done the same if I knew it meant you were safe."

I swallow hard, willing my eyes to keep their hold on his, not to break. I feel like looking at him, bare and all of my secrets before him, is the ultimate show of trust—this is me giving him my heart. I won't turn away, not now.

"I regret so much," I say, my voice hoarse with emotion.

"I know," he says, his lips grazing mine as he breathes the words again. "I know. But I'm begging you...no more regrets."

My eyes hold his a few seconds longer, and I nod *yes*. "No more regrets," I repeat, as if reciting my pledge. My arms around his neck, I pull him to me, the warmth of his chest crushing against mine, igniting something deeper inside of us both. Andrew's movements grow needier, his hands roaming my body more, gripping and clawing down my back as he kisses his way from my mouth down each of my breasts, sucking the peaks and pinching each between his teeth while I writhe beneath him.

He slides down my body, his lips pausing over my stomach, his mouth open and panting with a hungry need as he unhooks the button of my jeans and grips them around my waist, sliding them down my legs as he stands. My body shivers. He stands before me, slowly removing his jeans and boxers, letting himself spring free while I wait in nothing but my small, white cotton panties. I've never wanted to feel someone inside me more, to take someone completely, to give myself wholly. My legs part for him, and he groans, kneeling on the floor in front of me, and he slides his hands from the tips of my toes up the insides of each of my thighs, my core throbbing and my heart pounding.

"I...I waited," I say, biting my lip hard, my eyes intent on him as his long lashes lift and his eyes widen on mine. "For you. I...I haven't given this to anyone. I saved it. And I'm pretty sure I was saving it for you."

His breath catches once and he exhales slowly, leaving his gaze on me. He lowers his head to the inside of my knee, placing soft kisses all the way up my leg until he's at my very center.

"This," he says, running a finger slowly along the waistband of my panties, teasing me by slipping a finger underneath, but never far enough. His eyes boring into mine, he draws a soft line with a barely-there touch from my belly button, over the top of my panties and down to the wet center where he presses his thumb, easing my need and igniting it all at once. "This...is only mine?"

"Yes," I breathe.

His breathing ragged, his lips fall to my center, and he runs his tongue over the small strip of material, the only thing between us, and my body goes wild in response. The heat of his breath is almost too much to take. I feel his hand sliding along the inside of my leg, then pull aside the center strip, exposing me to him, and my body rushes with heat from blushing and desire. I grip at his pillow, pulling it over my face, biting the material hard as his tongue traces it's same path, this time no barrier there to stop it from dipping deeper inside me.

"Oh my god, Andrew..." I pant, arching against him. His hand tugs hard, tearing my panties until they're completely ripped away. Andrew's tongue caresses me as his thumb presses on the swollen center between my legs until finally his hand slides forward far enough for him to push a finger deep inside, leaving it there as he works me with his mouth. The pressure is so much that I pull my legs up, bending my knees, wanting to hold on, to make this last longer.

Andrew continues to suck and kiss me, letting his other hand find my breasts, running the rough pad of his thumb over each nipple and pulling them back to attention instantly until I cry out with the sensation of my first orgasm. The waves are almost too intense to take, and I pull away on instinct, but Andrew holds me to him, pressing his tongue into me hard, cupping my breasts and pushing his other fingers in and out at an intoxicating rhythm.

As I come down from my high, he kisses his way back up my stomach, worshiping my breasts until he's completely holding himself over me, his body matched up with mine, his hard cock hot against my skin. He takes himself in one hand, and runs the tip down through my wet and still-pulsing center in long, slow strokes that almost send me over the edge again. The sensation has me raising my hips, begging for him to penetrate me.

"Patience," he says, his mouth an arrogant grin as he dominates me. Andrew moves to his feet, stepping around to the side of his bed where he slides open his night table drawer to pull out a condom. I watch as he tears it open and slides it over himself, my mind a little worried over his size and how this is all going to feel. We've reached the limits of my sexual experience, but I'm also desperate for him to take me beyond them.

Andrew positions himself in front of me again, repeating the same teasing strokes along my center, his cock in his hand as he pauses and pushes just enough against me to have my body completely ready to accept him. Leaning forward, he runs his hand behind my neck, tilting my head back slightly as he kisses me hard, possessively, then drags his hand in a hard line down the side of my body, his thumb grazing my nipple as it passes. He reaches the inside of my thigh and pushes my right leg out, opening me to him more, my left leg following his lead as he guides himself to my entrance. His eyes concentrate on every movement, and I'm completely seduced by the vision of him looking at me like this, of him watching himself slide inside me, slowly.

His movement is slow at first, taking long seconds in one place to let me grow accustomed to his size before sliding back out and entering me again, each time falling deeper and deeper until he finally thrusts forward, filling me completely.

"Oh god!" I cry, arching again, his arms sweeping under me, holding me to him while his hips take over the work of pumping in and out in long, tortuous strokes.

"My dreams, Emma. This is better than my dreams," he says, his breath hot against my ear.

I wrap my legs around him, searching for ways to feel him even deeper inside, and Andrew responds, his hands moving to my ass, pulling me up into him with every pummel, our pressure meeting, the sweet ache growing and growing with every thrust.

I can feel the sweat beading on my body, and Andrew's back is moist as his muscles work to hold us together, to send us both over the edge.

"I'm so close, Andrew. Please...just a little more," I gasp, my teeth grazing his shoulder, my fingers digging into his skin as he rocks into me. The need to release builds until I can no longer breathe, and when I feel Andrew begin to push harder, I know he's with me, so I let everything go.

"Come for me, baby. Please...come for me," he growls into my neck. I cry out loud until all I have left in me are soft whimpers of pleasure as I feel Andrew thicken inside me, his breath held as he follows me into bliss.

"Emma! Fuck me, Emma," he grunts, pulling me into him harder and harder, exploding inside me until all that is left is exhaustion and two satiated souls in love.

Andrew doesn't still right away, sliding in and out in slow movements, wanting to drain every last moment of pleasure from my body. He finally pulls out of me completely, then kisses my scar softly before whispering against my skin. "For always, Emma Burke. For always," he breathes.

Showered and now nestled deep in Andrew's sheets and arms and clothes, reality begins to settle in, and I grow still and quiet. For long minutes, Andrew doesn't ask why, instead content to have me here and hold me, to stroke my hair and press his lips to the back of my head every so often as I lay here in the safest place in the world.

"Do you know that the only time I ever smoked a joint was that one time?" Andrew says, breaking the silence. I swallow hard. "Once. Ha! I'm like the perfect anti-drug campaign. *Don't do drugs, kids. Even just once could ruin your whole life.*"

His joke is the sad kind, and I squeeze his arms, pulling them tighter around me. "I'm sorry, Andrew," I say, kissing his hand and pressing it against my face.

"Don't be. I made my choices. I made every single one of them," he says. I'm not looking at him when he speaks, but there's something about the timber in his voice that lets me know he's smiling. Right now—with me—he's smiling.

"You still shouldn't have had to go through any of that," I say, shutting my eyes at the thought of his younger self at the hand of someone hurting him. "They shouldn't have punished you at all, let alone to that extent."

"I'm a Harper. We're *bad seeds*," he chuckles.

"No. You're not," I whisper.

"How you see me," he says against my neck, leaving a soft kiss there before blowing it away. "That's what matters."

His hand moves back up to my hair, and he continues the gentle strokes, combing his fingers through my long waves and letting them fall against my bare arm, my body hugged in the soft cotton of one of his shirts.

"Are you going to tell someone?" Andrew asks, and I turn a little, my head shifting to look at him, not sure what he means. I'll tell the world about you, about how I love you, Andrew. Why wouldn't I?

"About Graham," he explains, my gut sinking the second he utters his name. "I know it's hard, and I know you want to just forget, but he hurt you, Emma. He can't get away with that."

"I know," I say, letting my face fall back to the pillow, away from him.

"I'll go with you...to tell someone. We can go together," he says, and I squeeze him again, so thankful for him, but sick knowing I'm going to disappoint him.

"I can't," I say, my eyes shuddering to a close as his arm pulls away from me and he pushes himself up to sit next to me. I suck in a long, painful breath, feeling the bruises on my ribs as I do, as if those injuries mock me. I sit up to face Andrew, but never lift my eyes to his. "He's Dr. Wheaton's son. She...she's my mentor, and she was the one who..." I move my fist slowly to my chest, letting my thumb scratch over the space in the middle where my scar resides.

Andrew understands in an instant, breathing in once, sharply. His head bows and he nods. Slowly leaning to the side, he slides his phone from his small night table, then holds it up to me, his lips pursed, his forehead wrinkled with question. "May I?" he asks, pointing to the camera lens. I pinch my brow, but offer a small nod *yes*. I let my expression fall to nothingness as he clicks a photo of me then lays by my side.

He turns the screen to face us both, sliding his finger over my image, zooming in, the purple around my eye still very much there. I close my eyes remembering the feel of Graham's hand crashing into me.

"I understand, Em. I swear I do. I just...I thought you needed to see what I see," he says.

I pull his phone into my hands, zooming the image back out, hoping from farther away the bruise is less noticeable, but it's not—it's all I see. I push the small button at the bottom to share the image with me, sending it to myself. Then I move to Andrew's contacts screen and enter my number, biting my lip as I hand the phone back to him.

"I thought it was about time we exchanged numbers," I say through a half-hearted laugh. Andrew makes the same sound, pulling his phone in his hands and typing me a message. I read along as he types I LOVE YOU, then slides his phone back onto his table, pulling me into his arms again.

I have him. He's mine, and I'm his. And we've left this wake of destruction, disaster, and remorse all about us to get here, yet I hold onto him tightly feeling somehow justified that it was still all worth everything.

"I don't want you to fight him," I exhale, tucking my face into his arms, burying myself into him even more. His body grows rigid—he didn't realize I knew.

He doesn't answer, but I feel his chin adjust above my head, his breathing slow, a silent apology.

"I don't want you to get hurt," I finally admit, and he holds me tighter, kissing my head, then whispering one more promise in my ear.

"I won't," he says. "I can't walk away, Emma, but I won't let him hurt me...or you. I swear."

I nod *okay*, but stay in my cocoon of his arms, not sure that he can keep this promise. Graham is two different people, and they are both manipulative, each possessing a different kind of charm. And now that I've seen both sides, I worry that there's yet another side I haven't seen—one that doesn't live in the rational, human world, and one that holds grudges and seeks revenge at any cost. The thought that Andrew's exactly that type doesn't warm my heart either—and I'm afraid when they're forced together, the destruction will be impossible to come back from.

Chapter 20

Andrew

Well that went about as well as I expected.

I woke up early, leaving Emma a note, then rushed to her apartment before work so I could try and talk with Lindsey. She never unhooked the chain, only opening the door wide enough to gain some distance to slam it closed. I think if my fingers or face had been in the way, she would have used more muscle, too.

I slid the letter under her door anyhow, begging her to meet me after work this morning at the coffee shop on her corner. I figured it would be safe. I didn't think Emma would walk down this street until she knew it wouldn't result in a painful run-in with her roommate.

I glance through the window as I walk toward the entrance, and the café is nearly empty, minus one or two students holed up in a booth with their laptops and piles of books. I glance at my watch, which says I'm right on time, then take a deep breath as I walk through the door and prepare for my plan to crash and burn.

"I'll take a large iced coffee," I say to the guy behind the counter. He pulls out a cup and writes my order on the side of it, then rings me up on the register. I remove my wallet to pay.

"Add a non-fat soy latte to that," I hear over my shoulder. I don't startle, but I definitely breathe. I nod *yes* to the guy, then hand him my card, paying for both orders.

"Thanks for coming," I say, turning enough to the side to catch her profile. She's dressed in a business suit, her hair pinned back in a clip, and the look surprises me a little.

"I have an interview. It's for an internship at the clinic. You get fifteen minutes," she says through tight lips.

We both wait for our coffees in awkward silence, then I follow her to a small table near the corner windows. Might as well be on display for everyone that walks by; maybe it will keep her from hitting me again.

"Your chin looks like shit," she says, blowing on her coffee after removing the lid. I chuckle and run my finger along the rough stitches, then pull the lid from my coffee to take a drink.

"Look, I know you didn't want to come here this morning, so *thank you*. Thank you for coming," I say, setting my cup down and folding my hands together, my elbows resting on the table.

"I didn't come for you. I came because you said I needed to know about Emma," she says. Her tone is angry and clipped, but she admitted she came here for Emma, and that's all I need to hear.

"Right. Emma," I say, cracking my knuckles and looking at my hands.

"I swear to god, Drew, if you're here to tell me you made a mistake, and you're going to break up with her now, I will punch you again—right in those stitches," she says, pointing one of her perfectly polished nails right at my chin. I don't doubt her threat for a second, so I lean back in my seat to give me some distance, and inhale to calm myself and make sure I get through to her—about how much she means to Emma, and how much Emma needs her now.

"That Graham guy, the one she went out with a couple nights ago? He hit her, Linds. That douchebag hit her, and I...I don't know what else, but I know she fought, and it could have been worse," I say, my nostrils flaring as the anger boils inside. Lindsey holds her gaze on me, her brow lowering just a touch, her lips pursing tighter, and I can tell that she still loves Emma by the way her breathing turns into a charge of fury.

"What is she going to do?" she asks, her eyes not leaving mine.

I breathe in deeply and push my cup a few inches along the table, wiping away the cold, wet ring it leaves behind on the table. "Nothing," I say. I feel Lindsey lean forward with the urge to speak, so I keep going. "And I guess there isn't much she can do. He's that doctor's son, and it would make things complicated. Honestly, at this point? You probably know more about that part of her life than I do. I told her she should say something to someone, or at least talk to someone...other than me. She's just...she's just going to move on, though, I guess. But I think it would help a hell of a lot if you were around to help her."

I glance up at her, and she's still rigid, her mouth a firm line as she blinks and eventually looks down at her own drink. She pulls it to her lips, sipping slowly, and I can see there's part of her that wants to bend, but I also see the shattered trust and hurt, too.

"I know I'm a broken record, but I swear Lindsey—this entire thing—it's on me. And *you* were Emma's only priority. All she wanted was for you to be happy," I say.

"Then she should have told me the truth. The truth would have made me happy. Knowing my best friend trusted me enough to tell me everything...that's what would have made me happy," she says, her voice soft and distant.

"I get that. And I think if Emma could go back, she would. But she couldn't decide then what would hurt you less. And I didn't make it easy. I'm just asking for you to be open to the idea of forgiving her. She needs you, Linds. And I think maybe you miss her too," I say.

Her eyes meet mine for a few seconds before she pulls her wrist up, checking the time again, and tugging her purse close to her body. She takes a large final sip of her drink, plunking it on the table in front of me and dusting the corners of her mouth with a napkin she quickly folds and stuffs inside the empty cup.

"Thanks for the coffee, Andrew," she says, her mouth tight. "It's been...well, I'd say it's been real, but it never was...was it?"

"I'm sorry, Lindsey," I shrug. She nods once, then slides a pair of sunglasses on her face, turning, leaving, and never looking back.

With my failed attempt with Lindsey behind me, I jog into campus, making sure to make an appearance at my classes for the day. I've marked the dates for tests on my calendar, and I never miss those, but it seems I've missed a quiz or two in calculus. I'm still getting an A, but it's by the skin of my teeth, so I make a tentative promise to myself that I'll show for the rest of my classes this semester. Scholarships are like gold for me, and I have to piece them together—*B's* don't really help the cause.

I check my phone obsessively, waiting to hear from Emma, and by the time I'm in my last class for the day, I break, sliding my phone into my lap so I can send her a message. I glance at the photo I sent her first, and the purple around her eye sends a shock through my core, and my fists form on instinct.

I look up, checking the status of where we're at in my Neighborhood and Urban Poverty class, my last undergrad sociology credit, and a class I took in high school. Turns out they make you take a lot of shit again when you check out of honors college to do a stint in juvie.

Feeling confident that I know where the lesson is, I lean one arm over the small desktop in front of me to make it look like I'm listening, then glance down to type my text.

How are you today?

A few minutes pass, torturous seconds that feel like an hour before she writes back.

I'm good. I just bought my ticket for this hockey game tonight. Don't tell anyone, but I know one of the players.

I grin like a fool over the fact that Emma's coming to watch me, but then I think about the long walk she has from the rink back to my apartment—alone—and in a millisecond I've zipped up my bag and sprinted from the back door of the lecture hall.

It takes me about five minutes to catch up to where she is, and I see her standing at the stoplight on the busy corner, looking at her phone, waiting for me to write back.

You shouldn't text and walk that close to the road. You could get hit by a car.

I cross my arms and wait for her to read, and she immediately starts looking for me, her eyes finally finding me and her smile lighting up my world. She takes a few steps away from the curb then types me one more note.

Stalker.

I grin again and write back.

That's not what you called me last night.

I can see her blush from here. Rather than tease her any longer, I push my phone in my back pocket and jog over to where she's waiting, not giving her time to say another word as I pull her into me and kiss her so hard that it feels like I'm branding her with my affection.

"Wow," she says, stumbling back on her feet. "Do all ticketholders get one of those?"

I shrug and nod *yes.* "Trent makes out with the old ladies. I get the hot ones," I smile. She giggles before punching me lightly in the gut.

"You better not be giving those kisses out for free," she says.

"Not anymore, Em. Not anymore," I say, no laughter now.

I sling my arm around her shoulder and pull her into me tightly as we step into the intersection. We make idle chat at first, me asking her about her day, her mine. But I can tell there's something bigger on her mind, and part of me is worried it's me.

"Hey," I say, stopping our walk so she can face me as I lightly run my thumb over her chin. "What's buggin' you?"

She looks down, a faint laugh through a frown, then shrugs as she looks back up at me.

"Lindsey wasn't in class today. I know you said it would just take time, but I was kind of hoping I'd at least see her, ya know?" Her mouth twists into disappointment. I wish I had good news for her, a curtain I could pull back and her life would be perfect on the other side, just waiting for her to step right through. But I don't, and I *hate* that I can't cure her anxiety.

"She'll come back. I know it," I say, squeezing her close so I can kiss her head. It's not a lie. I saw it in Lindsey's eyes, and if I have to keep stalking her just to remind her of what she's missing, I will.

As we walk up the pathway to my apartment door, my phone buzzes in my back pocket. I pull it out to read, expecting an update from Trent on what time he wants to get to the rink for pregame. He likes to get there before everyone else, and I usually join him. I hold the door open for Emma and glance at my phone as she passes, my mind not understanding the message at first until I realize who it's from. It's Harley. And that fight he had scheduled for me for a few weeks from now—it's been moved up.

Rich boy wants to show off what he's got Sunday night. I can't get a venue, so it'll be here. The money line is trending big on your favorite round if you know what I'm sayin'.

My stomach rolls when I read his message, and I slow as I trail behind Emma toward my room. My eyes stay on my phone as I follow her through my door, closing it behind us, and my heartbeat is drumming out every other sound as I realize I'm going to have to tell her. I will never lie to Emma—ever.

"So can I wear one of your Tech Hockey shirts? I want to look like I fit in..." She stops talking the instant she turns to face me, the joy from moments ago sucked away into the black hole of doom that I can't seem to avoid when it comes to all things me-and-Emma-Burke.

She never asks. I don't wait for her to. She deserves to know, and my gut told me the second she asked me not to fight Graham that I would tell her the minute I got the call. There's also no way I'm letting her near him—she'll be safe, here, in my home with Trent, when I fight.

"That was my guy...at the gym. Graham set a date," I say, glancing back at my phone, sort of hoping that there's a follow-up saying everything's been cancelled. I won't back out—but I wouldn't exactly be upset if he did at this point.

"When?" she asks, falling to my bed, pulling her knees up and hiding her mouth behind the tops. Damn, I hate that she's stressed over this or worried. I hate that she's thinking about Graham. And I hate that bruise on her face. That's the one thing justifying what I'm going to do.

"Sunday," I say, my jaw flexing as I swallow. The part of me that wants to protect her hates to tell her any of this.

But I will never lie.

"That's in two days," she says, her eyes staring at her kneecaps, her fingers gripping her jean-covered shins.

I move closer, slowly, lifting one foot in my hand, pulling her leg from her grip and taking her shoe off. I rest that foot on the floor and do the same with her other leg. The entire time, her eyes never quite make it to mine. She's afraid to look at me, and I know it's because she's afraid to show me she's afraid.

I step in between her legs and kneel down, running my hands along her thighs and then around her, hugging her to me, my head resting on her lap.

"I will be okay, Emma. I won't let him hurt you, and he won't hurt me. I'm stronger than he is," I say, and deep down I know I am. He may have me in size, but my heart beats for this girl, and when I have that in my corner, there's nothing I can't defeat.

"I don't trust him, Andrew," she says, and I feel her body shake once beneath me, but she holds it in, not wanting to cry in front of me. I stand to my feet, taking her hands to pull her to hers, and the second she rises, I sweep her into my arms, sitting with her on my lap. She folds into me, her fit perfect, like everything I've ever been missing.

"I'm scared," she says, her eyes closed, her face pressed into my chest. Her breathing slows, but I feel every rise and fall.

"I'm so scared. I can't lie to you. I won't," she pauses, her voice trailing off. She rolls her head against me, her forehead pressed against my heart, her face still shielded from my view. "If you're going to stand in a ring with him...I want you to kill him."

I hold her tightly, and I feel her muscles tense. I feel her anger, and I feel her worry. I kiss her head and run my hands down her back, wanting nothing more than to make her worries disappear and her wishes come true. After a few minutes, I sway her playfully, but when it doesn't produce a smile, I stop. We are at a depth too deep for small gestures. What she needs now is love, protection, and a guarantee. I promise her the world, but the voice in the back of my head also reminds me who I am.

Good doesn't usually come to the Harpers.

Emma

Andrew is amazing on the ice. He's always been beautiful to watch out there—the grace with which he skates, such a contrast to the force he can deliver when he wants something badly enough.

He wants to destroy Graham Wheaton. I can see it in his eyes. What scares me is I want him to destroy him too. I want

302

Graham to pay, to repent, to disappear—I want him to vanish from all of my memories. But Andrew can't make that happen. Nobody can. And the risk that he might lose something bigger than the gamble he's making in that ring consumes my every thought.

Andrew was slow to return in the third period. He was missing from the bench, and I went absolutely insane as I sat here alone wondering where he could be. This is the trouble with having zero friends—no wing-woman of rationality, and all logic is lost.

He returned a few minutes into the third with the trainer, probably needing to be taped or iced for one of the blows he took on the ice. And as much relief that it gave me to see him there, where he should be, it wasn't enough to quell what was really worrying me. I'm afraid Graham Wheaton is going to play dirty and take out my rejection on him. I'm also afraid Graham is powerful enough to get away with it.

I'm in a haze for most of the final minutes, my mind on rapid-fire in search of a way to get Andrew out of this, something I could dangle as an incentive to deter him, a trick to keep him out of that ring and away from that gym Sunday night. But he wouldn't fall for it, and I don't want to trick him.

I wait as the crowd clears out, moving over to the small exit near the bench where Andrew told me to wait for him before the game. He and Trent are two of the first to leave. I notice a group of girls hovering above the bench waiting for the players to exit; they begin to maneuver their way closer. Andrew brushes by them, scooping me up against his side, his body warm from the shower he just took.

I kiss him hard, my hands grabbing at his face, and as I pull away, I stare down a pair of twins eyeing him. Andrew follows my gaze, then looks back to me, pressing his forehead against mine as he chuckles.

"They're not here for me," he says. "The chicks always swarm for Trent. They know which one of us is going to make NHL bank one day."

"I don't know, those twins were making googley eyes at you. I think you're selling yourself short," I say.

"Twins? Where?" he jokes, jerking away from me to look, but coming back quickly, leaning me back in his arms with a possessive kiss, the roughness of his stubble scratching sweetly against my cold cheeks and chin.

"Come on, let's get you home," he says, taking my hand in his, weaving his fingers through mine, his eyes watching our connection before dropping his hand between us. "That will never get old," he grins.

We walk to his car, dropping his gear in the trunk and waiting for Trent to take his compliments from his fan girls and catch up. Trent insists I take the front seat, and we make the short trip home, the conversation centered on their three-to-one win over Ohio State.

There's an actual skip to Andrew's step as he walks up to his apartment, and it makes me smile seeing it. He's happy, and his body can't help but reflect it. He keeps rehashing plays on the ice with Trent, and his friend gives Andrew credit where it's wholly deserved.

Their celebrating carries over as we get inside, and Trent walks into their kitchen, opening the fridge wide as he talks with his back to us, giving Andrew enough time to tug me to him, then lean me over and kiss me hard.

"Well shit! That's the problem with always going to Majerle's to celebrate our wins, we're never prepared with beer to celebrate at home. There's only one left," Trent says, twisting the cap and turning around just in time to catch us in a full-on make-out session. "Or maybe you don't *need* beer to celebrate," he chuckles, pressing the bottle to his mouth and drinking.

"Shut up," Andrew says, taking his keys back out of his pocket. "I'll run to the store. I'll be back in five minutes. You want anything...I don't know...girly?"

"I like beer," I blush.

His eyebrows lift in a teasing way, but he pulls my chin close and dusts my lips with a kiss, smiling and winking before he leaves. I watch the door close, then I shiver once at the realization he's gone. Even here in the safety of his home—with his roommate who I know won't hurt me—I immediately feel vulnerable. I never thought Graham would hurt me. But he did. And I hate that I feel so dependent on Andrew for safety.

I turn to Trent and hug my body, my lips in a tight smile. He sits on the back of the sofa, and I relax a little with the distance between us. I think Trent senses my edginess, and I know he at least has an idea of what happened with Graham. I'm sure Andrew's talked to him, and my bruises are still very much on display. I've quit looking in mirrors. I don't like what I'm reminded of when I do.

"Andrew is crazy about you, you know," Trent says, light laughter coming out as he looks down at his feet before raising an eyebrow at me. "You in this as much as he is?"

I hold his stare, then nod *yes*. He begins to nod with me.

"Good," he says, looking back down. "That's good."

I move to the stool by their counter in the kitchen, sliding it out enough to sit on top and rest my head on my hands. As safe as I feel here, I'm still not okay—I'm *miles* from okay. When Andrew's gone, all I see are Graham's lips curl into an evil grin, smoke trailing around his whiskers. I feel my skin burn from everywhere he touched, and I try to replace it with the feel of Andrew.

What holds me hostage, though, is the knowledge that it isn't over—that Graham isn't over. Andrew is going to face him, and I want to be there to keep *him* safe. But I can't—my body and heart literally wouldn't survive being in Graham's presence. I'm afraid one more look at him and my nightmare would never leave.

"Did he tell you about his fight?" I ask, unable to fully look at him. I feel like I'm sharing secrets behind Andrew's back.

"He did," Trent says, and I glance up to see his mouth paused open, like he wants to protest the fight too. But he doesn't, instead biting at his bottom lip and shaking his head.

"Don't let him," I beg, my voice breaking when I ask, and my eyes burning from tears. The emotion hits me fast; I pull my sleeves up over my wrists and push them into my eyes, squeezing them shut tightly until I can speak again with composure, without my voice feeling weak and frantic. I clear my throat and look down. "He'll listen to you, Trent. Please," I whisper.

It's quiet between us for several seconds, and I work to regain control of my emotions, knowing Andrew will return home any minute. I focus on every breath, thinking of Andrew's smile, and forcing out the thoughts of Graham and his devil eyes.

"He doesn't listen to me, Emma. Andrew Harper listens to Andrew Harper," Trent says through a faint laugh. "But he's been a lot more reasonable since you showed up, so maybe...just maybe...he'll come around before he does something really stupid. I know that's what I'm hoping for..."

The sound of the key in the door has Trent on his feet, and his face is a full smile as Andrew walks inside—no sign of the worry I saw seconds before.

Andrew slides two six-packs of beer into the fridge, pulling out a bottle for him and me before peeling away the caps and placing a cold one in my hand. Trent finishes his first, then reaches into the fridge to grab a fresh one to catch up to us, tapping Andrew on the shoulder as he moves to stand next to him, holding the top of his beer out to tap into one another.

"To friendship, and finally getting what you deserve," Trent says, his eyes flitting to me. I smile, knowing that he's trying to give a subtle hint to Andrew that he has so much going for him right now. Unfortunately, I fear those words ring about revenge in Andrew's mind.

"To getting what you deserve," he says, an ominous smirk on his lips. "Soon enough."

I can feel his body growing hostile at the thought of Graham, and I can tell how much he wants to make him pay. Panicked, I push my beer bottle into his next, just before he can pull it away to take a sip. I'm not satisfied with this toast, and I want to throw out a Hail Mary.

"And to remembering what you have...what's here to come home to," I say, causing him to turn to me, his head falling to the side and his eyes meeting mine instantly.

"To you," he says. "The reason I do anything," he adds with a whisper. I close my eyes, holding my breath as he pulls my head into him and kisses the top, cradling me in his arm.

"I'm drinking to this, but just so we're clear here, Em, that last part of the deal is just you two," Trent says, motioning his beer between Andrew and me. I laugh, but it's a façade. Andrew's is genuine, and as he tilts his beer to drink, Trent and I exchange one last glance—and I can tell he's just as worried as I am.

Chapter 21

Andrew

Saturday was a blur. We won our hockey game, and Emma came with me again. This time, we joined the team at Majerle's. Emma and I only stayed for an hour, anxious to race home to be alone. The newness of it all is part of it, along with the longing we've both endured—at least I know *I've* endured. But it's more than that, too. This all feels fleeting, like there are hurdles yet to clear. I know that's partly my fault.

She hasn't asked me not to go since we last talked about the fight. She won't ask—I can tell. But I also know she doesn't want me to. I know I could handle him. I think she knows it, too. She wants it. But she's afraid of the unexpected. The things we couldn't plan for have been our downfall so many times.

We've lain here the entire morning, her running her fingers up and down my arm and back while I press my face to the side in my pillow and stare at her. I like the way she looks at me—like I'm *someone.*

"You were really amazing last night," she hums.

I smirk, and bunch my shoulder. "That's not the first time I've heard that," I tease. Her hand stops moving and she brings it down on my shoulder with a quick *smack.* "Owwwww!"

I grab her, rolling her over so she's pinned beneath me, her eyes lit up with her laughter, her hair a chaotic storm of smoke around her.

"I meant at your hockey game, you cocky asshole," she says, rolling her eyes, but giving way to laughter again as I push my thumbs into the ticklish spots along her sides.

"I know," I say, my forehead against hers. Our laughter fades into a rhythmic breath and I close my eyes, feeling the tip of my nose brush against hers until I find my way to her lips. "I was just hoping I was amazing at other things, too," I speak against her mouth, biting my lip, then hers.

"You were," she says against me, her lips closing the slight distance until we're kissing so hard it feels as if it's for survival.

It feels as if it could be the last.

My phone buzzes with a text, and we both pause our movement until I lift myself enough to look into her eyes, neither of us happy.

"You should get that," she says, her face falling to the side, away from my phone.

Away from me.

I take a deep breath and lean to the edge of the bed, rolling away from her until I sit with my feet on the floor. It's nearly noon; we've slept most of the day away. I open my messages to find one from Harley. I knew it was him.

The fight is set for six at his gym. They're usually later, and it strikes me how rushed and unprofessional everything about this feels compared to the fights I've done for him before.

I text him back *OKAY,* then close my phone before turning to take in Emma, still lying in my bed with her back to me. I lay back down behind her, running my palm up the perfect line of her spine, sweeping her hair to the side and pressing my lips on the back of her hot neck.

"Was that about the fight?" she asks, her voice hoarse and quiet.

I press my head into the back of hers and breathe her in. "Yes," I say. I feel her nod against me, then eventually her hands find my arms and she pulls them around her tightly.

"When?" she asks, pulling my palm up to her chest, pressing it flat against her heart. It's beating so hard I can almost feel it working in and out.

"Six," I say. "But I need to leave in a couple hours to get ready."

She nods again, and her body quivers lightly. I know she's crying, but I also know she's trying to hide it from me. I let her think she has, and I run my thumbs over her knuckles as our hands caress each other.

"Hold me…like this…until you go?" Her voice is a whisper now.

"Okay," I say, snuggling into her more before pulling the blanket over us. I stroke her skin and hair until I can tell she's calm. She isn't asleep—she's too afraid of missing something. It takes me back to Lake Crest when I never let myself completely lose sense of where I was and what was happening around me. I learned early on that sleeping left me vulnerable—it's when others took advantage and stole away anything I had.

Nobody would be stealing anything from us today—not Emma's father, my history, or the ghosts of my past. I'd make sure of it. This small moment—it's Emma's and mine. And soon, when I'm about to face the sorry excuse for a man who marred her perfect face, I'll make sure he can't rob us of anything either.

Leaving her felt impossible. Emma has a paper due, so she buried herself in my bed, surrounded by books and her laptop. She played aloof as I packed my bag and left, as if it were just me getting ready to leave for practice, or class, or work. But her eyes were empty, and I know her thoughts were on where I'm really going.

I kissed her and promised her I'd call as soon as I was on my way back. She smiled, barely, nodding and pushing her ear buds in, her music turned so loud that I could hear it clearly on my end. I let her front. I know she needs this.

She never asked to come, which is good because I don't want to have to argue with her. I can't have her near him. I gave Trent orders to keep her home, too. He laughed at me at first, but quit when he took in my face—an understanding of how serious this is settling onto him.

I almost told Trent the truth—just so he would be able to stay calm, to do whatever he needed to do to keep her calm. But I stopped myself, still not one-hundred-percent committed to my midnight-hatched plan. I almost backed out at the bank when I withdrew every cent I had. I'm still not convinced I'll be able to follow through with it now as I step through the back door of Harley's gym—the street lined with expensive cars and the main warehouse filled with gambling men ready to spend their money on two twenty-something punk shits beating each other senseless for no title or ring.

I guess for some there's glory. For most of the guys I've fought, the prize has always been knowing they're ready for what's next, a gift of confidence as they head into the ring with someone real—someone who mattered. But today—there's not glory. There's grudge and hate and vengeance between two sick men. I'm well enough to admit I'm sick, to admit I like the feel of pain more than I should. I know the way I cope with what really hurts in my life is unhealthy. But now that I know how Emma feels, what it's like to have her completely fill the space inside my chest and heart, I'm not hungry for something to take me away anymore.

When life is good, I don't need the distraction of the rush. I've just never had *good* before, I guess.

Harley is still in his back office when I walk through the heavy metal door. It slams shut behind me, and Bill steps out from the office to see who's entering.

"Just me," I say, holding up a hand. He nods, then reaches his hand out to shake mine. His eyes glance around my body and his brow furrows when he realizes I don't have my usual training bag with me. All I have is a small envelope—nothing more. I nod and pat him on the back as I pass by, slipping into Harley's office.

"You're early. What, can't wait for that fix and need Bill to knock you in the head a few times now?" He snickers as he talks, amused at how predictable I am. Normally, he'd be right. But not today.

I plunk the heavy envelope on his desk then shove my hands in my pockets, staring at it, staring at *him* staring at it. He pokes it with a pen, turning it slightly, then tapping it.

"What's this?" he says, peering up at me, his hat turned backward so I can see the angry suspicion in his eyes.

"It's every cent I have to my name. Something like twenty-seven hundred. And I know I'll probably owe you more, and I'll get it to you, because I didn't want this to be a problem for you, to cost you anything," I say, my eyes meeting his. There's nothing Harley can do to me. I quit being afraid of people the day I stepped out of Lake Crest Academy.

He leans back in his chair, pulling the envelope in his hands and slicing it open on one end to look in at the small stack of money. He tosses it back on his desk, and folds his arms again, studying.

"What the fuck are you talking about?"

"I'm out, Harley," I say. I hear Bill chuckle softly behind me, and I glance at him, shaking my head. "No, I'm serious. I mean it. I'm out. I'm sorry, but I'm not fighting this guy today. I'm done fighting."

The air grows thick with quiet, the sound of chatter in the main gym faint in the background and the repeated thump of a speed bag working down the hall blurring into the rest of nothingness that fills Harley's hot office. He pulls his hat from his head, running his hand through his hair.

He leans forward, his palms flat on his desk on either side of the envelope, and he begins to shake his head, laughing to himself. I hold my breath, though, because I know better.

In a swift movement, he hurls the envelope at me. Money flies loose in all directions. He shoots his chair back against the wall, rounding his desk, slamming me into his door with enough force it closes behind me. His arm thrusts against my chest, knocking the wind from me. He slides it up my body until his forearm rests against my windpipe.

He. Can't. Hurt me.

"What the fuck do you mean, you're *done?* You are done when I say you're done, you crazy head-case motherfucker! I have a room full of high-dollar customers out there—with money they want to spend...*with me*...and that pathetic chunk of change you waltzed in here with is not even close to covering it—do you understand?"

I don't react. I simply hold his gaze, my mouth in a hard line and my breath working hard to pass through my nose and find a way into my limbs.

"You are going to get out there in an hour and stand in that goddamned ring and I don't give a shit if you raise your hand once. You can let him hit you until you go fucking blind! I don't care! All that matters is you go down in the fourth round, and then you can pack up all your shit and I never have to see your face again. Understood?"

His nostrils flaring, Harley leans into me, and my fingertips tingle from the lack of oxygen. I never let my eyes slip from his, and he loosens his hold on me just enough that I'm able to shake my head *no.*

He pushes into me again, this time rearing back and punching me in the gut and chest as his other arm brings renewed force against my neck.

"No," I choke out.

"Not an acceptable answer!" he rages.

"It's the only answer you're going to get," I say, my words cracked and hard to hear, but Harley hears them. His nose to mine, he's inches from my lips, and he reads them as I speak.

I watch his pupils dilate as the wave of realization comes over him. He's not going to win this battle. There's nothing he can say that's going to change my mind. Emma doesn't want me in the ring with Graham, so I'm not going.

"Fuck!" Harley says, punching a hole through the wall next to my head. His hand comes down three more times. I don't flinch.

"Harper, you better rethink this real quick! If you don't get your ass ready..."

"What are you going to do to me?" I interrupt. Harley flinches at my boldness, stumbling back a step or two, his brow lowering as his chest picks up speed, breathing in and out with more force. He opens his mouth, ready to lay into me again, but I ignore it all, talking right through him.

"This isn't about you, Harley. It's about me, and doing right by someone. And I never wanted to shit on everything you've done for me, have given me by letting me come here. You've given me an escape, so many times, man. And I am aware and grateful for you and your lack of judgment. Believe me...you've saved me from the brink more often than you'll ever know."

Harley looks up, his face still angry, his teeth gnashed.

"You could almost kill me and the answer would still be no," I say, and I watch as his chest stutters. "And that's only because I know *completely* killing me wouldn't do you any good either. You can't rule me, Harley. You never could."

I look over to Bill, standing, arms folded, against the wall across from us, his eyes switching from me to Harley and back again. Bill's doing his best to look armed and ready, but I can see the doubt and shock underneath it. He never thought I'd leave. I never thought I'd leave. Up until last night, I thought I'd be here today ready to pummel Graham, forgetting about the fourth-round rule, powering through until there was nothing left of him.

Then Emma cried in her sleep, her body cinching up on me, and her arms squeezing at her chest as if she were dying. That one vision—seeing her hurt when she wasn't awake and aware enough to hide the pain—was all it took.

I will never make her hurt like that again.

"Get the fuck out!" Harley yells. "Get your goddamned face away from me, get your car off my street, and leave."

His hand runs over his chin as his wide eyes look around his desk until he finds his chair, sitting in it and leaning back.

"I'm sorry, Harley. I really am grateful," I say, lifting my hand to shake his. He slaps it away, hard, then leans to the side, spitting on his floor and stomping the wetness into the ground with his heavy boot.

I look to Bill, my lips pursed, and I shake my head, perhaps a little in shame. I don't like leaving them in a position, but I weighed the pros and cons. Harley will be fine. Tomorrow, he'll have another me—another pawn to put in the ring. He'll get over today quickly, and Graham will live without the glory. And I will live without punishing him. As badly as I want to, I will live.

I step from the office and walk down the hallway slowly, letting my fingertips drag along the wood-paneled wall on my way out, remembering the feel of the tongue-and-groove pattern that I will never see again.

I don't know how I'm going to pay for next semester, and come three months from now, I'm not sure how I'm going to make my portion of the rent. But I'll figure it out. I'll take three jobs, beg coach to find more money for my scholarship portion, or hell—I'll sell my car. It doesn't matter as long as Emma's eyes are waiting for me, her arms waiting to hold me, her heart waiting to need me. I can live without so very many things. What I can't live without, though, is her.

Sliding into my car without a penny to my name, I turn my key, then adjust my mirror, looking at myself for the first time in maybe years. I stare into my own eyes and try to recognize something, and for once, I think I just might. My lip curls on one side, and I look back down, tugging my beanie on my head, my smile growing as I think about what I'm racing home to, shifting into drive and grinning all the way through the warehouse district.

I stop at the last light before I leave the shadows of the delivery bays—between two of the largest shipment buildings—and I think about calling Emma. I leave my phone in my pocket, deciding surprising her will be even sweeter. When I glance back into my review mirror, I see the swell of bright headlights racing toward me, and I don't have time to do anything but prepare my body for the blow.

The large SUV hauls through me, smashing my back-end, shattering glass, and pushing my car into the intersection—a passing car clips my front bumper, spinning me into the pole at the side of the road.

My arms are cut to shit, and my lip is bleeding badly, but my bones don't seem to be broken. I'm still whole. I kick at the door, the smell of gasoline rich. As I'm stepping out, I look toward the spot of the impact, the crushed SUV still revving, but the driver no longer inside. My head is ringing, and my body is tingling with adrenaline, but I somehow am aware enough to notice that both doors to the front seat are open. Two people were inside, and I have a strange sensation that they meant to hit me.

I wobble on my unsteady legs, and the faint sound of someone calling my name tries to force its way through the rush of blood passing over my eardrums. I spin in all directions, my head soon dizzy from my movement. I find the two people from the SUV—each grabbing one of my arms and kicking my legs out from under me, dragging me closer to the car that hit my front end.

"What the fuck, man!" I kick and jerk, but their hold is tight, and their size is nearly double mine. They stretch my body in opposite directions, kicking at my legs until they're able to drag me to the back end of the black Mercedes that hit me the second time.

"Always so unwilling, Harper. Always so quick to say *no*—to put up a fight. You never could just *do* what you were supposed to." His voice reaches down my throat and through my ears, strangling me…before seeping through the rest of my body and killing my spirit, one cell at a time.

I left Lake Crest when I was seventeen years old, never formally bidding farewell to the man who'd broken me more than any tragedy in my life had been able to before. I opted out of my exit interview, knowing nobody really cared to listen about my tales of corruption or reports of abuse. Instead, I let my last memory of that man be the beating he gave me and the round burn of his cigar on my wrist.

Standing before me, his hair grayed, but his body the same—his height somehow more than mine despite his age—I'm instantly filled with terror, and I fight to run, pulling and kicking against the beasts he's brought with him to hold me here for him to torture. I've been here, in this exact position with this man, so many times before.

"Graham was always such a good boy. He and I, we've had a great business relationship since he left my school. He saw the potential for our mutual gain—my…ability to persuade people for him, to make his indiscretions vanish. And we've made loads of money in return. I could hardly believe it when he mentioned your name a few weeks ago. What was it he called you? Oh yes, this *nuisance* that he wanted me to make disappear. But I don't do that anymore, Andrew. I don't make people disappear. I've…changed."

His grin is that of the devil, his mustache thin and his teeth yellow from nicotine. The acid in my stomach threatens to come up, so I will it down. I won't be weak in front of him. I'm weak for no one.

"So that's how Graham knew I went to Lake Crest," I say, spitting blood to the side, the spray of it hitting one of his beasts, who jerks me harder; I smirk, pleased that I've pissed him off.

"He was two years before you. Drugs…just like you," he says, and I jerk at the comparison. I'm nothing like Graham—not then, not now.

"I thought you would be another one I could trust, just like him. That's what I did at that shit-for-nothing school; I made apprentices, partners in my…*business*. But you were too stupid, weren't you?" His brow lowers, and he reaches into his side

316

pocket, pulling out a lighter before moving to the breast pocket of his jacket for a cigar. I wince at the sight, my wrist burning from the memory.

"I'm not weak, like Graham. That's all," I say, the blood from my lip choking me again. I lean forward and spit, turning to the side and grinning at the guy I spit at before. "That better?" I say, an eyebrow raised.

"Oh, I don't think Graham's weak. After all, he isn't the one being held down and beaten by the light of the moon and headlights of my car, is he?" His laugh is soundless, and my body grows rigid on instinct, expecting to feel his hand on me, his fist through me; the need to protect myself, strong. "Look at that. I can still get to you, can't I?"

I twist as he steps closer, and the hold on me grows stronger.

"You're pathetic," I spit out. "You can't do anything to me. You have nothing to gain," I say, my eyes darting around him as he saunters close enough to blow a puff of his smoke into my face.

"Maybe I don't have anything to gain. But I sure as shit don't have anything to lose, either. I had a shitload of money invested on this fight happening tonight, and you just cost me. You...*you!* You were always costing me, and when Harley said the fight wasn't on because one guy dropped out, I knew who it was. I got into this on a whim, when Graham mentioned it was you. I thought it would be a quick-and-entertaining way to make some cash. I booked thousands, and some assholes even bet on you. Ha! Imagine that," he says, his face close enough that I can smell the sourness of his breath. "Someone actually thought you would win. But you're just the pathetic coward you always were, aren't you?"

"I'm no coward," I seethe, my mouth once again full of blood. "I'm just not your pawn. *You're* the one who has always been afraid. I was a child, and I stood up to you. You're nothing."

I swallow hard, then let my lids fall closed for a brief second as I think of Emma's face, my heart beating, my hands on her. There's nothing he can take from me, and I've survived him before. I found her in the end.

I open my eyes and stare at him, almost challenging him, begging for his worst, when something shifts—a flash that makes my world tilt, my head dizzy. His thugs drop their hold under my arms and take off running back to the smashed-up SUV that brought them here. Nick Meyers walks away just as quickly, his step not quite a run, but his clip urgent. Their tires squeal and they swerve back into the direction they came from, their lights darting around buildings and disappearing around corners—the sound of their engines vanishing just as fast.

"That's right, you fucker!" I yell, lifting my arm and swinging it over my hand, giving my ghosts a giant middle finger. "Run away, you fucking loser! I will never belong to you!"

My legs collapse under my weight, and my knees hit the gravel hard, the rocks digging into my skin as I fall forward, my hands catching me before my face hits the ground. I'm instantly heavy. The ground begins to swirl, and despite the fact that the sun has fallen below the horizon, my world is bright. Everything yellow. Everything slow. My mouth is overcome with the taste of metal, and I let myself fall to my back, my head to the side as I vomit blood. The feeling sends a searing burn through my stomach, and I curl my knees up into my body like a child, my hands moving to my belly, wanting to make the pain stop.

Wet—so wet. Everything wet! I pull my hand up in front of me and immediately lurch with the desire to vomit again. The blood is everywhere. I look down to see my shirt soaked through, and as I pull the fabric up, I see the gaping hole in my belly, the round wound spilling out blood faster than I can think. My mind races with what to do, putting together what happened, then I remember it—the sound. I shut it out, but it was there—the loud cap of the gun, the acrid stench from the fire of it.

My hand finds my pocket, and I slide my phone out, hitting the emergency icon and letting it ring. A woman answers, and I choke on my blood as I lay myself more to the side. More vomit. Moaning...I need to make noise so they hear me. I moan, and I slap at the pavement, and then eventually, there's nothing.

Emma

I haven't written a single word. I've been sitting in here among the smell of Andrew, buried in his covers, my books all around me, and all I've done is blink. I haven't opened my laptop once, and the few times Trent has knocked lightly on the door, I've lied that I'm "fine" and "getting a lot done."

He doesn't believe me. I can tell. And his knocks have come more often as the day has shifted into evening, as six o'clock has passed and as nearly an hour after the time Andrew was set to fight has come and gone.

I'm giving him two more minutes. Two minutes, and then I'm calling. Two minutes, and then I'm dragging Trent out into the streets with me to find him. The soft knock comes again, and this time I invite him in.

"Nothing?" Trent asks, nodding to my phone, his own in his hand. I shake my head quickly, my eyes wide on my blank screen. Why is my screen blank? Why no ringing or message?

"I'm sure he's on his way," he says, sitting on the end of the bed near my feet. I nod *yes*, but I don't believe it. Something is wrong—I feel it in my gut.

The two minutes comes and goes, and as soon as my phone reads 7:01, I let the tear I've been holding in for hours fall down my cheek.

"We have to find him," I say.

"I know," Trent says, standing and walking from the room. "I'll get my keys."

I kick away the useless books on his bed, running to the restroom to pull my hair into a tie and shove my feet into my running shoes. I swallow my nightly round of meds with the feeling that I won't be home in time to take them, then I rush around the corner, still pulling my arms into the sleeves of one of Andrew's sweatshirts when I run into Trent. He's holding a hand up to me, his phone pressed to his ear with his other hand, and his face is completely blank.

"Yes, I'll call them. Yes, yes. Thank you. I'll be there soon, too," Trent says. I reach for his hand, grabbing onto his fingers, threading mine with his and holding his fist hostage. I have a sense that I'm going to need it to stand soon.

"Was that him?" I ask. He shakes his head *no*.

"Hospital," he says, his eyes wide, not looking at anything. "Someone...shot him, Emma. He's in critical..."

My lungs collapse and everything blurs. I fall down Trent's leg, my grasp on his hand too weak, and his the same as he stands limply, in shock.

"I...I have to call his mom. I...I don't think I can drive, Em. I..." Trent's eyes fall to mine, and we both look into each other. We should have tried harder. We could have stopped this. Andrew...I might lose Andrew!

"I'll call a cab. Where is he?" I fumble with my phone, dropping it on the floor and cracking a corner of the screen. Shit! I hope it still works. I click it *on*, and breathe out hard when it lights up.

"Mercy," Trent says, falling into one of the stools in his kitchen, his eyes forward on his phone as he chews at the inside of his mouth.

I manage to speak clearly enough to request our cab, and I listen as Trent delivers the painful news to a family that's had so much of it over the years. He ends his phone call, unable to give them many answers, just as our cab pulls up, and we both drag ourselves to it. As I close the door, I glance up and realize that we left the front door completely open, and I motion to Trent.

He shrugs, so I let the driver pull away. There's nothing worth anything in that apartment, anyhow. The only thing that matters is fighting for his life seventeen miles away.

"Hold on, Andrew," I murmur to myself. "Please, just...hold on."

Chapter 22

Emma

The *beeping* sound haunts me. I wait for irregularities. Though, I've learned now that even those sounds are meaningless. Andrew is being kept alive by a tangled mess of tubes and wires and liquids all working together. His body repaired as best as doctors could, the worry now is how long until he wakes on his own, and what state his brain was in after he was left to die in some back lot only miles away from our home.

Our home.

His family showed up minutes behind Trent and me, and his brother came in this morning. He looks so much like Andrew; it's hard to look at him. He's been kind, but very quiet. He rarely leaves Andrew's side. He lets me stay, too. I told him who I was, that staying here was important, and he just nodded once, never questioning that my need to be present was just as great as his.

He stepped out to grab coffee and call his girlfriend. They weren't able to both make the flight from Germany. I don't think they could afford it. It must have cost thousands as it was. I can tell Owen misses her, though, and I can tell she loves Andrew like her own flesh and blood. I heard her crying through the phone earlier.

She sounds like me.

"Here, I made it black, but brought a little of everything," Owen says, handing me a small cardboard box filled with sugars and creams along with a Styrofoam cup of steaming coffee. I nod *thanks*, then slide it onto the table next to me. He stares at it for a moment quietly.

"I'm not very hungry," I say.

"Yeah," he sighs, setting his cup down, no intention of drinking it either. "There's a girl here for you," he says, his eyes on his brother as he slides one of the tubes over Andrew's chest and away from his neck, wanting him to be comfortable even in this state. "She said her name's Nicole or Lesley or something like that."

"Lindsey," I whisper.

"Yeah, that was it," he says. "Anyhow, she's in the family room down the hall. I told her I'd come get you."

"Thanks," I say, my eyes zeroing in on Andrew's, willing them to open. "If anything changes…" I start to say as I stand. Owen raises a hand, acknowledging me.

I hate leaving his room. I'm so afraid I'll miss something. So afraid I'm what's helping him breathe—as self-centered as that sounds. The door closes lightly behind me, and I take small, sliding steps down the hall, my hand dragging along the cold metal of the railings until I get to the windows for the family room. Andrew's mom and stepdad took off for a nearby hotel to grab a room so they could shower and stay close for as long as Andrew would be here. The only one in the waiting room now is Lindsey. Her back is to me as I open the door, but she sits up fast and turns around, her eyes meeting mine as soon as I enter.

"Hi," I say, lifting my shoulders, not sure if I should hug her, or thank her, or apologize. Probably all three, but my body doesn't seem to want to leave the spot where it stopped walking.

"Hi," she says in return, standing, but not moving closer. We're both at the same impasse. Her head falls, and she laughs lightly with tears in her eyes. "Andrew said he'd find a way to get me and you together."

She bites her lip when she looks at me, her head shaking. I move to her, and the closer I get, the less worried I am over everything else. Her arms open to me, and she holds me tight as I cry into her. I cry hard and long, until my face is empty and my heart feels close to normal again. When I finally step away, I keep hold of her hand, and I shake it up and down as I speak, nervous to let her go and so happy to be touching my friend.

She's here. Of course, she's here.

"I'm so sorry, Lindsey. God, I'm so sorry," I say, my face puffy and my voice a pathetic rasp.

"I know," she says. She doesn't smile, and her eyes fall from mine quickly. "I was so hurt. I'm *still* hurt, and that's going to take time. It's not that I thought Andrew and I were going to run away and make a life together. Hell, I was starting to think he was gay because the boy never liked to make out for long, and it sure as hell never went anywhere. Though he was a good kisser. Moody as shit, but a good kisser."

She laughs at this, and I laugh, too. Hers fades, though, and she looks right into my eyes.

"I was hurt because you didn't tell me something important in your life. You can trust me, Emma. With anything. And the thought that you couldn't...with Andrew? It hurt."

I sit in a small chair next to her and look down at my hands. "I didn't want to hurt you," I say, not able to look at her when I speak. "It felt like I had to pick, you or him, and I'm so sorry I didn't have faith in how strong *we* were. That's on me, Linds. And I'm so...so deeply sorry."

I whisper an apology again, but I know its just words. And I know it's time, like she said, that's going to truly heal her and me. But she's here now, when I need her desperately. She's here. I sense her shadow as she sits next to me on the sofa, and I let myself go, catching her up on what I know—there's an investigation, they think it's some smalltime bookie who thought Andrew owed him money.

"So it wasn't Graham?" she asks. I shake my head *no*.

It grows quiet between us again for several minutes. I don't like the quiet. My mind gets carried away, starts imagining the whirling sounds of his machines and beeping and people rushing—Andrew leaving.

"You should try to go home, maybe shower?" Lindsey says, her mouth twisted on one side. "You can...you can come...*home.* It won't be easy, but I've had time to think, and I don't want this to be the end of the *Emma and Lindsey show.* I'm probably going to say bitchy things sometimes, and be totally passive aggressive, but I want to try to...you know...move past it?"

I suck in a sharp breath, my cry surprising me almost as much as her gesture. I reach over and squeeze her hand again, my eyes fluttering as they close and I nod, accepting her offer.

"I missed my classes today. I missed...Miranda," I say, tucking my lip in, waiting for Lindsey's response. I'm hoping she'll give me a solution.

"Yeah, that's...that isn't good," she agrees. "But I think you need to talk to her, Em. You know you can switch mentors, if something's uncomfortable or if it gets awkward."

I nod again, grateful for her suggestion—one I'd thought about myself. It's hard to give up time with the person I admire because her son happens to be an awful human being. Then again, I'm not sure how wonderful Miranda is after all. She saved my life, but maybe that doesn't make her a hero—maybe it just makes her good at her job. I've seen glimpses of the cracks in her selfless façade, and they're discouraging.

"Just promise you'll think about it," Lindsey says, her hand on my knee. "You have options."

My conversation with Lindsey stuck with me, even now, hours after she left.

I have options.

I'm not so sure I do, but looking at Andrew...watching him lay here—so much working on his behalf just so he can breathe—I feel a little angry with myself for letting Graham off without any punishment for what he did. I know he's not the hand that put Andrew here today, but he's partly the reason. And he *is* the hand that struck me.

I wonder how many others he's abused?

My mind keeps replaying the switch flipping in him. I go to all of those moments where he wasn't quite a gentleman in the first place. He was short, or rude, or curt during a conversation. His hands were always just *a little too assuming* with me, crossing the line *a little too far*; his presumption that I was his property happened quickly, and without my consent.

"You should take a break," Owen says, kicking my foot from the chair he and I have both commandeered as our footstool. He smirks, spreading his enormous feet out on the surface of the seat in a teasing way, taking up all the space.

I sit up, rubbing my face and sliding my advanced bio book back in my bag on the floor. I haven't slept but for a few minutes here and there, and I can feel the knots in my hair around the base of my neck. I think...maybe...I also smell a little.

"Go home. Take a nap. Get some rest. I promise I'll text you if *anything* happens," he says, holding out a fist for me to pound. I laugh at it, then squeeze it between both of my hands. Twenty-four hours together in this situation has formed an instant bond between Owen and me. I get why Andrew loves him so much.

I pull my bag over my shoulders and head through the door, spinning around before leaving and pointing at him. "You promise. If *anything* happens," I say.

Owen crosses his heart, and I believe him. I've learned that's part of the deal with Harper boys—they don't swear on their hearts often, and when they do, they mean it.

I think about going to my old apartment, and when I hail a cab out front, that's the address I give the driver. But when I step out of the car, my legs carry me to Andrew's. The smell is comforting, and I *feel* him alive here. I need that—the image of him living, him just being. I shower quickly and leave a note for Trent asking him to text me when he gets home. He was taking care of alerting the school and the coach.

My hair dried and my clothes changed, I feel a small reserve of energy kick in my body. I brew myself a double cup of coffee and fill one of Trent's mugs so I can carry it with me to stave off sleepiness for a few hours longer. I lock up and begin to walk back to the hospital, but I notice the light outside, the glow of late afternoon, and I check the time on my phone. It's not quite four-thirty, and Miranda's office hours end at five.

I don't want to go. I stop walking at least a dozen times, a dozen more I turn around. But Lindsey is right. And Andrew was right. I need to tell someone—I need to tell Miranda first.

By the time I get to her door, I can hear the sounds of her on the other side powering down her computer and packing up her things. With a deep breath, I knock lightly, and her door slowly slides open with the force of my touch. Her body leans back in her chair, and soon our eyes meet.

"Emma, hi. I was just packing up. I missed you today," she says, no longer looking at me. She's checking out, moving on to her next thing. I step into her office and watch as she pulls her makeup bag from her purse, pulling out a mirror and lip gloss that she circles around her lips twice. I wonder who she's wearing that for?

"Yes, I know. I'm sorry I missed today. I...a friend of mine was in a terrible accident. I've been at the hospital with him," I say, sitting down as she stands. She glances as our bodies play opposite, her lips pursing and her brow furrowing with inconvenience. She sits anyhow, because she's not a rude person. She's just not as selfless as I always thought.

"I hope he's all right," she says, and I notice how rehearsed her sympathy sounds. I think she may be a sociopath—I read somewhere that most successful people are.

"He's at Mercy, and it's...well...we're waiting for him to wake up," I grimace. On cue, she bows her head—more rehearsed sympathy on its way.

"I see. Well, I'm very sorry," she says. "We can catch up later this week. I understand, Emma. And I have somewhere I need to leave for soon, so—"

"Right," I say, standing, my bag in my lap sliding to the floor. I awkwardly bend and pick it up, squeezing my eyes shut as my head is down. *Be strong, Emma. Be strong.* "I...I'll let you get going. I just...I only had one thing I wanted to talk to you about first. It...it won't take long."

Really, it should take hours. Maybe even days. There should be wake-up calls and interventions discussed, but I get the sense that I have about two minutes to make my case. I pull my phone from the front pocket of my bag, clicking it *on*, sliding it across her desk, the photo of my face filling the screen.

Miranda remains standing, her head down and looking at the girl on my phone—the one with a deep-purple bruise around her eye, with matching handprints around her arm where Graham dug his fingers in. Miranda only stares, waiting for me to say it.

"I respect you. So much. And it's more than my heart, though...yeah...my heart has a lot to do with it. But that's not why I came here. I came here to learn from you, because I believe in what you do, and I want to be like you—professionally," I say. Her lip twitches at my addendum. "It's out of that respect that I thought I should tell you first. I'm filing a police report. I'm

326

leaving here and going to the student advocacy center first. And I'm not sleeping until I've documented my story. Graham...gave me that." I move my finger to the screen, pointing to it, then rolling my sleeve up on that same arm and turning it over, exposing the soft flesh of my forearm and the black, finger-sized marks left from his hold on me. "And this," I add.

Miranda's eyes dart around the evidence, her look almost analytical. I wait for tears. For an apology. For...something. But she only nods.

"If that's what you think is best, then do what you think is necessary," she says, her eyes rising to meet mine. I'm in shock at the complete lack of empathy in them, and I can't help my candor.

She doesn't believe me.

"Miranda," I say, and she straightens at my use of her first name. I've called her that before, but something tells me she'd rather show her dominance now. First names make us feel like equals. "Dr. Wheaton, your son needs help. I don't want *this* to happen to someone else...or worse," I say, swallowing hard at the thought of what could have happened. My nightmares play that version, even during catnaps at the hospital—it's nothing but a teeter-totter of Graham's anger and Andrew's pain.

"Like I said," she says, sliding her chair under her desk and walking to the door, encouraging me to follow. "You do what you feel is necessary. Now, I do need to make an obligation, so if we can talk more at our regular meeting later this week..."

Her lips are in a perfect smile, and I notice how her eyebrows are raised indignantly. I'm not sure what I expected from coming here, but I no longer feel beholden to her for what she's given me. A weight has been lifted.

I tug my bag over my shoulder and mimic her smile with a clenched-teeth version of my own. I step out of her office and she sends me away with one more condolence for my friend in the hospital, and I walk away, shaking my head and listening to the sound of her heels stamp along the floor in the other direction— all the way to the elevator on the other end.

I leave my sleeve rolled up as I take the stairs down two flights to the ground, and I look at the marks on my arm, renewed strength finding me that I'm right—that I owe nothing to anybody. I push through the main doors, out onto the campus mall, and move my own fingers to the marks on my arms, my hands not able to spread wide enough to meet every mark, and I think to myself how my bruises are like fingerprints—there's really only one, singular match.

I stop at the advocacy center first. I remember learning about it during orientation, thinking I would never need it. I'm so grateful for it now. It's after five in the afternoon, but there are people here at the front, waiting—with open arms. From the moment I step inside and utter the words "I was attacked," I'm surrounded by support. My advocate's name is Jane, and even her eyes on me while I'm talking let me know she's on my side. She believes me, and Jane and I—we've got this.

The forms with the advocacy center take an hour to complete, but I insist on filing my report with the police tonight. I don't want to wait—I'm afraid I'll change my mind, and I'm also afraid of closing my eyes at night. This act I'm doing right now, it feels like a much-needed antidote to the poison Graham left behind.

The officer who greets us at the campus police station is kind. Her last name is Rodriguez. She told me her first name, and I know it's on the card she handed me, but I can't take my eyes off of her tag. I'll remember her last name for now. I don't think she likes that I insist Jane comes with me. But I can't do this alone, and reluctantly the officer agrees, ushering me to a private room where I document every single moment of that night— what happened, and the people I know were there to see it. I give them Graham's phone number, and his friend Brody's name, the only friend of his I really spoke to. I'm sure his friends will stand up for him—*I'm sure they've seen a scene like mine before.* But I remembered other things from that night. The club's security guy was named Jax, and he helped me into a cab. I describe a few others, including the cab driver...he saw things, too.

I'm racking my brain, trying to dig out more details, things I can give Officer Rodriguez that will help even more. The longer I speak, the angrier I get, and eventually, the emotion builds up to a boiling point and my hand forms a fist, punching hard against the table.

"It's okay, Miss Burke. What you gave us, it's enough for now," the officer says, her hands still from writing in her notepad and her head cocked to one side. She's almost being kind, but yet the whole thing feels sterile at the same time—emotionless. My breathing is a little rapid, and it takes me a few seconds to let the heat dissipate from my face.

"I'm sorry. I haven't really...I haven't really gone through *anger* yet," I say, grabbing the bottle of water she brought for me, twisting the top off and drinking nearly half of it down.

"It's all okay," Jane says, her hand moving forward to mine, which is once again balled in a fist on the table. She pats it once, causing me to look up, my lungs finally taking a deep breath. "What you feel—whatever you feel, whenever you feel it—it's okay."

I take in Jane's words, and I unfurl my fingers, flexing my hand and sliding it along the surface of the table outward from me, laying forward and stretching before pulling my body back in.

"It's okay," I repeat in a whisper.

"Yes," she says.

After two hours of rehashing, probing questions into my background, and conversation that almost makes me feel as if *I'm* the one being investigated, Officer Rodriguez pulls all of the paperwork into a file, then makes some notes on the top cover before stacking it on top of several other folders. I wonder how many of those are cases just like mine?

Jane walks out from the back offices with me, and I can't help myself—I hug her. She hands me a few of her cards, encouraging me to share them with others I think might need help, and she also urges me to call—whenever. I'm going to. A lot. Then she guides me back out to the front lobby where a homeless man is passed out across four seats. All of his earthly possessions are tucked in a black plastic bag clutched in his hand while he slumbers.

Jane and I part ways when I leave the police station. The air is crisp and cold. I stop at the steps and pull on Andrew's

329

sweatshirt, then lift my bag over my back and make my way to the train stop near the edge of campus. My fingers are tingling and my feet feel heavy, and in the middle of my walk I have to pause and hold my arms over my head, reminding myself to breathe so I don't fall over. My stomach kicks in its two cents, and I bend forward and throw up the little contents that are in my stomach. The panic attack comes and goes, but it leaves me feeling even more exhausted.

I buy a ticket to take me back to Mercy and climb aboard the next train to arrive, hugging my bag in my lap—clutching something personal, just like the homeless man from the police lobby. It's late. Hours have disappeared while I've told my story. Time well spent. Empowering, though emotionally draining. No matter how tired I may feel, I don't dare shut my eyes. I left my half-full coffee mug in Miranda's office, and as much as I could use the caffeine, I smirk at the thought of how irritated she's going to be with the smell of stale coffee and the reminder of me, and my visit, there to greet her in the morning. In the midst of so much that's awful, at least I have this one small win.

Chapter 23

Emma

It's been sixty hours.

Six. Zero.

The doctors told us not even to consider worrying about things until we start to hit that seventy-two-hour mark.

Those numbers are arbitrary. I know they are, because they aren't in any of my books. Nothing is for certain, and throwing out hours is just a way for doctors to buy time to find consciousness. The cases run the gamut—some people waking up immediately, others taking weeks. Science points to medians, but medians are just clusters of numbers—they don't mean anything when the person you love is all that counts.

But I also know Andrew Harper, and I know if there is a number to beat, he's going to. I spent most of this morning talking to him. He doesn't talk back, which I jokingly told him was refreshing. Owen was in the room, and he just moved his phone low enough to raise a brow at me, then went back to texting his girlfriend.

When Owen stepped outside for a while, I whispered in Andrew's ear that I reported Graham. I needed to say it out loud, even in a whisper. I needed Andrew to hear it. I finally let myself exhale a little—the weight lifting for just a moment.

With every hour that's passed, I've watched him like a hawk, waiting...knowing any second I'd hear him. It's why I've ignored the raging growl building in my belly. The floor at my feet is lined with emptied cups, and my breath tastes foul, and the growling—it's getting harder to ignore, until finally one lingers so long I can actually feel the pang work around my intestines and climb up my esophagus.

"Okay, either you're shifting into a vampire and the sun coming in through that window is secretly melting away your skin, or you need to feed that monster in your gut," Owen says, his phone flat against his leg again.

"What?" I ask. My stomach betrays me, growling again—with a vengeance.

"It's gross. You sound like my grandfather. Seriously, go eat," Owen chuckles. I shrug and roll my eyes, standing, but stopping at the door. He raises a hand, never looking away from his phone screen. "I know, I know...text you the second something happens."

"The. Second," I point at him.

I've been very positive this morning. It's the first time I've felt this full of hope since my parents pulled me out of high school to head to the hospital for my surgery. Things feel brighter, and breathing feels easier.

Andrew is going to wake up today.

I have zero doubts.

I head down to the break room on the first floor where a few kids are lined up, all dressed in various costumes—ghosts, goblins, and superheroes with hospital gowns underneath. I'd lost track of time lately, and I realize it's Halloween.

I notice a line of doctors and nurses, all with pockets full of candy, positioned at tables around the cafeteria, and the scene paints a smile on my face. The girl closest to me is wearing wings, her bald head painted with beautiful designs and glitter. I'm amongst real fighters.

Andrew is right where he belongs.

I rush through the line at the gift shop across the hall, grabbing a granola bar for myself, and a row full of candy—the big bars—for the line of trick-or-treaters waiting in the hallway. I ask a nurse if it's okay if I help, too, and she smiles, nodding *yes*.

"The more we can do to remind them of life's good parts, the better," she grins.

I pause and watch as she moves to a table, placing her basket of small, crocheted angels in her lap, handing one along with a Hershey kiss to every kid that comes by.

"Hope and love," she says to me, laughing lightly. "I'm sure they just see the chocolate. But a few of them...they see the hope and love, too."

"I like that," I say. "Mind if I...take one? I know someone who could use it."

332

She nods, and pulls a blue angel from her stash, wrapping its soft arms around two kisses.

"You deserve something sweet, too," she says, winking at me.

"Thank you," I whisper, taking her gift and tucking it in the front pouch of Andrew's sweatshirt. I pull a chair out from the next table over and pour my candy bars on the table, loving the light in each child's eyes as they step up and whistle through missing teeth "trick-or-treat" and "thank you."

This is most definitely a good part.

Andrew

It's Christmas, and I'm eight. My grandpa bought me a pedal car from the Goodwill, and Owen and he are in the garage fixing it so I can ride it. The pedals were bent, so they're taking the ones from Owen's bike and putting them on for me. Owen always gives me his things. I hope I have something for him one day.

I'm waiting at the back door, my feet dangling outside over the stoop, but my body inside where it's warm. Mom keeps yelling to shut the door. We have a fire going, and I'm letting out heat I guess. But I want to watch them work. My other brother, James, didn't come to Christmas. We all woke up in the morning, and he wasn't home.

Owen told me James is lost, but he seems to find his way home. I think he didn't want to come here because we don't make him very happy. There's a lot of yelling when James is home. And my mom cries a lot, too. I feel terrible, but I'm sort of glad he wasn't here for Christmas. It was a really nice day.

My grandfather just swore and threw that wrench thingy down on the ground. I giggle, and he and Owen both turn to look at me. I pull my feet inside and start to shut the door, hoping I didn't make them mad, but Owen catches the door before I can close it.

"You think you can do better, hot shot? Come on out; let's see you give it a try." Owen hands me his work gloves and a screwdriver. I stare at them, and the box of tools spread around the garage floor, then look up at Owen's face. He's smirking, so I know he isn't mad. And I *would* like to be in the garage—with the men, doing man things, like swearing and stuff.

I pull Owen's gloves on, my fingers barely making it halfway down the finger slots, and I grip the screwdriver in my right hand. My grandfather holds a flashlight up and begins walking me through the way my car works.

"The chain has to loop through these gears, but it's tricky, because those gears are bigger than the ones from Owen's bike, so we have to somehow make his parts work with the car parts, and all of those things need to turn the front tires when you pedal. Make sense?" My grandpa's hair tufts down in his eyes, and he reaches up, smoothing it back and pulling his glasses from his face, wiping away the smudges on his shirt before putting them back on.

"I think...I think I got it," I say, letting my eyes run through the process, what my grandfather said, over and over.

Owen moves to a chair, pulling up a water bottle and guzzling down half of it before handing the rest to our grandpa. I hear them whispering in the background, something about how they'll give me five minutes to play, then step back in and finish, but eventually their voices fade away, and all I hear is my own voice in my head.

My eyes lock in on individual parts, on grooves and patterns, and suddenly everything becomes clear. "I need both chains," I say.

My grandpa laughs and continues to talk with Owen.

"No, Grandpa. The old chain. I need it," I say, my voice serious. Owen stands up and moves over next to me, kneeling down and following the line of my sight, staring at the same gears and parts I am.

"He's right," he whispers, snapping to my grandpa to bring over the chain. Our grandpa does, and Owen hands it to me. I start snapping and unsnapping gears, blending both sizes into one, asking Owen for help when I'm not strong enough. My hands can't work fast enough, and it's like my mind is already riding the pedal car down the hill while my hands are still busy screwing and clipping metal pieces.

334

Within the hour, the three of us are rolling my new car down the driveway, already dusted with a fresh layer of snow. I don't care, though, because I deserve a test drive.

"How did you do that?" Owen says as he buckles the helmet to my head. It's an old motorcycle helmet that we bought from a garage sale, so one of Owen's shirts is stuffed inside to make it fit.

"I don't know. I just...I could *see* it. Is that...am I...weird?" I ask.

Owen presses on my head, making sure the helmet is snug enough.

"Yes," he grins. "You're very weird. But you might also be a genius. Now go kick some ass down that hill and don't crash your present."

The wind hits my face with Owen's push, and soon I'm soaring down the roadway, pulling on levers and leaning to veer from the right to the left. The road is empty. In fact, there aren't any houses near me anymore. I look up, and the sky is clear, and the sun is bright. When I look back, my house is gone, and so are Owen and my grandpa.

I'm going so fast, though, I can't stop. I keep pulling on the brake, but nothing is working. I didn't look at the brakes—I should have checked them!

"Andrew...Andrew, stop!"

I hear Owen. I can hear him, but he sounds different.

"Stop fighting, Andrew. Stop fighting!"

I'm not fighting. Why does he think I'm fighting? I'm scared. I'm lying down and the roadway is bumpy. I can't stop. But I'm not fighting.

"Andrew!"

I see him.

A dream.

Where am I?

My body. My arms. My head, legs, chest.

Owen is holding my right arm down against a bed, and my eyes are fighting to stay open long enough to see him. I see him. He's older. I'm older!

The fight. I didn't fight. I didn't fight! That's what this is. They think I was fighting, but I wasn't. I left, and then there was a crash. And Nick. The devil was there, and—

He shot me.

"I need Emma," I try to say, but when I hear my words, they're mumbles, nonsensical—something is stopping them, choking me. I try to speak again, but it's impossible, and it makes me start to cry in frustration. Owen's hands are on me again, and I flail just wanting to yell, to scream. He needs to understand me.

"Andrew. Stop fighting me," Owen says, his head close to mine.

Stop fighting.

Yes, that's it. I breathe deep, everything hurts, the sensation of wires and tubes intubating me and poking me everywhere, but I keep my arms still. I will my legs to lay still. And soon my eyes focus—I see Owen. He's smiling, and he's talking to doctors, my mom's voice coming from somewhere behind me.

I jerk with my arms, wanting to see, but so many people are over me now. My eyes find Owen, and grow wide. A man with glasses and a white coat is hovering over me, and my throat burns as I try to speak. He's telling me to stop, and I finally feel it—the tube in my throat.

I hold Owen in my sight while the man removes the tube, and everything hurts. The doctor is telling me not to speak yet, but I ignore him.

"You flew here from Germany," I say, my voice gravely and my throat raw. Owen laughs, sliding his hand down my arm to my hand, holding it like he did when I was a kid.

"Yeah, you shit head. I flew here from Germany," he says, running his sleeve over his eyes to blot away tears.

"Where...is...is Emma here?" I ask, my voice still barely audible.

Owen smiles, though, hearing me clearly. He nods.

"Yeah, she's here. She's barely left this room, and man is she going to be pissed at me when she finds out I told her to go eat and that's when you wake up. I'll go get her," he says, and I close my eyes, nodding *yes*.

Yes. Emma. I need Emma.

336

Emma

I hand the last kid in line three candy bars, because that's all I had left.

"You should get a reward for being so patient," I wink. He smiles, reaching into his pillowcase to inspect the three chocolates I gave him.

I thank the nurse closest to me for letting me participate, then I tear a corner away from my granola bar, pushing part of it through and biting into the salty end. My stomach rolls in appreciation.

"Emma!"

Owen's voice startles me, and I jump, turning to see him racing toward me, his phone clutched in his hand.

"Andrew?" I ask, shoving the rest of my bar in my mouth, chewing manically. Owen nods, laughing and crying at the same time.

"I was going to text you, but I run faster than I type. Just now. He asked for you!"

I'm chasing behind him, trying to keep pace with his long strides as he takes the stairs three at a time.

"He asked for me," I repeat his words, smiling and pounding my feet as fast as they'll go. I toss my wrapper into a trash that we pass on our way down Andrew's hall after Owen buzzes us in through the large double doors. I see doctors and nurses all moving in and out of his room as I get closer, but I ignore them, weaving through and under until I'm at his bedside.

The instant I see his open eyes, I know—this is one of life's good parts, too, the kind of moment I will hold on to forever. My eyes swell with tears, and I lunge to his side, grabbing his hand and laying my torso across him, wanting to hug tighter but knowing he had so many open wounds underneath.

I feel his hand squeeze mine, his strength weak, but his movement very much alive and well.

"Oh my god I'm so happy to see you," I say, stepping back for a nurse to take vitals. I move around every person who needs him, but I never let go of my touch on him. His mom is sitting on the other side, her hands wrapped around his arm.

"How was your lunch?" he teases. His voice is scratchy, but I hear *him* underneath it all.

"You ass. I leave your room for five minutes, and *that's* when you decide to wake up?" I move my head to his shoulder, laying my face against his arm, feeling the beat of his heart with my hand. This entire time, his heart—it's been strong.

"You know me—flair for the dramatic," he says, swallowing hard.

"Andrew, I'm going to work on removing the tube in your nose, and it should make it a little easier to talk. But I'm going to need you to lie still and just be patient for a few minutes, okay?" the doctor says.

Andrew nods, and I squeeze his hand again, threading my fingers tightly with his. I roll his hand over in mine, opening his palm, and with the tip of my finger, I write *I love you* again and again. Andrew keeps his promise to the doctor, and we don't talk for almost an hour while they work around him, eventually removing many of the monitors and tubes attached to his body. My eyes never leave his the entire time, and even though he can't speak, I see the love in his eyes for me.

Eventually, the room clears, and for a small window of time, Andrew and I are alone.

"I didn't fight, Emma," he whispers, his voice still raw. I lay my head flat on his chest, the welcome stroke of his hand over my head and through my hair keeping time with the rhythm of his heart as I watch the lines zigzag up and down on the monitor.

"I know. Thank you," I weep against his chest. His hand stills as he leans forward as much as he can, his lips finding my head.

"That man...he would have found me eventually," he says, and I lift my head to look at him, my brow pinched.

"They said it was some bookie or something, and he thought you owed him money?" I stare deep into Andrew's eyes, and his mouth falls into a peaceful line.

"It was my demon," he says, rolling his arm over and motioning to the deep burn scar on his wrist. "He wanted to torture me one last time, I guess."

My eyes hover over his scar, and I pull his arm to my lips, pressing a soft kiss over the round mark, wanting to hide it all with my love. I rest my head back against him, knowing any moment his family will be back to break up our small bubble. They miss him too, but I'm selfish.

"Someone else took care of your demon for you," I sigh. "Owen can fill you in more, but I guess the investigators figured out where he lived, and when they got to his house to question him, they found him in the living room dead from a gunshot wound."

Andrew's chest pauses, and I tilt my head up to look at him. I don't like it when he's not breathing. Not breathing...it makes me nervous.

"Do they know who?" he asks.

I shake my head *no* and return my focus to the feel of his fingers in mine. Andrew does the same, and we both lay silently, our hands making long, methodic strokes along each other's skin. I can never get enough of the feel of him—life beating through his body, love pumping through his veins.

"My brother thinks you're cute," he teases after several minutes of quiet. I smile against him, turning my head just enough to press a kiss over his heart. "I mean, I'd understand if you want to jump ship and get on Team Owen. You could probably take Kensi in a fight."

"I like this Harper," I say, pulling my legs up onto his bed with me so I can lie next to him and snuggle in closer. Andrew leans his foot to the side, tapping his toe into the tip of my shoe. It makes me giggle.

"You always did have a thing for my shoes," he jokes.

I shove him lightly, then bury my face against his arm.

"Not true," I say, bringing my eyes to his, blushing and glancing to the side of his face. "It's the holes in your ears. I told you I liked them."

He laughs, moving his hand up to feel the small plastic circle tucked in his ear. The hospital took the metal gauges out, so Owen brought him new ones.

"Yeah, I'm a pretty sexy beast," he says, laughing and immediately wincing from the pain.

The chatter outside his door starts to build, and I know our time alone is done. There's so much I want to say, so many kisses I need to give and embraces that I need to savor. But I guess I have time now. Andrew Harper was a gift, a friend when I was scared and alone, a savior when I almost lost everything, and the love of my life that I got lucky enough to find a second time. He's all mine. And I'm his. And I am never letting go again.

His room fills with his family and Trent, Owen quickly putting a phone in his hand so he can talk to Kensi. Andrew tends to them all, hugging and talking and smiling for them—giving them light and hope—giving them the *good parts.* But he never lets go of my hand. And just when I think he's losing his grip, starting to move his attention from me to the other amazing and deserving people in his life, he turns my hand to the side, smoothing it flat and writing in it a letter at a time.

FOR ALWAYS.

Epilogue

Christmas Day

Andrew

Emma said I didn't need to bring a gift, but it felt wrong. The last time I was at her father's house, I noticed it was dark. That's half the reason we all used to pretend that house was haunted. When a home is built around the turn of the last century, the lighting is a little old.

It isn't much, but I carry the wrapped box in my arms, hoping her father will let me install the light in the foyer later today. I think it will make him happy—to have a little brightness in his house.

I know part of the reason I need a gift, though, is because of my nerves. I'm still consumed with wanting her father to like me. I've spent five years not giving a shit about others' opinions of me. Part of my own shelter, I just always assumed most people thought I was an asshole, so when they didn't, I was pleasantly surprised.

But Carl Burke—I care about his opinion. I care about his daughter, and that's the *only* reason I care about anything at all.

"Relax, he cooked all day, and he wanted you here," Emma says, dusting snowflakes from my arm. I wore the only nice jacket I have—it's black and wool...and hot as fuck!

I hold my arm out for her to take as we walk up the main path to the house. I'm driving a twenty-year-old Volvo. It's fast, and it sure as hell won't ever break. But it's not my Camaro.

When I got out of the hospital, my mom gave me a letter with a check inside. She said the man who delivered it was young, maybe mid-twenties, with blonde hair and a strong build. He told her he was from H and Sons, and they were handling the settlement from the insurance claim. But I know there was no claim, and I know it was just Harley's way of making sure the universe was right between us.

I always told you I take care of my business. Seems there were a few people who were bad *for business, and I wanted you to know, they won't be seeking you out anymore either. I'm sorry about your car; she was a beauty. This probably won't even come close to getting you in that kind of ride, but...I thought you deserved your money back. I never wanted a dime from you. You can't work for me anymore; I think you understand why. But, I'd be happy to give you a reference if you want to apply for a gym—a* real *gym, in the city. I know a guy who knows a guy, so maybe give this number a call.*

Glad to see you back on your feet.

H

My savings was just enough to buy a piece-of-shit from the auction, and Owen helped me tune it up a little before he left again for Germany. His season over there started a few weeks ago now, so I hope by the time he comes back, I can afford a Camaro again.

We spent the morning at my parents' house. Dwayne hooked me up with new gear and skates. Maybe I can break them in this winter so I can find my way back to the ice with the rest of the team. Coach was able to work my scholarship out with the financial aid department, diverting my money to next season since I was given a medical withdrawal from most of my classes this semester. I asked to take my finals anyhow, knowing I could pass, but they were rather insistent. Emma has about seven million years of school left, so I'm in no rush to leave.

My life took one enormous hiccup—everything about it thrown in all directions—yet somehow, when the dust settled, things looked brighter. I only hope that trend continues for one more hour, or at least through the second Carl opens the door and welcomes me inside.

"He knows I'm coming, right?" I ask Emma, my free hand now deeply rooted in my pocket, my other clutching my poorly wrapped box like a teddy bear.

"My god, Andrew. For such a bad-ass, you're pretty wussy right now," she laughs.

I mock her laugh, then let my mouth fall to a straight line. "I fail to see the humor in this. It's easy for you; you're the daughter. Last time I was here, I pretty much slammed the door in your father's face," I gulp.

Emma nods, pursing her lips in a tight smile, then reaches up to straighten my tie. For all that's holy, I'm wearing a tie. My jacket is a sweatshop and I have a noose around my neck.

"That was before he really knew you," she says, her eyes wide and bright. I love the way she looks at me. I wish *everyone* saw me through her eyes.

Emma is so very strong. She calls me the fighter, but I don't know—I kind of think that's her. After she filed her police report, others came forward, and Graham was sentenced to two years of counseling. I could tell Emma was disappointed, but she never let it show. There was a plea bargain, with many—but Emma didn't want anything. She only wanted to be sure Graham couldn't do what he did to her again. Maybe, just this once, penance will work.

Graham's mother ended up taking a position at Northwestern...something she said was *already* in the works. I have my doubts, but I'm thankful that Emma doesn't have to face a reminder of her nightmares on a daily basis. Her heart was holding her hostage, but no more.

I'm not prepared, but the door opens anyway, and Carl and Cole stand side-by-side, both greeting us and ushering us in from the cold. They each take turns hugging Emma, and I step to the side, not wanting to be in the way.

"Well...we're here. We're...we're all here," Carl says, his voice sounding as nervous as I feel. He glances down, then back up to me. "Andrew...can I take your coat, son?"

"That'd be great," I say, probably a little too anxious. Emma ribs me with her elbow, and I roll my eyes at her. "It's so hot," I whisper, and her mouth quirks up on one side with a smile.

I set the package down on the side table and pull my arms from my sleeves slowly, my movements still not as sure and strong as they need to be. My entire front was opened up in

343

surgery, and the healing is slow. Seems the only thing that heals slower than muscle is a broken heart; over the last few months, I've healed both.

I hand my coat to Carl, and he folds it over his arm, patting it and breathing in through his nose. "I'm...I'm really glad you're here, Andrew," he says, his eyes down at my jacket in his arms.

"Me, too, sir," I say, glancing to Emma then back to her father. He takes a slow step toward me, then raises his head to look into my eyes, his own delivering a heavy and honest message—an apology.

With one arm outstretched, Carl pulls me close, his heavy hand patting my back as he hugs me as if I'm his own. "I never thanked you, Andrew. What you did..." he starts, his voice clearly overrun with emotion. He's referring to my time at Lake Crest, to the trade I made with his daughter there on that highway—the lie I told to save her from the dark, and I know he's about to say more about it, but he doesn't need to. His simple thanks...that's enough.

"You don't have to," I say, hugging him in return, smiling at Emma over his shoulder before pulling away. "Really. I would do it all again."

He steps back, clearing his throat and running his hand under his eye. "Yes, I know you would," he says, pausing and lifting his gaze to mine. "I know you would, which is why I have peace."

Emma and Cole are walking down the hall, but I hear his words to me. He moves on quickly, hanging my coat before escorting me down the hallway to their simple dining room. I let him talk about things he needs to do to the house, and I eventually make him open my gift early, loving the smile on his ragged and tired face when he sees the small chandelier. I offer to stay late tonight, to help hang it and rewire a few things, and Emma sits back and watches as I form a bond with her father, as he trusts me with his most cherished possession, and I promise without words to never take her for granted.

On a day made for family and selflessness, I somehow become my brother—wanting to give all I have so others can feel joy. But it's not really selfless at all, because my heart is so full from it.

Full.

And beating.

And so very far away from *alone*.

THE END

Acknowledgments

I first learned about Hypoplastic Left Heart Syndrome during a drive home through the Arizona desert from my parents' house on a late Sunday afternoon. I listen to a lot of NPR, and someone had done a story on one of the first long-term survivors of the Norwood procedure. I tuned in, my son napping in the backseat while we drove, and listened as I felt blessed that my son was born with a complete and working heart. The story was hopeful, inspirational and heartbreaking.

It left a mark.

I've wanted to weave this rare diagnosis into one of my stories for a while now. I just didn't know when the fit would feel right...until I began plotting out Emma Burke. Emma felt like so many of the stories I'd read on the condition, and as I dug deeper, learning all I could from friends in the medical profession (thanks, Robin Meyers Bull!) and organizations that research and support HLHS, I knew this was the book for this very important story.

As I began plotting, I started following a blog on the Children's Organ Transplant Association for Sadie Chapman. Sadie and Emma—they share the same diagnosis. And they're both dreamers. Sadie wants to be an actress, Emma, a surgeon. As I was writing, Sadie was on a waiting list for a new heart. On July 8, 2015, it came.

The costs associated with transplant surgeries are tremendous. Beyond the surgery itself, there are medications and biopsies and endless doctors visits to ward off organ rejection and other complications. But COTA does an amazing job of helping those like Sadie share their stories with the public. She is one of so many in need of support. For more information, visit cota.org. For more on Sadie, visit cotaforsadiec.com.

And Sadie: we have never met, but the reach of your heart is far, and the beat is strong. It kicks throughout Wicked Restless, and I thank you for that.

Please note that Wicked is most definitely fiction—and Emma's path is not necessarily that of the typical patient.

To say I love these Harper boys and the world they live in would be selling them short. Getting to dive back into their town, their family, this time through Andrew's eyes, was pure joy. I have the readers who were hungry for Andrew's take on life to thank for that. Thank you for loving the Harper boys as much as I do. It means the world to me.

I must also send thanks to Tracey Breeden, my go-to knowledge base on all things police procedure, protocol and general "but what if *this* happened—would he get arrested?" questions. I am so blessed to call you my friend.

While I'm an ESPN addict, when it comes to college hockey, there were some nuances I wasn't so sure on—practice routines, schedules, conferences, travel. Thank you to Scott Young, director of hockey operations and assistant coach of the Boston University men's hockey team, for taking the time out to chat up this tomboy and very girly romance writer! You filled in the gaps, and gained a forever fan for the Terriers (unless they ever face the Sun Devils).

As with every work, I would get nowhere if it were not for my team of amazing beta readers and editors. Thank you, Shelley, Bianca, Jen, Debbie, Ashley, Tina and Billi Joy Carson (Editing Addict) for steering me right. You ladies can drive me anywhere! And of course, thanks to the hubs and kiddo for putting up with the laptop at dinner, ballgames, practice, batting lessons, the trip to the East Coast (this list is endless). I love you both to the moon!

As with Wild Reckless, Wicked Restless tackles some very serious topics. I don't believe in shying away from things—the effects of mental health and the far-to-common instances for assault and rape among college students is unfortunately not fiction. Below are some resources that specialize in helping you when you need it most. If someone you know could use a helping hand to find healing and strength, please consider passing these websites along:

National Child Abuse Hotline
1.800.422.4453 www.childhelp.org

National Domestic Violence Hotline
1.800.799.7233 www.ndvh.org

Rape, Abuse & Incest National Network
1.800.656.4673 www.rainn.org

National Teen Dating Abuse Helpline
1.866.331.9474 www.loveisrespect.org

National Suicide Prevention Lifeline
1.800.273.8255 www.suicidepreventionlifeline.org

As always, thank you for spending time on my book. If you enjoyed Wicked Restless, please consider leaving a review and/or sharing your recommendation with a friend. I'm thankful for every kind word, and I promise to work hard to give you more to swoon over. Consider this my foot tap to you ;-).

With love,
Ginger

Books by Ginger Scott

The Falling Series
This Is Falling
You and Everything After
The Girl I Was Before

The Waiting Series
Waiting on the Sidelines
Going Long

Harper Boys
Wild Reckless
Wicked Restless

Standalones
Blindness
How We Deal With Gravity

About the Author

Ginger Scott is an Amazon-bestselling author of nine young and new adult romances, including Waiting on the Sidelines, Going Long, Blindness, How We Deal With Gravity, This Is Falling, You and Everything After, The Girl I Was Before, Wild Reckless and Wicked Restless.

A sucker for a good romance, Ginger's other passion is sports, and she often blends the two in her stories. (She's also a sucker for a hot quarterback, catcher, pitcher, point guard...the list goes on.) Ginger has been writing and editing for newspapers, magazines and blogs for more than 15 years. She has told the stories of Olympians, politicians, actors, scientists, cowboys, criminals and towns. For more on her and her work, visit her website at http://www.littlemisswrite.com.

When she's not writing, the odds are high that she's somewhere near a baseball diamond, either watching her son field pop flies like Bryce Harper or cheering on her favorite baseball team, the Arizona Diamondbacks. Ginger lives in Arizona and is married to her college sweetheart whom she met at ASU (fork 'em, Devils).

Ginger Scott Online

@TheGingerScott
www.facebook.com/GingerScottAuthor
www.littlemisswrite.com

Made in the USA
San Bernardino, CA
26 April 2016